GW01034806

Brendan
Bracken

To Meliani, thank you for the support and encouragement over the course of this literary journey.

Aria

A Symphony of Love

BRENDAN BRACKEN

authorHOUSE®

AuthorHouse™ UK
1663 Liberty Drive
Bloomington, IN 47403 USA
www.authorhouse.co.uk
Phone: 0800.197.4150

Published by AuthorHouse 04/11/2018

ISBN: 978-1-5462-9034-6 (sc)
ISBN: 978-1-5462-9036-0 (hc)
ISBN: 978-1-5462-9035-3 (e)

Library of Congress Control Number: 2018903452

Print information available on the last page.

Synopsis

This is the love story of Consuella, a young girl from the convent in Verona, and Antonio, a dashing young man from Milan. While Antonio is visiting his former teacher and mentor Father Martine in Verona, his teacher persuades him to stay for a special celebration in the monastery chapel. Father Martine's objective is to make sure Antonio gets to hear young Consuella singing in the choir. On hearing her voice, he immediately recognises her special gift.

After many battles and much persuasion, Antonio brings her to Milan; she takes the opera world by storm. Over the next two years, Antonio and Consuella fall in love. Antonio's dearest wish is to marry Consuella. He returns to Verona to seek her father's consent.

During his absence, Don Barcese, an influential figure in the opera community, begins to cause mischief. He promises Consuella that, under his management, she will become the most famous opera star in the world.

By the time Antonio returns, the damage is already done. Antonio reluctantly terminates his role as Consuella's manager, and with a heavy heart, he travels to Vienna and takes up a position with the Vienna Court Opera.

Meanwhile, Don Barcese arranges major engagements on Consuella's behalf throughout Europe—all of which are hugely successful. Before embarking on a much-anticipated American tour, Consuella and Antonio secretly meet and reconcile. Their plan is that, on her return from America, they will announce to the world their undying love for each other and be married.

CONTENTS

CHAPTER 1

The Monastery

It was approaching noon on a pleasant spring day in Verona in early March 1909. Antonio, a dashing young man of twenty-five, had just completed auditions to recruit three musicians for La Scala Opera House in Milan. Since Verona was the city of his birth, and he wasn't due to return to Milan until the following day, he took this opportunity to meet with his Sister. He also decided to pay a visit to his former teacher and mentor Father Martine, the very person who instilled in him his abiding love of the opera. Although Antonio had never excelled as a musician, he considered himself very fortunate to be associated with La Scala. He believed that he owed his good fortune to the support and encouragement he'd received from his teacher over the years.

Passing through the monastery gates, he felt himself drawn back to his student days and fond memories of former pupils and teachers. Knocking on the solid oak door, he wondered if things had changed much since his last visit.

The door was opened by Father Damiano. Although getting on in years, he immediately recognised Antonio and greeted him warmly. "Antonio, what a pleasant surprise. My goodness. We haven't seen you for!!! how long has it been since you last paid us a visit?"

"It has been almost two years now, Father, and I must say it is always such a joy to return."

"Well then, come in. Take a seat in the drawing room and make yourself comfortable. I will let Father Martine know you are here."

Antonio gazed around the room, thinking that, even after so many years, it's power to intimidate was still very much evident.

Some moments later, the sound of quick footsteps coming down the hall alerted him. The door suddenly opened, and Father Martine strode in purposefully. Despite his slight stature, at fifty-three he was still a remarkable fit and strong individual. Taking one look at Antonio, he exclaimed, "So my former pupil decides to finally visit his old master! Even though he has been here several days now!"

Taken slightly aback by Father Martine's accusing tone, Antonio then saw his mentor's stern countenance melt away. With a broad smile, Father Martine came over and gave him an affectionate hug. Taking a seat on the couch by the large bay window, he invited Antonio to join him.

"Come, come, my dear boy. Sit yourself down and tell me all that's happening with you since we last met."

Taking a seat, Antonio replied, "If you are already aware of my presence, then I am sure you know the purpose of my visit."

"By the way, how did the auditions go? Did you hire the musicians?"

"Seeing you are so well informed, I really don't see the point in bothering you with boring details."

"There's not much that goes on in Verona that escapes my attention. It is not that I am interested in, however. I want to know more about your involvement with La Scala."

"Well, there have been major changes since we last spoke, and I am happy to report that my position has improved somewhat."

"Please continue. I'm so excited."

"Recently the director of the opera, Señor Guilio Gatti, resigned. The Metropolitan Opera of New York offered him a similar position, which he accepted. My superior has been promoted to the vacant position, and I'm happy to say these changes resulted in my appointment as events director."

"Bravo, bravo! So with your new exalted position, you will be able to secure me a private box for the next performance of *Figaro*."

"A private box—I don't think so. My influence is not that great. A ticket for the stalls certainly."

"So tell me, when did all this take place?"

"Oh, about five months ago, though there was another significant development that did not affect me personally."

"And what was that?"

"Before his departure, Señor Guilio persuaded our principal conductor, Arturo Toscanini, to accompany him."

"This is dreadful news. You mean to tell me one of our greatest conductors has left Italy to perform in America?"

"I am afraid so, even though I don't necessarily believe it was such a bad thing."

"How did you arrive at that conclusion?"

"I realise their departure will be a disappointment to all opera lovers here at home. However, I am pretty confident the two of them will play a major role in raising the profile of Italian opera in that great nation."

"Well, maybe I shouldn't be too disappointed. After all, I suppose in a roundabout sort of way Italy's loss is a beneficial gain for your good self."

Antonio, not quite certain what Father Martine meant with this last comment, decided a polite response would be best. "Why thank you, Father. I will take that last remark as a compliment."

Father Martine just smiled back and replied, "My dear boy, of course it was a compliment. How could it be otherwise?"

Antonio, not wanting to be there all night, shifted the conversation in another direction. As he reminisced about days gone by, Father Martine just sat there, making a determined effort to mask the bored expression on his face. To his relief, Father Damiano entered. He set a tray on the table laden with assorted cheeses and a carafe of wine. He then asked, "Will there be anything else, Father?"

"No, thank you. Father, these are just fine. You will see to it we are not disturbed."

"Of course, Father."

"Antonio, please have some refreshments. They will fortify you for our celebrations later this evening."

"Please, Father, I have an early journey back tomorrow morning and still have paperwork to complete. An early night and a restful sleep is what I am looking forward to. Anyway, I don't have a change of clothes to hand."

"Not to worry. As we speak, one of our friars is already on his way to settle the account and collect your valise from the boarding house you were lodging in. For a director of La Scala, your choice of accommodation surprised me. I would have been much more impressed if I were sending Father Adolfo to the Palazzo Victoria. But then again, maybe I should be thankful for small mercies. The boarding house I can afford. The Palazzo Victoria, I fear, would have stretched my purse a little too far."

Antonio knew to protest further would be fruitless. He resigned himself to the fact he was going to be a guest at the monastery, whether he liked it or not.

Father Martine, detecting his air of surrender, continued. "Well, don't you want to ask me about this evening's special event?"

Trying to convey an air of enthusiasm, Antonio replied, "Why of course, Father. Please continue."

"Our celebration is in honour of the two hundredth anniversary of the founding of this great monastery. We will start the evening with the rosary, followed by benediction. I will have the honour of being the principal celebrant. Finally, the service will end with a performance by the choir from the convent of St Mary Magdalena."

"It sounds so exciting. I can hardly wait."

Detecting the slight cynicism in his voice, Father Martine continued. "Antonio, I know you're being polite. I can promise you something very special awaits you this evening. I am asking you just this once to trust your old teacher."

Slightly embarrassed, Antonio replied, "I realise how important this event is for you and the community. So please Father, forgive my bad manners just now."

Father Martine stood up and guided Antonio to the door. He finished by saying, "Your valise is already in one of our guest rooms. Father Damiano will take you there. Rest awhile, and later you can join me for a light meal. I will then accompany you to the chapel, there you will have the honour of being seated among our many important guests."

Entering the room, Antonio found it refreshingly cool, despite the warm spring sunshine. Loosening his clothes, he lay on the bed and reflected on his conversation with Father Martine. He wondered what this special event could possibly be. With these thoughts, he drifted off into a gentle slumber.

He awoke to the sound of the Angelus bell, freshening up and changing his clothes, he then made his way to the dining room. Father Martine was sitting with some members of the community and beckoned Antonio to join them.

"Ah, there you are, Antonio. Come join us."

"I hope I haven't kept you waiting Father."

"Not at all, dear boy. As a matter of fact, you are just in time. Have some food, and when you are ready, I will escort you to the chapel."

As he was eating, Father Martine enquired, "In your time at La Scala, did you ever consider sponsoring or managing a promising new talent?"

"I have certainly given it some thought. At the moment, it is not really on my agenda, though on the other hand, if an opportunity presented itself, I am sure I would give it careful consideration. Presently in Milan, the world of opera management is controlled and dominated by one powerful individual."

"And who might this person be?"

"His name is Don Marco Barcese. Sponsors and families with young, talented hopefuls make their way to his office. He auditions these aspiring artistes, and if he is satisfied, he signs them to a binding one-sided contract that keeps them under his control for the remainder of their career—or until such time he deems they are of no further use to him. For this privilege, he extracts 30 per cent of their earnings. A close colleague of mine who is a voice coach will have nothing to do with this character."

Father Martine, listening intently, replied, "Come, Antonio. It's time for us to go. Who knows? An opportunity may present itself when you least expect it."

Making their way from the dining room, Antonio wondered what exactly Father Martine meant by this remark.

On reaching the chapel, Father Damiano guided him to one of the seats in front of the altar. Looking around, he could see the congregation had already taken their places in the pews. They seemed to be praying fervently for a miracle or the avoidance of some unforeseen catastrophe. His side of the altar was occupied by the mayor and other dignitaries. The far side was reserved for monks and friars from two of the other monasteries. Father Martine entered, bowing to the faithful. He then knelt at the altar rails and began reciting the rosary quite passionately.

Antonio, leaning back, resigned himself to a long evening of excruciating boredom. As Father Martine went through the rosary, Antonio found himself thinking back to his childhood—the family kneeling down each evening to say the rosary. All he could remember was the glorious, the sorrowful, the dull, and the boring.

As the rosary ended, Father Martine stood up and returned to the vestry. Antonio looked down into the congregation, he noticed some of the parishioners had dozed off and seemed perfectly happy in their slumber. He was somewhat envious and very much aware his highly visible seating position denied him the same privilege.

Father Martine re-emerged robed in elaborate vestments. He proceeded with the benediction. For Antonio, this part of the service seemed to take even longer than the previous segment. Eventually, it came to an end. Two assistants helped Father Martine disrobe. Now dressed in his humble black cassock, he took a seat on the other side of the altar.

Looking over in Antonio's direction, his eyes seemed to say, *Thank you for your patience. The remainder of the evening is for you.* Antonio returned his gaze. He did not have time to dwell on what it was he thought he saw in Father Martine's expression because just then the sound of singing from the choir of Saint Mary Magdelena filled the small chapel.

Sitting back, he listened as the choir performed. Their melodic harmonies had a soothing effect on his senses. And then, to his surprise, he heard the sound of a single voice inexorably rising above the others. It reached into every corner of the building.

Hearing this voice, he knew instantly he was in the presence of something very special. In all his time listening to wonderful memorable arias, never before had he heard anything quite as beautiful as the voice now filling the chapel. It was angelic and pure, full of innocence and yet quite passionate. As he listened in total rapture, he glanced over in the direction of Father Martine, who silently responded with a smile. This time he seemed to be saying, *I told you I would have a great surprise for you. Now do you believe me?*

When the choir finished, the ceremony concluded. The parishioners stood and waited as the friars made their way down the aisle, followed by the other guests. Antonio joined the procession as it made its way to the main community room, which had been turned into a banqueting hall. There were tables laden with assorted meats, cheeses, breads, and wine. Everyone seemed to be in a festive mood. There was much talk about the historic occasion, the wonderful ceremony, and the choir's performance. Just then, Sister Maria, a tall authoritative-looking figure in her early fifties, entered the room accompanied by another nun. The choir of young girls followed behind. Father Martine made his way over. On the way, he spotted Antonio and invited him to join them.

He introduced him to the two sisters. "Antonio, I would like to introduce you to Sister Maria, Mother Superior of the convent, and her able assistant, Sister Francesca, who conducted the wonderful choir you heard this evening."

Bowing graciously, Antonio complimented the two of them on the choir's performance.

Father Martine chimed in, "Sisters, I am quite certain you will appreciate the compliment. You see, Antonio here is not only my former pupil, he is also a director at La Scala and is a person of great influence in operatic circles throughout Italy."

"Mother Superior, Sister Francesca, my teacher flatters me greatly. I am events director at La Scala, and I must confess my influence in the world of opera is not as great as the good Father's imagination. Anyway, enough about me. I do not wish to repeat myself, but the choir's performance was truly magnificent, especially the soloist. Her voice was quite beautiful. She has a natural gift and a wonderful talent."

"Why, thank you, Antonio. And please call me Sister Maria. Perhaps you would like to meet our young star."

Before he had time to reply, she turned to Sister Francesca, "Dear Sister, would you be so good and bring Consuella over?"

Sister Francesca went over to where the girls were having some refreshments. Plucking a young girl from among them, she ushered her across the room. Antonio took a moment to observe. He saw a young girl, perhaps seventeen or eighteen. She had a pretty face and long dark hair. Although tall for her age, she seemed self-conscious and slightly awkward.

"Consuella this is Señor Antonio from La Scala in Milan. He enjoyed your singing and would like to compliment you."

She blushed slightly and bowed in his direction.

Sister Maria continued, "Consuella has lived with us at the convent for some time now. She is a wonderful student and never gives us any cause for concern.

Antonio, taking her by surprise asked, "May I have your permission to escort Consuella over to the other choir members? I would like to congratulate them also."

Without waiting for a reply, he took Consuella by the hand and propelled her across the room.

Sister Maria, momentarily taken aback, remarked, "Well it looks like he has my permission whether I like it or not."

Suppressing a smile, Father Martine answered her. "That boy was never bashful. It must have something to do with his upbringing. So impetuous, so impetuous."

She replied in a tone slightly scornful but without any real malice, "Or maybe it might have something to do with the influence of his former teacher."

Antonio chatted with the young singers, who were giggling and enjoying themselves enormously. Then, turning to the assembled gathering, he tapped the side of a glass. The room fell silent as he began to speak. "Reverend Sisters, Reverend Fathers, distinguished guests, on behalf of everyone gathered here this evening, I would like to offer our heartfelt appreciation to Sister Maria and Father Martine for this wonderful joyous occasion celebrating the two hundredth anniversary of this historic monastery. Please raise your glasses and join me in a toast to the future continuance of their good works and spiritual endeavours we all sincerely hope and pray continue for many years to come."

All present raised their glasses. Sister Maria and Father Martine, slightly taken aback, nonetheless bowed somewhat awkwardly in response.

"Finally, I would very much like to congratulate Sister Francesca and the young ladies of the choir for a truly wonderful performance. I sincerely believe if this group of talented young singers were to perform on any stage in this great country of ours, they would indeed do us proud."

The room burst into enthusiastic applause, accompanied by shouts of, "Bravo, bravo."

As the applause subsided, Sister Francesca gathered the girls around her. With a silent command, they placed their capes over their shoulders. Standing in formation, they bowed to the guests and then marched from the room, led by the indomitable Sister Francesca.

Antonio made his way back to Father Martine, who couldn't resist teasing him. "Well my dear boy, I think you missed your vocation."

Quite pleased with his little speech and with a satisfied grin he asked, "What vocation would that be, dear Father?"

"Well, maybe you should have chosen politics as a career."

"Dear teacher it has always been my opinion the two professions I lack the requisite skills to survive in are politics and the priesthood."

"And what skills would they be?"

"Well a gentleman named Machiavelli comes to mind."

Before Father Martine had a chance to reply, a parishioner approached, accompanied by two young adults. Quickly recovering from his verbal joust, Father Martine greeted them and shook hands and then turned to Antonio saying, "Antonio, may I introduce you to Señor Pellegrini, a most-respected member of our community. This is his daughter, Dominique, and son, Adamo."

Antonio shook hands with the three guests.

Father Martine invited Señor Pellegrini's son and daughter to help themselves to some refreshments at a nearby table. Just then, Sister Maria joined them. Father Martine, putting an arm around Señor Pellegrini's shoulder, continued, "Pietro, you may not know this, but my former pupil here holds a most prestigious position as a director of La Scala Opera, and he was very impressed with Consuella's performance."

Antonio took over the conversation, "Señor Pellegrini, every time the reverend father discusses my role with La Scala, my position becomes grander. If I was paid a salary matching the lofty status he confers on me within that great institution, I do believe I would be a person of some considerable means. No matter, I really was impressed with the young señorita's performance. Have you by chance heard her sing before?"

Before he had a chance to answer, Father Martine interrupted, "Antonio, Señor Pellegrini has probably heard Consuella sing more often than any other person in this room."

"How is that so?" Antonio queried.

Father Martine, in a casual tone, replied, "Because, Antonio, Señor Pellegrini is Consuella's father."

Now acutely embarrassed, he stumbled over his reply, "Please forgive me, Señor Pellegrini, you see I thought Consuella was an orph—" He stopped short of probably causing considerable offence. Looking over in Father Martine's direction, he gave him a look expressing his discomfort.

His glance was returned with a wry smile, which seemed to say, *Machiavelli indeed.*

Sister Maria, noticing the slight tension, interceded. "Antonio, Consuella is not an orphan. I do apologise if I misled you when I said she resides with us at the convent, I fully understand the conclusion you may have drawn. Let me explain. Some four years ago, Señor Pellegrini's wife passed away, leaving a grief-stricken husband with three children to raise on his own. He turned to Father Martine and myself for support and guidance. We agreed a temporary practical solution would be for Consuella to live with the sisters at the convent.

Adamo continued working with his father in their small vineyard. Dominique, being the first born, was old enough to look after the household. Consuella was just fourteen years of age. Being the youngest, she was given into our care. She has settled very well into our community and continues her studies under our supervision. As I said earlier, she is a wonderful student and delights us frequently with the beautiful voice gifted to her by God. Father Martine and I have been given the privilege of being Consuella's guardians. So now she has three parents, and we protect her like we would a precious jewel because that is how special she is to us."

Antonio turned to Señor Pellegrini. "Please accept my deepest sympathy on the sad loss of your beloved wife, and please forgive my indiscretion just now. I am truly sorry."

Señor Pellegrini graciously accepted the apology.

Just as he was about to depart, Antonio asked if he could make a suggestion concerning Consuella. The three of them looked at him without saying a word.

Father Martine broke the silence. "Go on, Antonio. What is it you would like to suggest?"

"As you all know, I am employed as events director at La Scala."

"Antonio," interrupted Father Martine. "All of us are aware of your position at La Scala. Now if it is not too much trouble, can you please enlighten us with this suggestion of yours?"

"Thank you, Father. I think we all agree Consuella has a great talent and, as you so aptly describe it, Mother Superior, an angelic voice. I am convinced, with the able assistance of a voice coach, she could very well become a successful soprano."

Señor Pellegrini looked puzzled and replied, "If, as you say, she has a beautiful voice, why then would she need the services of, what did you call it?"

"A voice coach."

Chimed in Father Martine, deciding to press Antonio a little further, "Antonio, please explain for us if you will, exactly what is the role of a voice coach?"

Antonio, trying his best to remain composed, endeavoured to explain the complexities of voice training. "In my time at the opera, I have had the pleasure of witnessing many great performers. In most cases, a voice coach was present. The assistance of such a professional in nearly all instances enables a singer to deliver a performance of the highest standard. What I am really trying to say is, although Consuella has a beautiful voice, for her to perform professionally, she would need the services of a professional coach."

"So tell me, Antonio," enquired Sister Maria, "What exactly, does a voice coach do?"

"A voice coach teaches breath control, voice projection, timing, and many more disciplines. These techniques, when taught by a competent professional, enable a singer with natural ability to develop their talent to a very high degree. Although Consuella undoubtedly has an excellent voice, I firmly believe she would still need the services of such a person to achieve her full potential."

Sister Maria and Pietro seemed to be grappling with Antonio's remarks concerning the complexities of voice training. To them, singing was singing. An individual could either sing or could not. For those who could, there were two categories—good voices and bad voices. Father Martine, quite happy to stand back and observe the exchanges, waited patiently to see how Antonio was going to deal with the situation as it unfolded.

Sister Maria threw in an acerbic remark, "Very good, Antonio. I must say I would never have thought singing was such a complicated business. I suppose I will have to take your word for it. After all, you are the expert."

Antonio was not sure if this was a compliment or an insult. Looking in Father Martine's direction, all he got was a look of passive disinterest. Sister Maria continued with a number of questions in quick succession, "Where will we find such a person? Would he be prepared to come to the convent? Most importantly, how much would these lessons cost?"

"I very much regret, Mother Superior, the person I have in mind would be unable to carry out the training here in Verona. He has many other students, and his studio is in Milan. It would be necessary for Consuella to travel there to avail herself of his services."

Sister Maria, absolutely outraged, shot back, "Out of the question, young man. Have you completely taken leave of your senses? Do you think for one moment we would allow that young innocent child be dragged all the way to Milan for voice training lessons by an individual we know absolutely nothing about."

Antonio felt an urge to beat a hasty retreat. Instead, he endured the full force of her wrath. He could also see Señor Pellegrini wasn't looking too pleased either. As he looked in Father Martine's direction for a comforting glance or gesture, all he got in return was the same look as before. He reminded himself to thank his teacher some time later for the embarrassing situation he now found himself in. He decided nevertheless, whatever damage had been done, it would be no worse if he just carried on and put forward the remainder of his proposal. "Dear Mother Superior, Señor Pellegrini, please? Indulge me for a few brief moments. Having heard Consuella sing this evening, I have come to the conclusion that, with sound management and professional training, she could have a very successful career. I can assure you my intentions are most honourable. The voice coach I have in mind is a devout Catholic and a man of impeccable character. I give you my solemn word, if you were to allow me bring Consuella to Milan, I would protect her as I would my own sister. There is a very respectable family in Milan that provides accommodation for female students of a similar age. They are good friends of mine. With your permission, I believe I would be successful in prevailing upon them to allow her stay at their home during her training. At the earliest opportunity, I would endeavour to arrange an audition. If it were to go well, I would then do all in my power to at least secure a supporting role for her in one of the new season's productions."

Having made his case, Antonio looked apprehensively from one to the other wondering what sort of reaction if any he was going to receive.

Sister Maria responded, "Señor Antonio, the only reason I indulged you these past few moments is in part due to Father Martine's favourable comments concerning your character. Now regarding these proposals of yours, there are elements that may have some merit, but I have to caution you; some of your suggestions would not be acceptable under any circumstances."

Antonio thought for a moment to ask if she could be more specific. A telling glance from his teacher banished the thought. Instead, he decided the more sensible course would be to allow her finish without interruption.

Sister Maria continued, "Pietro, Father Martine, is there anything you wish to add?"

They just shook their heads and remained silent.

"Very well then. I believe our discussions have concluded, I am sure you don't expect an answer from us this evening. It is getting late. Señor Pellegrini and I must take our leave. We will discuss your proposals among ourselves sometime tomorrow. If there is an outcome, we will surely let you know."

With that, the pair went over to Dominique and Adamo. Father Martine accompanied them to the door, leaving a very chastened Antonio standing alone in the middle of the room, feeling quite alone.

Having bid the others farewell, Father Martine headed back to a forlorn-looking Antonio. "After that performance, I certainly won't be recommending you for a post with the diplomatic service."

"Dear Father, thank you so much. You promised me earlier my life may change. You were most certainly correct. I feel as if I have aged ten years."

"Oh come now; it wasn't that bad. You should see her when she really gets angry. Under the circumstances, I think you came out of the encounter relatively unscathed. Though there is one thing you need to be very much aware of. Consuella's welfare is of paramount importance to her. You should also consider yourself very fortunate."

"Why so?"

"Well, despite your less than subtle approach, she didn't reject your suggestions completely."

"So please explain. Exactly what does that mean?"

"It means she will give your proposals careful consideration."

"What about Señor Pellegrini?"

"No need to worry. Consuella's father will be more than happy to agree with whatever Sister Maria decides. He trusts her explicitly."

"And you, Father, what decision are you likely to take?"

"Me? I have already made my decision."

"Would you care to enlighten me?"

"Why of course. I have decided Consuella will travel to Milan and, in time, become a great opera singer."

"Well then, why did you not speak up when I was floundering?"

"I didn't want to give them the impression we were colluding in any way."

"But we weren't."

"Actually we were. You just didn't know it at the time."

"Honestly, Father, I am beginning to think you put me through this as a form of punishment for some terrible deed committed in the past."

"Not at all, dear boy. Despite your inept performance I believe you did reasonably well in the encounter. Now it is getting late. You must be tired after all the excitement of today. Off you go and get a restful night's sleep. I have an early mass tomorrow morning. Before your departure, you may join me for breakfast if you wish."

In the privacy of his room, Antonio berated himself for allowing Father Martine to steer him into a situation that, on cold reflection, made him appear naive and foolish in the extreme. How could he have been so stupid to think Señor Pellegrini would allow him, a practical stranger, drag his daughter off to Milan, on a half promise of turning her into an opera star? He was even more upset with the realisation it was most likely he would not have an opportunity to apologise in person to Sister Maria and Señor Pellegrini. He surmised, however, that maybe this wasn't such a bad thing, for who knows what further damage he might cause if such an encounter took place? With these thoughts, he drifted off into an uneasy sleep.

CHAPTER 2

The Following Morning

The sound of hens cackling and an early sunrise awakened Antonio from his restless slumber. After washing and dressing himself rather hastily, he made his way down the broad staircase. Leaving his valise in the hallway, he apprehensively entered the dining room.

He was greatly surprised to see his three protagonists and another sister sitting at the table, seemingly enjoying breakfast and cheerfully chatting among themselves. His initial reaction was to grab his bag and run as fast as he could rather than face another inquisition.

Father Martine, seeing the pained expression on his face, beamed a broad smile in his direction. "Come, come, Antonio, please join us and have some breakfast before your departure."

As Antonio nervously took a seat, the thought going through his mind was to say nothing. He just wanted to avoid reigniting Sister Maria's wrath.

After an uncomfortable silence, except for the noise of cutlery on plates, Sister Maria finally spoke. "Antonio, let me introduce you to Sister Lucia. She is one of our dedicated teachers, and Consuella is most fortunate to be one of her pupils."

Antonio nodded politely but still remained silent.

"Now, Antonio, before we discuss the issues raised by you last night, is there anything you wish to add?"

He decided there and then he now had nothing to lose, so he might as well say what was really on his mind. ", there is, Reverend Mother."

Father Martine prayed silently Antonio wasn't going to say something foolish and jeopardise his plan.

"Reverend Mother, I would like first of all to apologise to the three of you for my overzealous approach in our previous discussions. My comments most likely caused you and more particularly Señor Pellegrini some offence. Please, believe me that was not my intention. I am still of the opinion, though, that Consuella has a very special talent and someday, with the proper training, may yet do you all proud. Any decision relating to her future is yours and yours alone to make. If I can assist in any way, I would consider it a great honour."

Father Martine, now slightly more at ease, waited for Sister Maria's response.

After a few brief moments she continued. "Thank you, Antonio. Your apology is both timely and gracious. Now, let's see if we can proceed in a calm rational manner. I said last night that we would discuss your suggestions among ourselves. This we have done, and I will now inform you of the outcome—though I must caution you in advance, our decision is final and non-negotiable. Can I take it you accept these conditions?"

"Yes, Reverend Mother. Please continue."

"We are in broad agreement with your suggestions. It is the method you wish to employ that causes us the most difficulty. So here is what we're proposing. You will leave for Milan later today. As soon as is practical, we expect you to make an appointment with this voice coach of yours. By the way, does he have a name?"

Answering her enthusiastically, Antonio replied, "He certainly does, Mother Superior. His name is Señor Francesco Cipriano. He is most reliable and is also a very close friend."

Father Martine interrupted. "Antonio, his name will be sufficient. We don't need a biography. Now, would it be possible for Sister Maria to continue?"

"I do apologise, Mother Superior. Please. You were saying just now?"

"Will you, for goodness sake, stop apologising? And please, for the last time, call me Sister Maria."

Silently blushing and lowering his head slightly, Antonio waited for her to resume.

"As I was saying, you will meet with your colleague Señor Cipriano and make the necessary arrangements for these voice training sessions. In the coming days, Consuella will travel to Milan in the company of Sister Lucia. You were probably wondering about her presence here this morning. Well, I thought it appropriate you meet with our good sister, as she will be Consuella's constant companion during her time there.

"Sister Lucia was to have taken up a teaching post in our convent there, but at my request, she has agreed to act as chaperone. There will be no need for you to bother the family you had in mind for accommodation, as both of them will reside at the convent. At a time you and your companion deem appropriate, you will arrange an audition. We are prepared to give the two of you three months to carry out this task.

"During this period, you will report to Father Martine on a weekly basis and keep him up to date on your progress. Sister Lucia will, of course, keep me informed on Consuella's well-being. At this stage, we don't see the need for a written contract. For our part, we are prepared to support you and your associate in any way we can. A modest fee for the lessons and your expenses will be paid for by the convent and the monastery.

"If your efforts are successful, at some later date, we will then revisit the issue of payment for yourself and your colleague. Oh, I almost forget. There is one further condition. For as long as you are in charge of her career, you will be required to take on the additional role of guardian. These are our proposals. The objectives, I believe, are much in line with your own, though the implementation is somewhat different. As I stated earlier, the terms are non-negotiable. The question I suppose is, are they acceptable or not? A straight yes or no will suffice."

A brief silence followed with nobody uttering a word. Father Martine observed Antonio and wondered, had he perhaps pushed him to far and drawn him into a situation that was beyond his reach at this stage in his career? He didn't have to wait very long for his answer.

"Sister Maria, with humility and gratitude, I willingly accept this exciting challenge. Your proposals are sensible, fair, and well thought out. I look forward to working with Sister Lucia and Señor Francesco, together we will become a formidable team. I am confident the three of us will be successful in our efforts on your behalf and of course Consuella's."

"Thank you, Antonio," she curtly answered.

Father Martine, brought the proceedings to a close by announcing, "I believe I can say with some confidence, our business here today is concluded. We have a lot to do in the coming days. It is imperative we give of our best to achieve a positive outcome. I would sincerely like to thank you all for your patience and courtesy during these delicate negotiations."

Sister Maria finished by saying, "I think now is a good time for us to take our leave. There's still a lot of work to be done in preparation for the forthcoming journey."

Addressing Antonio in that formal way of hers, she continued, "Thank you, Antonio. Have a safe trip. I look forward to our next meeting."

Before he had a chance to reply, she was gone.

Pietro approached him. They shook hands. As they did so, he asked, "Antonio, as a father, I'm asking you to take good care of Consuella. Promise me you will protect her. I'm placing her future in your hands because of the faith Father Martine has in you. Finally, from here on in, please, if you will, just call me Pietro."

A very relieved Antonio replied, "Of course, Pietro. I give you my solemn word Sister Lucia and I between us will take very good care of your daughter."

Father Martine and Antonio bid all three of them farewell. Teacher and pupil found themselves alone once more.

"Antonio, you've hardly touched your breakfast. Aren't you hungry?"

"As a matter of fact, I'm starving, but I was too frightened to eat while she was speaking."

"Well you can relax now."

He called Father Damiano to bring a hot breakfast and order a cab. As Antonio tucked into the food, the sense of relief he now felt was not lost on Father Martine.

"Well, my boy, how do you feel in light of all that's taken place over the past twenty-four hours?"

"To start with, I'm convinced, and I don't think anything in this wide world will give me cause to change my mind, that you purposely led me into the lion's den to be savaged. I am also of the opinion that today's outcome was something you desired from the first moment of my arrival."

"Oh come now, Antonio. You only sustained one or two bruises in the encounter and most likely to your pride. However, in relation to the other matter, you are most perceptive. You know better than anyone the abiding passion I have for the opera.

"I've known for some time the great gift this child possesses. It would have been very difficult for me on my own to win over Sister Maria and her Father. Fortuitously, your unexpected arrival yesterday gave me the perfect opportunity to execute my plan.

"I suppose in a way you became my Trojan horse. Though there is one thing I want you to know. It was only after I saw the expression on your face in the chapel as you listened to her sing—it was only then that I decided to manoeuvre you into the lion's den as you so aptly put it.

"Now in the final analysis, I think it's fair to say we've both achieved our objective. You get to realise your ambition of becoming the manager of a future star. I get to see a young girl who is practically an orphan given the opportunity to achieve her full potential, as she so rightly deserves."

"I suppose there's no point in arguing with your logic, but why didn't you just take me into your confidence when I arrived yesterday?"

"Good question. The only answer I can honestly give is I was probably afraid you would over rehearse your role, thereby raising Sister's suspicions."

"Well, it's not much of an answer, though under the circumstances, I suppose it will have to do."

Now it was Father Martine's turn to feel relieved. "Antonio, I want you to know, you've performed a great service for me today. I greatly appreciate it, and I promise it won't be forgotten."

With that, Father Damiano entered. "Excuse me Father, Señor Antonio's cab has arrived."

The pair walked together into the hallway, Father Martine picked up Antonio's valise and carried it to the waiting cab. Antonio, about to bid him farewell, was surprised to see him climbing into the cab alongside him.

"Antonio, it would be my privilege to accompany you personally to the train station."

As they drove away from the monastery, their conversation once more reverted to times past. At the station, Father Martine accompanied him all the way to the platform. "Have a pleasant journey. And remember, there's a daunting task ahead of you, though I'm fully confident you will prevail."

Antonio couldn't resist one last jibe. "You know, Father, if I didn't know you better, I believe the only reason you escorted me was to make sure I leave Verona."

With that, Father Martine gave him an affectionate hug. "How right you are, my son. I fear another twenty-four hours would be too much for both of us. Now go with God's blessing. Become the best operatic manager in this land and make an old priest happy."

With these parting words, Father Martine turned around and left the platform. As Antonio boarded the train, he looked back and smiled with deep affection as he watched his teacher walking in that distinctive way of his towards the exit.

CHAPTER 3

Milan

On his arrival in Milan, Antonio immediately made his way to Francesco's residence, rang the doorbell, and waited.

Francesco's wife, Carlota, a tall elegant thirty-four-year-old with sallow skin, deep brown eyes, and a winning smile, opened the door.

She greeted him warmly and invited him into the study. "Antonio, before I fetch Francesco, what will it be, tea or coffee?"

"Carlota, today can I have a coffee?"

"Okay, Antonio. Take a seat, and I'll get it right away."

Having brought him the coffee, she then went to fetch her husband.

Francesco, a tall handsome thirty-six-year-old with smiling grey-green eyes and chestnut brown hair reaching his shoulders, entered the room and greeted him with a question. "Well, Antonio, how was your trip? Did you manage to hire the musicians?"

"I did indeed, but not only that. Do you recall on a number of occasions the two of us often spoke about discovering a new talent showing great promise? Such an opportunity we agreed would enable us to break the monopoly currently enjoyed by your friend and mine Don Marco Barcese."

"I do indeed, and that's the stuff dreams are made of."

"Yes without doubt, that is the stuff dreams are made of."

"Well, you've certainly grabbed my attention. Go on. I'm listening."

"Dear friend, I have good news. In fact, I have spectacular news. I'm so excited I don't know where to begin."

"Well Antonio you were never shy, so from the beginning might be a good start."

Antonio took Francesco through everything that had taken place from the afternoon he called on Father Martine through hearing Consuella's

21

voice in the chapel, Father Martine's intrigues, and his battles with Sister Maria. He finished his narrative by proudly declaring, "So now you see here before you the proud manager of an exciting new talent. With my organisational skills and your coaching abilities, I believe our efforts will have a significant impact on the opera community here in Milan and even beyond."

Francesco, in a detached kind of way, threw out a casual question. "Is there anything else you wish to add?"

"Oh yes. I nearly forgot. They will arrive three days from now. Their place of residence will be the convent, you know, the one where your two daughters attend school."

"So now there are two individuals, and I suppose you're going to tell me both of them are nuns."

"Only one of them is a nun. The other is practically an orphan, and for the duration of her voice training schedule, I'm obligated to perform the role of guardian as well as manager."

"Then do I take it the nun's role is to pray for divine intervention?"

"No not at all. She will be Consuella's constant companion, escorting her from the convent to your studio and vice versa."

"Okay, Antonio. I think you've told me enough for now. When the two ladies arrive, bring them around, and we'll take it from there."

"Thank you, Francesco. I promise you won't be disappointed."

Antonio headed to his apartment with great expectations. He was convinced as soon as Francesco had an opportunity to hear Consuella sing, he would be completely won over.

Three days later, Consuella and Sister Lucia travelled to Milan. At the convent, they were welcomed by Sister Colombina.

To Consuella, it seemed more like an induction than a greeting. Sister Lucia did her best to reassure her,

"Consuella, there's no need to be so terrified. Sister Colombina is Reverend Mother's deputy here in Milan. Sometimes she can be a little overzealous. Believe me, she really means well. Just stay close to me, I'll take good care of you."

Antonio, at the earliest opportunity, brought them around to meet Francesco.

After what could only be described as a stiff formal introduction, Francesco decided to prevail upon his wife to somehow take the frost out of the air.

Breezing into the study with her two twelve-year-old daughters trailing behind, she immediately made her way over to Consuella. "My dear Consuella, welcome to Milan. I am Francesco's wife, Carlota, and these two young ladies are our twin daughters, Adriana and Carla. Antonio has told me so much about you. He tells me you have a rare talent. We hope to have the pleasure of hearing you sing for us very soon."

Consuella immediately felt more relaxed with Carlota's friendly manner. She then exchanged warm handshakes with the girls while Carlota greeted Sister Lucia.

"Francesco tells me the two of you will be staying at the convent during your time here in Milan. Our two girls attend school there. The good sisters tell me they are reasonably well behaved. Perhaps you can do a bit of spying and find out if this is so?"

Sister Lucia, now looking at the girls with a mischievous smile on her face, replied, "What were those names again? Ah yes, Adriana and Carla Cipriano. I will keep a close eye. If I discover any transgressions, I will report back to you straight away."

As she was saying this, she beamed a big friendly smile in the girl's direction. They weren't entirely sure if she was joking or being serious.

Carlota then invited them into the sitting room for some refreshments. Francesco brought matters to a close by announcing, "Sister Lucia, if you and Consuella can be here tomorrow morning, let's say by ten—my studio is the annex at the side of our house—we can then get started and see how we progress from there."

"Thank you, Señor Francesco, for the time and courtesy you and Señora Carlota have shown us on this our first visit to your home. We are both looking forward to being here at the appointed hour tomorrow."

Sister Lucia and Consuella joined Carlota and the girls. After they'd had some refreshments and chatted some more, they then took their leave and headed back to the convent.

Over the following weeks, Sister Lucia accompanied Consuella on a daily basis to and from Francesco's studio. He was charming and polite on all occasions and was somewhat amused by Sister Lucia's constant presence. Eventually, it became so routine he began to treat the two of them as a single person.

Antonio kept in touch and dropped by on a regular basis. On one occasion, he asked Francesco his opinion regarding the quality of Consuella's singing voice.

"I don't have an opinion."

Antonio somewhat puzzled questioned him, "How come?"

"It's quite simple really. I haven't heard her sing yet."

Antonio, now greatly confused continued, "But surely you need to hear her sing so you can establish her capacity and range?"

"No not really. I've heard her speak, and that's sufficient for the moment. Any more questions?"

Now acutely embarrassed and with the other two enjoying his discomfort, he just stood there with a forlorn expression.

Francesco came to his rescue. "Antonio, we'll make a pact. Let Sister Lucia be the protector, you be the manager, and I'll be the voice coach. Then if we all do our job, why who knows, Consuella may even get to sing one of these days."

All Antonio could do was smile in agreement at the simple logic in the argument put forward.

Francesco continued, "At this stage, I don't need to hear her sing. but I can report she is making excellent progress.

"Two weeks from now, Consuella will sing an aria. I will accompany her on the piano. You and her guardian angel here can then give your opinion."

Antonio looked seriously at Sister Lucia and Francesco for a brief moment. The two of them suddenly burst into laughter. He joined in enthusiastically. As the laughter subsided, Antonio finished by saying, "Now I know we a are formidable united team, and with our guardian angel protecting Consuella, there is nothing we cannot achieve. Now I must go and do my job. There is the small matter of an audition to be arranged."

From then on, they all worked very closely together. Antonio reported back to Father Martine, while Sister Lucia kept Sister Maria up to date.

Within two weeks, Antonio's effort to secure an audition was successful. The judging panel agreed to his sponsorship of her candidacy. He came to the studio and gave them the good news.

"Ladies and gentleman, Tuesday week next, Consuella will have the privilege of performing before a panel of experts from the operatic community.

Francesco, looking slightly concerned, replied, "I would have preferred more time. Not to worry. We will work a little harder and make sure she's ready for the occasion. Consuella, there's no doubt in my mind you can do this. The important question is, how do you feel?"

"Quite frightened actually. I'll do my best not to let you down and pray my nerves hold out."

"That's a natural reaction. I've seen it many times before. Right now, I'd be more worried if you were feeling confident. What we're going to do is audition you every day for the next two weeks starting right now. Sister, you and Antonio can be the judging panel."

Sitting at the piano, he selected a piece from Mascagni's opera *Cavalleria Rusticana*. "Consuella, close your eyes. Don't open them until you hear my signal. I want you to imagine you are standing on the stage of the Arena Verona. You're playing the part of Santuzza, the peasant girl. You are going to sing her magnificent aria on my command. One, two, and three."

He began the introduction. With perfect timing, she joined in.

Sister Lucia and Antonio sat there, and as they listened, they could see Consuella had entered a different realm—no more tension, no more nerves. It was as if she was being guided by a heavenly presence. Her voice, with its perfect pitch and beautiful tone, filled the entire room. It left them in no doubt they were in the presence of something very special. As Francesco finished the piece, she gave a gentle bow and returned to her seat, reverting to the shy but not so awkward girl Antonio had met after he had first heard her singing on that fateful night in the monastery chapel.

"Well, judges, may I have your opinion on the performance of our candidate?"

Sister Lucia responded, "Señor Francesco, she certainly has my vote."

"How say you, Antonio?"

"The singing was absolutely delightful; the piano accompaniment I suppose was adequate."

"Maybe next time I will arrange for a full orchestra. Will that satisfy you?"

Smiling broadly, Antonio replied. "Maybe a cello and a violin. Seriously, though, I was absolutely enthralled by how effortlessly she took on the persona of that peasant girl. For me, I was no longer looking at Consuella. Instead, I was gazing at Santuzza singing this beautiful aria so passionately. In two weeks, if her performance is as good, there is absolutely no doubt in my mind she will win the panel over."

Francesco replied, "That's all very well and good. I need to remind you, though, these judges can sometimes be most conservative in how they adjudicate. To them, a talent as outstanding as Consuella's might just be a little too overwhelming. So I'm suggesting she tone down her performance just a little to get her through this first hurdle. If our efforts are successful, and she lands even a small part in any of the coming season's productions, she will then have an opportunity to show the opera-loving audiences of Italy a once-in-a-lifetime star has arrived."

On the morning of the audition, Antonio accompanied Consuella into the auditorium. Sister Lucia and Francesco were already seated among the small audience. Taking their seats among the other sponsors and contestants, Antonio spotted Don Barcese, who was sponsoring two candidates, one female and one male. There were three other sponsors with one contestant each.

A group of four musicians were already present—two violins, a double base, and a grand piano. The auditioning panel comprised of three judges were seated at the other side of the stage.

The chairperson rose and outlined the procedures. "Ladies and gentlemen, today we are holding auditions for our forthcoming opera season. Two candidates will be selected—a tenor and a soprano. They will undergo an intensive programme of training. The level of progress achieved and how they perform over this period will determine what future role, if any, they might have with this great institution."

Looking through the roll call, Antonio was rather pleased to see Consuella listed as last to sing. This, he believed, would afford Francesco the opportunity to gauge the strengths and weaknesses of her competition.

The auditions commenced with Don Barcese's two candidates performing, followed by the other three. The panel now invited Consuella onto the stage.

Francesco rose from his seat. "Forgive my interruption. If the panel could indulge me for the briefest moment, I need to speak with our candidate before she begins."

The chairperson replied, "This is highly irregular, Señor Cipriano. Of course, if the other sponsors have no objection, you may proceed."

Don Barcese, now feeling very confident, was convinced Señor Antonio's faith in his own candidate was diminishing, and his companion was making one last desperate effort to boost her confidence. He gave his approval with a dismissive wave of his hand. The other three sponsors, slightly intimidated, also complied.

Francesco bowed in appreciation. He took Consuella to one side of the stage. "Consuella, I want you to forget everything I said about toning down your performance."

"Why this late change? What's the reason? I'm slightly confused."

"I've been observing the judges. They're bored. They need a performance to convince them they've not wasted their time here today. So before the music starts close your eyes. This time, picture yourself on the stage of La Scala. When the music starts, open your eyes and give a performance as if your very life depended on it."

"Thank you, Francesco. I will do my best."

Returning to his seat, he gave Antonio and Sister Lucia a reassuring glance.

Consuella sang two arias, the first from Mozart's *Don Giovanni*. Her second offering was from Puccini's *Tosca*.

During the performance, Francesco continued observing the judges. He could see by their demeanour they were very pleased, not only with her singing. her stage presence and confident manner seemed to impress them as well. Antonio, discreetly glancing around, could see the effect her singing had on those present. Even Don Barcese was paying close attention.

Having completed the two pieces, Consuella bowed to the audience and the judging panel. As she returned to her seat, Francesco caught her eye and gave her winning smile.

The judging panel spent less than five minutes conferring. When they had completed their deliberations, the chairperson rose and made the following statement, "Ladies and gentlemen, I would first of all like to thank all the candidates for their efforts here today. We are very much aware there will be four disappointed contestants. We urge you nonetheless to continue practising. Six months from now, there will be further auditions. Your participation would be most welcome.

"Now it gives me great pleasure to announce the results of today's contest. For the role of tenor, the judging panel has chosen Señor Alberto Caffarelli's candidate Stefano Pavello."

Señor Alberto stood up with a delighted Stefano. The two of them hugged each other and then bowed in the direction of the adjudicators. There was polite applause from the other sponsors and contestants.

Everyone in the auditorium was now waiting with bated breath to see who had been chosen for the soprano's part. Don Barcese wasn't too displeased his tenor hadn't won. He was fully confident his soprano would be chosen ahead of the other contestants.

The chairperson, having congratulated the young tenor, continued, "Selecting a winner for the soprano's role was a most difficult task, as all three contestants performed to a very high standard. However, our unanimous choice is Señor Antonio Fabrizio's candidate Señorita Consuella Pellegrini."

Sister Lucia and Francesco leaped from their seats and dashed over to Consuella and Antonio. Consuella remained speechless. She could hardly believe her ears. Sister Lucia gave her a rapturous hug. The applause from all present seemed to indicate the decision of the judges was a popular one.

Don Barcese approached Antonio. "Congratulations, Señor Antonio. You certainly surprised us today." Ignoring Sister Lucia and Francesco, he turned to Consuella, "Well done, señorita. I look forward to seeing you perform very soon. I will follow your progress with interest."

Antonio, noting Consuella's discomfort, answered on her behalf. "Thank you, Don Barcese, for your gracious remarks. We will do our best not to disappoint you."

With that, Don Barcese gave a perfunctory bow and departed.

Francesco and Antonio thanked the panel.

As they left the auditorium, Francesco announced, "This calls for a celebration. I would like the three of you to accompany me to my home. Carlota and my two girls have prepared a luncheon to celebrate the occasion."

"You were that confident."

"Sister Lucia, I never doubted for a moment. On our way, we need to stop at the telegraph office and send the good news to Verona."

Consuella was still almost speechless. Francesco asked her, "Well, how does our young star feel right now?"

"I am stunned and completely overwhelmed. I just can't find the words to express what it is I'm feeling right now. The three of you have been so wonderful during these past few months. I don't think I could have possibly succeeded without your dedication and support."

Francesco continued, "As I've said in the past, this is just the first hurdle. Tomorrow, the real work begins. After all, we wouldn't like to disappoint the great impresario."

"Are you referring to the gentleman in the auditorium just now?"

"Consuella, that individual is many things. But a gentleman he certainly is not.

"What's most important for you to remember is, never allow that creature into your company under any circumstances. Though I have to say I'm happy in the knowledge you have Sister Lucia and Antonio to make certain such a situation never arises. So, now let's all go and enjoy the rest of this special day."

Throwing himself feverishly into preparations, Antonio had to balance his duties as events director and his commitments to Consuella.

Francesco provided crucial support during this challenging period.

Sister Lucia, as always, was on hand, assisting in any way she could and performing many tasks.

Consuella was making excellent progress. To the others she seemed to be completely unaffected by the enormity of the challenge lying ahead.

Sister Lucia and Francesco never left her side. They accompanied her to and from all rehearsals.

Antonio, despite his hectic work schedule, dropped by as often as he could to keep himself up to date on her progress.

As each day passed, he could see the improvements for himself. Although his workload was tremendous and at times very demanding, he nevertheless met all the challenges with great calm and perseverance.

The major driving force in all of this was his belief Consuella would rise to the challenge and take the opera world by storm. There was no doubt in his mind La Scala's audience, even with its demanding reputation, would be completely won over by the sheer force of her talent.

The organising committee had chosen six operas for the upcoming season. Consuella was selected to perform in three of the productions, these being *Cavalleria Rusticana*, *Palliachi*, and *The Marriage of Figaro*. They provided Antonio with the list of dates on which she was selected to perform. From this schedule, he calculated she would be required to sing on at least eighteen occasions. With four short weeks left before opening night, he knew there was no time to lose.

CHAPTER 4

Opening Night

Finally, after frantic weeks of exhaustive rehearsals, costume fittings, and elaborate set construction, it was now time to open the opera with a three-night run of *The Marriage of Figaro*—probably the most popular and best loved comic opera of all time.

Consuella had a major role, playing the part of Susanna, maidservant to Count Almaviva's wife. Antonio had invited Sister Maria, Pietro, and Father Martine.

As this was going to be a special occasion, Sister Maria suggested to the others, that Dominique and Adamo should make the journey with them.

Arriving by train in the afternoon, the five of them had just enough time for some refreshments and a change of clothes before they made their way to the theatre.

Antonio greeted them in the main foyer. "It is such a joy to see all of you here. And now, if I may, I would like to finally introduce my dear friend Francesco Cipriano; his charming wife, Carlota; and their two lovely daughters, Adriana and Carla."

Once all had exchanged warm greetings and handshakes, Sister Maria enquired, "How is our dear Consuella? I'm quite certain she must be somewhat nervous."

"Not to worry," Antonio answered. "Why as we speak, she is in her dressing room. Sister Lucia is assisting her with her costume. You will get to meet the two of them later this evening.

"Now if you can please excuse us," he added. "Francesco and I have to return backstage for some last minute preparations. Carlota will escort you to your seats; we will join you before the curtain rises."

Carlota gently took Sister Maria by the arm. "Sister Maria, if you and your group just follow me, I will show you to your seats."

She led them to a box with a perfect view overlooking the stage. "Sister Maria, Señor Pietro, Father Martine, please make yourselves comfortable. Antonio and Francesco will join you shortly. Dominique, Adamo, my two daughters, and myself will be in the adjoining box."

Before she left, Father Martine turned to her, saying, "This for me, Carlota, is like a dream come true. I could never have imagined one day I would have the privilege of sitting in a private box at La Scala. Add to that a young girl who has had such an impact on all of our lives is actually going to be on that stage performing. Please excuse me Carlota. I'm becoming quite emotional right now."

"Dear Father, I quite understand the emotions all of you must be experiencing just now. If someone that close to me was performing on this stage tonight, I believe for me it would also be a very emotional experience. Now I want you to relax and enjoy the rest of the evening."

Pietro, taking the other two by surprise, replied, "Thank you, Carlota, for those kind words."

"Well, Señor Pietro, Sister Lucia and Antonio have always spoken very highly of you and Sister Maria. Why Antonio even said Father Martine can be quite charming when he is getting his own way."

Father Martine looked at her with a scornful expression. The other two were greatly amused by her remarks and quite enjoyed his temporary loss of composure.

Carlota, now with a beaming smile on her face, added, "Though in fairness, he did say, in spite of your cantankerous nature, there is nobody else's opinion he values more than yours, and he dearly loves you as a son should love a father."

Father Martine, with a broad smile on his face, responded, "I do believe we have a formidable lady in our presence here this evening. So if I may suggest, we better be on our best behaviour. After all, we don't want a negative report making its way back to our illustrious hosts."

Sister Maria then added, "Carlota, I'm happy in the knowledge we have forged a new, lasting friendship here in Milan and thank you for taking care of us this evening. Why even Father Martine is impressed."

Ignoring her last jibe, Father Martine concluded, "I have to say, I think we're all still a little bit nervous on Consuella's behalf."

Carlota reassured them. "I know how dearly the three of you care about her. You have all more than likely listened to her beautiful voice many times in the past. Antonio has told me on more than one occasion her voice is even better now than before she left Verona. My husband, God bless him, who is not easily impressed, is delighted with the progress she's made over these past three months. As a matter of fact, I've heard him say this to Antonio on a number of occasions, particularly over the past three weeks or so. He says that she is one of the best sopranos he has ever heard. And believe me, he has listened to many fine performers in his time. So now, if you will excuse me, I think it's time for me to join my guests in the adjoining box."

With those final reassuring comments, she took her leave.

After a few minutes their two hosts joined them.

As they took their seats, Father Martine, now quite nervous, asked in an anxious manner, "Is everything okay? Are you satisfied all necessary arrangements have been made and carried out as they should be?"

Antonio answered in a reassuring voice, "Please don't worry, Father. Everything is under control. Just try and relax. Believe me. Nothing has been left to chance."

Just then, he spotted Don Barcese across the other side of the theatre in his private box with a retinue of guests. He nudged Father Martine, saying, "That's Don Barcese over there. Can you see him?"

"You mean the gentleman in the flashy suit?"

"Yes that's him that's the famous Don Barcese, impresario to the stars."

Francesco, over-hearing Antonio, chimed in, "Forgive my interruption Father, Antonio is quite correct. He just left out two letters in the description. So if I may rephrase, that's the *infamous* Don Barcese."

Father Martine had to make a special effort not to laugh out loud. He did this by reminding himself he was in the most prestigious opera house in the world.

Just then, the lights dimmed. The orchestra came to life. Father Martine leaned across to Antonio and quietly whispered, "My dear son, I have been waiting for this moment for so many years now. Thank you. Thank you so very much for making it possible. I earnestly pray God will guide our Consuella to give her best."

From the opening curtain, the musicians and cast were quite superb. The audience was savouring every single moment. They were completely enthralled by Consuella's beautiful voice. Her delivery and timing was spellbinding.

During the entire performance, she showed no signs of nervousness or stage fright. As the curtain closed, the whole theatre rose in tumultuous applause. Shouts of "bravo, bravo" were followed by the audience chanting Consuella, Consuella. Antonio and Francesco glanced over at their guests and could see they were completely overcome; they had tears of joy running down their faces.

They, however, remained composed, because deep down there was absolutely no doubt in their minds, she would rise to the challenge and give a remarkable performance. For the others, it was a revelation. The fact that Consuella, on this the night of her debut, managed to captivate this audience so convincingly with a performance so exquisite, it just left them overawed and practically speechless.

Father Martine emotionally exclaimed, "Antonio, Francesco, please accept on behalf of us all our profound gratitude for what you have achieved here on this very special evening. What we witnessed in this great theatre was absolutely spellbinding."

Francesco answered him, "Dear Father, it was our great pleasure to have played some small part in what all of you have joyfully experienced. Antonio, Sister Lucia, and myself performed our tasks as best we could. However, it was Consuella who, from the moment she walked onto that stage, showed her bravery and commitment. Her performance was quite remarkable, so your gratitude and praise should really be reserved for what she has achieved. To see the joy and appreciation on the faces of the audience, that for us was reward enough."

Antonio continued where Francesco had left off. "Now, dear friends, I would very much appreciate it if all of you do us the honour of attending a post opera dinner to celebrate Consuella's debut. Francesco will accompany you to the Hotel Galileo. Carlota and the girls have already gone ahead with Dominique and Adamo. I will follow on shortly with Consuella and Sister Lucia. An evening of great celebration awaits us. And if you are on your best behaviour, I might even introduce you to the star of tonight's performance."

Francesco escorted his guests the short distance to the hotel.

Antonio waited backstage until the cast had changed out of their costumes. He then gathered them together, "Tonight, as events director on this opening night, I want to congratulate all of you for a superb performance. In all my time working here, this production is probably the best I've ever seen. I would now like all of you to accompany me for a well-deserved celebration supper.

"On our arrival, I want you to assemble in the foyer. As soon as the music starts, I will give the signal for the cast to enter the ballroom, followed by the Countess Almavina, and her husband, the count. Finally, our two young stars, Susanna and Figaro, will enter. I will then guide all of you to the main table, where you'll be seated in the company of our invited guests."

Antonio and Sister Lucia led the group from the theatre to the grand ballroom of the hotel.

Francesco had already guided his group to where Carlota was now seated.

A group of musicians were on stage performing popular pieces from different operas.

As soon as everyone was seated, Antonio entered and approached the stage. The musicians ceased playing, and he made the following announcement: "Ladies and gentlemen, distinguished guests, I'll be very brief. Tonight, we were very fortunate to witness an absolutely wonderful opening to our opera season. I now invite you to show your appreciation for the cast of tonight's performance."

With that, the musicians immediately launched into the overture. The doors swung open, and the cast trooped in, followed by the Countess Almavina; her husband, the count; and finally the two young stars, a dashing Figaro and the very pretty servant girl Susanna.

As they took their seats, the guests applauded them enthusiastically.

Father Martine rose from his chair. "Dear friends, you may remain seated. I would like you to join me in giving thanks to the Lord for this memorable occasion and the supper we are about to share in God's name. Amen."

As the meal progressed, the conversation around the tables was all about the evening's performance, the orchestra, the chorus, and the wonderful stage sets.

In most instances, though, the main topic of conversation inevitability turned to the outstanding performance of the new discovery, Consuella Pellegrini.

Most of the guests, having now finished their supper, were delighted as the musicians began playing popular waltzes. The ballroom floor was now filling with couples, happily waltzing in a carefree manner.

Sister Maria, now beginning to grow slightly impatient, turned to Father Martine. "Dear Father, I was wondering just now, what are the chances of us getting to meet Consuella anytime soon?"

Meanwhile at the main table, a constant group of well-wishers was arriving non-stop, offering their congratulations to the cast and, in particular, to Consuella.

Now beginning to feel quite overwhelmed, she responded graciously nonetheless.

Antonio decided now would be a good time to rescue her from the throng of well-wishers.

Taking her by the hand, he guided her over to where the others were seated. Bowing formally he announced, "Ladies and gentlemen, may I take this opportunity to introduce you to the star of tonight's wonderful production, Señorita Consuella Pellegrini."

Making her way around the table, she greeted everyone with hugs and kisses and then took a seat between Sister Maria and her father.

Sister Maria took Consuella's hand in hers. Barely able to hold back her tears and quite overcome with emotion, she said, "My dear child, it seems so long since we last saw you. The day you left Verona was a sad day for all of us. We often wondered, had we made a terrible mistake? There were many, many days when all I wanted was to see you in the convent chapel, singing those beautiful hymns. Our only contact with you was through our dear Sister Lucia. She lifted our spirits with her wonderful reports on the tremendous progress you were making. This evening, as I watched you on that stage, it was one of the happiest moments of my life. I will cherish this experience for a very long time to come."

Consuella, now feeling quite emotional, responded, "Thank you, thank you, Reverend Mother, for those kind, kind thoughtful words. Thank you."

Then, leaning over to her father, she embraced him. "Dearest Papa, thank you for bringing Dominique and Adamo. It was such a wonderful surprise. Tonight as I was singing, my thoughts were of dearest Momma. I had a sense she was looking down on all of us from heaven."

With tears in his eyes, Pietro replied, "I too was thinking of your dear Mother and how proud she would have been to be here among us on this special occasion. You were shining a light on our family, and I pray this light burns brightly for you and for all of us in the years to come."

To Father Martine, Consuella just smiled and said, "Dear Father, I hope you were not disappointed tonight."

"Consuella, when you left Verona, I sometimes wondered had I placed too big a burden on one so young? Happily, tonight all those fears and anxieties were banished. Your singing was sublime. Bravissimo."

After some moments of pleasant exchanges, Carlota and Francesco brought their two daughters over. "My two girls have school tomorrow, so I best get them home to bed," Carlota said.

Consuella replied, "Carlota, thank you for the kindness you've shown me since my arrival in Milan."

"It was my pleasure, Consuella."

Taking his two daughters by the hand, Francesco, in a sort of lecturing tone, said to her, "Young lady, you have a day off tomorrow. Nonetheless, I'll be expecting you in my studio the following morning. We still have a lot of work to do."

With that, Carlota grabbed his sleeve. And as she dragged him away, she said, "Don't pay attention to him, Consuella. This is your night. Enjoy it."

And so she did—the music, the conversation, family, and friends.

It was a fitting end to the first night of what promised to be a glittering career.

The following morning, Antonio and Francesco joined Father Martine, Pietro, and Adamo for an early morning breakfast at the hotel.

"Francesco," Father Martine inquired, "I have to ask, how confident were you before the opening curtain Consuella was going to perform as sublimely as she did?"

"That's an interesting question. The answer, I suppose, is you never really know. There was no question in my mind concerning her ability.

That was obvious after the first few coaching sessions. Pietro, I hope you'll forgive me for saying this. When I first met your daughter, my initial thought was, would this shy slightly awkward young girl have the confidence to walk onto a stage and hold her nerve in front of a large, maybe even hostile audience?

"It wasn't until one afternoon in my studio, in the presence of Sister Lucia and Antonio, I sat at the piano and played the opening to an aria from *Cavelleria Rusticana*. With perfect timing, she joined in. For several minutes, we observed as she sang this beautiful piece. What we witnessed was not the shy young girl from Verona, but a beautiful young lady performing an aria in a heavenly voice with superb grace and confidence. From that day on, we knew this opening night would hold no fear for her whatsoever. That's about as good an answer as I can give."

Father Martine replied, "Amazing, quite amazing."

Pietro joined the conversation. "Francesco, I suppose we may never quite understand this gift my daughter possesses. For me, as Consuella's father, I would just like to express my deepest gratitude for all you and Antonio have achieved. It was truly remarkable."

Having finished breakfast, they gathered their suitcases and travelled the short distance to the convent. Sister Maria, Sister Lucia, Consuella, and Dominique were in the drawing room chatting among themselves.

Antonio knocked on the door and entered. "Good morning, Sisters. Good morning, ladies. I take it you all had a restful night's sleep. So when you're ready, we can join the others for a final farewell."

Consuella, hugging her sister and brother, tearfully requested, "Dominique, Adamo, please take good care of Papa. Promise me you will."

She gave her father one last hug. "Have a safe journey. And please, Papa, don't work too hard in the vineyard."

"My dearest Consuella, last night you gave me cause for great joy. I'm so proud of you and what you've achieved in such a short time. So please, don't worry about me. I'll be fine. I'm happy in the knowledge you're in very capable hands. And for that, I'm truly grateful."

Sister Maria and Father Martine bid farewell to Sister Lucia. As they headed for the front door, Consuella called out, "What about me? Are you going to leave without saying goodbye?"

The two of them turned around. Sister Maria held out her two hands. Consuella clasped them tightly in her own.

"My dearest Consuella, it's so difficult for me to say goodbye. So, until we meet again. I promise to keep you in my thoughts and prayers."

Father Martine placed his arm around her shoulder. "Consuella, always remember, this voice you possess is a heavenly gift. Use it wisely and take good care of it. Your destiny is to become a great opera singer. This is something I have always believed. Your performance last night was an affirmation."

Taking both their hands, she walked them to the door.

As the two auto-mobiles pulled away, she and Sister Lucia stood there waving until they faded into the distance.

At Milan Central railway station, just before their guests boarded the train, Francesco purchased copies of *la Repubblica* and *La Stampa* newspapers. He gave a copy of each to Father Martine. "These should make interesting reading on the journey home. Both papers have extensive coverage on last night's performance, and at a quick glance, I'm happy to say Consuella has been singled out for some praiseworthy comments."

"Why thank you, Francesco. That's most thoughtful. I will read them on the journey home, very loudly of course."

Sister Maria had some final words. "Francesco, before I came here, I really didn't know what to expect. It was certainly a great pleasure to finally meet you and your charming wife, Carlota. When Antonio spoke so highly of you back in Verona, I should have of course trusted his judgement. Thank you for your efforts. They are greatly appreciated."

"Thank you, Sister Maria. Have a safe journey. And hopefully, we'll meet again very soon."

Francesco then shook hands with Pietro, Dominique, and Adamo. "I'm sure the three of you on your journey home will agree with me when I say, Consuella's remarkable performance on stage last night must have been an occasion of great happiness and joy for all of you."

As they exchanged handshakes, each of them thanked Francesco for his kind words.

Finally, taking Father Martine's hand in his own, he said, "Father, it was a great honour finally making your acquaintance. Until we meet again, have a safe and pleasant journey."

Antonio, having said his goodbyes to the others, finally turned to his mentor. "Well, Father, any last words before you depart?"

"You know, my son, over the past three months or so, I often asked myself, was I asking too much when I set you the task of transforming a young inexperienced convent girl into a competent soprano? Well I'm delighted to say, that question was answered most emphatically last night. It was truly wonderful. There's no doubt in my mind you and Francesco will give us many more opportunities to celebrate her progress in the months ahead."

As he gave his former student a fond embrace, he whispered quietly in his ear, "Although my mind was doubtful, my heart never lost faith. Thank you, thank you, my son."

With that, they gathered their luggage, made their way along the platform, and boarded the train for the journey back to Verona.

Antonio and Francesco gave a final wave.

As the train pulled out from the station, the two of them walked along the platform at a leisurely pace and then left the station and made their journey home.

CHAPTER 5

The Angel of Verona

Returning to the convent that same afternoon, Antonio proudly set the newspapers on the table. Consuella and Sister Lucia sat silently while he read a sample of what some of the critics had to say.

He quoted from an article in *la Repubblica*. The theatre critic had written, "The performance of this newcomer was a revelation. Her timing and delivery never faltered. Her stage presence was so impressive I had to remind myself many times that this young soprano was making her debut. As she sang, I studied the audience to gauge their reaction There was absolutely no doubt in my mind, the audience was completely enthralled by this young señorita's beautiful voice."

Antonio, with a broad smile, waited for her reaction to this glowing newspaper report.

She calmly replied, "Are you waiting for me to say something, Antonio?"

"Well, are you not excited by what this critic had to say?"

"Antonio, a journalist's job is to sell newspapers. They print words they believe their readers want to hear. That is all this means to me."

"Oh come now, Consuella. Surely you don't mean that. Just let me read you one more from *La Stampa*. In this piece, the writer opens with the heading, 'The angel of Verona captures the—'"

"Antonio, please," Consuella interrupted. "Sister Lucia and I cannot listen to any more of this nonsense. Now, can we talk about something more important instead?"

"Such as?"

"Such as the rest of the season, the productions in which I am due to perform, and the preparations we need to make. After all, we would not like those nice journalists writing nasty things about me, now would we?"

Putting the papers aside, he replied rather sheepishly, "As you wish, Consuella."

"Why thank you, Antonio. Now, let us see. Where should we start?"

Despite her distain for the journalists, the newspaper articles, nonetheless, had a profound effect on the opera-going public. The media coverage guaranteed packed houses. The crowds flocked in their thousands to hear and see 'The Angel Of Verona', a title now popularly bestowed on her by an ever-increasing number of enthusiastic opera lovers.

Whenever she heard this description, she just cringed in embarrassment. Nevertheless, she continued with her daily routine—convent to studio, convent to theatre—and always in the company of her constant companion, the indomitable Sister Lucia.

Over the following weeks, Francesco tirelessly prepared her for the two remaining operas, *Cavalleria Rusticana* and *Pallachi*. With each performance, she went from strength to strength. Sister Lucia's role expanded to that of wardrobe assistant, nurse, and doctor, all rolled into one.

Antonio managed her performing schedule and opened a bank account to accommodate the fees being generated. In addition, he found himself dealing with numerous offers and requests from many other opera houses. He had to balance all of this with his official duties and responsibilities as events director.

After six long arduous weeks, La Scala's curtain finally closed on what had been a most successful opening to the season. Consuella had performed on no less than eighteen occasions. There was absolutely no doubt in the minds of the operatic community; this new discovery, Señorita Pellegrini, was indeed a rising star with huge potential.

While she spent a few days enjoying a well-deserved break from performing, Antonio and Francesco spent the time available planning the continuing development of her career. During one of these sessions, Antonio gave Francesco a selected number of venues he had chosen in the larger cities. He listed the titles of the operas to be staged, including a corresponding calendar of dates.

He then asked Francesco, "When you have an opportunity, would it be possible to study these and give me your opinion?"

Francesco took one look at what was staring at him from the page and replied, "I can see you've been busy. But what exactly is this?"

"As you know, Francesco, I've received numerous invitations from many opera houses requesting they be included in her forthcoming schedule. So I drew up this list of venues. I then cross-referenced them with the titles of the operas they plan to stage and the calendar of dates on which they'll be performed. Finally, I listed the names of the conductors who will be conducting at each venue. That's basically it. Do you have any questions?"

Francesco looked at the sheet of paper one more time and then refocused his attention on Antonio. "You want my opinion on what I have here in front of me?"

Antonio replied rather hesitantly, "Yes, but in your own time; there's no immediate hurry."

"Well, if you like, I'll give you my opinion right now."

Antonio, now quite apprehensive as to what Francesco was about to say, replied in a barely audible voice, "Please? If you will, I'm listening."

Taking a deep breath and staring straight ahead, Francesco replied, "This paper I have here before me is probably the most brilliant piece of preparatory work I have ever come across. I am going to study it in great detail. When I'm done the two of us can then sit down and draw up a schedule that suits her best. This information will enable us to select the most appropriate venues and the operas that match her abilities the most. Finally, we can decide the dates and frequency of all appearances, thereby allowing appropriate intervals of rest to ensure she doesn't experience bouts of fatigue. Well done, young Antonio, well done."

All Antonio could say in reply was, "Really? You think it is that good?"

"Yes I do. It really is that good. And to show my appreciation, I am going to treat you to a fine meal at Marios."

"I humbly accept but with one condition."

"Pray tell, what is the condition?"

"You allow me buy the wine."

"Agreed."

CHAPTER 6

Francesco Confronts Don Barcese

On entering the restaurant, Antonio and Francesco were greeted by Mario, owner and occasional head waiter.

As he was about to show them to their regular table, they couldn't help but notice Don Barcese holding court with his usual retinue of hangers-on.

"Mario, it's a little noisy here. Antonio and I have some business to discuss. Could we possibly have that table over there in the corner?"

"Of course, Señor Francesco. Please follow me."

As they sat down, Mario enquired, "Gentlemen, this is the quietest spot in the restaurant. I do hope it's to your liking?"

"This is just fine, Mario. Now what would you recommend from your extensive wine list?"

"Well, Señor Antonio, your choice of wine very much depends on what it is you choose for your main course."

"The fish."

"And yourself, Señor Francesco?"

"The same."

Handing Antonio the wine list with a dramatic flourish, Mario continued, "In that case, Señor Antonio, I would have absolutely no hesitation, no hesitation whatsoever, in recommending the Nivasco Piomonte. This most definitely has to be the one."

Glancing at the price Antonio responded, "It seems somewhat expensive to me."

"Oh, Señor Antonio, what is price between old friends? Trust me. I know deep down in my heart of hearts you and Señor Francesco will savour every last sip."

"And if we don't, can I take it then there'll be no charge?"

Mario just smiled. "Ah, there you go, Señor Antonio, always making with the jokes. I will now personally go to the wine cellar and select your wine. In the meantime I will send Angelo over to take your order. So now, gentlemen, relax and enjoy the rest of your evening in my humble establishment."

With a theatrical bow worthy of a character in a Shakespeare play, Mario headed for the wine cellar.

The two of them just watched as he glided across the floor.

After a moment or two, Francesco, in a casual kind of way, remarked, "There's no doubt in my mind, if I were to take Mario for a few voice coaching sessions, you'd be able to land him a part in a Puccini opera."

With a broad smile on his face, Antonio replied, "Of that, I have no doubt. For a head waiter, he certainly does add a theatrical touch."

While the two friends were eating, chatting, and enjoying their wine, suddenly there was a commotion over in the direction of Don Barcese's table.

A very angry-looking individual who was not a patron entered in a somewhat agitated state. He walked over to where Don Barcese was sitting, lifted a glass of wine from the table, and threw it in his face. As Mario and Angelo attempted to restrain him, Don Barcese wiped his face and the front of his shirt with a napkin. Then slamming his fist forcefully down, scattering glasses in the process, he bellowed, "What's the meaning of this outrage? How dare you come in here and attack me in this barbaric fashion? Who on God's earth do you think you are? I demand to know. In God's name, tell me, tell me, you worthless wretch. Mark my words; you will pay dearly for this unprovoked assault. Do you know who I am? Do you have any idea who you are dealing with?"

Despite being restrained, Don Barcese's assailant somehow managed to answer. "I know who you are, you abominable creature. Now just in case you've forgotten, I'll tell you who I am. My name is Alberto Mollinaro. I am the father of Violetta Mollinaro, and you are the monster who destroyed my daughter's life. I pray you rot in hell, Don Marco Barcese."

Staff and customers alike, now in total shock, could only stare in stunned silence at the drama being played out in front of their very eyes.

Francesco laid his cutlery down and stood up from the table. "Excuse me, Antonio. I'll be back in a moment. There's something I need to attend to."

He made his way across the room to where Mario and Angelo were having some difficulty in holding on to Señor Mollinaro.

"Mario, please, if you will release your hold on this gentleman, I give you my word I will escort him from your dining room and out of the restaurant. I promise you I will do this. So please, just let him go. Trust me. I will do as I say."

Mario hesitated momentarily and then motioned to Angelo. Slowly, very slowly, they released their grip. Francesco took Alberto Mollinaro by the arm and very slowly walked him from the dining room to the main entrance and out into the street.

Mario, now in somewhat of a panic, announced, "Ladies and gentlemen, please accept my deepest apologies for this minor disturbance just now."

Being Mario, he couldn't resist inserting a touch of drama. "One has to ask oneself, why do such things happen? Who knows? I suppose the only thing I can say for certain is they do, unfortunately, happen from time to time. So please, I promise no more disturbances. Finally I would like all of you present to accept a glass of wine of your choice, with my compliments of course."

He now rather reluctantly made his way over to Don Barcese's table. "Don Barcese, please forgive me for the inconvenience visited upon you this evening. I would be so glad if you were to accept, with my compliments of course, a bottle of my finest wine."

"Is that what you call it, an inconvenience? And what was all that nonsense about 'these things happen'? Now you can bring me two bottles of wine. And at the end of the evening, don't bother presenting me with a bill."

Mario who didn't know the meaning of the word embarrassing, asked quite innocently, "Pray tell, Don Barcese, why would I not bring you your bill?"

Answering him in a voice the whole restaurant could here, Don Barcese bellowed, "Because, I have no intention of paying it. And when I leave this restaurant, I will give very careful consideration as to whether I will ever dine in this establishment again. Have I made myself clear?"

"Yes, Don Barcese, that's indeed very clear. Now, if you'll excuse me, I'll bring you your wine—that is, your two bottles of wine."

Having managed to escort Señor Mollinaro from the restaurant, Francesco guided him to a vacant table under the awning on the outside of the building. Looking around and making sure they were quite alone, he sat him down and waited just long enough to allow him to gain some degree of composure and then spoke to him in a calm reassuring tone, "Alberto, can you please give me some reason, perhaps some kind of explanation, anything at all that might explain why you did what you did in there?"

With tears in his eyes and in a state of utter despair he replied, "My daughter's life is in ruins because of him. Yet there he is, being chauffeured around town in his fine auto-mobile, wearing expensive suits, dining in the best restaurants, and enjoying the luxury of a private box at the opera. This isn't fair, Señor Francesco. It's just not right."

"I know, but I'm trying to understand, why this evening of all evenings? What was it that prompted you to do what you did? Because if I recall correctly, it is at least nine months since Violetta's unfortunate incident."

"That was no unfortunate incident; it was, in fact his greed and negligence that brought about her breakdown. Since the night of her collapse and humiliation on La Scala's stage, she has never recovered. During these past months, I've nursed and taken care of her as best I could. Most of the time, I just about managed to avoid meeting him. It was never my intention to provoke a confrontation.

"Today, however, was quite different. In the afternoon, Violetta took a bad turn. I rushed her to the doctor; his diagnosis was, as before, deep depression and acute melancholia. He gave me a prescription and then advised me to get her home to bed. This I did. When she was finally settled, I made my way to the pharmacy to purchase her medication. On my way home in the last hour or so, I was passing this very building and saw him stepping out of his auto-mobile with not a care in the world. There and then, I could feel my blood boiling. The rest you and the entire restaurant witnessed."

"Okay, Alberto. Here's what I'm suggesting you do right now. I want you to go home straight away and take care of Violetta. When she's well enough, bring her to my studio. If there's anything I can do to assist her, I will be more than willing to do so. I'm asking you to do this, not for my sake, but for the sake of your precious daughter, Violetta."

"Thank you, Señor Francesco, you are a decent, kind person. I will do as you suggest."

Gently taking Alberto by the arm, he led him to a waiting cab. "Driver, my friend and I were having a meal, and he suddenly felt unwell. Can you please take him home straight away?"

He paid the cab driver the fare, bid Alberto good night, and waited until the cab had pulled out of sight.

As he returned to the dining room, Don Barcese addressed him as he was passing his table. "Ah there you are, Señor Francesco. May I offer you my gratitude and humble thanks for your timely intervention. My dining companions and I are most appreciative for the effort you made in dealing with this unfortunate incident."

"Don Barcese, any effort I made was certainly not for your benefit or on behalf of your sycophantic group of yes-men. The reason for my intervention was to escort a gentleman of my acquaintance from your obnoxious presence. I came to his aid as any decent human being would do in similar circumstances. You of all people, with your deceitful sense of outrage, know very well the reason behind this 'unfortunate incident' as you prefer to call it."

The entire restaurant, in the course of less than half an hour, once again found themselves looking on in disbelief.

Francesco continued, "You, Don Barcese, exploited the promising talents of his daughter, Violetta for your own selfish ends. Then when you had no further use for her, you cast her aside in a despicable fashion. You, señor, have no shame; you don't even know the meaning of the word."

With that, he just walked away and rejoined Antonio.

Don Barcese, now desperately trying to control the anger and resentment building up inside him, attempted to make light of the situation with a feeble remark. "That, gentlemen, was the voice of the voice coach. In the operatic world, these so-called experts have great difficulty in determining what it is they actually are. All I can say is, they're neither fish nor fowl."

On cue, his dining companions cackled like hens at his desperate attempt to appear witty and urbane. Then quite abruptly, he turned the two empty wine bottles upside down in the ice buckets. He stood up, and just as he was about to leave in the company of his companions, Mario, ever alert, made it to the front door ahead of him.

Holding the door open, Mario enquired, "Dear Don Barcese, despite that little setback earlier, I really do hope you and your guests enjoyed your evening."

Don Barcese, eyes bulging and face red with anger, practically roared, "This very evening, I have been insulted and slandered in this establishment of yours, not once, but twice. When I walk out this door, I can promise you one thing."

"And what would that be, Don Barcese?"

Now ready to explode, he screamed, "I promise you, you jumped-up waiter posing as a restraunter, I will never, and neither will any of my companions ever, darken your door again."

Mario remained silent just for the briefest of moments and then calmly responded, "There's no need, no need at all, for you to even contemplate such drastic action."

"I challenge you here and now. Why shouldn't I do as I say?"

"Because, Don Barcese, as of this very moment, I am barring you and your bunch of cronies from eating in my restaurant ever again. Now, if you don't mind, I will bid you a good night."

With that, he practically slammed the door in his face.

Back in the dining room, he made his way over to Antonio and Francesco. "Let me be the first to congratulate you on the manner in which you dealt with that earlier situation. Though I have to say. Señor Francesco, your words to Don Barcese on your return seemed to upset him somewhat."

"In what way?"

"Well, as he stormed out, he stated he would never darken my door again. I will certainly miss the excitement, but somehow I think I'll manage. Señor Antonio, Señor Francesco, I will now leave you to enjoy the remainder of your evening. By the way, was the wine to your liking?"

"Yes indeed. As a matter of fact, you made an excellent choice."

"So, can I take it we won't be quibbling over the bill?"

"Yes, Mario, you can take it we won't be quibbling over the bill."

"Excellent, excellent. In that case, would you do me the honour of accepting a complimentary glass of wine?"

"One glass?"

"Ah, there you go again, Señor Antonio, always making with the jokes. But tonight, I'm feeling generous, so let's make it two glasses."

Once more with a theatrical bow, Mario departed to fetch their wine.

While enjoying their wine, Antonio queried Francesco on his reasons for becoming involved in the earlier confrontation. "When you interceded on behalf of that poor unfortunate individual, I was somewhat perplexed. How well do you know him?"

"I knew him reasonably well for about a year before his daughter Violetta collapsed. I've hardly seen him since. His unfortunate daughter, I haven't seen since that tragic event. But surely, Antonio, you must have come across her in your role as events director?"

"Yes, now that you mention it, I did meet her on one or two occasions. Though on the night in question, if I recall, I was in Verona attending my sister's wedding. When I returned, another soprano was already rehearsing her role. I have to confess she just faded from my memory rather quickly.

"So tell me, when you took him outside, were you able to ascertain what it was that prompted him to act in such a way? More importantly, did you find out any more about his daughter and how she's doing?"

"Firstly, the reason I was so angry on my return was the fact that, on the many occasions I've met him in the past, I've always found him to be a pleasant individual. The relative success his daughter was having meant so much to him. She is all he has in the whole world. He's a widower and has no other children. He invested his whole life in her career.

"Then that creature came along. Poor Alberto, he was completely taken in by that scoundrel. Well, the rest you know. Violetta isn't the first to be badly represented and mistreated by this individual, and she certainly won't be the last. The heartbreaking part is, outside this restaurant tonight I was looking at a broken man and a broken life. And what he told me about his daughter leads me to believe she is in a worse state."

Antonio, quite shocked as he listened to this harrowing tale, replied, "This is such a shame. What is to become of father and daughter? What kind of future can they possibly have after suffering such trauma?"

"Before I sent him home, I asked him to call to my studio whenever her condition improves."

"What do you have in mind?"

"Well, I've heard her sing, and so have you. She has an excellent voice. It's my belief a course of voice training and some positive encouragement would enable her to resume her career sometime in the near future."

"May I make a suggestion?"

"Of course."

"When you have this meeting, would it be possible for me to attend?"

"Do you have a reason?"

"Well I would like to find out more and if I can offer some assistance."

"That's an excellent suggestion. When the time comes, I will put it to him. I'm sure he won't have any objections."

With the excitement of the minor commotion now behind them and finally having the opportunity to relax a little, Francesco continued, "When we came in here earlier, I was anticipating a quiet pleasant evening, you know two friends having an agreeable meal, sharing a bottle of wine. Who would have predicted it was going to end in such drama? That's the interesting thing about life, I suppose. You never really know what's waiting for you around the next corner.

"Now it's getting late. I think it's time we settle our bill with Mario and take our leave. We're not due to meet Consuella until the day after tomorrow. I suggest we use the time available to plan her schedule for the next three months or so."

"That's an excellent suggestion. I'll come by at ten in the morning. Now I wonder, where Mario has gotten to?"

After some friendly haggling, they settled their account with Mario and bid him a fond farewell.

Chapter 7

Sister Colombina

The following morning at the convent, Consuella and Sister Lucia were having breakfast with the other sisters. The rather loud ringing of a bell startled her somewhat.

"Goodness me, Sister. What on earth was that? Is the convent on fire or something?"

"No, no, Consuella. It's nothing of the sort. That's the bell calling the students to assembly."

"But why have I not heard it before?"

"Assembly call generally takes place at beginning and end of term or on such other occasions Sister Colombina decides there is something of sufficient importance to justify it. Surely you haven't forgotten your time at the convent in Verona already?"

"Oh yes, now I remember. We'd all troop into the assembly hall. The sisters would file onto the stage. Finally, Reverend Mother would make her dramatic entrance. On most occasions, if I recall correctly, her favourite topics would be the parlous state of the convent finances, the leaking roof, and its current state of disrepair. But without fail there would always be a collective chastisement for some minor infractions, like splashing our fingers in the holy water font, hastily making the sign of the cross, or genuflecting using the incorrect knee. These disrespectful acts, she would remind us, at the very least were serious enough for us to remember at our next confession. But still, I have to say I do remember those assemblies quite fondly. Do you have any idea what topics Sister Colombina has on her agenda for today's assembly?"

"Just one."

"Good, so it won't take too long. And do you know the subject matter?"

"Why yes indeed. The theme of today's topic is you."

"Why on earth would I be the topic of discussion in front of students who've probably never even heard of me?"

"Believe me, Consuella, they've heard of you. And Sister Colombina wants to hold you up as a shining example of what can be achieved with hard work and dedication. When you're ready, I'll accompany you. And by the way, Sister Colombina wants you to make your entrance with her onto the stage."

"Very well, Sister. Lead the way. I have to say, though, that I would be a lot more comfortable sitting among the students instead."

Sister Lucia took her place on stage with the other nuns.

Consuella stood rather nervously next to Sister Colombina, who was just standing there waiting for the students to take their seats.

Looking in Consuella's direction, Sister Colombina gave her precise instructions. "Now, my dear, I would like you to accompany me onto the stage. I will address the assembly. All you have to do is stand close by looking as pretty as you possibly can. When it's appropriate, I'll permit you the occasional smile. Do you think you can manage that?"

Slightly intimidated, she meekly replied, "I'll do my best, Sister. That is, I mean I'll try to smile when you deem it appropriate."

As she followed Sister Colombina out to face the students, she couldn't help but notice the manner in which they were just sitting there with bored blank expressions on their faces.

Sister Colombina, now at the lectern, adopted a formal pose and then began her address.

"Dear children, today I would like to introduce you to this charming young lady beside me. Her name is Señorita Consuella Pellegrini. Consuella is a guest here among us. You might have seen her coming and going in the company of our dear Sister Lucia. Now it might come as a surprise to you, Consuella is a former pupil from our convent in Verona. During her time there, she studied hard and was always obedient. In addition she also sang in the choir. Her wonderful voice left a lasting impression on the sisters and the wider community.

"One day, a very important person from La Scala happened to be visiting. By chance, he got to hear Consuella singing in the monastery chapel. He immediately recognised her talent and arranged an audition.

Now as Consuella stands here before you on this very stage, I'm delighted to say she was chosen to sing in three operas in that most famous theatre, the very heart of Italian opera, La Scala in Milan.

"Now, children, the reason I summoned you here was to give you an opportunity to see our own dear Consuella standing here beside me. When you return to your classrooms I want you to bring an image with you. I want all of you to concentrate your minds. If, like Consuella, you follow the path of study, hard work, dedication to the task, and most importantly obedience, you too can achieve great success.

"So now I would like you to show your appreciation for what Consuella has accomplished and the wonderful example she has set—not just for the students of Saint Mary Magdalena's convent in Verona, but also for all of you young ladies here today."

Sister Colombina turned to Consuella and beckoned her to step forward. This she did smiling and bowing as previously instructed.

The students stood up and gave her a rapturous applause.

For a moment, Consuella felt she was back on the stage of La Scala. Still bowing and smiling, she was thinking maybe she should say a few words to encourage the students.

One glance from Sister Colombina banished the thought. As she left the stage in the company of Sister Colombina and Sister Lucia, she made a valiant effort in finding the appropriate words to thank Sister Colombina for her glowing remarks. "Dear Sister, thank you so much for the honour bestowed on me just now. I really do appreciate it. But honestly, I really don't deserve it."

"You don't deserve what exactly?"

Now utterly confused, she hesitantly replied, "Those, those very kind words you spoke just now."

"Oh, you poor deluded child, that little exhibition out there wasn't for you at all at all. I was just using you and the fortunate position you happen to find yourself in to urge those obstinate stubborn young girls to greater efforts. That's all. So now if you'll excuse me, I have a very busy day ahead of me."

Before Consuella even had a chance to make any kind of response, Sister Colombina in a very matter-of-fact kind of way whirled around and headed in the direction of her office. Her long black habit swishing from side to side as she marched down the corridor.

Sister Lucia took one look at Consuella, who was now in a momentary state of shock. She just smiled and said, "That, Consuella, was your official welcome to the Milan branch of the convent of Saint Mary Magdalena."

"Well it's reassuring to know I'm so highly thought of, especially by Sister Napoleon. Is she always like this?"

"Oh don't take it to heart; her bark is much worse than her bite. In fact, she's very proud of what you've achieved, and she really does think very highly of you. Believe me; she has said this to me on more than one occasion.

"I think a cup of coffee right now would be most helpful. What do you say?"

"That is the most sensible and, may I say, welcome suggestion I have heard so far this morning."

As they walked towards the dining room arm in arm, Consuella, with a smile on her face, continued, "You know, if I hadn't had you by my side these past few months, I think by now, I would have probably run all the way back to Verona."

"Come on, Consuella. I know you are much tougher than that. Now let us go in and enjoy that well-earned cup of coffee."

CHAPTER 8

Remaining Concert Dates

During the time Sister Colombina was waging her charm offensive, Antonio and Francesco got down to the serious task of planning Consuella's forthcoming schedule.

The itinerary included cities in Lombardy—Brescia, Bergamo, and Piacenza. Following this, Antonio planned a three-night appearance at the Teatro Comunale in Bologna. From there, his intention was for them to travel south-west to Tuscany and the beautiful city of Florence.

"Francesco, have you ever been to Florence?"

"Yes, I've visited once or twice. It's very beautiful."

"I promise you, this segment of the tour will be something very special. Instead of Consuella appearing in Puccini's *Tosca* at the Teatro della Pergola, my suggestion is we book her to play the tragic heroine, Violetta, in Verdi's *La Traviata*. The four-night production will be staged at Saint Mark's English Church. This venue is steeped in history and is part of the Medici Palace."

Francesco replied, "You might be interested to know, Machiavelli in his time acquired the entire estate and actually lived there."

Antonio couldn't help but smile at the mention of the name.

Francesco, somewhat puzzled, asked, "Did I say something amusing?"

"No, no, not at all. It's just when you mentioned Machiavelli, it reminded me of something I said to Father Martine not too long ago."

"Nothing too serious I hope."

"No, it was just on an occasion when we were having a discussion, or rather, he was having the discussion with me. All I remember is making a remark along the lines that one would need the skills of Machiavelli to succeed in the priesthood."

"How did he react?"

"I think you know him reasonably well by now. He just smiled and took it in his stride. Maybe we should invite him to Florence."

Francesco, with a smile on his face, replied, "Now who's being amusing? Let's get back to your schedule. I must say though, your idea in relation to the venue in Florence sounds exciting and quite different. So where to next?"

"At this stage, we'll be into September. My suggestion is we journey north to Padua for the staging of Rossini's, *The Barber of Seville*. The part of Rosina would be perfect for her. The next city on my list is Venice. The Teatro Malbran has scheduled four performances of Verdi's *Il Travatore*. In this production, she can take on the role of the noble lady Leonara. I would very much like to hear her sing the beautiful aria, 'Di Quella Pira.'"

"When this programme of appearances comes to an end, we have but one stop before the season closes. Would you care to hear my suggestion?"

"Well so far, I see no fault with the schedule you've outlined just now. So please, enlighten me."

"For her final performances of the season, Consuella will take on the role of Micaela in Bizet's *Carmen*. The venue for this production will be the Arena Verona, the city of her birth and the very place where this grand adventure first saw the light of day. Now on this occasion, do you suppose I should invite Father Martine?"

"Oh, maybe you might just mention it in passing."

Antonio just looked at him with a bemused smile, "Could you imagine Consuella performing in Verona without him being present?"

"Well if that were to happen, I doubt very much you would ever be able to show your face in Verona again."

"Is that all? I think I would have to leave Italy altogether. Now on a more serious note, I will brief Consuella and Sister Lucia tomorrow morning. I will start booking the venues, make the travel arrangements, and arrange hotel accommodation. When this task is completed, I will issue a gilt-edged invitation to Father Martine for the performance in Verona, though I think I'll just skip Florence."

"Good thinking, Antonio. I'm beginning to think this job is making you wise beyond your years."

Antonio just smiled in return.

The following day, Antonio began preparing the schedule as agreed with Francesco. He sent a detailed report of the dates and venues to Verona.

That same afternoon, he briefed Consuella and Sister Lucia on the planned programme. "Unfortunately, Francesco's schedule doesn't allow him to accompany you for the duration of the full tour. Though he will make every effort to meet with the conductors and check the acoustics at the various venues. He promises to be definitely in Verona for the final stage. There's five days left before the first performance in Brescia. Sister Lucia, can you make the necessary arrangements for yourself and Consuella?"

"Of course. Regarding accommodation, our order has convents in most of the locations. I believe Reverend Mother would expect us to avail ourselves of these facilities during our travels."

"That's fine, Sister. I'll leave that entirely up to you. It will be one task less for me to worry about.

"Consuella, you and Francesco will need to go through the entire programme. I don't want to leave anything to chance. Any questions?"

Consuella responded, "I'm quite overwhelmed. All of this has happened so fast. I can hardly believe it. You really mean it Antonio, when you say I will actually sing an aria on the stage of the Arena Verona."

Antonio replied, "Consuella, it will be more much more than that. You will play the part of Micaela in Bizet's opera *Carmen*. It's not the lead role. The reason I made this choice is because Micaela is a most gentle and sensitive character compared to the more aggressive Carmen. In this production, you get to sing the best-loved and most-remembered aria. It's simply called 'Micaela's Aria'."

And so the grand tour began. With each city and with each performance, Consuella was fast becoming the most talked about performer within the operatic community—not just in Lombardy, but throughout the other regions as well. Her modest lifestyle generated even more interest among her ever-growing number of admirers.

By the time they reached Verona in mid-September 1909, there was a keen sense of anticipation among the population at large. After all, one of their own was returning in triumph to perform for them in the great arena.

As their train pulled into the station, there to greet them were Father Martine and Pietro.

On their way to the convent, Consuella chatted excitedly with her father about all the marvellous cities she had visited since her departure from Milan.

As they were driven through the convent gates, both sides of the drive were lined with students. As she passed by, they waved and cheered. She was quite overcome with the warmth and affection being shown to her from a group who, only six months past, were fellow students.

Sister Maria and the other nuns were waiting at the main door.

As the cab came to a halt, Pietro, Father Martine, and Antonio stepped out. They then assisted Sister Lucia and Consuella from the cab.

Sister Maria greeted them enthusiastically. "Welcome, welcome back to Verona. I've been waiting a long time for this day. So please, everyone, I would like you to join us in the dining room. I'm so excited I can barely catch my breath."

As they were eating, Antonio brought them up to date on all that had taken place over the past number of weeks—the cities, the theatres, and the many performances.

Father Martine enquired, "Tell me, Antonio, looking back on this, Consuella's first tour, did you ever fear the schedule and maybe the number of performances might have been too much of a burden for someone just starting her career?"

He replied matter-of-factly. "I believe Consuella would be the best person to answer that question. Before she does, I'd just like to say, Francesco and myself devised a system, a methodology if you like, that factored in everything. This enabled us devise a plan we thought would best suit Consuella. As I said earlier, though, the best person to answer this question is Consuella herself."

Father Martine asked, "Well Consuella, as you're nearing the final part of your first operatic season, I'd be most interested in what you have to say."

"Looking back, at times I found the schedule quite challenging, but not once did I feel overburdened or fatigued. I have to say their planning was measured and well thought out. However, there are still four performances left. And these are, without doubt, much more important than anything that's gone before. So I hope I haven't spoken too soon."

Sister Maria answered, "Not at all, Consuella. I believe you'll do us all proud when you step onto the Arena stage."

"Thank you, Reverend Mother. I will do my best. Now, if I may be excused, would it perhaps be okay if I took a rest?"

"Of course, my dear. Sister Serafina, would you be so kind and take Consuella to her room?"

With the five of them remaining, Father Martine continued. "Now, Antonio, when can we expect Francesco?"

"Oh, sometime later this evening."

"Excellent. When he arrives, we can get together. With this first tour almost completed, it would certainly be desirable to have a more permanent arrangement in place."

Sister Maria joined in. "That's a sensible suggestion, Father. Do you have any thoughts, Antonio?"

"Not really. I think Francesco and myself will be happy to go along with whatever you suggest."

"Well then, as soon as he arrives, we can get started. Pietro, could you speak with Consuella and get her thoughts?"

"If it's all right with you, Sister, I would much prefer if you spoke with her."

"Of course, Pietro. Now that that's settled, if we can be excused, Sister Lucia and I have some tasks to attend to. When Francesco arrives, I'll join you."

The three of them remained.

An hour or so later, Francesco arrived. When Sister Serafina showed him in, Father Martine greeted him warmly. "Ah, Francesco, there you are. Please, come and join us. Would you care for some food?"

"No thank you, Father. A cup of coffee though would be most welcome."

"Sister, could you bring a pot of coffee and let Reverend Mother know our guest has arrived."

As they were having their coffee, Sister Maria returned. She began by saying, "Well, now that we're all present, I think we can get the meeting under way. Before we begin, does anyone have any questions?"

Antonio asked, "Have you spoken with Consuella?"

"Yes I have. But before I get to that, if I may, I would like to take you back to our initial discussions last March. Back then, we weren't certain if this project was going to be successful or not. I'm happy to say what you and Francesco have achieved is truly remarkable. I remember us agreeing on a modest fee for your services and a more permanent arrangement to be discussed at a later date.

"We have now reached that stage and are prepared to enter into an agreement that fairly reflects the effort put in by both of you. Before we do, I have two questions. The first is, are the two of you prepared to enter into this more permanent arrangement? And if so, how would this impact your other responsibilities?"

Francesco was first to respond. "For me, personally, this new situation wouldn't affect me greatly. I will still be available to assist Consuella in her preparations for any opera in any theatre. I intend reducing my coaching activities in the near future, though that has to do with a different project I've been developing."

Father Martine, ever alert, jumped in. "Francesco, I've only known you a short time. You are certainly a most intriguing character. So tell me, what's this big mysterious project of yours?"

"Father Martine, I promise you, when this project is ready for implementation, you'll be the first to know."

"Francesco, I'm going to hold you to that promise." Then in mock seriousness, he carried on. "Antonio, when are you going to answer Sister Maria?"

Well used to Father Martine's mischievous sense of humour, Antonio knew better than to rise to the bait. Ignoring him, he answered her question. "Sister Maria, if we agree to terms this evening, it would be a great honour for me to continue guiding Consuella's career into what I believe will be an exciting future."

Again, a mischievous Father Martine cut in. "Antonio, we don't need the Gettysburg address. Can you just please answer the question?"

"Thank you, Father. As always, your interventions are both timely and diplomatic. Now, Sister, to your second question. At the earliest opportunity, I will resign my position at La Scala. Also, I would like to reserve the right to manage other aspiring artistes. Finally, I promise, Francesco and I during our tenure will do everything possible to assist Consuella in becoming the best operatic performer throughout Italy. My apologies, dear Father, for the long-winded response."

Sister Maria answered him, "Antonio, you and Francesco have been very clear. Don't pay any heed to Father. Now, I spoke with Consuella earlier, and this is how she would like her fees dispersed. For yourself and Francesco, she has requested 30 per cent be allocated for your services. How you split it she is leaving up to the two of you to decide. Another 30 per cent, she will retain for her own use. She has very generously allocated 5 per cent each to the convent and the monastery. The remaining 30 per cent will be lodged to an account on her father's behalf. This will enable him develop his vineyard and winemaking enterprise. Regarding Sister Lucia and the selfless tasks she's performed, Consuella suggested Father Martine and myself assist her nieces and nephews from time to time with their tuition fees.

"Finally, with her nineteenth birthday just two weeks away, I'm suggesting we agree a two-year contract. This will take us up to her twenty-first birthday. Who knows what sort of discussions we'll be having when that day comes?"

Antonio and Francesco sat for a few moments without saying anything. Father Martine, now slightly anxious, decided to gently push them into some kind of response. "So there you have it, gentlemen. I think the proposals put forward are fair and reasonable. So how say you?"

Antonio glanced at his companion; they made eye contact, nothing more.

Father Martine was busy looking from one to the other, desperately trying to read the passing signals.

Noting his anxious expression, they played out their little charade for another moment or two.

Finally Francesco responded, "Father Martine, if it is okay with you, Antonio would prefer it if it was myself answering on our behalf."

Father Martine had a heart-stopping moment. He couldn't help but feel a rejection was coming, and Antonio, not wanting to be impolite had signalled his companion to deliver the bad news. Putting on his best smile, he replied as calmly as his nerves would allow. "Why of course, Francesco, of course it is okay. Please, in your own time, please continue."

Francesco, with a roguish smile, replied, "We accept your proposals."

Father Martine, having feared the worst and totally surprised by the positive outcome, uncharacteristically stumbled over his response. "What? You what? You mean you accept. Haven't you any questions, any conditions of your own you would like us to consider?"

At this stage, Sister Maria intervened. "Father, I believe our two friends have given us their answer. What we need to do now is draw up the necessary papers. By tomorrow, we will have ourselves a contract."

Father Martine replied in as much as his fractured nerves would allow. "Of course, Sister. I was confident all along they would accept our proposals as fair and reasonable."

Antonio made the following suggestion concerning the contract: "Sister Maria, Francesco and myself are satisfied with what has been agreed just now. So there is no need for a written contract. We both take you at your word, and that's good enough for both of us."

Father Martine, now slightly confused, looked to Sister Maria.

She responded, "Well said, Antonio. We now have an agreement that is so much more valuable than words written on a piece of paper. I congratulate you both on your integrity and willing cooperation."

Standing up, she shook hands with the two of them. Father Martine and Pietro did likewise. Sister Maria brought the proceedings to a close. "Well, it is getting late. I am sure you gentlemen would like to be getting back to your hotel. Have a safe journey, and I look forward to seeing you all at the Arena Verona."

Father Martine was now in quite a happy mood. "Antonio, why don't the four of us share a cab," he suggested. "We can drop Pietro off on the way, and I will take you and Francesco to your hotel. How does that sound?"

"You know, Father, that may be the best suggestion you made all night."

As Father Martine scowled back, the other two couldn't help but smile.

Francesco chided him. "My oh my, Father. I think you may have trained your pupil a little too well."

"How so?"

"Well, from where I'm standing, I do believe young Antonio here is beginning to beat you at your own game."

"You know, Francesco, I think you are quite correct. That's my weakness. I have always been too generous, and some of my students have not always shown me the respect I deserve, present company excluded of course."

Then with a broad smile, he finished by saying, "I think now would be a good time to go, before I change my mind about that cab ride to your hotel."

Having been dropped off, Antonio and Francesco decided to have a light supper.

During the meal, Antonio brought up Consuella's method of reward and the possible dilemma it posed. "Francesco, I was just wondering, do you have any thoughts on how we should deal with the payment Consuella allocated for us?"

"Well, she certainly found a novel way of providing us with an opportunity to test our friendship. For me, personally, I'm happy to leave it to you."

"You see, now you have given me the difficult task."

"It's not a difficult task. All you have to do is offer me what you think my services are worth."

"That's just it. If I offer you a sum you feel is inadequate, you will think I am quite mean and selfish. On the other hand, if I offer a sum you feel is too generous, you will most likely draw the conclusion I am naive and foolish."

"Antonio, please. I have a lot of work to do tomorrow. I don't want to be here all night. So here is what I'm suggesting. I will write down on my napkin what I think I'm worth. You do the same with yours."

"You mean I write down on my napkin what I think you are worth."

"Goodness gracious, I really am beginning to believe we will be here all night. Antonio, you write down on your napkin what you think you are worth. We then exchange napkins, and on the count of three, we turn them over to see the figure each of us has written."

"Oh I understand now, kind of like a duel but without the pistols."

Francesco wearily replied, "At this stage, I am fast coming to the conclusion a duel would be a more practical solution. Now, Antonio, can we just do this?"

They exchanged napkins. And then on his count—one, two, three, go—they turned the napkins over.

Francesco's had the number fifteen. Antonio's had the number five.

"Ah, now I see. You are really saying I am worth 25 per cent, and I am saying you are worth fifteen per cent."

"No, that's not it at all. Each of us has revealed the value we have placed on ourselves. Looking at these figures, the next part is simple. My suggestion is you increase your estimation of your own worth by 5 per cent. You recommend I increase mine by the same amount. The sum does not change. It is still 30 per cent. Yet both of us have gained on where we were when we started out. This way, neither of us has insulted the other."

"Francesco, sometimes you amaze me."

"Well, Antonio, maybe I should be in the amazing business. Now if you don't mind, I would like to take myself off to my room and get some sleep, I'm tired and there's a lot of work to be done over the coming days."

As they headed out of the dining room, Antonio was somewhat relieved the fee issue had been settled amicably and most sensibly between them.

For her last and final performance, Antonio and Francesco were joined by Sister Maria, Father Martine, Pietro, Dominique, and Adamo. This occasion was even more special than the night of her debut. They shared an overwhelming sense of euphoria. After all, this was her native city.

Carmen by George Bizet, the organisers' choice, was the third most popular opera of all time. With Consuella singing Micaela's beautiful aria, they and the audience had an overwhelming sense that she belonged to them and the wonderful city of Verona.

After the final curtain, Antonio invited all of them to the post opera supper at the aptly named Hotel San Pietro. The seating arrangements, he made sure, enabled all of them to be seated together in the large dining room.

During the course of the evening, Sister Maria stood up and delivered a short speech, "Dear friends, it is such a joy and a great honour to be here this evening celebrating with our very own dearest Consuella on this her triumphant return to her home city of Verona. She has indeed done us proud these past four nights. I am delighted to announce we have reached an agreement with Señor Antonio and Señor Francesco, which will take us through to her twenty-first birthday. Finally, I would like to take this opportunity to thank Consuella for the donations she has so generously bequeathed to the monastery and the convent. Father, would you care to say a few words?"

Standing up, he cleared his throat as if preparing for a speech to a synod of bishops. He then began. "What can I say? I believe Reverend Mother has already said what needs to be said. I would just like to add, over the past few months there were many occasions I asked myself, was I expecting too much from Consuella? I must confess, even though I'm sure you are all very much aware, that from the very start, this was always my ambition for her.

"On that fateful day when Antonio came to visit, I seized my opportunity. I drew an unwitting Sister Maria and a very trusting Pietro into my grand scheme. The end result, I am delighted to say, is the wonderful experience we all shared in the Arena Verona on this very special occasion. So now, let us all enjoy the remainder of this wonderful evening."

As he sat down, Sister Maria thanked Consuella once more for her generosity.

"Oh think nothing of it, Reverend Mother. At least now you will be able to fix that leaking roof."

"Consuella, did you not know? I fixed the roof a long time ago. I just use that line from time to time to get the students' attention. And on most occasions, I am happy to say it actually works."

Father Martine couldn't resist joining in with some comments of his own. "Consuella, despite your very busy schedule, you won't forget our carol service this Christmas and the anniversary celebration next spring?"

Taking a few moments to answer, she replied rather impishly and loudly enough to make sure everyone could hear. "Dear Father, may I suggest you take this matter up with my management team? I am sure they will do their utmost to accommodate you and agree to an appropriate fee."

He made no response. He just sat there sulking while the rest of them enjoyed his temporary embarrassment.

Francesco decided to take him out of his misery. "Oh there now, Father. No need to be so gloomy. Antonio and I will prevail upon our young star to put in an appearance. What's more, we won't even charge a fee. Now how does that sound?"

With a broad smile, he replied in that famous mischievous way of his, "Well, under the circumstances, I suppose it will have to do."

And so the evening drew to a close on Consuella's very first season as an operatic performer of some significance. The following morning, they journeyed back to Milan. Consuella and Sister Lucia returned to the convent. Francesco resumed his voice coaching activities. Antonio continued performing his duties at La Scala, though he wondered to himself, for how much longer would he be doing so.

CHAPTER 9

Don Barcese

In opera circles and even among the much wider business community, the source of Don Barcese's wealth had always been a hot topic of discussion. The rumours circulating described diamond mines in South Africa and gold fields in Alaska. He was quite happy to be the subject of such speculation. He believed it added a certain mystique to his persona. It certainly afforded him the opportunity to mingle in the best social circles and enjoy the many privileges such a position merited.

On rare occasions, if someone in his presence had the temerity to raise the subject, he always responded with a stock answer delivered in a tone of fake humility: "Oh, I am but a humble businessman who has enjoyed some modest success in my career. And I am truly grateful this blessing has given me the opportunity to enjoy the number one passion in my life—the opera, particularly the opera in this great city of Milan."

Statements like this, at least in his presence, always put a stop to any further probing. He was happy in the knowledge no one, despite all the gossip, had the remotest idea as to the actual source of his wealth. This secret he guarded zealously. He was determined that nobody would ever know he was an arms dealer and an illegal one at that. He had been engaged in this activity since his arrival in Milan from Sicily some years earlier.

All transactions were handled through a network of agents spread across other European cities. The methods employed were quite ingenious. A set of false procurement documents purporting to be from military establishments and defence ministries representing countries such as, Greece, Portugal, and even Belgium would be presented, along with letters of credit from banks in Berlin and Paris. Once the paperwork was complete, the consignment would be loaded onto a cargo vessel at a designated port and then shipped to destinations in Southern Europe and North Africa for resale.

After perfecting this process in Europe, he then took it to America and was successful there in completing even bigger arms deals. His agents took care of all procedural matters, such as verification, loading, transport, shipping, and distribution.

He maintained his control over the whole enterprise with a rigid system of compartmentalisation. Each operative was responsible for a single task. This ensured that no one person had full knowledge of how the process worked from initial purchase to final resale. Obtaining the false documentation from the various countries was something he kept under his own control through a system of bribery targeting low-level officials. In all cases, the captain of the vessel and a most reliable associate by the name of Carlo were the only ones, other than himself, who knew the whereabouts of their final destination. Once the cargo was warehoused, Carlo would then initiate the last and most delicate stage of the whole process. His task was to make contact with the end users.

These invariably included revolutionary groups from Hungary, dissidents from the Balkans, separatists from the Basque regions, and tribal warlords across North Africa. The procedures followed never varied. Documentation listing type and quantity of weapons including a non-negotiable price would be handed over to the potential buyers. A twenty-four-hour period of grace was allowed for the monies to be lodged to a numbered account in any one of two designated banks. Once verification was complete, the arms would be delivered to a prearranged location for collection. After expenses and payment to all those involved, he generally realised a threefold increase on the initial investment. These ill-gotten gains he kept on deposit in German and French banks. All activities related to this lucrative illegal trade were transacted outside of Italy. He firmly believed that, by sticking rigidly to this modus operandi, he could ensure nobody in his social circle would ever have any knowledge as to the extent and scale of his illicit activities.

On occasions, when the mood took him, he would reflect on his standing in respectable Milanese society, his lofty status within the operatic community, and his magnificent palazzo. It was a far cry from the grinding poverty of his Sicilian youth and the precarious life of petty crime that he had once known. When he left Sicily, he brought with him the street skills and guile that had served him well in the tough neighbourhoods and back alleys of Catania, his home city, which stubbornly lay in the ever-threatening shadow of Mount Etna.

The respect he now commanded was, in his mind, the result of his entrepreneurial skills and a fitting testament to how far he had come in a relatively short space of time. He was now determined more than ever to guard these hard-won privileges and crush anyone bold enough to threaten his exalted position. Revenge, he believed, was not only sweet; it also had a long and patient memory. One incident not forgotten was the embarrassing encounter with Señor Francesco Cipriano in Mario's restaurant sometime back. He vowed that sometime in the not-too-distant future, he would make this troublesome individual pay a very heavy price for the humiliation inflicted on him during that particular confrontation. Meanwhile, he would do everything in his power to win control of Consuella's career. This goal now became his primary objective.

CHAPTER 10

Violetta Mollinaro

Some months passed. Alberto Mollinaro eventually made contact with Francesco. He informed him Violetta had made some progress and was ready to discuss her current situation. Francesco spoke with Antonio, who agreed to collect father and daughter the following morning. Arriving at Señor Mollinaro's house, a modest dwelling in a respectable suburb on the edge of the city, Antonio rang the bell and waited. Opening the door, Alberto thought he recognised the face but, in the moment, was not quite able to place it.

"Good morning, Señor Mollinaro. I am here on behalf of Señor Francesco Cipriano to accompany you and your daughter Violetta to his studio."

"Ah yes, of course. Please come in."

As they entered the front room, Alberto suddenly remembered. "Please forgive me, but for just a moment, I did not recognise you. You are Señor Fabrizio from La Scala, are you not?"

"I am indeed, Señor Mollinaro. Forgive my bad manners. I should have introduced myself when you opened the door just now."

"No problem, Señor Fabrizio. So now if you will excuse me, I will go and see if Violetta is ready."

"Please take your time, Señor Mollinaro."

"Please just call me Alberto."

"I will do as you ask if you do something for me."

"If I can, I certainly will."

"I will call you Alberto, if you call me Antonio."

"That, if I may say, is a most sensible suggestion. Here we are. We have been talking for less than two minutes, and already, we are on first-name terms. So please take a seat I will be back in a moment with Violetta."

Antonio nodded politely and sat down.

After a few short moments, Alberto returned. Violetta followed behind, moving very slowly with her head slightly bowed. Antonio was quite taken aback by her general demeanour and could see she was in a rather fragile state. Standing up, he tried to think of something to say that might be conveyed in a polite and respectful tone.

"Good morning, Violetta. It is nice to make your acquaintance again."

She answered in a voice signifying her discomfort, "Thank you, Señor Fabrizio."

About to respond with a friendly, *Oh, please call me Antonio*, he caught a telling glance from Alberto that soon changed his mind.

The three of them just stood there for what seemed like an eternity. The surreal atmosphere prompted Antonio to speak in a calming and hopefully reassuring voice. "Well, Alberto, if you and Violetta are ready, I have a cab waiting for our journey to Señor Francesco's studio. If you just follow me, we can be on our way."

"Very good, Antonio. Come, Violetta. We don't want to be late for our appointment."

She replied in a detached kind of way, "Yes, Father."

As the cab made its way across the city, Alberto and Antonio made some effort at inconsequential small talk. They discussed the weather, the passing traffic, and even the architecture of the buildings they encountered along the way. Both of them intuitively knew the steady rhythmic tone of their voices would at least have some kind of calming effect on Violetta's senses. She just sat there gazing straight ahead as if lost in her own world.

Finally the cab came to a halt outside Francesco's residence. Stepping down, Antonio waited for Alberto while he assisted Violetta onto the pavement. He led them to a door leading directly into the studio.

Once they were inside, Francesco, dispensing with formalities, greeted them in a friendly manner. Then broaching the subject of Antonio's presence, he asked, "Alberto, Antonio is a trusted colleague. Would it be acceptable to you and Violetta if he were to remain and participate in our discussions?"

She nodded in her father's direction, signalling her approval.

Alberto warmly responded, "Antonio is more than welcome to remain and participate. This is the first time in quite a while my daughter and I find ourselves in the company of two people we can trust."

"Thank you, Violetta. Thank you, Alberto. Now if both of you are ready, we can begin our discussion."

As they took their places, Francesco invited Alberto to bring them up to date on everything that had taken place over the course of her career and a brief explanation as to their current situation.

"Thank you, Señor Francesco. I will be as brief as I can. About four years ago when Violetta began her professional career, her bookings generally came through various agents. For about a year under this arrangement, she made reasonable progress. Around this time, I myself took the decision to manage her career in the mistaken belief dedicating myself to the task would improve her prospects even more. Regrettably, my skills as a manager were somewhat lacking. Despite my ineptitude, she was still relatively busy. Within a year, I had a sense something different was needed.

It was around this time the great Don Barcese arrived on the scene promising great things. We signed a three-year contract; foolishly I did this without seeking an informed opinion. To my regret, I now realise I should have consulted a person such as yourself or Antonio. Initially, her career flourished. For the first nine months or so, everything seemed to be just right. Then quite unexpectedly I noticed on a number occasions she was not giving of her best. I expressed my concerns to Don Barcese."

Antonio queried him, "What answer did he give you?"

"He just fobbed me off, telling me most performers experience a low patch from time to time."

"Alberto, I would like to clarify something in relation to that specific period in Violetta's career."

"Please, Señor Francesco, please continue."

"I seem to recall around that particular time I attended a production of Verdi's *Rigoletto*. It was in the Lyric Theatre. Violetta was playing the part of Gilda. Would that be correct?"

"Yes indeed. Your description just now is remarkably accurate."

"Now, Alberto, do you remember I had a brief conversation with yourself and Violetta in the foyer after the performance?"

"Why yes indeed. You had some complimentary words concerning her performance."

"Is that all? Do you not recall the rest of our conversation?"

During these brief exchanges, Antonio was quietly observing. He could see Violetta, despite her delicate state, was nonetheless paying close attention. Poor Alberto, on the other hand, was beginning to exhibit some early signs of stress.

Francesco, taking cognisance of this, continued in a friendly reassuring manner. "Alberto, it is certainly not my intention to cause you or Violetta any discomfort. With your permission, I would like to proceed, and please, it would be much easier if you just called me Francesco."

"Of course, Francesco. Please continue."

"Towards the end of our conversation, I suggested some voice coaching sessions would enable Violetta to improve her performance. I offered my services, and as I recall, you seemed receptive. Your parting words were you thought it was an excellent suggestion. You said you would discuss it further with Violetta and get back to me with what you believed would be a positive response.

"That was the last conversation you and I ever had. Of course we bumped into each other on numerous occasions and exchanged pleasantries. But we never again discussed that particular topic. Violetta never did have her voice coaching lessons. And from that day to this, I have been somewhat curious as to why you never did get back to me."

"Francesco, over these past few months, on many occasions, I have reflected on the suggestions you made that particular evening."

"So tell me, Alberto, what changed your mind?"

"It is not so much a matter of *what* it was, more a matter of *who*. Following our conversation that evening, Violetta and I were more than happy to proceed with your suggestions and advice. Violetta even told me some of her fellow performers had spoken very highly of you."

"Why thank you, Violetta. It is nice to know someone had a few kind words to say on my behalf."

As he was speaking, he glanced over in her direction. For a very brief moment he could see her eyes were slightly more alert. Also her face didn't quite have the lifeless expression that was clearly evident at the time of her arrival.

"Sorry, Alberto. You were saying just now?"

"Yes, as I was saying, the next morning, I made my way to Don Barcese's office to inform him of our intentions. This I did as a matter of courtesy."

"Did he respond or offer an opinion?"

"He contemptuously dismissed them as pure rubbish and stated these so-called voice coaching techniques had no place in the world of professional opera. The practitioners of this dubious craft, he added, were nothing more than a bunch of confidence tricksters, extorting money from gullible victims. He followed this with a remark that was definitely not an opinion, but what I can only describe as a direct threat. He stated that he, as Violetta's manager, would be the one to decide what was in her best interest, and he was certainly not going to waste money on these costly useless pursuits. So there you have it, Francesco. That is the reason we never did discuss that particular topic again."

"What happened next?"

"Violetta struggled on as best she could. He, on the other hand, continued to intimidate and bully her constantly—booking her for parts that were totally mis-matched with her abilities, dramatically increasing the frequency of her appearances. On many occasions, she was exhausted before she even set foot on a stage. Not too long after these episodes, she suffered that awful humiliation."

With tears of pain, his voice now choked with emotion, and holding his daughter's hand close in his own, he somehow managed to continue. "Francesco, please forgive me. You were there that night. You saw what happened.

"Every time I think back on that dreadful incident, it breaks my heart. Before that monster invaded our lives, my daughter was a wonderful generous person with a beautiful voice. All she ever wanted to do was sing in the opera. Tell me, can somebody just please explain to me? Was I asking too much for my daughter? Was I being too selfish and ambitious on her behalf that she had to suffer in this way?" With that, he leaned forward and placed his head in his hands, making a futile attempt to subdue his sobbing.

Antonio and Francesco just sat there helplessly looking on.

It was now Violetta's turn to comfort her father. She reached out her arm, placed it around his shoulder, and held him in a caring comforting embrace.

Giving Alberto a few moments to recover, Francesco asked two final questions. "Since that terrible episode, Alberto, what was Don Barcese's reaction and how have you and Violetta coped?"

"As I told you on the last occasion we spoke, he discarded her like something you would just throw away. Not once did he enquire or offer any kind of assistance. One week later, I received a document by special messenger. It stated, 'Due to Señorita Mollinaro's continued unavailability, I have been instructed by Don Marco Barcese to terminate this contract forthwith.' Since then, Violetta has only made a partial recovery. In all of that time, she has neither sang nor appeared on a stage, not even once.

"Presently, we are surviving on my very modest pension. Despite all of that, I still pray and thank God on a daily basis. We are still alive, and I have faith there will be a brighter future for my daughter—because, in my heart, I believe she deserves nothing less."

Francesco waited for a few moments and then responded. "Alberto, I want to thank you for your detailed account just now. You spoke most eloquently. Your description of the events and the impact they have had on you and, more particularly, on Violetta will be most helpful to Antonio and myself when we discuss the practical steps we can now take in assisting her to regain her confidence.

"Hopefully these measures will guide her back to the stage, which has been such an important feature in both your lives. May I suggest a short break. And please, if you can excuse me for a few moments, there is something that requires my attention."

As they waited, Antonio wondered if he should try and engage Violetta in some polite conversation to maybe lift the gloom hanging in the air.

To his relief, Francesco returned, accompanied by Carlota. Each of them was carrying a tray laden with refreshments and snacks. Having placed them on the sideboard, Carlota approached Alberto. Reaching out her hand she introduced herself. "You must be Señor Alberto, and this has to be Violetta. Please have something to drink, and I've prepared some snacks as well. I'm sure you could do with some sustenance after your discussions just now."

For the first time since her arrival, Violetta smiled. She stood up from the table and replied, "Thank you, Señora Carlota. That's most thoughtful of you."

"You're most welcome, Violetta." Then in her best matronly tone, she called Alberto and Antonio. "Gentlemen, are the two of you just going to sit there and stare?"

The two of them practically jumped up from their chairs.

As they were enjoying the short break, Carlota decided to leave and let them get on with it. "My dear, I will leave now and allow you and your guests to continue on with your discussions."

The others bowed graciously, showing their appreciation.

With her departure, they continued enjoying the few moments of relaxation the short break afforded them. Francesco, reasonably happy the interlude had lifted Alberto's spirits, suggested they resume. "If you are ready, we can be seated and continue were we left off. This time, Alberto, I promise you, no more awkward questions."

Taking his seat, Alberto was somewhat relieved.

"Alberto, just one or two questions for Violetta if I may?"

Alberto glanced in her direction; once again she nodded, signalling her willingness to proceed.

"Now, Violetta, may I ask what age you are?"

"I will be twenty-four next birthday."

"Can you tell me your favourite operas?"

Concentrating for a moment, she then continued, "I would say without doubt *The Marriage of Figaro*, *Carmen*, *Rigoletto*, *La Traviata*, and *Il Travatore*."

"Excellent choices. In operatic terms, you are still a very young person. With proper application and sound management, there is no reason, none whatsoever, that you shouldn't have a successful career sometime soon. I need to know. Is this something you desire? And more importantly, is it something you believe you can achieve?"

To his surprise, she replied in a remarkably clear voice, "From the day I finished school, all I ever wanted to do was sing. Whenever I was performing, those occasions were, for me, the happiest of times. Thankfully now, although you would not think it to look at me, my health has improved. And I would dearly love to return to the stage sometime in the future, not just for my sake but for my dear Papa's sake also."

Francesco, encouraged by her articulate answer, replied, "Young lady, despite all the setbacks and heartbreak you have endured, you have shown remarkable courage coming here today. I know it was not easy after all you have been through. I can promise you that, from today on, things will improve. As your dear father has already stated, you deserve nothing less.

"You obviously know Antonio manages the career of Consuella Pellegrini. I play a lesser role, mainly in the area of voice coaching. Consuella and her patrons, I am quite certain, would have no objections if Antonio and I were to take on the additional task of guiding the career of one more talented performer. You not only fit the bill; your past record speaks for itself.

"So going forward, Antonio will take responsibility for the day-to-day management of your career. I will be your voice coach. A week from now, I will have a vacant slot in my schedule. If you wish, I will keep it open for you. That is really all I have to say. If you and your father wish to discuss the matter in private, please, take all the time you need. You can get back to us with your decision. We will still be here. Now, Antonio, is there anything you wish to add?"

"I would just like to say I concur with everything Francesco said just now. If you agree with the proposals, I will see to it your reintroduction to the stage will be timely and gradual. To assist you in regaining your confidence, I will select smaller venues and parts that should not be overly challenging. When we deem it appropriate, with yours and your father's permission, we will then relaunch your career on the stage of La Scala. When that time comes, you will be able to regain what was so callously taken away from you."

Alberto looked to his daughter and asked, "Violetta would you like to comment on what Francesco and Antonio have proposed just now?"

"Señor Francesco, Señor Antonio, when I came here today, my expectations were very low. Now for the first time in well over a year, my faith has been restored. I know my dear Papa will not mind me speaking for both of us. Actually I think he will be overjoyed his daughter is finally capable of answering in a rational sensible manner.

"I am truly grateful for the opportunity the two of you have given me here today. I am really looking forward to the coaching lessons. I promise to present myself as a lively healthy human being for their duration. From the bottom of my heart, please accept my heartfelt gratitude."

Francesco stood up and, with a broad smile, brought proceedings to a close, saying, "Well, Alberto, it looks like you and Violetta are going to turn Antonio and myself into two wealthy individuals. I would have been so disappointed if you and Violetta had rejected our proposals. You see, we really do need the money."

Even Violetta was smiling. All four of them shook hands enthusiastically.

As father and daughter and Antonio were preparing to leave, Francesco had one last word. "Violetta, over the course of next week, please feel free to visit my studio any day you wish. You will have an opportunity to observe some of my students going through various coaching techniques. It should be of some benefit to you when you start your lessons."

With a warm smile, she graciously accepted his offer and then took her leave with Antonio and her father.

CHAPTER 11

One Year Later, September 1910

A year had passed. It was around the occasion of Consuella's twentieth birthday. Everyone had an opportunity to reflect on the year and how quickly it had gone by.

Consuella, despite her pre-eminence and ever-growing popularity still continued living modestly at the convent. She paid very little attention to the newspaper reports, which often featured articles about her unique stage presence and wonderful singing voice. They would regularly make favourable comparisons between her and some of the great opera stars of the past.

Some other, less reputable journals printed articles that had little or no basis in fact. One scurrilous article falsely portrayed the life she lived prior to her arrival in Milan. It shamelessly stated she was no more than a penniless orphan, living off the sisters' charity at the convent in Verona. This brand of irresponsible journalism, to say the least, was most insulting to herself and her Father and showed a total lack of respect for the memory of her dear departed Mother.

On one occasion she commented to Antonio, "Heaven forbid, if I were to be found guilty of even the most minor infraction, these bloodthirsty creatures would be calling for my public execution!"

Other than these one or two unpleasant incidents, the year had been a resounding success.

For Antonio, this period had been a busy and productive one. Apart from the day-to-day management of Consuella's concert schedule, he took care of all correspondence and managed her financial affairs, which by now were substantial. He continued the practise of furnishing Father Martine with monthly reports.

Some months earlier, he had resigned his position at La Scala. This decision now made it possible for him to accept bookings from Trentino in the north to Calabria in the south. With this expanded though carefully managed schedule, Consuella was fast becoming the most recognised and adored operatic performer throughout the whole of Italy.

There were other related and unrelated events taking place for Antonio during this period. One of them was the decision he and Francesco took to relaunch Violetta Mollinaro's career. Out of courtesy, he informed Consuella and sent a detailed account to Father Martine.

Two other important developments were most likely to have a much greater impact on anything that had taken place heretofore. The first was the issue concerning offers from other European Countries and even the United States of America. It was now obvious to Antonio, Consuella's reputation had travelled far beyond the borders of Italy. The second one concerned him personally. The Vienna State Opera Company had written and offered him the position as director of opera.

He decided to discuss these opportunities in greater detail with Francesco at the earliest opportunity.

Francesco as ever played an important role. Consuella, now finding herself taking on more complex operatic challenges, depended on him even more. His extensive knowledge of acoustics and, through his father, the positive relationship he had with many conductors ensured her preparations were always of the highest standard.

He also made sure the performing schedule allowed for her presence in Verona during the Christmas carol service and the anniversary celebrations. These, after all, were two promises he'd made to Father Martine. Coaching was still his main occupation, and he was delighted that Violetta Mollinaro was now a client.

Pietro's life changed quite dramatically. His youngest daughter's continued success and financial support enabled him to purchase more land for vine harvesting. He increased the capacity of his wine presses and established himself as a quality wine producer of some note, particularly throughout the Tuscany, Venetto, and Lombardy regions.

Adamo, now a handsome young man, was able to discontinue his hard physical toil in the vineyards. He was now responsible for overseeing production and distribution.

Dominique no longer had to concern herself with household chores. The family was now able to afford the services of a housekeeper. Presently, her main occupation was the marketing of the ever-growing brand of Pellegrini wines. Some months earlier, to everyone's delight, she had become engaged to a fine young man by the name of Paolo Gasparini.

For Sister Maria, life carried on as usual. Consuella's generous contributions enabled her to take on projects that, in previous years, were nothing more than unfulfilled dreams.

Father Martine continued running the monastery as he had always done—though, financially, his task was much more manageable, and he was truly thankful for that.

Sister Lucia, as always, performed her tasks in a pleasant unselfish manner. She still regularly updated Sister Maria on all the exciting developments taking place. During breaks in the performance schedules, she took the opportunity to assist some of the teaching nuns.

There were many instances when Adriana and Carla Cipriano found themselves in her classroom. At first, they were somewhat suspicious. But as time passed, they became very fond of her, and she of them.

Don Barcese, meanwhile, remained warily in the background—always watching always waiting. It was still a cause of tremendous disappointment to him that the most important operatic talent to come along in more than a decade was being managed by someone other than himself. He observed and followed Consuella's progress with great interest. Whenever she appeared at La Scala, he made sure never to miss a performance. On occasions, he would have a large bouquet of flowers delivered to her dressing room. The accompanying note always contained gushing sentiments praising her performance. He decided all he could do in the interim was bide his time and wait for an opportunity to present itself sometime in the future.

From previous experience, he was certain in the knowledge that even the slightest incident might enable him exploit the situation to his advantage. As a Sicilian, he didn't necessarily believe patience was a virtue. For him, it was more a matter of pragmatic necessity.

At one of their regular meetings, having drawn up Consuella's schedule for the following three months, Antonio and Francesco then turned their attention to the planned relaunch of Violetta Mollinaro's career. Having introduced her to Consuella some months past, they were quite pleased with the outcome. The two young sopranos had seemed to hit it off reasonably well, and there was certainly no hint of petty rivalry. On many occasions, Consuella had actively supported and encouraged Violetta.

As their meeting was drawing to a close, Antonio raised the issue concerning the offers from outside of Italy; he also sought Francesco's advice regarding the offer from Vienna. "What do you suggest I do in relation to these latest developments?"

"Well, first of all, let's take ourselves down to Mario's we can discuss these matters over an enjoyable meal."

On entering the restaurant, as usual they found Mario on hand to welcome them. "Señor Francesco, Señor Antonio, welcome to my humble establishment. For you this evening, I have the best table in the house." Leading them to their table, he proudly presented them with the wine list. "I have some new very exciting wines for you to savour."

"Yes, these look very exciting. And the prices, they're also quite exciting. Mario, don't you know the meaning of the words *reasonable* and *inexpensive*?"

"Oh, Señor Antonio, there you go again. The moment you walked through that door I said to Angelo. By the way, he will be your waiter tonight. I said to Angelo, here comes Señor Antonio, and I know he will be making with the jokes like he always does. And you see, I'm right. Here you are making with the jokes."

"Now, gentlemen, down to the serious business of food. What will be your choice—the fish or the meat?"

"Tonight, Mario, both of us are going to have the pasta, a nice simple Italian dish."

"Señor Francesco, in other restaurants the pasta is, as you say, a simple dish. But in my dining room, there is only one word to describe the pasta."

"And what word would that be?"

"Dear Señor Francesco, that word would be *magnifico*."

"Well then," Antonio queried, "may I ask what wine you'll be recommending for this evening's feast?"

"You know, gentlemen, sometimes I amaze myself. You see, for me, the fact you've chosen the pasta means it has to be red. And from my extensive wine list, it can only be the Bardolino—a most beautiful full-bodied wine from the Veneto region."

Francesco, hearing the name, recognised it straight away as one of Pietro's. Now deciding it was his turn to be amazing, he remarked, "Mario, how would you feel if I were to tell you we know the producer of this excellent wine and his daughter has actually dined here on more than one occasion?"

"Señor Francesco, if that were so, I would be truly amazed."

"Well then, prepare to be amazed. The gentleman in question is a colleague of ours. His name is Señor Pietro Pellegrini, and his daughter's name is Señorita Consuella Pellegrini."

Mario, now almost speechless, just stood there momentarily, his mouth hanging open with no words coming out.

Francesco and Antonio sat there with serious expressions, even though they were doing their best to avoid laughing out loud.

Finally, Mario regained enough composure to answer, "That, Señor Francesco, is truly amazing. Please, if you would be so kind, I will leave you alone now. I need a few moments to recover. I will send Angelo over to take your order. As soon as I've regained my composure, I will of course personally fetch the Bardolino from the wine cellar. Excellent choice, excellent choice. And to think, you are friends with the producer of this exceptional wine. Also the fact he is the Father of Señorita Pellegrini. Señor Francesco, Señor Antonio, tonight I have to humbly acknowledge, I am truly, truly amazed." Again with his usual dramatic bow, Mario departed.

Antonio, still smiling, remarked, "You know, Francesco, I believe we come here as much for the entertainment as we do for the food."

"I couldn't agree with you more. Unfortunately, we live in a world where too many people take themselves far too seriously. It restores my faith in humankind when I encounter people such as Mario. He brings a certain energy to every situation, and he takes nobody seriously, including himself.

"Now, where were we? Ah yes, we came here to discuss these latest developments. So, Antonio, whenever you're ready."

"These offers have been coming in for some weeks past—from Vienna, Salzburg, Berlin, Barcelona, Paris, London, and even New York."

"Have you informed Consuella or Father Martine?"

"Not yet. I thought it best to discuss them with you first and get your thoughts."

"Well let's see, we now have less than a year left in the agreement. Consuella's programme for the next three months is already in place. For the following nine months here in Italy alone, we could fill her schedule three times over. Your mandate from the very start was to develop her career. This you have done way beyond everyone's expectations. There were never any discussions as to where and when she should perform. These decisions they left entirely to you, and in my opinion, you've done a remarkable job."

"What would you suggest I do now? Should I raise the issue with them?"

"Whatever you do, don't say a word to any of them, at least not for the time being. As things stand, we both know there's no practical way it would be possible for her to perform outside of Italy for at least another twelve months. Raising this issue now would only confuse them and most likely cause you tremendous stress. This you don't need, certainly not now. I suggest the first thing you do is reply to all these societies, committees, whatever. Thank them for their kind and welcome invitations. Politely inform them her schedule is already planned for the coming twelve months. Finish by letting them know you will contact them nine months from now to negotiate concert dates for the following year. This way you haven't rejected their offers. In the interim, it should keep them reasonably happy.

"A month or so before the current agreement ends, make sure to discuss these developments with Father Martine. His understanding and support will enhance your position in whatever negotiations follow.

"There is one exception to everything I've said so far, and it's this. For now and the immediate future, exclude the United States of America from any planned schedules. Don't misunderstand me; I admire that great nation. Unfortunately, I haven't the time just now to explain my reasons. All I'm asking is your trust."

"Francesco, I trust your judgement. I'm happy to go along with what you've suggested."

"Very good. Now this other matter concerning the Vienna State Opera Company."

"Well, as you already know I've been offered this prestigious position in Vienna, and I really don't know how I should respond."

"Antonio, it's really quite simple."

"Simple. Can you please explain it to me?"

"All you have to do is make the decision, do you wish to continue managing Consuella's career as well as Violetta's? Or should you take this opportunity and accept the offer from Vienna? It would certainly be a step up for you when you compare it to the position you held at La Scala. The main difference would be you'd be working in Vienna instead of Milan. Now, whether you like it or not, you have to make a decision. I fully understand your dilemma. There's nothing more I can say to help. It really is down to you."

Antonio sat quietly for several moments, silently turning over in his mind Francesco's comments. "Francesco, as usual, you are quite right. And I admire your gift for simplifying complex matters. I will continue managing both their careers and decline the offer from Vienna. I will write straight away and let them know my decision."

"What about Father Martine? Are you going to mention any of this to him?"

"I think under the circumstances it would be best to say nothing. There's no point in worrying him in relation to something that has no further relevance."

"Very good, Antonio. I believe you've made the right decision. Don't concern yourself too much with next year. If you find yourself in other European capitals, I will be more than willing to fill the gaps here at home."

"Thank you, Francesco. Your support, as always, is appreciated.

"Now what about this secret project of yours, the one you alluded to in one of your conversations with Father Martine?"

"Oh that, not to worry that won't be happening until my two girls have completed college, so it won't be today or tomorrow.

"Now I wonder where Angelo's got to. I think we should treat ourselves to some dessert."

Angelo appeared in an instant, took their order, and delivered their deserts.

As they finished, Mario drifted over. "Gentlemen, I trust everything was to your satisfaction. And the wine, was I not spot on with my selection?"

"Why yes, Mario," Antonio replied. "Everything was just fine, including the wine. The next time Señor Pellegrini is in Milan, we'll bring him here for a meal and introduce you. How does that sound?"

"Oh, Señor Antonio, it would be such an honour. You will really do as you say?"

"Of course, Mario. All you have to do is give us a discount on tonight's bill. Then on his next visit to Milan, we will bring him here as promised, and we won't tell him the exorbitant prices you're charging for his wine."

"Señor Antonio, you've really wounded me just now. I am but a humble waiter trying to make an honest living. However, to show my gratitude for your valued custom, please accept a freshly brewed cup of coffee, one for each of you, with my compliments of course."

Antonio couldn't resist. "What about the desserts?"

"What about the desserts, Señor Antonio? Have you not just eaten them? Were they not to your liking?"

"On the contrary, they were delicious. I just thought maybe you would throw them in with the coffee, you know with your compliments of course."

"Señor Antonio, this time I know you are not making with the jokes. Me, I'm a generous fool. The desserts and the coffees, no charge. I will now go and prepare your bill. I fear if this conversation goes on much longer, it will be me paying you to eat in my own restaurant."

Antonio just smiled. "Mario, you are a rogue, but you know we love you very much."

"Oh, Señor Antonio, you do say the nicest words. And as always, it's a great pleasure for me when you come here to dine, especially now we no longer have to tolerate that overblown self-important buffoon."

Francesco decided to draw him out. "Pray tell, Mario, who is this gentleman you are referring to?"

"Señor Francesco, the person I'm referring to is certainly no gentleman; it's that Sicilian gangster, Don Marco Barcese."

"Surely you must be mistaken, Mario. What in heaven's name leads you to the conclusion Don Barcese might be a gangster?"

"Well for a start, that scar on his face."

"Maybe he cut himself shaving."

"Then if that's the case, it must be a very large razor."

Francesco couldn't resist drawing him out even more. "Mario, I by chance saw Don Barcese the other day, and he had his hands in his own pockets."

"Well then, all I can say is, for him to have his hands in his own pockets instead of someone else's, it must have been a very cold day indeed."

They couldn't help but smile at his sardonic wit.

Mario, satisfied at having the last word, departed with a flourish to prepare their bill.

Having enjoyed their free desserts and coffees, Francesco and Antonio settled their account, bid farewell to Mario, and took their leave.

During the following months, the well-established routine continued. Performing, touring, voice training, and rest periods.

During these intervals, Antonio prevailed upon Sister Lucia to allow him to accompany Consuella on short trips outside the convent. He took her to museums and art galleries. She enjoyed these outings enormously.

Without either of them seeming to notice, they were actually becoming quite attached to each other.

CHAPTER 12

Dominique's Wedding

In June 1911, the other happy news was the forthcoming marriage of Dominique and Paolo. Consuella, Antonio, Carlota, and Francesco travelled to Verona for the occasion. Violetta and Alberto also made the journey with them.

The twins stayed with Sister Lucia at the convent.

Consuella, as the principal bridesmaid and this being the most important day in her sister's life, made the decision not to sing. She wanted to be absolutely certain all the attention would be focused exclusively on Dominique. With her father's approval, she prevailed upon Violetta to do the honours.

On the journey down, Carlota, ever perceptive, couldn't help but notice the growing affection between Consuella and Antonio. She reminded herself to observe and see how this situation might develop over the coming two days.

The wedding itself was a joyous happy occasion for the Pellegrini family. The ceremony was performed by Father Martine in the monastery chapel, the very place where Antonio had first heard Consuella sing.

As he sat there, Antonio reflected on that faithful evening two years and some months past. He remembered the shy awkward eighteen-year-old. Watching her now, he could see she had grown into a beautiful elegant lady quite literally before his eyes.

The reception was held in the Hotel San Pietro.

After the speeches and the many congratulatory messages, the music started. As was the custom, the bride and groom took to the floor for the first waltz of the evening.

For the second waltz, they were joined on the floor by many of their guests.

Antonio was in conversation with Carlotta, Violetta, Sister Maria, Francesco, Alberto, and Father Martine. As they were speaking, Consuella came across the room and joined them. Oblivious to their compliments about her dress and the happy occasion, she asked in a rather coy sort of fashion. "Dearest Antonio, aren't you going to ask me to dance?"

Carlota and Violetta certainly noticed the almost flirtatious manner she had adopted.

Antonio, adopting a slightly bashful tone, responded, "Of course, Consuella. But I feel I must warn you I'm not much of a dancer."

"Oh, come now, Antonio. A waltz can't be that difficult." Grabbing him by the arm, she practically dragged him onto the dance floor.

As they waltzed to the music, Father Martine remarked quite casually, "Don't they make a lovely couple?"

Sister Maria shot a disapproving glance in his direction. "Shame on you, Father. Consuella is still practically a child."

"Oh come now, Sister. I believe you will always see her that way. When are you going to allow her grow up?"

Francesco joined in. "Well, from where I'm standing, I think I would have to say she is definitely no longer a child."

Now it was Carlota's turn to give her husband a disapproving look.

Adamo was next to come over. Bowing graciously to Violetta, he asked her if she would care to dance.

"Why certainly, Adamo. How very gallant you are."

Sister Maria couldn't resist. "I suppose the two of you are going to tell me they make a lovely couple as well."

They didn't respond. Alberto just smiled.

As the evening drew to a close, Carlota, Violetta, Francesco, and Alberto stayed at the hotel. Antonio stayed at the monastery as Father Martine's guest.

Consuella, stayed over at her father's house. Although the day had been a very happy occasion, she felt he might feel a little sad, as this was going to be the first time Dominique would not be spending the night at home.

The following morning, the six of them made the journey back to Milan. On the journey, they chatted about the wonderful day and how radiant Dominique had looked on her special day.

Carlota in a casual kind of way remarked, "You know, Antonio, when you and Consuella were dancing, Father Martine remarked that the two of you make a lovely couple."

"But of course we do, Carlota. Don't we, Antonio?"

Blushing slightly, Antonio looked over in Francesco and Alberto's direction. The two of them, enjoying his temporary loss of composure, sat there quietly smiling without saying anything likely to cause him further discomfort.

Violetta then joined in. "You never know, Carlota. Maybe someone will have an announcement to make in the not-too-distant future."

Consuella just smiled. Antonio was acutely embarrassed.

To his relief, however, the remainder of the journey passed off without any more teasing from the two of them.

Back in Milan, life continued on as usual, though at a slightly more frenetic pace. Antonio found himself travelling to the other regions, arranging and organising Consuella's schedule.

Francesco, in addition to coaching, handled Violetta's programme of performances. Although not as hectic as Consuella's, nevertheless Violetta and her father were delighted her career had well and truly been relaunched.

On one particular occasion, Antonio happened to bump into Don Barcese quite by chance. Not wishing to be rude, he greeted him politely.

Don Barcese in that flattering way of his enquired, "Ah, there you are, Señor Antonio. Pray tell me, how is Señorita Pellegrini these days?"

Antonio, slightly annoyed, replied, "I would've thought you'd know the answer to that question yourself, as you never seem to miss a performance."

"Forgive me, dear Antonio. I was just making polite conversation. I was figuratively speaking of course. What a wonderful talent. What a wonderful voice."

"Well in that case, I'm quite sure you'll be happy to know Violetta Mollinaro is not doing too badly either."

Don Barcese, about to give him a contemptuous answer, instead masked his displeasure by responding with an insincere concerned look on his face. "You know, Antonio, it was so upsetting when that poor girl had that unfortunate breakdown. I have to say, though, I'm so pleased to see your good self and your colleague have been successful in relaunching her career."

"Then I'm sure you will be delighted to know, Señor Francesco and I are planning her return to La Scala very soon."

Now absolutely seething with rage, Don Barcese nonetheless managed to reply with a forced smile. "Why, that's wonderful news. It certainly restores my faith in human nature when I see sadness turning to joy."

Antonio, growing tired of the hypocrisy, replied, "I'm sure you must be very busy, Don Barcese, so I'll bid you a good day." With that, he walked off, leaving a most disgruntled Don Barcese standing quite alone without his normal group of hangers-on.

As Don Barcese watched Antonio depart, he made the following remark to himself: 'Someday, someday, Señor Antonio, I promise, you will pay a very high price for the dismissive way you've treated me just now.'

As the weeks passed, Antonio found himself having to deal with the conflicting emotions he was now experiencing regarding his professional responsibilities on the one hand and his growing affection on the other. With just four weeks left before Consuella's final concert and twenty-first birthday, he decided to seek Carlota and Francesco's advice.

On his arrival at their home, as usual, Carlota greeted him. She was about to go and fetch Francesco when, in a slightly awkward tone, he made a request. "Carlota, I would be very grateful if you could possibly join us. There's something weighing heavily on my mind. I would like your opinion and, more importantly, some advice."

"My word, Antonio, this sounds most intriguing. Please take yourself into the drawing room. I will fetch Francesco right away."

As he waited, Antonio tried to work out in his mind how best to explain his dilemma. He didn't have to wait very long. Almost immediately, Francesco and Carlota joined him.

"Well, Antonio," Francesco began, "Carlota tells me you have some weighty matters you wish to discuss, so let's make ourselves comfortable. You explain what you need to explain. Then let's see if we can find a solution to this dilemma of yours."

"Thank you both for giving me this time. Carlota, there maybe elements of what I have to say you may feel are not relevant to your presence here. But please, I've good reason to believe they are all related in one way or another."

"Antonio, please continue. And take all the time you need."

"Thank you, Carlota. As you both know, there are approximately four weeks left before Consuella's final concert and her twenty-first birthday. All arrangements are in place. I am planning on travelling to Verona in the coming days to discuss with Father Martine and company their travel arrangements. Sister Maria, will most likely stay at the convent. Dominique, Paolo, Adamo, Pietro, and Father Martine will stay at the hotel."

Francesco queried, "I take it you are still going to raise the issue concerning the offers from outside of Italy?"

"Yes, I'm going to discuss them with Father Martine first and get his thoughts."

"What about the offer from Austria concerning you personally? Are you still of the same mind?"

"Yes, and the fact I've declined the position at this stage pretty much renders the subject irrelevant."

"I agree. There's no sense in bothering Father Martine on a subject you say has no further relevance. In relation to the offers concerning Consuella, you've made a wise decision. I believe Father Martine will deal with this issue in an appropriate manner. Whether he discusses this information with the others or not will be his decision.

"Well now that that's out of the way, Carlota has been waiting patiently. So again in your own time you can explain this matter you feel requires her opinion and advice."

Antonio, feeling somewhat awkward continued, "Thank you, Francesco, for your thoughts. Carlota, I'm most grateful. You've been very patient. Most of what you've just heard probably doesn't interest you very much. But I felt it was important for you to be present. As you can see, I'm reasonably confident in matters concerning the management of her career. My dilemma, however, is Consuella herself."

"Okay Antonio, just relax. Take your time. Continue in your own words. We're both listening. You know if there's any way we can assist, we most certainly will."

"Thank you, Carlota. When I say Consuella is my dilemma, what I mean is.... Oh goodness me, how do I put this? You remember some time back—actually it was on the occasion of Dominique's wedding. On the journey back, you referred to a comment you said was made by Father Martine whilst Consuella and I were dancing."

"Why yes, Antonio, I do remember, quite well actually. Now what is the point you wish to make?"

"The point is, I'm wondering, was Father Martine being mischievous? What prompted you to mention it on the journey home? And lastly, do you have any thoughts on what was said?"

"Well, Antonio, you know the good father better than I do. It's my belief he was being his usual mischievous self—though I'm convinced he was gently, just gently, putting out a very subtle sign or signal for others to pick up on. For as long as I've known him, there is one thing I'm absolutely sure of."

Antonio, now becoming somewhat anxious, asked, "What is that, Carlota?"

"Well, despite his light-hearted and mischievous comments, I'm convinced every word, every sentence he uttered on that particular occasion was very carefully thought out in advance."

Antonio, just sitting there, thought about some of his past encounters with his teacher. He quickly came to the conclusion her perception of Father Martine was remarkably accurate.

Francesco joined in. "You know, Antonio, I would have to agree 100 per cent with Carlota's assessment of Father Martine. He has a unique gift in pushing an agenda that suits his objectives."

Antonio, finding himself in complete agreement, then asked, "Carlota, I'm curious to know. What was it that prompted you to raise this matter on the journey back?"

"Before I answer your question, Antonio, there is something I need to ask you."

"Of course, Carlota," he replied hesitantly.

"What feelings do you have for Consuella?"

"Well, she's a wonderful person, and I have to say I'm quite fond of her."

"Antonio, if as you say you are quite fond of her, then why are we having this conversation? And what could this dilemma you've been talking about possibly be?"

Following these comments, he decided the most sensible approach was to speak from his heart. "Carlota, Francesco, please forgive me. My comments just now were probably somewhat disingenuous. When I say I am fond of Consuella, what I am really trying to say is I have very strong feelings of affection for her. That's my dilemma."

"Antonio, people fall in love all the time. So where's the dilemma?"

"That's just it, Carlota. I've fallen in love with Consuella. This situation must surely compromise my position as manager and guardian. I don't think our friends in Verona will be too impressed with this development. In fact, I believe they will feel very disappointed indeed."

"Whether they're disappointed or not shouldn't concern you. The important thing is how you feel about Consuella and, more importantly, how Consuella feels about you. We know the answer to the first part. I will now give you my reasons for saying what I said on our journey home and also my thoughts on what you should do next. Maybe then we might come close to getting an answer to the second part.

"For some time now, I have noticed small but nonetheless evident signs that an affectionate bond was developing between Consuella and yourself. When Father Martine said what he said, I believe he detected it as well and just floated his comment out to see what the reaction would be. Despite Sister Maria's matronly response, her reaction was not a negative one. On the journey home, I was more interested in how Consuella would respond. I'm happy to say I was pleasantly surprised.

"So now the question is, what next? Here's what I'm suggesting. Before you make your journey, meet with Consuella. Tell her you will be travelling to Verona to confirm their travel arrangements. At this stage, there's no need to mention the offers concerning herself. Give her a hint as to the main reason for your trip. Tell her there's another matter of some importance you need to discuss with them. Let her know that, if all goes well, you might have some exciting news for her on your return.

"When you get to Verona, confide in Father Martine. Let him know your feelings. I'm absolutely certain he won't be surprised in the least. Ask him to guide you in pleading your case with her father and Sister Maria. This is what I'm advising. All I need to know is, do you have enough confidence and belief in yourself to embark on this quest?"

"Yes I do. I believe Consuella and I are destined to be together for the rest of our lives. I will make the arrangements right away and do as you suggest. Thank you, Carlota. Thank you, Francesco. Wish me luck."

They both bid him a fond farewell and wished him luck in his quest to win Consuella's hand.

CHAPTER 13

The Fortune Teller

On one particular occasion when Don Barcese was holding court with his usual group of hangers-on in Trattoria Guardia—this establishment had become the restaurant of choice following his embarrassing encounter with Alberto and Francesco in Mario's some time back—Carlo reminded him of a practise the restaurant owner allowed from time to time for the amusement of patrons. Tonight was one of those nights.

The activity involved a gypsy woman sitting at a vacant table, inviting customers to have their fortunes told. Her methods involved palm reading and an ordinary deck of playing cards.

Carlo pointed her out, saying, "Don Barcese, the old lady sitting over there, she's the gypsy woman I told you about. She has the ability to read people's fortunes and predict their future."

"Carlo, you deluded gullible fool. That old witch over there, who has probably never seen the inside of a bathtub, is nothing more than a cheat playing on outdated superstitions held by people such as yourself."

"No, honestly no. She read the cards for me a little more than a year ago, and she was remarkably accurate."

"What did she predict? You were going to have a long life and an army of grandchildren?"

"No, truly she told me something about my family, my sister in fact, what she predicted actually came to pass just recently."

"Indulge me, what was this momentous event concerning your sister?"

"Well, my sister, having been married for some three years, was having difficulty in conceiving. As a matter of fact, she was beginning to lose all hope of starting a family. That gypsy woman sitting over there told me a close relative of mine would give birth to a baby boy within the year."

"Tell me what happened?"

"Just four months ago, my sister gave birth to twin boys."

"Bravo. So the old hag was 50 per cent right, and if my sums are correct, it also means she was 50 per cent wrong." Pushing back his chair and standing up in front of his dining companions, he exclaimed, "Let's see if that bundle of rags over there can tell me anything, anything at all that convinces me she is something other than a cunning thief."

Strutting across the dining room in his usual arrogant fashion, he sat himself down and, eyeing the old lady disdainfully, exclaimed, "Now gypsy woman, my name is Don Marco Barcese. For the benefit of my dining companions and the other witnesses gathered here, please, if you will, tell me something about myself."

"That I will, Señor. But first you must cross my palm with gold or silver."

Calling him *Señor* irritated him slightly, though he still couldn't help but smile at her brazenness. "Carlo, give this creature two gold sovereigns and let's see if she can conjure up some magic for our amusement."

Raising her hand in a mild gesture of defiance, she responded, "Señor, if you wish me to tell what the cards have in store for you, then it is you who has to cross my palm. Otherwise, I will be unable to reveal your destiny."

Thoroughly enjoying being the centre of attention and feeling rather generous, he extracted three gold coins from his waistcoat and rather mockingly remarked, "Oh so sorry, I thought I might have had thirty pieces of silver to hand. Instead, these will have to suffice." He gratuitously placed the coins in her palm. As he did so, she placed her other hand over his and held it momentarily in a strong grip.

Slightly alarmed, he attempted to loosen her grasp, but to no avail. As she held on, she fixed him with a penetrating gaze. "Please, Señor, relax. All I am doing is getting a sense of your spirit and inner self."

In an instant she released her hold. "Now, Señor, if you're ready, I will begin."

Wiping his hand with a napkin, he replied rather impatiently, "Yes of course I'm ready. Just get on with it, and let's dispense with the theatrics. I don't find them at all amusing, and I'm sure neither do my companions."

"As you wish, Señor. I would like you to once more give me your hand. I will read your palm and reveal what lies therein."

He smirked back. "Which hand would you prefer, left or right?"

"It matters not to me, Señor. But seeing as you ask, you may give me your left hand."

With a sly grin on his face and in a further effort to humiliate her, he thrust out his right hand, saying, "You will have to perform your black magic on this one."

"Please, Señor, why so?"

"Because, gypsy woman, this is the hand that crossed your palm. When we're done here, I will only have to wash this one."

Taking his hand and placing it in her own, she took a moment to observe his group of hangers-on grinning like Cheshire cats. His insulting remarks and their infantile giggling didn't disturb her in the least.

Studying the lines of his upturned palm, she informed him he was of Sicilian birth.

He replied quite contemptuously, "A blind monkey could have told you that."

"Please explain, Señor?"

"You and everyone else in this room know quite well when people address me, the title they use is Don as in Don Barcese, for that is my name. And it is a well known fact this title is reserved for eminent persons of Sicilian birth."

"You are of course quite correct. You are indeed a person of some eminence, Señor, or should I say Don Barcese? But this line I am reading tells a somewhat different tale."

"Pray tell me, witch lady. What would be the nature of this tale?"

Without hesitation, she replied, "This line reveals your life in Sicily was one of hardship and deprivation. Your existence was somewhat precarious and vastly inferior to your current position of pre-eminence."

With a concerned look on his face and fully aware of his audience, he decided to brazen it out by responding, "That's no shame. It is a well-established fact some of Italy's most successful businessmen, entrepreneurs, and leading statesmen had very humble beginnings. It comforts me to know I am counted among this group of exceptional individuals. And yes, I am very proud of my humble origins, which were endured in poverty, honest hard-working poverty. Now, gypsy lady, what more can you tell me?"

"Well I can see you are a person of substantial wealth."

"Which line on my palm told you this?"

"It wasn't your palm. I drew this conclusion from your fine clothes and the expensive rings on your fingers."

Releasing his hand she continued, "If you desire it, Don Barcese, I will now reveal what destiny awaits you in the cards."

Turning to his companions, who were enjoying the encounter enormously, he answered her, "Indeed. Why not? Let's see what hocus-pocus these cards of yours have in store for me."

Silently picking up the cards and with deft handling, she fanned them out in front of him face down. "Please, Don Barcese, I would like for you to select a card and turn it over."

This he did. Reaching out his hand, he selected a card. It was the queen of hearts. He questioned her, "What does this card tell you about me?"

"All in good time, Don Barcese. I will now select some other cards, place them with the queen, and tell you what they signify."

Turning over a number of cards and placing them face up, she continued in a voice now almost a whisper but loud enough for him to hear. "This is most interesting. You selected the queen. In itself, this is not particularly significant, but the cards laid out beside the queen tell me much."

Growing somewhat impatient, he retorted rather irritably, "Just get on with it. My time is precious, and I don't have all night to listen to much more of this superstitious nonsense."

Placing both hands on the table, fixing him with a steely glare, and raising her voice an octave or two, she answered in a fashion others would never even dare contemplate. "Don Barcese, from the moment you sat down at this table, you've done everything possible to insult and humiliate me in front of this gathering. Although you enjoy great wealth and prestige, it still does not give you the right to treat me in such a fashion. I may not have riches, a fine mansion, or exclusive garments. What I posses is by far much more valuable than any of these worldly possessions. I have a gift that enables me to look into a person's soul. You, on the other hand, have nothing more than these props. You delude yourself in the belief they define you as a human being. They are nothing more than a facade. A person's humanity is defined by what is in their heart. You, on the other hand, are a person without humanity, and you have no heart. All you believe in is the power of money. The loyalty, obedience, and acquiescence you receive from your companions over there is bought and paid for by you. They are shallow individuals indeed. In truth, they are nothing more than a sad reflection of your own pathetic existence. This evening at this table you had an opportunity to learn something about yourself, but you have been undone by your own self-important arrogance."

Standing up, she gathered her cards, extracted the gold coins from her apron, and laid them on the table, saying, "I believe these coins belong to you. I was taught never to accept reward for a service not provided."

Before he had the slightest chance to make a response or indeed make any kind of gesture, she was gone. It was so sudden it was as if she just vanished into thin air.

His audience just stood there open-mouthed, not knowing how to react. They were somewhat fearful and all too aware from past experience that, whenever anybody had the audacity to stand up to his ill-mannered foul-mouthed abuse, someone among their number would generally become the target of his displeasure. With this uppermost in their minds, they soon made themselves scarce by scattering to different corners of the room.

For several moments, he just sat there silently brooding.

Carlo, who was probably much more adept at handling these situations and somewhat more courageous than the other spineless warriors, ordered the waiter to pour two glasses of wine. Bringing them over, he sat down and placed a glass in front of him saying, "Don Barcese, I deeply regret this unfortunate incident. It would not have happened if I had not told you what I told you earlier. Please accept my apologies."

To his surprise, Don Barcese picked up the wine, drank it rather slowly, and then responded, "Not to worry, Carlo. Maybe I pushed the old hag a little too far with my ungenerous remarks. My only regret is that she didn't proceed with the episode concerning the cards."

"Would I be correct in assuming you are now a convert to this mystical practise?"

"Absolutely not, though on the other hand I did have a sense she was going to reveal something of substance—that is, of course, she had continued with this card reading business of hers."

Carlo, although surprised by Don Barcese's calm response, felt maybe, just maybe, he was beginning to regret his abusive conduct during the palm reading encounter. He braced himself and decided to probe a little further. "I hope I'm not being impertinent when I ask, whether, if by chance an opportunity presented itself, let's say to re-engage with this fortune teller, gypsy, or whatever it is you wish to call her, would you avail yourself of it?"

Sitting there pondering what might have been revealed, Don Barcese replied, after a moment, "Perhaps. Maybe on another occasion, should I feel the need for further amusement, I might just consider revisiting this card reading nonsense—though I doubt very much the old hag would indulge me after this particular encounter."

"If I were you, I wouldn't be to put out by this episode just now."

"Why ever not?"

"That gypsy, I am pretty certain, has a fairly thick skin. Creatures like her have to battle every single day just to stay alive. I'm absolutely convinced that, by tomorrow morning, to her, this incident will be nothing more than a faded memory."

Don Barcese, quite impressed with Carlo's astute observations remarked, "You're quite certain by tomorrow she will have forgotten?"

"Yes, I'm quite certain."

"But how can you be so sure?"

"Don Barcese, you are an intelligent man. Please forgive me. I don't mean to be impertinent. Earlier this evening, she mentioned the poverty you experienced in your childhood and youth."

"What has that got to do with it?"

"Well if you can cast your mind back to those difficult days, on each waking morning, what was your overriding priority?"

He answered without hesitation, "During those hard years of deprivation, over the course of each and every day, my main objective was to survive the next twenty-four hours. What scheme or racket would I need to employ to enable me to obtain money by any means, any means whatsoever, even if it meant stealing or cheating? That was my daily challenge. I had to accumulate a sufficient amount to purchase food for the table in the hovel my widowed mother and siblings called home."

"So then, each waking morning, did you give any thought or dwell on the insults and disappointments of the previous day?"

"In my battles for survival, reflection was a luxury I could ill afford. Yesterday was gone. There was only today, and that was all that mattered."

Carlo took a moment and then responded, "Your graphic description just now, I believe, answers your own question most emphatically."

"Why yes indeed, Carlo, I do suppose it does really. By first light tomorrow, that gypsy woman will most likely have forgotten me and my inconvenient remarks."

"Would you be any way interested in discovering what might have been revealed if the card reading had continued?"

"Yes, I suppose I would. But I don't think that's going to happen now."

"Leave it to me. Let me see if I can persuade her to reconsider."

"Very good, Carlo. Do what you can. But I don't want it done here."

"Would you prefer if I brought you to her?"

"No, no. If you can persuade her to reconsider, I will want you to bring her to my home."

"I'll see what I can arrange. Leave it to me."

"Very good. Now be a good fellow and fetch George. This place is beginning to bore me."

After two days, Carlo was successful in persuading the fortune teller to reconsider. He brought her to Don Barcese's residence.

On opening the door Henry the butler was somewhat startled by the appearance of the person standing before him. By his reckoning, she was an old lady, small in stature, with a dark oily complexion and wrinkled skin. Her eyes, however, told a different tale. They were lively, alert, and penetratingly blue. Her dark hair was covered by a scarf or some sort of multi-coloured bandana. She was sporting a large pair of earrings; her clothing consisted of a single not quite threadbare garment covering a slight frame. Observing her, he was thinking the slightest breeze would most likely blow her away.

"Carlo, if you and your guest accompany me, I will take you to the master."

He ushered them into the study. Don Barcese was already seated at a table. With a dismissive wave of his hand, he bid her to sit opposite him. "Thank you, Carlo. You may stay. That is, of course, our guest has no objections."

She nodded her approval and took the seat opposite him.

"Now gypsy lady, I would like you to continue where you left off on the previous occasion we met. I believe the queen of hearts was the card selected by me."

Without saying a, word she extended her hand and waited.

"Ah yes, of course, the small matter of reward." This time he took five gold coins from his waistcoat and placed them in her hand.

Taking them she replied, "Why so generous, Don Barcese?"

"Well let's just say there's a little extra for any inconvenience caused during our last encounter."

"Your gesture I accept. But I must warn you. If you insult me again, without hesitation, I will discontinue this reading."

"It's not a subtle point you're making. Nevertheless, I agree. There will be no inappropriate remarks. So when you're ready, please continue."

To his amazement, the cards she turned over were the exact ones she had placed beside the queen on the previous occasion. He wondered how could she possibly pull such a trick. He decided to remain silent and allow her to proceed without interruption.

After silently observing the cards for some moments, she began the reading. "The queen of hearts on its own, as I said earlier, is not especially significant. However, the cards I've placed beside the queen tell me much about a matter that is of some importance to you, Don Barcese. A question if I may?"

In his reply, he decided to tread very carefully and make sure the reading continued. "Yes of course, madam. Please ask your question?"

"Could you please tell me what it is you do here in Milan, what profession are you engaged in?"

"Oh I'm so sorry," he answered, not quite rudely but not exactly politely. "I thought you already knew. Actually, my main activity involves the opera. I manage the careers of some of our leading performers."

"But not this one," she replied, pointing her finger to the queen.

Her response amazed and startled him. Now somewhat impressed with her astute observation, he replied, "This is intriguing, most intriguing indeed. Please tell me more."

With her finger still pointed at the queen, she continued, "The queen is a prominent person in the opera community. She is not within your orbit, though this is something you desire very much. If you were to secure this prize, it would be, for you, a crowning achievement in your career."

Now greatly excited, he couldn't help but interrupt. "Can you tell me what it is I need to do to achieve this objective?"

"I'm sorry, Don Barcese. My purpose here is not to tell you what to do. I can only reveal what's in the cards. If you allow me to continue, I will do this. You will then have an opportunity to decide the manner in which you wish to proceed."

"I promise, no more interruptions. Please, please continue."

Moving her hand, she deftly placed the first two cards alongside the queen. They were the three of hearts and the three of diamonds. She continued, "These two cards reveal this person has six people who are close to her. Three of them are always present in her day-to-day life. The other three perform a guardianship role and are generally some distance away. They have her absolute trust, and it would take a significant event to disturb this equilibrium. The next two cards are the knave and ten of clubs. These reveal a possible rift in the relationship around a significant event in her life."

As she continued, he was focusing and paying close attention to what was being revealed. He came to the conclusion this gypsy did indeed have a psychic gift of sorts, and it was highly unlikely she could have gained this insight prior to the reading. He was also beginning to realise how the process worked. Her cryptic revelations, he decided, would require his careful evaluation.

What she had revealed so far told him the queen was none other than Consuella. The first three cards represented Antonio and his two assistants; the other three was a reference to the group in Verona. The ten and knave at first puzzled him. He thought hard. Then it suddenly came to him. These two, when added together, totalled twenty-one. Could this be the significant date? Was the fortune teller perhaps referring to Consuella's twenty-first birthday three months hence? He now began to ponder what event or action might be the cause of a possible rift.

Rather pleased with the reading and how it was progressing, he waited for her to continue.

The next and last card in this sequence was the seven of diamonds.

He wondered what was about to be revealed concerning Consuella Pellegrini's future.

Holding the card and looking directly in his direction, the gypsy continued. "This card tells me, should difficulties arise in or around this occasion or event, it is possible your influence may have some effect, though I must caution you, there is one among this group who will vigorously challenge you."

"Can you per chance shed some light on who this might be?"

"Regrettably, this is as much as the cards reveal concerning this person and yourself."

His realisation that his earlier remarks questioning her abilities had been totally misplaced prompted him to question her concerning a matter of particular importance. He began by saying, "As you can see for yourself, I am a person of some means. Can you perhaps tell me, will I enjoy this privilege even into my old age?"

Pondering his question, she invited him to turn over another card. The card he selected was the ace of spades.

Before she turned over any other cards, he interrupted once more by asking, "Please tell me, how significant is this card and does it have any bearing on my question?"

She answered, "This card Don Barcese, is the card of death. It tells me you will die."

Now totally panic-stricken, his breathing becoming quite laboured. He blurted out, "How can this be? Please tell me. How can this be possible? My doctor tells me I am remarkably healthy. Is a calamitous accident going to befall me? This is too dreadful to even contemplate."

Carlo, who up to now had been sitting quietly in the background suddenly sat up and paid close attention. Don Barcese now sweating profusely waited anxiously for her to continue.

"My apologies for any alarm caused. If you had not interrupted me, you would not now be experiencing this distress."

He replied rather hesitantly, "Please, I humbly beg you, please continue."

"Before your reaction, I was about to make the same comment I made earlier concerning the queen of hearts. This card on it's own does not have any particular significance. All it tells me, Don Barcese, is you will die. I will die. And even your companion over there, Señor Carlo, some day even he will die."

Carlo, experiencing a tightening in his throat, coughed slightly and loosened the collar of his shirt to relieve the constriction.

Don Barcese, just ever so slightly, relieved decided to let her continue without any further interruptions.

"As I've thus far indicated, someday we will all die. In your case, I cannot tell you when. It could be tomorrow, next week, next year. Who knows? It could be ten, twenty, even thirty years from now. The life you have, Don Barcese, was given to you by God and it is God who will decide when to take it away. Although I have certain gifts that enable me to reveal aspects of your well-being and existence, the only thing I can say with certainty concerning your life and death is this: Today is the oldest you've ever been, and it is the youngest you will ever be. Everything else is in God's hands."

She now proceeded to turn over four additional cards. As she did so, he was slightly more at ease. He paid close attention as the cards were placed alongside the ace.

The cards turned over were the queen of diamonds, the king of diamonds, the seven of clubs, and the four of clubs.

He waited with bated breath for her to reveal their meaning.

Placing her hand over the queen, she continued, "Your wealth, Don Barcese, during your lifetime, will not diminish."

Shifting her attention to the king, she added, "This card tells me nobody will steal your wealth from you. With the passage of time, your wealth will substantially increase. When you come to the end of your life's journey, it will still be under your control. And it might comfort you to know, it will be close by."

Overjoyed with this welcome news, he exclaimed, "Wonderful, marvellous. Now, madam, can you reveal what this next card has in store for me?"

"I will indeed, Don Barcese, and what it reveals will not in any way have an impact on what I have just now told you regarding your wealth. This card, the seven of clubs, tells me you will make a voyage sometime in the future."

He replied enthusiastically, "Why yes of course, I will be making an important journey to the United States of America. Now what does this last card, the four, tell you?"

"The four indicates your voyage will be a short one. That is all I can tell you, Don Barcese. If you have no objections, I would now like to bring this reading to an end."

By this stage, he too was satisfied with her decision to terminate the reading.

Feeling very pleased with himself, he stood up from the table. Taking two more gold coins from his pocket he declared, "Thank you, madam, for this most interesting experience and your insightful comments just now. Please accept this small additional sum in appreciation."

She accepted the coins and replied, "Thank you for your generosity, Don Barcese. These revelations will come to pass. Of that I am certain."

"Well, madam, we shall see, we shall see. Again, I thank you for your efforts. With your permission, I would like my driver to take you safely back to your home."

With that, he rang the bell.

Henry promptly entered. "Yes, master?"

"Ah, there you are, Henry. Be a good chap. Escort this lady out and have George drive her to wherever it is she needs to go."

Without saying anything by way of reply, the fortune teller bowed slightly and took her leave with Henry.

On their own once more, Carlo now somewhat anxious to establish his boss's frame of mind, asked him his opinion. "Forgive me for asking, Don Barcese. What the gypsy told you, was it relevant in any way? Do you have any thoughts?"

Taking an envelope of money from his jacket, Don Barcese handed it to Carlo. "You've performed a valuable service today. Here's a little something for your toil. What that gypsy woman revealed was most interesting and I was certainly not displeased. For the moment, I'll wait and see how events unfold. I'm sure something will come to mind, enabling me to somehow sow a degree of discord into the relationship Señorita Pellegrini has with these individuals."

Carlo, breathing a sigh of relief, answered, "Excellent, Don Barcese. If I can be of assistance, please just say the word."

"Actually, there is something you can do for me."

"Just name it."

"I would like you to keep an eye on Señor Antonio Fabrizio. Nothing too obvious. Just observe. If you see something unusual or maybe a change in his routine, report back to me at once."

"As you wish, Don Barcese. I will make this my mission."

With Carlo's departure, Don Barcese sat silently reflecting on the gypsy and her remarkable insights. He came to the conclusion his best option in achieving his objective was to continue his charm offensive and patiently wait for the opportunity he believed must surely present itself, especially now following his intriguing encounter with the fortune teller. Her prediction concerning his financial affairs was of tremendous comfort and filled him with a sense he would never again have to endure the grinding poverty of his Sicilian childhood and youth.

CHAPTER 14

Antonio Travels to Verona

Over the following days, Antonio made all the necessary arrangements and sent a cablegram to Father Martine.

On Thursday, the day before his departure, he visited the convent. As usual, Sister Agostina greeted him warmly, showing him into the drawing room. She then went and informed Consuella of his arrival.

A moment or two later, Consuella entered with a beaming smile on her face. "Well, Antonio, I wasn't expecting you today. Pray tell, what brings you here? Or is it possible you were just missing me?"

"Consuella, whenever I'm not in your company I of course always miss you. However, the purpose of my visit is to let you know I will be travelling to Verona tomorrow and will be away for a number of days. I have spoken with Francesco. He will take care of things during my absence, and I know Sister Lucia will take very good care of you while I'm gone."

She responded in a frivolous manner. "Oh, Antonio, how very thoughtful of you. I'm wondering if per chance you might have brought some chocolates.

With a puzzled expression he replied, "Chocolates, why would I bring chocolates?"

"Because, Antonio, your comments just now would lead one to think I was an eleven-year-old child. I'm practically a fully-grown woman. Or maybe you haven't noticed. Oh how terribly sad."

"Dearest Consuella, you are not practically a full grown woman. In fact you are a full grown woman and, I would like to add, a beautiful one at that."

"Oh, Antonio, you do say the nicest things. I will miss you very much while you're away from me. Now, please, tell me the reason for your journey?"

Encouraged by her response, which he felt was pleasantly intimate, he continued on in a slightly more confident manner. "Thank you, Consuella. I of course will miss you too. The reason for my trip is to discuss their travel plans and your forthcoming birthday."

"Why that's wonderful, Antonio. How very thoughtful you are."

"It's my pleasure, Consuella. I'm also hoping to discuss another very important personal matter with them."

Now somewhat curious she enquired, "An important personal matter? How intriguing. Is there a chance you might perhaps confide in me? I promise it will be our secret."

"Dear Consuella, all I can say is, if my discussions result in a positive outcome, then on my return I may have some exciting news for you."

"Antonio, you are being so mysterious. Not only are you leaving me behind, you are also leaving me in a state of suspense. Goodness me. I do believe I'm going to be quite ill."

"Oh come now, Consuella. You'll be so busy you won't have time to think of anything other than your upcoming performances. I must take my leave now. So promise me you will take good care of yourself while I'm away." With that, he leaned over and gave her a gentle kiss on the cheek.

Before she had a chance to react, he was gone. Closing the door behind him, she gently put her hand to her cheek and just lovingly smiled.

The next day Friday, Antonio travelled to Verona. On his arrival, he was pleasantly surprised to see Father Martine waiting for him at the train station.

"Welcome, welcome, Antonio. I trust you had a pleasant journey?"

"Yes indeed, Father, most pleasant."

"Well then, let's get you to your hotel. We can have a spot of lunch, and you can then bring me up to date. Monthly reports are all very well, but I would much rather hear from you in person how things are actually progressing."

"That's an excellent suggestion, Father. Please lead the way."

Over lunch, Father Martine invited him to begin their discussion. "Now, Antonio, you have my attention. So when you're ready, please proceed?"

"Thank you, Father. I need to know what thoughts you may have regarding Consuella's final performances and her upcoming birthday celebration."

"Ah, yes indeed. I've already had preliminary discussions with the others. We will travel to Milan Friday next. Dominique, Paolo, and Adamo will make their journey the following Monday. The venue and guest list we can discuss in further detail when we have our meeting."

"Excellent. That gives me plenty of time to make the necessary arrangements. I take it Sister Maria will be staying at the convent, and I will book the hotel for the rest of you."

"That's fine, though I have to say these arrangements could have been organised with an exchange of cablegrams. So was your journey all that necessary?"

"Actually there are one or two other important matters I would like to discuss with you privately."

"Okay. In your own time; I'm listening."

Antonio explained as best he could the offers and their likely impact concerning Consuella.

Father Martine, paying close attention, queried, "Did you discuss these developments with Francesco?"

"Yes. In fact the two of us discussed them in great detail."

"Did he make any suggestions?"

"He advised me I should write to them. This I have already done. He also suggested I discuss the matter with you privately and get your thoughts. Regarding the offers from the United States, he stated we shouldn't even consider them for at least two years."

"Did he explain why?"

"Not really, though it's my belief there is no good reason for me to question his judgement."

"Well, you know Francesco better than I do. If this is what the two of you have decided, so be it. When it's appropriate, I will speak with the others. Have you mentioned any of this to Consuella?"

"No. I thought it best to speak with Francesco and yourself first."

"Good. No point in confusing her until we decide how best to proceed."

"Thank you, Father. There is one last very important subject I need to discuss. It involves Consuella and myself."

"Please, Antonio, I hope you're not going to tell me the two of you have had a quarrel or some sort of disagreement."

"It's not that at all. In fact, it's quite the opposite."

"Okay, I'm listening."

"Well, let's see where should I begin. Ah yes, from the very first day of our agreement, I have done my utmost to carry out my duties in an honourable and professional manner. My main concern has been her career, as well as her safety and well-being. I now have a dilemma. You see, over some months past, I've developed a deep affection for Consuella."

"Did you discuss any of this with her?"

"Not yet."

"Why so?"

"Well I believe to have done so would have been in direct conflict with my duties as manager and guardian. I did, however, speak with Carlota and Francesco."

"How did they react?"

"Carlota wasn't so terribly surprised. She suggested I should speak with you first and get your thoughts."

"That's a reasonable point. So tell me. Do you have any inkling how she might feel about you? And what would you like me to do now?"

"I believe she is experiencing similar emotions and that she would respond positively if I had her father's approval, as well as yours and Sister Maria's of course. My reason for sharing all of this with you first, is to get your thoughts and, more importantly, prevail upon you to assist me in gaining her father's agreement."

"Antonio, I will support you in every way I can. Let's just say I will now have the opportunity of becoming your Trojan horse. You might recall sometime in the past there was an occasion you performed a service for me. I told you then I wouldn't forget it."

"Indeed you haven't, Father. Indeed you haven't."

"All right then. Here's how we proceed. Tomorrow Saturday we can all meet at the convent. We can discuss the travel arrangements and the plans for her birthday celebration. The next day Sunday, not really a suitable day for meetings, I will suggest we get together on Monday. Before then, I will let them know you wish to speak with them on a personal matter concerning Consuella and yourself. I should be able to gauge from their reaction the likely response you'll receive when you get the opportunity to plead your case. One word of advice though."

"Yes, Father. I'm listening."

"When you're speaking, focus your attention on Pietro. Under normal circumstances, you tend to address Sister Maria or myself. This situation is very different, as it will be Consuella's Father making the final decision."

"Thank you, Father. I will do as you suggest. One final question, if I may?"

"Of course."

"What I told you just now concerning Consuella and myself, did it surprise you in any way?"

"Antonio, I may be an old-fashioned priest, but I've always been a keen observer of human nature—people's strengths and weaknesses if you like. Your situation is nothing terribly unusual. You've simply fallen in love with a most talented and beautiful young lady. It doesn't surprise me in the least, and I, for my part, will do all in my power to bring about an agreeable outcome.

"So now, I think we're done for the moment. Tomorrow we'll have our meeting. Sunday you're free to do as you wish. Have you made any plans?"

"Yes. I intend spending some time with my sister."

"Very good. Please pass on my good wishes. Come Monday, we'll see what fate has in store for you."

Before leaving the hotel, Father Martine raised the topic of Violetta Mollinaro and her father, Alberto. "I'm just curious. How did yourself and Francesco become involved?"

Antonio gave him the short version of events that had resulted in them taking over the management of Violetta's career. "So as you can see, it was a very sad and tragic chapter in both their lives," he concluded. "But I'm happy to say both father and daughter are now doing quite well. The credit for Violetta's rehabilitation and successful return to the stage is due mainly to the efforts of Francesco. My role was a very minor one in comparison. Your question just now has me somewhat curious. Do you have any particular interest in them?"

"No, nothing special. It's just when I met them at Dominique's wedding, I was curious how your association with them came about, that's all. I have to say, she has an excellent voice. And her father seems a decent sort of fellow."

"Father, why do I have a strong feeling you brought up the subject for a very specific reason?"

"Well, now while we're on the subject, I'm just wondering, if you're going to be spending more time in other countries, how are you going to balance your role managing two careers?"

"That won't be an insurmountable task. Francesco and I have already discussed and agreed a workable strategy. If and when I have to travel to other countries on Consuella's behalf, here at home, her schedule and Violetta's will be handled by Francesco. Does this explanation clarify the situation?"

"Indeed it does. You see, I was just exploring all avenues. That's all. I just didn't want to be caught off guard by Sister Maria. You of all people know how tenacious she can be."

"I do indeed, Father."

As Father Martine, departed Antonio cast his mind back to what Carlota had said about the measured way he uttered every sentence. He just smiled in the knowledge it was a most perceptive observation indeed.

CHAPTER 15

Meanwhile in Milan

On the Friday morning of his departure, Antonio made the short journey to the train station unaware he was being followed.

Carlo, who had been following him on and off for the past few weeks, felt there was something different on this particular day. Observing Antonio board the train for Verona, he casually remarked to the porter on the platform, "Was that Señor Fabrizio I saw just now?"

"It was indeed, Señor."

"Very good, very good. I was hoping to call on him this coming Monday to discuss an important matter. Would you by chance have any clue as to when he might be returning?"

"Tuesday next, Señor."

Handing the porter a fifty-lire note, Carlo replied, "Thank you so much. You have saved me a wasted journey."

He immediately made his way over to Don Barcese's residence and gave him the news of Antonio's departure.

Don Barcese questioned him thoroughly. "You're sure he was travelling alone?"

"Yes, Don Barcese, quite sure. He was definitely unaccompanied and will be away until Tuesday next. The information cost me some money, but I can assure you it is reliable."

Escorting Carlo to the door, Don Barcese answered, "Well done, Carlo. I won't forget this. You'll be well rewarded for your efforts."

Returning to his study, Don Barcese crafted a carefully worded note inviting Antonio and Consuella to join him for lunch the following day. Placing the contents in an envelope, he then wrote both their names and the words "most urgent" on the outside.

He summoned his driver George and gave him explicit instructions. "I want you to deliver this letter to the convent of Saint Mary Magdalena. Tell them you were unable to deliver it to Señor Fabrizio due to the fact he was unavailable when you called to his residence. Impress upon them your instructions in such a circumstance was to deliver the letter to Señorita Pellegrini."

George drove to the convent as instructed. On his arrival, Sister Agostina answered the door. She was somewhat surprised to see a total stranger standing on the doorstep. Also, she didn't fail to notice the rather grand auto-mobile in the drive.

"Forgive me for the intrusion, Sister. My task was to deliver this most important letter to Señor Fabrizio. Alas, he was unavailable. My instructions, however, were quite explicit. They stated, should my efforts in this instance prove to be unsuccessful, I was to then personally deliver it here for Señorita Pellegrini's attention. By any chance would Señorita Pellegrini be available?"

Sister Agostina, now quite flustered, replied, "Oh I'm so terribly sorry, señor. You see, Consuella! I mean Senorita Pellegrini is not available right now. Well when I say she is not available, I'm really saying she's not here at the convent at this particular moment."

Noting the sister's nervousness, George decided to press her just a little to see if he could glean a little more information. "That's such a pity. When did she leave Milan?"

Now really flustered and in that innocent trusting nature of hers, Sister Agostina replied, "Oh no, goodness gracious me no. Señorita Pellegrini hasn't left the convent or even Milan for that matter. She left here just an hour ago in the company of Sister Lucia for her voice-coaching lesson with Señor Cipriano. They will return within the next hour or so."

"Sister, you have been most kind, and I thank you for your patience. With your kind permission, I would like it if you could accept this important letter into your care. From our conversation just now, I am more than satisfied you will make sure Señorita Pellegrini receives it on her return."

Now quite relieved this brief exchange was drawing to a close, Sister Agostina accepted the letter and bid the driver of the fine car a good day. In the kitchen, she put the letter in a safe place and reflected on the conversation that had taken place between herself and this stranger.

She came to the conclusion that, despite the fact that the man had spoken Italian, he was most definitely not Italian. She also regretted the fact that, in her confusion, she had forgotten to ask him his name and on whose behalf he was delivering the letter. She decided all she could do now was pass the letter on to Consuella as soon as she returned.

Earlier that same morning, probably around the time Antonio's train was pulling out from the station, Sister Lucia accompanied Consuella from the convent to Francesco's studio.

He started the session by taking her through the scales. His method was straightforward. Sitting at the piano, he played a note. Holding up his right hand, he signalled her to sing the note. The exercise lasted almost thirty minutes and didn't finish until she had faultlessly gone through all the scales.

After her breathing and voice projection exercises, he handed her the sheet music for Verdi's *La Traviata*. "Now, Consuella, you know this opera very well. As in the past and also on this occasion, you will sing and perform the role of Violetta, the courtesan whose tale of love, betrayal, reconciliation, and tragic death is the central theme of this great Verdi masterpiece. We have seven days left before your last four performances. So let's go through the entire programme, see how we get on, and then decide if we need to do any more preparatory work later in the week."

"Well, Francesco, I can promise you during this rehearsal I will be appropriately sad."

Somewhat puzzled, he asked her, "How so?"

"With dear Antonio's departure this morning, I am missing him already, and it's making me so sad."

"It seems to me, young lady, we now have the perfect sombre mood for your rehearsal. Anyway, not to worry. He'll be back before you know it, and I'm sure he's missing you also. Why, who knows? He might even have a surprise for you when he returns."

"Francesco, why do I have the feeling you know something?"

"Well, Consuella, the only thing I know is we need to get through this rehearsal, or we'll be here half the night."

While they carried on with the rehearsal, Sister Lucia chatted with Carlota and the twins in the drawing room.

Consuella and Francesco eventually joined them.

Carlota took one look at Consuella and exclaimed, "My dear child, you look exhausted. Francesco, you ought to be ashamed of yourself. You're driving this young lady far too hard. Sit down, dear. Carla will bring you a nice cup of tea. Francesco, I insist, Consuella should have the rest of the week off."

"Dearest, we've done what had to be done. And I agree. We won't have to do any more work, at least not until early next week. So may I have a cup of tea as well?"

As they sat enjoying their tea, the conversation turned to Antonio and his trip. Carlota casually remarked. "Well I suppose he's probably halfway to Verona by now."

"Yes indeed." Consuella sighed. "Though I'm very cross with him."

Carlota inquired, "Why ever so?"

"Well he's left me here in a state of great suspense, telling me he might have exciting news for me on his return."

Carlota tried to lift her mood with some encouraging words. "Oh come now, Consuella. It's not so bad. Antonio will be back in a few days from now, and I must say, I do believe we'll all be looking forward to hearing his exciting news."

"I suppose you're right, Carlota. I will just have to try and be a little more patient."

Sister Lucia stood up said goodbye to the twins. Then thanking Carlota and Francesco she said, "We probably won't meet again, at least not until Antonio returns. So in the meantime, I will try and get Consuella to relax a little."

Consuella joined her. They both took their leave and headed back to the convent.

Arriving at the convent, Consuella was about to go to her room when Sister Agostina told her about the letter.

Somewhat surprised, Consuella responded, "A letter for me? How strange."

Sister Agostina headed for the kitchen, fetched the letter, and handed it to her.

Sister Lucia, not paying too much attention, headed to her own room.

Consuella, having received the letter, took it with her; she could see it was addressed to both Antonio and herself.

Alone in her room, she opened and read it. She then sat down and read it again.

At first, she didn't know how to react. Here was an invitation from Don Barcese, inviting Antonio and herself for lunch the following day at his residence. Somewhat puzzled, she wondered to herself, what should she do. Should she just ignore it, give it to Antonio on his return and let him deal with it? Should she perhaps inform Sister Lucia or maybe even Francesco?

She decided to do no more about it for the time being.

The remainder of the evening passed off without any mention of the letter.

Sister Lucia was of the opinion that, if Consuella didn't bring the letter up during dinner, then it wasn't her place to raise the subject.

CHAPTER 16

Consuella Meets Don Barcese

The following morning, just before breakfast, Consuella read the contents of the letter one more time.

She decided to make the journey to Don Barcese's town house and see for herself what was behind this invitation.

Sometime around midday, she casually remarked to Sister Lucia that she needed to visit Francesco's studio to check on something relating to her forthcoming performances.

Sister Lucia replied, "Just give me a moment, and I will get ready."

"Sister, I know you had alternative plans for today. So please, I'll be fine. I can make the journey on my own. After all, I will be twenty-one in little over a week."

"Very good, Consuella. But please take good care. Mother Superior would never forgive me if some calamity were to befall you whilst travelling alone."

"Don't worry, Sister. I'll be quite safe."

With that, Consuella left the convent, making sure she had the letter with her.

She took a cab, gave the driver the address, and made the journey over to Don Barcese's town house. On the way over, she couldn't help but feel somewhat guilty for the earlier deception. She decided all she could do now was complete her journey and see what motive lay behind his surprising invitation.

Arriving just after one o'clock, she couldn't help but notice the sheer grandeur of his residence. It really was quite impressive.

She rang the bell. Almost immediately, the door was opened by Henry. His formal manner and mode of dress surprised her somewhat. She had never had this kind of experience before.

She introduced herself saying, "Good afternoon. My name is Señorita Pellegrini. I am here by invitation of Don Barcese. Is he by chance available?"

"Indeed, Señorita. Please, if you will, just follow me. I will take you to him."

She followed Henry down a long expansive hallway. He led her into a large dining room.

Don Barcese was sitting on a couch to one side of the dining table. As she entered, he stood up and greeted her effusively. He took her hand in his and kissed it.

Somewhat taken aback, she didn't quite know how to respond.

Noting the slight discomfort his gesture caused, he released his hold and invited her to sit on the rather large armchair adjacent to the couch. "Please, please, Consuella. Please take a seat. And may I ask, will Señor Antonio be joining us?"

"I'm afraid not, Don Barcese."

"Oh how disappointing," he lied.

"I was so looking forward to the two of you joining me for lunch. Has he been detained somewhere?"

"No, as a matter of fact, he had to travel to Verona on some personal business."

"What a pity. Anyway, let's have a spot of lunch." He guided her over to the dining table and invited her to take a seat.

Having seated himself, he rang the bell.

Almost immediately, Henry entered with Mildred trailing behind carrying a large tray of food. She stood to attention while Henry served the lunch.

With the food in front of her, Henry enquired. "Will there be anything else, master?"

"Forgive me, my dear. Would you care for some wine perhaps?"

"No thank you, Don Barcese. The water will be just fine."

"Very good, very good. Thank you, Henry, Mildred. That will be all for now."

With their departure, he invited her to begin.

"I do hope the food is to your liking?"

"It looks quite delicious, Don Barcese. Thank you. And I hope you don't think me impertinent. But may I ask the reason you chose to invite Antonio and myself to your beautiful home on this particular occasion?"

"Oh it's something I've been meaning to do for some time now. I suppose all I can say is better late than never. Now, Consuella, I take it you're looking forward to your final performances this season."

"Yes indeed. It has been a wonderful season, and I feel very privileged having had the opportunity to perform throughout the entire country."

"Why yes indeed. Antonio and his companion have done an exemplary job in guiding your career on the national stage. However, I find myself wondering, what next for Consuella Pellegrini—the most accomplished soprano to appear on an Italian stage in over a decade?"

Beginning to wonder where exactly he was going with these particular comments, she decided to make it abundantly clear the future management of her career would continue on in exactly the same fashion as it had from the very first day of her arrival in Milan. "Don Barcese, as we speak, Antonio is most likely discussing these very issues with my father, Sister Maria, and Father Martine. In case you didn't know, it was they who placed the development of my career into Antonio's capable hands. And to date, I think you will agree he has done a remarkable job. Sister Maria, my father, and Father Martine will be travelling from Verona later this week. And I dare say we will be finalising a new agreement for the foreseeable future."

He decided the time was now right to try and plant even the smallest doubt in her mind concerning Antonio's abilities. "Yes of course, of course. Antonio has done a remarkable job here in Italy. But I have to ask myself, does he have the expertise and the breadth of vision to take your career to the next level?"

Growing slightly uncomfortable, she decided nevertheless to question Don Barcese a little more to see exactly where he was going with this line of conversation. "When you use the term 'breadth of vision', can you please explain exactly what it is you actually mean?"

Now somewhat relieved she hadn't terminated the conversation, Don Barcese decided now was the moment to impress upon her the level of expertise and experience he possessed managing the careers of operatic performers on the international stage. "Consuella, from the first time I heard you perform here in Milan, I have followed your career with great interest.

"Please forgive me I'm fully aware I'm repeating myself just now. But I have to say you are, without doubt, the most outstanding soprano the opera world has seen emerge in at least a decade. I am convinced the voice and talent you possess should be heard in every European capital and even in the Grand Metropolitan of New York. For you to attain this goal, I believe I am the person most suited for the task."

Having finished making his case, he sat back and waited to see if she was going to react or make any sort of comment.

After a few brief moments, she replied, "Thank you, Don Barcese, for a most enjoyable lunch and an interesting conversation. I no doubt will have cause to reflect on it over the coming days. And now if I may be excused, I really need to be getting back."

"Please, Consuella, one more question if I may?"

"By all means."

"I don't mean to be impertinent. I couldn't help but notice you've lived at the convent since your arrival here in Milan. Is it your intention to reside there for the foreseeable future?"

"As a matter of fact, no. As soon as I find a property that suits my needs and, more importantly, my budget, it will then no longer be necessary or even practical for me to reside there. I'm curious. Why do you ask?"

"I was of the opinion you were not going to spend the remainder of your career there. This fact you've just confirmed. My reason for asking is it just so happens a colleague of mine has an office quite near the theatre. He deals in real estate." Taking a card from his waistcoat, he offered it to her and continued, "If you wish to speak with him, take this card. It contains his details. Tell him I sent you. He owes me a favour or two. I will see to it personally he shows you a property that suits your needs and your budget."

For the first time since her arrival, she felt slightly more at ease. Taking the card, she replied, "Why thank you, Don Barcese. I'm most grateful for your kind offer."

"Think nothing of it my dear."

With that, he rang the bell summoning Henry. In an instant, he appeared. "You rang, master?"

"Yes. Please tell George to bring my auto-mobile around to the front door. I need him to drive Señorita Pellegrini back to the convent."

"Very good, master."

Slightly embarrassed she stood up. "Please, Don Barcese, there's no need to trouble your driver."

"No trouble at all. I just want to be certain your journey back is a safe one."

"Thank you for your thoughtfulness."

"You're most welcome, Consuella. Could I perhaps make one final suggestion?"

"You may."

"With your permission, I would like to set down on paper some aspects of our discussions just now and have them delivered to you over the coming days."

"You may if you wish. Just mark the envelope for my attention. I will study the contents when time allows. Again thank you for your hospitality."

Henry escorted her to the auto-mobile.

As Consuella made her journey back, she reflected on this her first real encounter with the famous, or on the many previous occasions, she had heard him being referred to as, the infamous Don Barcese.

She thought there might be no harm in receiving this document of his. After all, the least it might do is give her an alternative view on the future path of her career.

CHAPTER 17

Sister Lucia's Confrontation With Consuella

While Consuella was meeting with Don Barcese, Sister Lucia decided to collect some items from the stationers. On her journey, she quite literally bumped into Carlota and Francesco. Greeting them, she then enquired, "No classes today, Francesco?"

He replied, "No classes. So Carlota dragged me into the city. She insists I need some new clothes."

Carlota chimed in. "And so you do. We're certainly not rich, but I won't have people forming the opinion I'm married to a pauper."

Sister Lucia quite amused, replied, "Oh come now, Carlota. Why even if Francesco were dressed in rags, he would still be most dashing."

Francesco couldn't help but smile at the compliment. He then continued, "I can now see why our girls are so fond of you. Thank you. Maybe now I can avoid having to visit every tailoring establishment in Milan."

Carlota, enjoying the friendly banter, took her husband by the arm. "We're leaving now before you try to change my husband's mind. Say hello to Consuella from both of us."

"Of course I will."

On her way back to the convent, Sister Lucia reflected on Consuella's comments at breakfast about needing to visit Francesco. She was now certain no such meeting took place. It was very clear to her Consuella had a somewhat different agenda. She couldn't help but draw the conclusion she had been deliberately deceived, but why? In all their time together, nothing even close to this had ever happened before.

It suddenly dawned on her—the letter from the day before. Could this be the reason behind her deception?

She decided to get back to the convent as speedily as possible and see if Sister Agostina might be able to reveal something about its origin.

On her return, she headed straight for the kitchen. "There you are, Sister. Do you know if Consuella has returned?"

"No, Sister, not yet."

"Sister, I need to ask you something of a personal nature concerning Consuella and the letter she received. Please trust me; it is a matter of some importance."

Sister Agostina nodded in agreement.

"Thank you, Sister. Now what can you tell me about this letter?"

"It was addressed to Señor Antonio and Consuella. The person who delivered it stated the instruction given to him was, in the event of Senor Antonio being unavailable, he was to then deliver it to Señorita Consuella."

"That's most interesting. So then the letter was intended for both of them?"

"Yes, that is my understanding."

"How did she respond when you gave it to her?"

"She really didn't seem all that interested."

"The person who delivered the letter, is there anything you can you tell me?"

"He was a tall gentleman. I would say he was between thirty-five and forty."

"Did you happen to get his name or the name of the person who sent him?"

"Unfortunately no. I realise now I should have been more diligent."

"Not to worry. Is there any other detail you can recall?"

"Yes, although he spoke Italian, I could tell he was most definitely not of Italian birth."

"How did you arrive at that conclusion?"

"Well, it was his accent."

"What about his accent?"

"It sounded so foreign."

"Could he perhaps be German or maybe Spanish?"

"No, he was none of those. If you asked me to make a guess, I would have to say he was English."

"Thank you, Sister. You've been most helpful."

As Sister Lucia was about to leave the kitchen, Sister Agostina remembered one last important detail. "Please, Sister, I almost forgot. That foreign gentleman who delivered the letter, he arrived in an auto-mobile."

"An auto-mobile. Can you describe it for me?"

"I'm really sorry. I'm afraid my knowledge of such machines is totally non-existent. The only thing I can say for sure is, it was kind of grey in colour and rather splendid."

"Again, Sister, thank you. You've been most helpful."

With Sister Lucia's departure, Sister Agostina carried on with her chores. Fretting slightly, she wondered if everything was all right between Consuella and Sister Lucia.

Sister Lucia decided to stay downstairs and await Consuella's return. She went into the library and left the door slightly ajar.

Consuella arrived back. As she passed the library, she noticed the open door. She looked in and was surprised to see Sister Lucia sitting there. "Oh I'm sorry, Sister. I didn't mean to disturb you."

"Not at all, Consuella. Please come in and join me. I'm just sorting out some paperwork. Anyway, how did your session go today?"

"Well it was scale after scale after scale. I am totally exhausted."

Sister Lucia, now convinced Consuella was being deliberately untruthful, decided to probe a little further. "Consuella, I need to ask. Is there something troubling you?"

"Of course not. I'm just fine. Why do you ask?"

"Well you seem a little tense. I was just wondering; maybe it has something to do with the letter you received yesterday."

Consuella replied somewhat caustically, "That letter is really none of your concern."

Sister Lucia, quite appalled, shot back, "Everything you do, Consuella, is my business—more particularly while Antonio is absent."

"I beg to differ, Sister. In little over a week from now, everything I do, everywhere I go, and anyone I decide to meet will be none of your business. So you might as well get used to it. Oh, and by the way, I will be leaving the convent again Monday morning, and I intend to do so alone."

"Consuella, I am asking politely. What reason do you have for leaving the convent this coming Monday? Another coaching session perhaps?"

"No. I will be attending to some personal business."

"Does it have anything to do with the letter delivered by the person who I believe was driving a very fine auto-mobile?"

"Again, Sister, it really is none of your business or, for that matter, Sister Agostina's. This conversation is beginning to bore me, so unless you have something important or useful to say, I think we're done talking for now."

"Before you go, Consuella, there is something I need to say. I would never have thought you of all people could be capable of such rudeness. You are right about one thing though. Very shortly, what you do and where you go will no longer concern me. However, when Antonio returns, I will be speaking to him about this incident. I also intend to speak with Reverend Mother when she arrives."

"Well, Sister, you do what you think is best. Now if you'll excuse me, I have other more important matters to attend to." Without waiting for a reply, she abruptly left.

Sister Lucia just sat there. Not only was she appalled, she was also quite upset about the way Consuella had spoken to her just now.

The following morning at breakfast, Sister Agostina sensed the tension between them. She tried lifting the mood by engaging in some small talk. "Well, Consuella, what a beautiful morning. Do you have any plans for today?"

Consuella took one look at her and replied, "Are you asking out of idle curiosity? Or by chance are you being prompted by our dear sister?"

Sister Lucia immediately stood up from the table. "Consuella, being rude to me is one thing, but I will not tolerate you being rude to Sister Agostina. You will apologise immediately."

Consuella answered in a very severe tone, "Oh really, Sister. You want me to apologise? Well maybe both of you should be apologising to me."

Sister Agostina, now acutely embarrassed, just sat there waiting to see how Sister Lucia was going to react.

Sister Lucia replied for both of them, "Consuella, do whatever it is you have to do. If you are waiting for an apology, don't hold your breath. Sister Agostina and I have nothing, absolutely nothing, to apologise for. As from today, I will play no further part in whatever it is you decide to do. I think it only fair to remind you, though, I will be making a full report to Reverend Mother when she arrives."

"Do as you wish, Sister. Now if I may be excused, I am going to my room and don't expect to be disturbed." With that, she abruptly left the dining room.

Sister Agostina, with a concerned look on her face asked, "How can this be, Sister? I've never seen her behave this way before. Is this perhaps something that happens to a person when they become successful and famous?"

"Unfortunately, Sister, fame and great success on occasions can affect people in that way. I must confess though, I would never in my wildest dreams have thought Consuella could possibly behave in the way she has just now. I firmly believe that letter has something to do with her strange behaviour. All we can do now is wait until Antonio returns and see if he can bring some sense to this strange situation."

For the remainder of the day, Consuella remained in her room.

Sister Lucia surmised this was a deliberate ploy adopted by her to have no further contact, thereby avoiding further questions.

On Monday morning, Consuella, unescorted, made the journey to meet with the property agent. As she travelled, deep down she couldn't help but feel somewhat guilty about the way she had behaved towards Sister Lucia and Sister Agostina.

On her arrival at the estate agent's office, she introduced herself and received the following reply.

"Please, Señorita Pellegrini, please take a seat. My name is Giovanni Bellini. Don Barcese told me to expect you. So now, how can I be of assistance?"

Deciding to keep the encounter on a formal footing, she replied in a businesslike manner, "Thank you, Señor Bellini. I am interested in acquiring a modest town house, as close as possible to La Scala. Nothing too grand you understand, as I have a limited budget."

"Of course, Señorita. There are many fine dwellings in this general area. With your permission, I will compile a short list of properties I believe may suit your needs. Would it be possible for you to call on me again, let's say early next week? I'm confident by then I will have something of interest to show you."

"How long will this process take?"

"In the happy event one of these properties suits your needs and we are able to satisfactorily complete all legal and financial issues, it shouldn't take more than three to six months."

"I may not be able to wait that long. Do you perhaps have any other suggestions?"

"In circumstances such as these, a short-term rental might be a suitable alternative."

"Very good, Señor Bellini. I will leave it to your good self to choose something to suit my immediate needs. My preferred date for occupancy would be around the fifth or sixth of October."

"Señorita Pellegrini, I will give this matter my fullest attention. By the end of this week, I will have a rental property I'm sure will be satisfactory."

"Thank you, Señor Bellini, for your valuable time. I will call on you this coming Friday. Hopefully we can then conclude our business."

"Of course, Señorita. And may I say what a privilege it is for me to be of assistance to a friend of Don Barcese's—especially a lady as pretty as your good self."

Bristling slightly from his closing remarks, Consuella nevertheless managed to mask her displeasure and then took her leave.

CHAPTER 18

The Necklace

Saturday morning in Verona, Antonio, Pietro, and Father Martine made their way to the convent. There they met with Sister Maria and discussed the travel arrangements for later that week.

Father Martine made no mention of the offers from abroad or the matter concerning Antonio's feelings for Consuella. He brought the short meeting to a close. "Well, Antonio, I think we've covered everything. So off you go and enjoy the rest of your weekend. I'll stay behind, as there is something I need to discuss with Sister Maria and Pietro. Monday morning, we can all have breakfast here at the convent. Then we can pick up where we've left off today. What do you say?"

"Thank you, Father. I'm looking forward to it already." With that, Antonio stood up. Bowing graciously to the three of them, he then took his leave.

Later that same afternoon, he took a leisurely stroll. Finding himself on Piazza San Nicolo, he spotted a quaint jeweller's shop. Looking at the displays in the window, he wondered, would it be appropriate to purchase a gift for Consuella? His initial thought was it might be somewhat premature, as he wasn't sure if Father Martine had even spoken to the others. Nonetheless, he decided it would do no harm to just have a look.

On entering, he could see there were no other customers. He observed an elderly gentleman sitting at a workbench. He had stooped shoulders, a mop of grey hair, a matching full beard, and a pair of rimless spectacles perched precariously on his nose. He wore a black work apron over his garb and was sporting a rather splendid pair of arm bands to keep his sleeves at an appropriate length so as to not impede his delicate work.

Looking up, he greeted Antonio warmly. "Good afternoon, Señor. If I can be of assistance, please let me know."

Antonio answered him, "I am looking for something special for a very special person."

"May I ask what it is you have in mind—a ring, a bracelet perhaps, or maybe a necklace?"

As he was speaking, something caught Antonio's eye.

The jeweller quickly spotted what it was that had drawn his attention. "I do believe, Señor, you have seen an item that is to your liking. Would you like me to show it to you?"

"Yes indeed, though I'm curious to know how you can possibly select the item that interests me from the many fine pieces on display?"

"Well, Señor, if you allow me, I will select the item, and you can tell me if I have made the correct choice."

More out of curiosity than anything else Antonio replied, "Please proceed."

Unlocking the cabinet, he chose an exquisite necklace. It was mounted on a purple velvet pad. Placing it on the counter in front of Antonio he enquired, "Have I chosen correctly, Señor?"

For a few brief moments Antonio remained silent. He just gazed at the beauty and craftsmanship of the object. The chain was made up of very delicate gold links, not too big but sufficiently strong. The links were attached to a brilliant blue sapphire surrounded by a cluster of sparkling diamonds.

When Antonio finally spoke he just said, "This necklace is even more exquisite than I first thought."

"Then, Señor, can I take from your reaction I have chosen correctly?"

Momentarily taking his eyes off the necklace, Antonio answered, "Congratulations, Señor. I do believe you know my mind and heart better than I do myself.

"Now, let's get down to the business of price. And I must warn you; I am a very stubborn negotiator, particularly in matters to do with financial transactions."

The jeweller looked at him and pleaded, "Oh please, Señor. You seem like an honourable gentleman. So please, I beg you. Don't take advantage, for I am but a humble craftsman. The greatest joy for me is not how much money I make on the transaction. That's not my overriding objective. The most important thing for me is the certain knowledge that, when a person of noble intentions such as your good self, having purchased something as beautiful as this necklace, receives in return from the recipient the full affection you so richly deserve. For I do believe you must love this person very dearly."

After some friendly haggling, they eventually agreed a price. Placing the gift in a small case, the jeweller also produced a card. Giving both of them to Antonio, he explained, "If you wish, Señor, you may write some words on the card. As you can see, it has my name and address on the back. Hopefully, if the lady is pleased with your gesture—who knows—maybe the two of you might someday return and choose something even more significant."

Looking at the card, Antonio couldn't help but smile. The old man, having successfully completed this sale, was already lining him up for the next one. "Domenico, not only are you a master craftsman; I can also see you're a pretty shrewd businessman as well."

Taking a pen from his jacket, he wrote the following: "To Consuella. Love and best wishes, Antonio."

Taking the card from Antonio, the jeweller placed it in an envelope. He handed them back with the following comment, "Consuella, what a beautiful name. Dear Antonio, I wish you every success in winning this fair lady's hand."

"Thank you, Domenico. I hope and pray this gift helps me in my quest. I promise, if the outcome is a happy one, I will revisit you in the company of this fair lady. You can then assist us in choosing an engagement ring."

Placing the case and the card in the inside pocket of his jacket, Antonio shook hands with Domenico and bid him farewell.

On the way back to his hotel, every now and again, he placed his hand over his breast pocket to reassure himself the contents were secure.

Monday morning, as previously arranged, Antonio made the short journey to the monastery. Feeling somewhat nervous, he nevertheless decided, at this critical stage, there was definitely no turning back.

So rather hesitantly, he entered the dining room and joined his group of protagonists.

Father Martine opened the conversation. "Good morning, Antonio. Please take a seat and have some breakfast. Later, we can use the drawing room and continue our discussions. By the way, did you have a pleasant visit with your sister?"

"Thank you, Father. I did indeed. And she asked me to pass on her good wishes to all of you."

Sister Maria and Pietro made no reply. They just carried on eating their breakfast.

Antonio thought to himself that this wasn't exactly an encouraging sign.

Father Martine, noting his obvious distress, continued on, "Excellent, excellent. When are you planning on returning to Milan?"

"Tomorrow morning early. I want to make certain all preparations are in place for the performances next week."

To his relief, Sister Maria finally joined the conversation. "You know, Antonio, when I think back to the fateful day two and a half years ago when we sat at this very table, who could have predicted back then the outstanding success Consuella would achieve in such a short space of time? Would you agree, Pietro?"

Antonio was eager to hear what Pietro had to say. He wondered if his response would contain some clue as to his feelings in relation to the subject yet to be discussed.

Pietro, in that quiet manner of his, replied, "Not only do I agree, I would also like to acknowledge the important role played by Antonio here. What has been achieved is quite remarkable. And for me, as Consuella's father, the entire experience has filled me with overwhelming pride and joy."

Antonio thanked him. He glanced over in the direction of Father Martine, who gave him a winning smile. He was now feeling slightly more hopeful than earlier.

As they finished their breakfast, Father Martine invited the other three to join him in the drawing room. Filing in, the three from Verona took their seats at a table. Father Martine motioned Antonio to take the single chair facing them.

As he sat down, Antonio couldn't help but feel the scene was reminiscent of past job interviews endured more than enjoyed.

Sister Maria opened the discussion. "Well, Antonio, Father Martine has spoken to us concerning a matter of some importance you wish to discuss. I believe it concerns Consuella and yourself. Would that be correct?"

"Yes, Sister."

"Okay. When you're ready, you may begin. We're listening."

Remembering Father Martine's advice, Antonio focused his attention on Pietro and began, "For two and a half years now, under your guidance, I have managed Consuella's career. From your previous comments, it would appear the three of you are satisfied with the outcome to date. So there's probably no need for further discussion on that particular topic. My main reason for requesting this meeting is to let you know of certain developments that have, let's say, evolved over some months past, which may have a bearing on any future decisions you may take in relation to the future management of her career and personal life." He paused briefly to gauge their reaction to his opening remarks.

Sister Maria replied, "Very good, Antonio. What you've said so far makes reasonable sense. Now, if you can just get to the heart of what it is you wish to say or propose. And please, if you will, can you explain what you mean by certain developments?"

Antonio surmised, although she was being very matter of fact in her comments, she certainly seemed to be affording him a degree of latitude to make his case. "Thank you, Sister. The developments I referred to concern Consuella and myself. For some months now, my feelings of affection for her have grown steadily day by day."

Pietro, now very attentive, asked him, "Have you spoken with my daughter concerning these emotions you say you're experiencing?"

"This I have not done."

"Why not?"

Again, making sure he focused his attention on Pietro, he continued, "To do so, I believe, would have been a breach of the trust the three of you placed in me at the outset. I have never forgotten the words you yourself spoke to me the day I left for Milan. This is the reason for my presence here today. I wanted to let you know my feelings for Consuella, thereby affording you the opportunity to discuss the matter with Sister Maria and Father Martine so the three of you could then decide what's best for her future well-being and happiness."

Pietro answered, "Is there anything else you wish to add, you know, something to convince us your feelings are truly sincere?"

Sitting there momentarily, he wondered, *What can I say? What can I do to convince them?*

Placing his hand on the outside of his breast pocket, he could feel the outline of the case containing the necklace. He decided to take a huge gamble. "Yes there is."

Sister Maria interrupted, "Yes there is what exactly?"

"Actually there is something I'd like to show you." Without waiting for a response, he reached into his breast pocket. Taking the case out, he laid it on the table and opened it, revealing the necklace.

For some moments, nobody uttered a word.

Antonio began to wonder, had he made a fatal error? Might they draw the conclusion his gesture might be that of an overconfident suitor trying to impress them with an extravagant gift?

Father Martine, noting the surprised expressions on the others' faces, intervened in an attempt to rescue the situation. "My, my, Antonio, what a superb piece of jewellery. I take it this is a gift for Consuella?"

"Yes, indeed it is, Father."

"How very thoughtful, though would you not agree maybe a little premature?"

Antonio contemplated mounting a strong argument to justify his purchase. A telling glance from his teacher quickly changed his mind. "Yes, Father, I have to agree it was somewhat premature to purchase such a gift before a decision has even been made."

Again focusing his attention on Pietro, he continued, "Please accept my apologies for what can only be described as an impetuous gesture on my part. The other day, having some time on my hands, I found myself in a jeweller's shop. I made the purchase and just thought at the time it would be an appropriate gift for Consuella. That's all I can say."

Then reaching out he closed the case, returned it to his pocket, and continued, "That's it really. I know now I should not have shown it to you. Finally, I would like to thank you for your time and courtesy. I will humbly accept whatever it is you decide."

Pietro answered him. "That's fine, Antonio. Now if you would kindly wait in the other room, we will discuss your request. I promise we won't keep you waiting very long before you have an answer."

Rising from his chair, Antonio bowed courteously and took himself into the adjoining room. Sitting there, nervously awaiting his fate, he wondered, could he have made a more impressive presentation? Should he have been better prepared?

He resigned himself to the fact that all he could now do was watch the clock.

As the minutes passed by agonisingly slowly, he waited.

Eventually, Sister Maria entered. "Please, Antonio. We've completed our deliberations. We are ready to see you now."

Following her in, he was trying to see if there was anything in her demeanour that might give him some clue as to how they were likely to respond. Her formal impassive manner told him nothing.

Returning to the chair, he sat silently waiting and wondering which of them was going to speak.

Father Martine opened the conversation, informing him Pietro, as Consuella's father, would be the one making the final decision.

Pietro more or less took up where he had left off. "Now, Antonio, before we give you an answer, is there anything you would like to add—some final word perhaps—before we pass sentence?" Pietro not known for making witty remarks was smiling as he said it.

Antonio, not sure if this was a good or bad sign, nervously replied, "I would just like to say that, if you—I mean the three of you—give me your approval and blessing, I will then do all in my power to prove myself worthy of Consuella's affection."

Pietro made no response. He just looked in the direction of Sister Maria and Father Martine.

No words were spoken. The other two just nodded back in his direction.

Antonio, now experiencing unbearable tension, knew this was the moment of truth. The next words spoken by Consuella's father would determine the shape his future would now take.

Pietro turned his attention to Antonio one last time. "Well, in that case, you have our permission to plead your case with Consuella."

The brief response took him totally by surprise. "You mean the answer is yes? I have your approval?"

"Yes, Antonio, you indeed have our approval. I hope and pray your endeavours result in a favourable outcome for the two of you. That's all I have to say. I think that concludes our business here today."

Sitting there for a moment or two, initially dumbstruck, Antonio could hardly believe his good fortune.

Excitedly getting up from his chair, he shook Pietro's hand enthusiastically, saying, "Should Consuella willingly agree and allow me to be her fiancé, I promise you, I will do my utmost to make her happy. Thank you, thank you so very, very much."

As he was speaking, he had momentarily forgotten the other two.

Father Martine let out an audible sigh.

Antonio turning to the two of them and continued, "Sister Maria, dear Father, please excuse my bad manners. You see, I am so overwhelmed by this wonderful news. I do declare this day is probably the happiest day of my entire life."

"Not so fast, not so fast, dear boy," replied Father Martine. "Although Sister Maria and myself played some small part in what for you must be a most favourable outcome, the battle is not won just yet. This is but the first hurdle in what might prove to be an arduous campaign. Now let's just see if, on your return to Milan, you can win the fair Consuella's hand."

Sister Maria finished by saying, "Now, Antonio, make your journey. It is our fervent wish your quest is successful and receives an agreeable response from our dearest Consuella. We will, of course, keep the two of you in our thoughts and prayers."

Antonio replied, "Thank you, Sister. Seeing today is my last day, would the three of you do me the honour and be my guests for dinner later this evening?"

"Thank you, Antonio. I'm sorry, but I'll have to decline your kind offer, though I'm sure Pietro and Father will be happy to join you."

Father Martine and Pietro graciously accepted his invitation. Then with that, Sister Maria and Pietro took their leave.

Once again, teacher and pupil found themselves alone.

Father Martine remarked, "Well, I can see from your expression you are most certainly happy with the outcome."

"Indeed I am. And may I say how grateful I feel that your support was most certainty crucial in the favourable decision Pietro made."

"You know, Antonio, the truth is, I didn't have to battle too hard. Both of them are really very fond of you, and they made their decision without any real persuading from me at all."

"Thank you, Father. That's good to know."

"You're welcome. By the way, producing the necklace, although at first it seemed to be somewhat premature, in fact, it actually helped your cause."

"In what way?"

"Well they both thought it was quite beautiful. We were just wondering how much such an exquisite item actually costs?"

"Father, why do I have the feeling it is you who is curious about the value of the necklace and not the other two?"

Smiling back at him, Father Martine replied, "Okay. Of course it's me whose curious. So come on, tell me."

"Well, let's just say the amount I spent on purchasing that gift would most likely get you a box in La Scala for most of the season."

"My goodness, if it was me, I would have chosen the box at La Scala."

"Indeed you would. Now if I may be excused, I think it's time for me to head back to my hotel. Would seven this evening be suitable for Pietro and yourself?"

"Fine, fine, Antonio. Now off you go and have a pleasant afternoon."

That evening, the three men had a very enjoyable meal. The wine on the table was from Pietro's own vineyard. It reminded Antonio of his promise to Mario. "Oh by the way, Pietro, this coming Friday in Milan, Francesco and I will have a wonderful surprise for both of you, and it concerns your wine."

"Please, Antonio, tell me more."

Antonio gave them a brief account of his and Francesco's many dining experiences in Mario's restaurant. "So you see, on our last occasion there, we promised him we would invite you as a guest," he concluded. "I think you will find Mario a most interesting individual."

Father Martine joined in. "Well as long as his food is reasonably edible, I really don't care what sort of character he is."

Antonio couldn't resist the opportunity to deflate his mentor's ego ever so slightly. With a wry smile on his face he answered, "Oh you don't have to concern yourself too much, Father. Pietro is the person Mario is most anxious to meet. In our conversations with him, your name never really came up. But of course you are more than welcome to join us."

Father Martine, knowing he was being gently provoked, replied, "Well, let's see if I have no other plans this coming Friday. I might consider accompanying you to this eating establishment, whatever it's called."

Pietro then asked Antonio, "This restaurant, does it have a name?"

"It's simply called Mario's and is quite close to the theatre on Piazza della Scala in fact."

"Very good. Excellent. Well I for one have to say I'm quite looking forward to the occasion. Thank you, Antonio, thank you very much for your thoughtful gesture. Now it's getting late. You have an early journey ahead of you tomorrow. So I think it's time for us to take our leave. Come on, Father. I'll drop you off at the monastery on the way."

As they stood up, Pietro spoke his final words to Antonio. "When we arrive on Friday, I certainly hope you have exciting news for us. I know deep down in my heart, if my daughter accepts your proposal, you will do everything you possibly can to make her happy. If this comes to pass, I too will be very pleased."

"Thank you, Pietro. I promise I will do my best."

Father Martine added, "I too agree wholeheartedly with the sentiments expressed just now. So after what's been, for you, an event-filled day, I'm sure you must be tired. Take yourself off to your room and have a restful night's sleep. I will pick you up early tomorrow morning and take you to the train station."

"Honestly, Father, there's no need. I can make the journey myself."

"I know you can, but as in the past, I just want to be certain you're on that train, more particularly now that you have an important mission to accomplish."

As they took their leave, Antonio bid Pietro a heartfelt goodnight.

Later in his room, he placed the necklace on the bedside table. As he gazed at it, he reflected on the events of the day and, most especially, on how it had ended.

As he drifted off into a peaceful slumber, the last thought on his mind was Consuella Pellegrini.

CHAPTER 19

Antonio Returns to Milan

The following morning Tuesday, as promised, Father Martine took Antonio to the train station and sent him on his way. He bid him a fond farewell and gave him an affectionate hug.

Arriving in Milan later that afternoon, Antonio stopped by his apartment, dropped off his valise, and picked up his mail.

He noticed one letter postmarked Austria. On opening it, he was quite surprised by the reply to his previous communication. Despite his polite refusal concerning the offer, it stated, should he wish to reconsider, the position would be held open until the first week in October.

Bringing the letter with him, he then made his way over to Francesco's.

Carlota greeted him. "Welcome back, Antonio. How was your trip?"

"Excellent. And I have exciting news."

Before he had a chance to continue, she ushered him into the drawing room saying, "Don't say another word until I return with Francesco."

When they returned, Francesco opened the conversation. "Carlota tells me you have good news. So please enlighten us?"

"You remember before I departed for Verona, I told you about the offer from Austria."

"Yes, as a matter of fact I do. Please go on."

"If you recall, I wrote to the Vienna State Opera Company politely declining their offer."

Francesco could see Carlota was now becoming slightly impatient, as was he. Nonetheless, he decided to allow Antonio to proceed. "Yes, Antonio, Carlota and I are fully aware of the offer and your response. But what has any of this to do with the other more important issue?"

"Nothing whatsoever. I just thought it would be a good idea to bring you up to date on this latest development before I give you my news from Verona."

Carlota wearily replied, "Okay, Antonio, please proceed. You have our attention."

"On the way here, I stopped off at my apartment. I picked up my post and noticed this letter from Austria."

Passing them the envelope, he waited for their reaction.

Francesco responded, "So, they're keeping the position open momentarily. That's wonderful, delightful. What more can I say? Now, before Carlota dies of boredom, could you by any chance bring us up to date on the outcome of your trip, in your own time of course?"

Antonio, now feeling rather foolish, apologised. "I'm sorry, Carlota. It's just whenever I'm discussing something concerning myself, I'm not in any way articulate. And at times I can be quite awkward. I don't know why. That's just me I suppose."

"Not to worry, Antonio. You're doing fine. And you know Francesco is merely teasing you. Take all the time you need."

Antonio, slightly more at ease, continued, "On my arrival in Verona, Father Martine met me at the station. We spent the remainder of the day together. As we were on our own, I decided to raise the issue concerning my feelings towards Consuella."

Carlota asked, "How did he react? Did he seem surprised?"

"No, he didn't seem surprised at all and was quite supportive. On Saturday, the four of us met. We discussed their travel arrangements for the pending trip and also the birthday preparations. I spent Sunday visiting with my sister. Then Monday morning, I was afforded the opportunity to plead my case. True to his word, Father Martine had already put forward a compelling argument in my favour. Rather nervously, I let the others know of my growing affection for Consuella."

Carlota asked, "How did they react to this revelation?"

"The amazing thing is they didn't seem terribly surprised."

"Then what?"

"Then I made my case just as you advised."

"Their response?"

"They politely asked me to wait in the adjoining room and allow them to discuss my request among themselves. After what seemed like an eternity but in actual fact was probably no more than a few minutes, Sister Maria invited me to rejoin them. Father Martine informed me Pietro, as Consuella's father, would be the one making the final decision."

Carlota, in anticipation, was now practically pleading. "Please, please, Antonio, the suspense is killing me. What was his answer? What did he say?"

"He asked me one or two questions. Then in that understated way of his, without any hesitation whatsoever, he informed me I had his permission to make her aware of my feelings and also let her know he would not object should she consent to becoming my fiancé."

"What about the other two? How did they react?"

"You know them reasonably well by now. They didn't display any great sense of emotion. But even so, I could see they were happy with his response."

Carlota, in her excitement, not knowing whether to laugh or cry, just said, "Antonio, this is wonderful news. I'm so happy for you and Consuella. In fact, I'm completely overwhelmed. Congratulations. From the bottom of my heart, congratulations."

Then turning to Francesco, she added, "Darling, isn't Antonio's news just wonderful?"

"My dear, you are such a romantic, and that's one of the reasons I married you. You may think me rather old-fashioned when I say this, but I'm going to say it anyway. When I see young Antonio here and the fair Consuella walking through the park arm in arm, then I'll be excited, overjoyed, and even overwhelmed."

With a playful smile on her face, Carlota responded, "Oh don't pay any attention to him, Antonio. When I think back to the time before we were married, there were occasions he was actually quite romantic and even sometimes ever so charming. I'm beginning to think he was just pursuing me for my money."

Antonio couldn't help but smile at the way they sparked off each other and could clearly see there was still a deep affection between them. "Carlota, I purchased a gift for her. I would like your opinion. I just need to know when would it be appropriate for me to present it to her?"

Taking the case from his jacket, he handed it to her.

Opening it, she exclaimed, "Oh, Antonio. This is such a beautiful and appropriate gift. You really must love her very much."

"Thank you, Carlota. Do you think I should present it when I'm making my proposal?"

"Of course, Antonio. The big question is, when are you going to give her your news. And more importantly, are you prepared for whatever decision she makes?"

Carefully returning the case to his pocket, he replied, "I was thinking tomorrow morning would be a good time, though up to now, I haven't given much thought to how she might respond."

Carlota replied rather impatiently, "Well then, you have to let her know straight away. Don't dwell on it. Go over there right now and tell her how you feel."

"What if she rejects me? What then?"

"Then, you'll be no worse off than you were before you began."

Francesco couldn't resist throwing in the following remark. "Well if that happens, judging by the number of diamonds on that gift of yours, you'll have saved yourself a considerable sum of money."

Carlota scolded him, "Darling, that's so cruel. You of all people should be encouraging and supporting Antonio in his efforts."

Antonio, knowing Francesco was gently teasing him, replied, "Thank you, Carlota. I agree. I will go over there immediately."

"Francesco darling, do you have any encouraging words you would like to add?"

"Not really, I am inclined to agree with you, dear. Antonio, you should just go over there right now, say what you have to say, and see what happens."

"Okay. I'll do it straight away. Now before I leave, may I ask how things were during my absence?"

"Absolutely fine. She came over here the day you left," Francesco informed him. "I went through the entire programme with her, and everything was perfect. I suggested she take a well-deserved break. Carlota and I haven't seen her since."

With that, Antonio bid them a fond farewell and made his way over to the convent.

Upon his arrival at the convent, Sister Agostina greeted him. "Señor Antonio, welcome back. Did you have a pleasant trip?"

"Very pleasant, Sister. I got back this afternoon and decided to come over and see how Consuella and Sister Lucia are doing."

She rather reluctantly replied, "Oh they're doing fine just fine. So while you're here, would you care for some food or a beverage perhaps?"

"Anything you have to go with a cup of coffee would be most welcome."

"I'll see if I can find a morsel or two. Please take a seat in the drawing room. I will let them know you're here."

"Thank you, Sister."

On her way to Consuella's room, Sister Agostina met Sister Lucia in the corridor. "Ah, there you are, Sister. Señor Antonio is in the drawing room. I'm on my way to let Consuella know he's arrived."

"Thank you, Sister. I'll just go in and say hello."

As he sat down, Antonio was turning everything over in his mind. How he should begin? What should he say? How he should say it?

Just then, Sister Lucia came in. "Welcome back, Antonio. May I ask regarding your mysterious journey, did you per chance achieve your objective?"

As she was speaking he couldn't help but notice the broad smile on her face. He responded with an even broader smile. "Well, let's just say the outcome of my mission was, relatively speaking, very successful indeed."

"Antonio, your mission and its successful outcome, does this mean you will have some exciting news for Consuella?"

"You know, Sister, if I didn't know you better, I'd say you were trying to read my thoughts."

"Oh come now, Antonio, you know me better than that. It's just that Consuella has been dying of curiosity since your departure."

Just at that very moment, Consuella entered, "Who's been dying of curiosity, Sister?"

Sister Lucia, though momentarily taken aback, regained her composure and replied, "Isn't it wonderful, Consuella, Antonio has finally returned following his important journey to Verona. And I was just telling him of your curiosity during his absence. That's all, Consuella. It was nothing more dramatic than that."

Antonio couldn't help but notice the apparent tension between them. Consuella's response, however, alarmed him even more.

"Thank you, Sister," she said. "I'm quite certain Antonio hasn't the slightest interest as to my degree of curiosity. You may leave us now. Antonio and I have important matters to discuss."

Sister Lucia made no effort to leave.

Antonio, now quite shocked, could hardly believe what he was actually hearing. He decided to intervene straight away. "Consuella I can't believe my ears. I've never heard you speak this way before."

Replying in a somewhat insincere manner, Consuella said, "I'm sorry, Antonio. I'm probably somewhat nervous about my final performances. Please do forgive me, Sister Lucia, for being so rude."

Sister Lucia answered in a voice showing no emotion, "It's quite all right, Consuella. I understand."

Antonio had a sense Consuella's apology to Sister Lucia was somewhat less than enthusiastic. He decided to continue the conversation and act as if everything was normal. "Well now, I just dropped by to see what's been happening during my absence."

Consuella, speaking in an effusive manner, replied, "Oh you know yourself, Antonio, the usual stuff. Voice training, costume fittings. There's a dress rehearsal tomorrow. That's about it really."

Sister Lucia decided to set a very small cat among the pigeons. "So you see, Antonio, Consuella has been very busy. Why she even told me she had been to Francesco's studio on Saturday, and this was even after our visit Friday last."

Consuella shot a disapproving glance in Sister Lucia's direction. She did her best, however, to mask her displeasure with the following comment, "Well you know Francesco. He leaves nothing to chance. He decided two voice training sessions were required, and we were both happy with the outcome. I'm probably as well prepared as I'll ever be."

As she was saying this, Antonio cast his mind back to his earlier conversation with Francesco. He distinctly remembered Francesco saying she was only over once during his absence.

Before he had a chance to query Consuella on this apparent inconsistency, Sister Agostina entered. She laid a tray on the table. "Señor Antonio, it's just a light snack. Please enjoy."

The brief interruption was, he felt, fortuitous. It would give him a few moments to decide how best to proceed.

Just then, he noticed Sister Agostina was holding a large somewhat bulky Manila envelope. Handing it to Consuella, she informed her, "Consuella, this arrived by special messenger just a few moments ago."

Consuella answered her in an offhand manner. "Just leave it on the sideboard. I will attend to it later."

"But it's marked urgent. I just thought you might like to see what's inside."

Consuella, this time making no effort to conceal her displeasure, angrily replied, "Do I have to repeat myself? I'm ordering you to leave it on the sideboard. Then you may go and make sure we're not disturbed. Have I made myself clear?"

"Please accept my apologies, Consuella. I promise, it won't happen again." Taking the envelope, Sister Agostina placed it on the sideboard.

As she was leaving, Sister Lucia and Antonio could clearly see how terribly upset she was. Consuella didn't give her a second glance. The three of them just sat there with no one uttering a word. Antonio was completely stunned by the severity of her remarks.

Sister Lucia, observing the two of them, remained impassive. She was wondering to herself which of them was going to be the first to say something.

Consuella, putting on her best smile and behaving as if nothing untoward had just taken place, took up the conversation. "Now, Antonio, please, how was your trip? And what news do you have from Verona?"

Still in a state of shock, he decided, however, not to challenge her in front of Sister Lucia. Instead, despite the strained atmosphere, he responded as politely as he could. "The journey was just fine. The good news is, our party will be here around midday this coming Friday. Dominique, Paolo, and Adamo will arrive Monday next, in plenty of time for your birthday celebration."

Sister Lucia, deciding she need not partake in any further discussions, replied, "Why that's wonderful news, Antonio. I'm so looking forward to seeing all of them again. Now if I may be excused, I have some homework to correct. I'm sure the two of you have much to talk about."

As she took her leave, Antonio stood up and bowed courteously. There was no reaction from Consuella.

With the two of them now alone, she continued in a slightly coquettish manner, "Well, Antonio, what other news do you have from Verona?"

"Before I get to that, there are one or two issues I believe need to be clarified."

"Okay, Antonio. Please continue."

"Consuella, are you feeling all right? Did anything happen while I was away? Maybe you were upset by something or somebody."

"Why no not at all. Every-thing's just fine."

"I hate to bring this up again, but why were you so appallingly rude to Sisters Lucia and Agostina just now? In all the time I've known you, I have never heard you speak like that to another human being."

"As I've already explained, end of season final performances. You know I become a little tense. And as you can see, I've already apologised to Sister Lucia."

"What about Sister Agostina?"

"Well then, if it satisfies you, I will go and apologise right now."

"Consuella, it's not about how or when you apologise. It's the fact you shouldn't have spoken like that in the first place. That's all." As he said this, he looked directly at her to see if she was inclined to respond.

She just averted her eyes and remained silent.

He decided to continue. "The envelope on the sideboard, may I enquire as to the contents?"

Suddenly alert, she replied, "Oh it's nothing really. Just some documents I have to study. If I need your assistance, I will certainly let you know."

Antonio, now somewhat annoyed, answered her, "Consuella, during the past two and a half years managing your career, I had been responsible for all negotiations. I've managed your financial affairs. I've taken care of administrative tasks and handled all correspondence. These tasks I performed to enable you focus exclusively on your operatic career. Has something changed since I've been away?"

"Why no, Antonio, of course not. Everything is just the same. Nothing has changed. So, please, can you just trust me? I promise I will discuss this with you in a day or two."

Though dissatisfied with her reply, Antonio felt there was probably not a lot he could do at this point. He decided to end the conversation, consult Francesco, and see if he might be able to shed more light on this unusual situation. Then he would wait for Father Martine's arrival and get his opinion as well.

Any thoughts he might have had concerning his proposal and gift, he decided to postpone certainly for the moment—or until he could get a clearer picture as to what may have brought about this very strange behaviour on Consuella's part.

Having considered these options, he then responded, "That's fine, Consuella. You will be twenty-one in a week's time. And I suppose I will probably have to get used to the fact you may wish to take more control of your personal life from there on."

"Oh, Antonio. I'm sure that won't be the case at all. So now, please do tell what other news do you have for me?"

He promptly stood up and looked at his watch. "Goodness me, is that the time? There's some other business I have to attend to. I promise I will bring you up to date as soon as possible."

Bowing politely, he quickly left without giving her an opportunity to respond.

He immediately headed for the kitchen. Sister Agostina was there, and he could see she was still quite upset. "Sister, I'm leaving now, and I just wanted to say thank you for spoiling me with the wonderful food you brought me at such short notice."

With tears in her eyes she blurted out, "Señor Antonio, it was no trouble at all. And please, please forgive me for my insolence in front of Señorita Consuella."

"Sister, you have nothing, absolutely nothing, to reproach yourself for. As a matter of fact, it is Consuella who should be apologising to you, and I insisted she do so at the earliest opportunity."

"Thank you. Thank you so much, Señor Antonio. You are such a gentleman."

"Oh, I don't know about that, Sister. But thank you for not judging Consuella too harshly. So on my next visit, you promise you will feed me again?"

Now with a smile on her face and the tears gone, she replied, "Señor Antonio, not only will I prepare something nice, I might even consider providing a linen napkin to mark the occasion. Now how does that sound?"

"Sister, I am going to hold you that promise. Until my return, please take good care of yourself and keep on doing what you do very well."

As he left the kitchen, she called out after him, "Don't worry, Señor Antonio. I promise, I will, I will."

Back in the corridor, he gave a gentle knock on the library door.

Sister Lucia opened it. She was surprised to see he hadn't left as yet. "Oh I'm sorry, Antonio. I thought you'd already departed. Please come in. I can see you're somewhat confused as to what happened just now."

"To say I'm confused is an understatement. But before I left, I just wanted to make sure Sister Agostina was all right."

Sister Lucia replied, "She is such a gentle soul. So how is she now?"

"We had a brief chat, and I think I managed to at least cheer her up a little."

"That's wonderful, Antonio. You are a true gentleman."

"You know, Sister, I think I will have to visit more often."

"Why is that?"

"Well not two minutes ago, Sister Agostina said the very same thing."

"Well there you are, Antonio. The two of us can't be wrong."

"Sister Lucia, thank you for the gracious compliment. I suppose now I will have to try and live up to these high standards. On a more serious note, I really was appalled by the way Consuella spoke to both of you. I told her so in no uncertain terms. Right now, I can't help but feel something must have happened during my absence that's caused this very strange behaviour. Can you shed any light on the matter?"

"All I can say is I agree. Her behaviour has been somewhat erratic. At first, I put it down to end-of-season fatigue. But I know it's not that. She's never behaved in this way before. So it has to be something else. But what it is, I really have no idea."

"Tell me, Sister. Do you know how many coaching sessions she had with Francesco?"

Caught off guard by this direct question, she now faced the dilemma of how best to answer. Should she just tell the truth and be disloyal to Consuella? Or should she try and give a more diplomatic response?

She chose the latter option. "On Friday, I accompanied her to Francesco's. The following day, she informed me she needed to visit Francesco one more time. This journey she made without me."

"I'm sorry to be pressing you on this issue, but when you say she left the convent on Saturday unaccompanied, it leaves me somewhat confused.

It's always been my understanding the practise from the very start was, any occasion Consuella ventured outside, you travelled with her. Has something suddenly changed?"

Sister Lucia, now feeling somewhat uncomfortable, answered as best she could. "Antonio, on the day of your departure, Consuella and I travelled to Francesco's studio. When the coaching session ended, Francesco expressed his satisfaction and stated there was no need for additional lessons, at least not until just before her forthcoming performances. He advised Consuella to rest and relax a little. As I've already told you, the following morning she informed me she needed to go over to Francesco's, and my company would not be required for the journey."

"What was your response?"

"To be quite honest, Antonio, I took the view that, with just one week to go before her twenty-first birthday, she was quite entitled to make such a decision. I felt my role as chaperone was going to be ending very soon anyway, so I didn't object."

"Did anything else unusual occur during my absence?"

"Yes something did happen. At first, I didn't think it was significant. On the day of your departure, she received a letter. So when she left the following day, I became slightly concerned. I asked Sister Agostina if she could she tell me anything about the person who made the delivery."

She filled him in as best she could on the sketchy details as relayed by Sister Agostina, including the fact the person who delivered the letter had arrived in an auto-mobile. She also informed him the letter was addressed to both of them.

"On her return later in the afternoon, I queried her about the letter," she added. "All I can say is she became somewhat agitated. The situation deteriorated even further. The following morning being Sunday, nothing out of the ordinary took place. She spent most of the day in her room. I think she was purposely avoiding myself and Sister Agostina."

"What happened after that?"

"On Monday morning, she again left the convent unaccompanied. Where she was going, I have no idea."

Antonio was shocked at these alarming revelations. He decided to return to Francesco's at once and discuss these strange developments.

Meanwhile, as they were having this conversation, Consuella was still sitting in the drawing room quite alone. She was annoyed with Antonio for not being more forthcoming. His sudden departure puzzled her even more.

She was even more annoyed with herself for her own inexplicable behaviour. She wondered if her relationship with Sister Lucia was now damaged beyond repair.

Anxiously taking the envelope from the sideboard, she headed towards her room. As she did so, to her surprise, she observed Antonio leaving the library.

Somewhat annoyed she called out, "Antonio, you left at least a half an hour ago. You said you had something important to do, yet you're still here. Can you please explain?"

"Consuella, I really don't feel inclined to explain, particularly following your shameful behaviour in the presence of Sisters Lucia and Agostina. If you must know, I went to the kitchen to see Sister Agostina. And just now, I was saying goodbye to Sister Lucia. Now if I may be excused, I will take my leave." Without giving her another glance, he walked past her and left.

Quite stunned by his abrupt departure, Consuella entered the kitchen. Approaching Sister Agostina she began by saying, "Dear Sister, please forgive my rude behaviour earlier on. I do apologise. I promise it will not happen again."

"Thank you, Consuella. Señor Antonio was here and he managed to cheer me up. He is such a gentleman."

"Yes indeed. That he certainly is. Anyway, thank you for graciously accepting my apology. I'm sure you must be busy, so I won't take up any more of your time." With that, she left the kitchen and knocked on the library door.

Sister Lucia responded by calling out, "Come in."

As she entered, Sister Lucia looked up and then continued, "Please, Consuella, I'm very tired right now, and I have no wish to argue with you again. So can we just leave it at that?"

"I didn't come here to argue, Sister. I came to apologise and to let you know I also apologised to Sister Agostina."

"Your apology is accepted, and I appreciate the gesture concerning Sister Agostina. I have no wish to appear rude. But just now, I would prefer to be alone."

"Thank you, Sister. I understand."

Sister Lucia, although feeling quite tired and hurt, decided to say what was on her mind. "Consuella, I wonder to myself, do you really understand? I really don't know what's happened to you over the past few days. And to be honest, it's probably no longer any of my business. But I do know something of significance has occurred. Whether it has something to do with the letter and that envelope you're holding is of no further interest to me. When you arrived here as a young innocent eighteen-year-old, you did so with a protective shield around you. In that time, you have achieved great success and have also grown into adulthood. You are now about to embark on the next phase of your life. It is you who will decide what sort of future you wish to have.

"My role is coming to its inevitable end. I don't know what role you have in mind for the others or even if you have given it any thought. I would strongly advise you, though, to consider carefully what your future path will be. Whatever decision you take, it will more than likely shape your life for the next five years or more."

Sister Lucia now feeling quite emotional concluded by saying, "For the past few years, it has been my great pleasure to have been of some assistance in the exciting development of your very successful career. Apart from our fractious relationship these past few days, I have to honestly say, for me personally, it was a wonderful experience. And I really do wish you well in your future, whatever form it takes."

Consuella, with tears welling up in her eyes, felt even more ashamed of the hurt her harsh words had caused. "Dear Sister," she replied, "thank you for those kind words. I will do my best not to forget them in the weeks and months to come. And please, I'm so terribly sorry." With these final words, she took her leave.

Sister Lucia remained seated for a few moments longer. She couldn't help but draw the conclusion, that Consuella was indeed deeply troubled.

CHAPTER 20

Antonio Revisits Francesco

For the second time since his arrival from Verona, Antonio found himself travelling once more to Francesco's home.

Carlota, opening the door with a concerned look on her face, asked him, "Antonio, you look somewhat troubled. Did things not go according to plan?"

"I'm afraid not, there seems to be something not quite right between Consuella and Sister Lucia. So I decided to come back here and see if you and Francesco can throw some light on this strange situation,"

She immediately fetched Francesco and returned promptly.

As they sat down, Carlota took up the conversation. "Now, Antonio, please continue. You were saying something seems to have happened between the two of them?"

"Before I get to that subject, I need to clarify something for myself," Antonio said. "How many coaching sessions did she have during my absence?"

Francesco answered, "As I stated earlier, just one. And that was last Friday, the day of your departure. We haven't seen either her or Sister Lucia since."

"Actually, darling, that's not quite correct," Carlota said. "You remember Saturday last, we met Sister Lucia."

"Yes of course. It was such a brief exchange I almost forgot. But from my recollection everything seemed just fine."

Antonio continued, "That's strange. I spoke with Sister Lucia at length. She didn't mention that fact. But worse than that, Consuella deliberately lied to me."

Carlota asked him, "Can I then take it you didn't have any discussions concerning your feelings towards her?"

"No I didn't. The atmosphere had become so strained I decided the most sensible option was to leave and return here."

Antonio gave them as much information as he could recall—the letter, the person arriving and departing by auto-mobile, her unescorted departure from the convent both Saturday and Monday, her unbelievable rudeness to both of the sisters, and the mysterious envelope delivered earlier. "I think under the circumstances, I made the right decision," Antonio concluded. "But what should I do now, have a confrontation and force her to explain?"

Francesco answered his question in a remarkably calm manner. "Let's not be too hasty. I think it best we examine the facts. There may be something that may explain her apparent deceit and uncharacteristic behaviour."

"What do you suggest?"

"Well, from the first day she arrived here, Carlota and I, on all occasions, have found her to be a most polite and charming young lady. Also, her companionship with Sister Lucia was a joy to behold. Then you travel to Verona for four days. On your return you're faced with this catastrophe. How so?

"It's my belief the letter, the unescorted excursions from the convent, and the envelope from earlier have a major bearing on the situation as it now stands. Do you have any thoughts yourself, Antonio?"

"At the moment, no. I'm just completely shocked and confused."

"Okay then. For my part, I have to say these incidents are not random or accidental. They are all inextricably linked, although I don't have sufficient proof. I have a pretty good idea the individual behind this mischief is none other than Don Marco Barcese."

"But, Francesco, how could he have possibly known of my absence? Also, if you are correct, then surely we have to do something about it."

"What do you suggest we do—barge into his office without a shred of evidence? I'm afraid we would look very foolish indeed, and we would be playing right into his hands. No that's exactly what we're not going to do."

"Then do we just do nothing?"

"Oh we will do something. And this is what I'm suggesting. We will carry on as if everything is normal, make sure Consuella does not make any more unescorted journeys. With the strained atmosphere between herself and Sister Lucia, I think it best you accompany her should the need arise.

"When the others arrive on Friday, you and I will need to speak with Father Martine. He will then be in a position to brief Sister Maria. I have tremendous faith in her ability to get to the heart of the matter. Consuella will find it rather difficult to fob her off. I strongly recommend we don't involve her father at this stage. In this instance, I am prepared to be guided by Father Martine. I believe he will speak with Consuella's father at the appropriate time. Antonio, I think that's about as much as we can do for the moment—that is unless you have some other suggestions."

"No I don't have anything to add. Again I find myself indebted to both of you. At this stage, you must be weary listening to me saying thank you."

Carlota brought the discussion to a close. "Not at all, Antonio. To us, you are a very dear friend. And maybe the situation will improve over the coming days.

I have tremendous confidence in Sister Maria and Father Martine to somehow achieve a satisfactory outcome."

With that, Antonio took his leave.

Over the next two days, he spent his time making the final arrangements for Consuella's final performances, the birthday celebration, and the group's arrival. He was somewhat relieved the strained relationship between the two hadn't gotten any worse. If anything, a sort of reluctant degree of civility seemed to have been re-established.

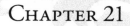

CHAPTER 21

Sister Maria and Co. Travel to Milan

The following Friday, Sister Maria, Pietro, and Father Martine settled into their compartment for a pleasant train journey to Milan.

Father Martine took them through the itinerary. "Now let's see. Antonio has hired an auto-mobile and a driver for the duration of our stay. He'll be at the station to welcome us. We can have lunch at the convent. Antonio will bring us up to date on the arrangements. The driver can then take Pietro and myself to our hotel. Later this evening, Antonio and Francesco have invited the two of us to meet some character who runs a restaurant of sorts.

"Tomorrow morning Saturday, with your permission, I would like to celebrate Holy Mass at the convent. Everyone, of course, will attend. Francesco and Carlota will be present. So will Violetta and her father, Alberto. You remember she was the young lady who sang at Dominique and Paolo's wedding. After Mass, we will have breakfast. Following on from that, we will have our meeting to discuss Consuella's progress to date and all the other options open to us concerning Antonio and Francesco's future role in her career.

"There is nothing scheduled for Sunday, so we're free to rest. Sister, it may give you an opportunity to catch up with Sister Colombina. I'm sure there's plenty the two of you might wish to discuss.

"Monday morning, Dominique, Paolo, and Adamo arrive. Later in the evening, we'll all be gathered together to celebrate her twenty-first birthday. Pietro, you must be feeling very proud right now."

"Indeed I am, and so should you and Sister Maria."

"Why so?"

"Well I firmly believe the friendship and support the two of you have given me these past number of years has made all of this possible."

Sister Maria replied, "Well, Pietro, I have to say you've been a wonderful friend also. And believe me, it has been a great joy for the two of us to watch the splendid development of Consuella's career. Pietro, you look concerned. I hope I haven't said something to upset you?"

"No, no. Not at all. Every-thing's just fine, except for Father's comment about poor Mario."

"Who's Mario?"

"He's the gentleman Francesco and Antonio are taking us to meet this evening. If I didn't know you better, dear Father, I do believe you might be a little bit jealous, just a little bit."

"Why I'm sure our dear Father hasn't a jealous bone in his body, though I'm somewhat intrigued. Please continue, Pietro."

"Well on the last occasion Antonio and Francesco were in his restaurant—and believe me, it is a fine establishment; I happen to know because I checked it out with my distributor—anyway, Mario served one of my wines. When they informed him I was a colleague, he impressed upon them that he would be most anxious to meet me on my next trip to Milan. Poor Father never got a mention. I think he may be feeling somewhat excluded. It's such a shame."

Sister Maria, greatly amused by Pietro's acerbic wit, decided nonetheless to console a dejected looking Father Martine. "Never mind, Father. I have every confidence when this Mario person meets you, he will be totally smitten by your undoubted charm. What do you think, Pietro? Would you agree?"

"Why of course, Sister. Nobody knows better than you and I how very charming our dear Father can be."

Now realising they were just teasing him, Father Martine smilingly responded, "Oh all right then. I'm sure this Mario character is a sterling chap. And I must say, I'm now really looking forward to making his acquaintance."

As the train trundled on, Sister Maria posed the following question: "You know, Pietro, I was just wondering if Antonio has spoken with

Consuella. And if so, how did she respond? I'm also curious to know if, perhaps, he presented her with the exquisite gift."

"Actually, Sister, I was just having the same thoughts myself."

Father Martine rejoined the conversation. "Well if he hasn't, there's nothing more we can do short of proposing to Consuella on his behalf. This, I'm sorry to say, would make poor Antonio look rather foolish. Anyway we're going to find out soon enough."

Sister Maria replied, "No need to worry. As soon as we arrive in Milan, his demeanour will tell us all we need to know."

Father Martine responded, "You seem pretty certain."

"Not only am I certain, I can guarantee it as well."

"Okay then. When we arrive we shall see how perceptive you are, because I'm not going to raise the subject."

Pietro added his voice. "And neither will I."

Bringing the subject to a close, Sister Maria answered both of them. "Very well then. Let's just see what awaits us at journey's end. Now if you two gentlemen have no objections, I would like to relax and look out my window at the beautiful countryside for the remainder of our journey."

Her two travelling companions simply nodded their heads in compliance and did likewise.

As the train pulled into the station, Antonio was waiting. He greeted the threesome warmly. "Welcome to Milan. This is Emilio. He'll be our driver during your stay."

With that, himself and Emilio assisted with the luggage and escorted the trio to the auto-mobile.

During the course of their journey from station to convent, they engaged in the usual small talk. Sister Maria was content to just quietly observe Antonio.

On their arrival, they were welcomed by Sister Colombina. "Welcome, welcome, dear Mother Superior!" she said warmly. "Please, if you and your guests would like to be seated in the dining room. Sister Agostina has prepared a light meal. I will let Consuella and Sister Lucia know you and your party have arrived.

"Antonio if you would be so kind, bring Mother Superior's bag and follow me."

Antonio did as she requested.

With the three of them alone for what was going to be a very brief period, Father Martine took the opportunity to quiz Sister Maria. "Sister, before anyone enters, I have to ask, do you think Antonio put his proposal to Consuella?"

"I can most emphatically say without hesitation he most definitely has not."

Father Martine, now slightly confused, replied, "But how come? You remember how excited he was when Pietro agreed to his request?"

Pietro joined in, "I must say, Sister, I'm as puzzled as Father Martine. On our arrival, I was half expecting Antonio to announce he and Consuella had already set a date for their engagement."

"Regrettably I'm as confused as both of you, though there is one thing I'm sure of."

The two of them, almost in unison, asked, "And what's that Sister?"

"In the next short while, when everybody is present, more will be revealed. Well anyway, that's what I'm hoping."

Consuella and Sister Lucia joined them. On seeing her father, Consuella immediately ran over and embraced him. "Dear Papa, it's so wonderful to see you again. Antonio told me Dominique, Paola, and Adamo will arrive Monday next, just in time for my birthday. I am so excited I can hardly wait."

He responded tenderly, "My dearest Consuella, we've all been waiting sometime now for this special day. My one and only wish is that it will be a memorable and happy occasion for all of us."

As he held her in a fond and loving embrace, the others exchanged the usual handshakes and greetings.

With the formalities completed, all present took his or her place at the dining table. Sister Colombina, accompanied by Sister Agostina, entered with two trays of piping hot food. Sister Colombina addressed her guests. "Please, please, everyone. I would like you to enjoy this lunch so lovingly prepared by our own dear Sister Agostina. As I always say, there's nothing like a long journey to whet the appetite."

Then turning to Sister Agostina, she added, "Come, Sister. Let's take our leave. I'm sure our guests have much to talk about."

After their departure, Sister Maria decided to address Consuella first. "Well, Consuella, next week promises to be one of the most exciting you've ever experienced. How are you coping? No nerves, I hope?"

"Yes indeed, Reverend Mother. Next week, I believe, will be quite exciting. I suppose with everything that's been happening, I probably am a little nervous."

As Consuella was speaking, Sister Maria quietly observed Sister Lucia and Antonio. She couldn't help but notice both of them seemed to be displaying an air of passive disinterest.

"Now, Antonio, my question for you is, do you think our young star is sufficiently prepared for what lies ahead?"

His reply she found slightly disturbing. "Consuella informed me that, during my absence, she has actually had two coaching sessions with Francesco. On my return, he gave me his assurance that she is as well prepared as she will ever be."

With mock enthusiasm, she exclaimed, "Excellent, excellent. That's wonderful news. And you, dear Sister, do you have anything to add?"

"No not really, Reverend Mother, except to say I totally agree with Antonio's comments just now."

With Sister Lucia's last remark, Consuella found herself growing more uncomfortable by the minute. Her discomfort certainly didn't go unnoticed by the others.

Father Martine decided a timely intervention was now required. Pietro just sat there patiently and observed.

"Consuella, all of us have tremendous faith in your proven ability to perform to the highest standard," said Father Martine. "This four-night run of Puccini's tragic opera *Tosca* commences Tuesday next, the day following your birthday. You know, I had the privilege of being present for the first performance. Let me see now. Ah yes, it was in Teatro Costanzi in Rome— January 1900 in fact. That was my last time to see this production. I have every confidence, and I'm sure everyone here will agree, your performances next week singing and playing the part of Floria, the tragic heroine, will be nothing short of brilliant."

With a warm smile on her face, Consuella replied, "Thank you, Father, for your encouraging words and the vote of confidence."

"That statement, young lady, I made in an effort to make you smile. And I'm pleased to say it worked. You're actually smiling, and that pleases me. Now I think we're done for the moment. Sister Maria has granted me the honour of celebrating Mass tomorrow morning for all of us present and some invited guests. What time suits, Sister?"

"Eight o'clock I think would be most suitable. Then after breakfast, we can have our meeting and, hopefully, with God's blessing, agree a plan to take us to the next exciting phase of Consuella's career. Can I take it we're all in agreement?"

Everyone around the table nodded in agreement.

Although Consuella nodded her approval, Sister Maria couldn't help but feel her response was somewhat less than enthusiastic.

Father Martine brought the discussion to a close by saying, "Then eight o'clock it is, Sister. Now I think it's time Pietro and I got to our hotel. We need to prepare for our exciting encounter with this Señor Mario later this evening. Antonio, would you be good enough and let Emilio know we're ready to depart."

"Of course, Father. And please, if you will allow me, I'll accompany both of you."

"It will be a pleasure, Antonio. Thank you."

As Antonio left to fetch Emilio, Sister Lucia and Consuella stood up together.

As they did so Sister Maria addressed them. "Now if the two of you would be so kind, I would like to have a brief word with Father Martine and Pietro before their departure. Hopefully, I will see the two of you here later this evening. We will then be able to catch up on all that's been happening over the past few months."

As both of them bowed and took their leave, Sister Maria turned to Father Martine and Pietro. "Well, gentlemen, any thoughts on what has just transpired this last hour or so?"

Father Martine answered, "Strange, very strange. I just don't know what to make of it. Pietro, what do you think?"

"I don't know what to think either. There's definitely something not quite right. Have you any thoughts, Sister?"

"All I can say is I agree and am most disturbed. The atmosphere was stiff and formal. The three of them hardly looked in each other's direction during the entire discussion."

Father Martine asked, "What should we do now?"

"Here's what we do. When you get to the hotel I think it would be a good idea, Father, if you invite Antonio to join you for a tea, coffee, whatever. Pietro, I hope you'll understand me suggesting this. I want you to excuse yourself on some pretext. Leave Father and Antonio to themselves. I'm quite certain Father will be able to find out what exactly has occurred over the last few days.

"In the meantime, I will speak separately with both of them later on and see if I can somehow get to the bottom of just exactly what is going on. After Mass tomorrow, we can meet briefly and see if we are any wiser. I believe it is absolutely imperative we have some additional knowledge before the meeting.

"Pietro, please understand me when I say this. Your daughter's future and well-being may very well depend on how we proceed from here."

Pietro, now visibly upset, replied, "Dear Sister, dear Father, for many years now, both of you have assisted me in all the difficult and testing times I've been through. You've always been there for me and my children. Should I now turn away and say thank you very much, no further assistance required? Both of you know, on most occasions, I am a person of few words. But I have to say this. During all the difficult years, if I had not had your support, I really don't think I would have been able to cope. So tonight, whatever you learn following these discussions, I will be most grateful. Both of you have my complete trust in whatever you decide or however you wish to proceed."

Sister Maria responded, "Dear Pietro, you know how much you and your family mean to both of us. You and your children have been a constant in our lives for many years now. It would be inconceivable for us to ever contemplate ending a friendship that's been forged over many years. We are part of you and, by extension, part of your family. So now, make your journey with Father. Let's see what he can learn from Antonio. In the meantime, I will endeavour to see what I can accomplish."

With that, Pietro and Father Martine stood up. They joined Antonio and Emilio.

At the hotel, Father Martine casually remarked, "Antonio, dear boy, would you care to join Pietro and myself for a night-cap?"

"You know, Father. It has been a long day. I think a refreshing beverage would be most welcome. Thank you."

As they entered the foyer, on cue, Pietro cut in. "Father, Antonio, please, if you will, may I be excused? I would love to join you. But alas, the journey and all the excitement, I'm sorry to say, has left me rather tired. If you don't mind, I'll just go to my room and take a short rest. I want to make sure to be refreshed for our exciting event this evening."

Father Martine, delighted with Pietro's choreography, replied, "Okay. Dear friend, don't worry. I, your trusted guardian, will call you at the appointed hour. Rest well."

As both of them sat down in the lounge, Antonio asked Father Martine his choice of coffee. "Well, Father, what's your choice, white or black?"

"You know, Antonio, I think I'll just have an Irish whisky, a Jameson in fact, with just a touch of soda nothing more, because, you see, too much additives spoil the essence of a malt that's been in a timber casket for maybe the best part of a hundred years."

"Father, whatever you wish, I am at your service."

With that, he summoned the waiter and ordered a black coffee and a Jameson and soda.

As Antonio sipped his coffee, he watched as Father Martine slowly very slowly tasted the essence of the elixir he had ordered for him.

Father Martine, in an expansive mood, exclaimed, "My dear boy, the Italians, the Spanish, and the French make excellent wines. But it is only the Irish and the Scots who can make a decent whisky.

"Well now that we're finally alone, what news do you have?"

"None actually."

"Please explain."

"An opportunity didn't present itself for me to speak with Consuella."

"You mean to tell me no discussions took place between the two of you even though you've been back since Tuesday."

"Oh there have been plenty of discussions but none in relation to the main purpose of my trip to Verona."

Father Martine's next comment was as much to himself as to Antonio. "So Sister Maria's conclusion was quite correct,."

"Sorry, Father, can you explain what you mean?"

"On our journey here, she stated she would be able to ascertain by your general demeanour whether you had spoken to Consuella or not."

"So tell me, what conclusion did she reach?"

"Well, just before we left the convent, she told Pietro and myself quite emphatically that no conversation had taken place between the two of you. Antonio, I have a sense this may be somewhat difficult for you. If you want to talk about it, I'm listening. If, on the other hand, you don't wish to, I will mind my own business."

"Father, I've no difficulty confiding in you. I'm just wondering where to begin."

"This sounds ominous. Why don't you take me through what happened from the time you got back? Who knows? Maybe there's a simple explanation."

Antonio did his best to outline everything that had taken place over the past few days—the letter; the envelope; the unaccompanied excursions from the convent; her deception in relation to the number of coaching sessions; and, most importantly, her appalling behaviour, including the obvious breakdown in her relationship with Sister Lucia. "That's about as much as I can think of for the moment," he concluded.

"Dear Lord, Antonio, I sincerely hope there isn't more. Tell me, have you spoken to anyone else about this?"

"Yes I did. I confided in Francesco and Carlota. With you in Verona, I needed to speak with someone."

"Under those particular circumstances, I believe you did the right thing. They are both good people. How did they react?"

"Naturally enough, Carlota was quite upset on my behalf. Francesco, on the other hand, had a very definite opinion as to the cause of her erratic behaviour." He then explained the conclusion Francesco had arrived at in relation to Don Barcese's possible involvement.

Father Martine, now gravely concerned, asked him, "Who is this Don Barcese?"

"Oh you've seen him before. Actually it was on the occasion of Consuella's debut in La Scala. I pointed him out to you. He was the person sporting the flashy suit in the box opposite ours."

"Ah yes, I remember. And if I'm not mistaken, Francesco certainly didn't have a high opinion of him."

"And quite rightly so."

"I'm curious, why on earth would this creature be causing such mischief? And what's his motive? That's assuming Francesco's suspicions are correct."

"After you, Father, Francesco is the person whose judgement and opinion I value most. He has never let me down. I would be inclined to agree with his analysis. The only thing is, we have no proof—short of Consuella admitting she has had some sort of contact with this individual. Judging by her actions so far, I don't think she's going to enlighten us anytime soon."

Father Martine sat there for some moments without saying anything. He was mulling over everything Antonio had just told him.

When he finally spoke, he did so in a measured fashion. "Okay, Antonio. Here's my suggestion."

"I'm listening, Father. Please continue."

"I'm not going to say anything to Pietro, well at least not for the moment. I find myself in agreement with Francesco. To confront this Don Barcese character would be unwise. We will need to establish whether some kind of meeting did in fact take place. Then perhaps we can ascertain the reasons behind her apparent untruthfulness and get an explanation for these unaccompanied excursions of hers.

"Later this evening, Sister Maria will make it her business to speak with both of Consuella and Sister Lucia. You're well aware how determined and persuasive she can be. Following tomorrow's Mass, she will update Pietro and myself on the outcome.

"All we can do now is wait and see how events unfold. You never know. It's possible all this recent pressure might have unnerved her. And maybe, just maybe, there's a simple explanation. In the meantime, there's probably not a lot we can do. So if I might suggest, take yourself off. Try and take your mind off these unfortunate incidents. Later, when you collect us, we can have an enjoyable evening, and hopefully, everything will work out for the best."

"Thank you, Father. Maybe there is a simple explanation. I'll be back at six thirty to pick you up. Francesco will be waiting for us at the restaurant."

With Antonio's departure, Father Martine made his way to Pietro's room.

"Well, Father, is there anything we should be concerned about?"

"Hard to say really. Sister Maria was certainly spot on. Antonio didn't get to put his proposal to Consuella."

"Oh this is most frustrating. What did Antonio have to say?"

Father Martine, not wanting to worry him too much, decided to give him a less damaging account. He finished his narrative by saying, "You know, these last few weeks have probably put some degree of pressure on both of them. It's probably nothing too serious. Hopefully, over the coming days, it will be resolved to everyone's satisfaction."

"Do you think we should discuss it at the restaurant this evening?"

"I'd rather not, unless of course Antonio brings it up. Instead, I'd prefer to discuss what plans they might have concerning her future. He has already informed me of some exciting developments in relation to some European capitals and even the United States of America. I think it would be a really good idea for you to get involved—you know, ask questions and even challenge them. After all, it is your daughter's career we'll be discussing.

"So now, dear friend, if you'll please excuse me, I think I will take a short nap. We can meet in the foyer at six thirty."

Pietro nodded his agreement. Both of them left the lounge together.

CHAPTER 22

The Restaurant

Antonio picked up Father Martine and Pietro at the appointed time. On entering the restaurant, they could see Francesco was already seated. In an instant, Mario appeared.

"Welcome, welcome, Señor Antonio. Please allow me show you and your guests to your table."

Guiding them over and bowing conspicuously to Francesco, he continued. "Señor Francesco, your guests have arrived."

"Thank you, Mario. Gentlemen, welcome to Milan. If I may, I would like to introduce you to our host. Father Martine, Pietro, this is Mario, head waiter and owner of this fine restaurant."

Mario shook hands with the two of them and said, "Gentlemen, welcome to Milan. Please, please be seated and make yourselves comfortable." As he passed around the menus he continued. "Your waiter this evening will be Angelo, but it would be an honour for me to assist you in choosing the appropriate wine for your dish of choice."

Francesco responded, "Mario, why don't you let Señor Pellegrini decide. After all, he is a wine producer. Surely you haven't forgotten our conversation some time back?"

"Señor Francesco, how could I possibly have forgotten that occasion? What you promised back then has now come to pass. Señor Pellegrini, welcome to my humble establishment. It would be a great honour for me if you were to choose the wine."

Pietro, not quite used to being made a fuss of in this fashion, decided nevertheless to humour Mario. Taking the wine list, he studied it, putting on his spectacles, taking them off again, running his finger very slowly down the list and back up again, all of this to try and convince a now anxious Mario that choosing a wine was a very serious business. Eventually, looking directly at Mario, he queried him, "Can I take it you have these wines in stock?"

"Without doubt, Señor Pellegrini. I have an excellent wine cellar that keeps all of these wines in perfect condition until the very moment they reach the table. Perhaps, Señor Pellegrini you would care to inspect my wine cellar."

Francesco and Antonio were enjoying themselves enormously. Father Martine just sat there with a bored expression on his face, wondering if he was eventually going to get a glass of wine.

Pietro continued, "Oh that won't be necessary, Mario. When I sample the wine, I will be able to tell straight away how good your wine cellar is."

Mario responded with a pained expression on his face, "Of course, Señor Pellegrini. After all, you are a wine expert, are you not?"

"Very good, Mario. Now let me see. Do you have the Arcole?"

"I do indeed, Señor Pellegrini."

"The white and the red?"

"Yes, the white and the red."

"What about the Bianco di Custoza and the Breganze?"

"These two, I'm happy to say, are also sitting in my wine cellar."

"Very good. Now here's my suggestion. You can bring the white and red Arcole straight away and keep the other two standing by. We will have them later as our meal progresses."

"Señor Pellegrini, what can I say? Your choice is perfection itself. Tonight the wine accompanying your meal will be like a symphony."

Father Martine couldn't resist intervening rather acerbically. "Well, Mario, if you're quite ready, maybe you should conduct yourself off to that wine cellar of yours. Then maybe we'll get to experience this symphony of yours before we die of thirst. And while you're at it, could you send Angelo over to take our order before he gets any older?"

"Ah, there you go, Father Martine, just like Señor Antonio, making with the jokes. Now if you'll please excuse me, I will send Angelo over at once and conduct myself off to the orchestra pit. Sorry, Father, that's my little joke. I will straight away go to the wine cellar and select Señor Pellegrini's excellent choice of wine."

With that, he was gone. Father Martine and Pietro just sat speechless.

Francesco couldn't resist commenting, "Well, gentlemen, Mario is the main reason we enjoy this restaurant so much. This is why Antonio booked it for this evening. He wanted the two of you to experience it first-hand.

As Angelo took their order and departed, Mario returned. He poured some wine into Pietro's glass. Waiting anxiously for him to taste it, he stood there motionless, bottle in hand.

Pietro lifted his glass very slowly and tasted the wine. "My dear, Mario, this is quite excellent. I can tell by just tasting these few sips, your wine cellar is more than adequate. Well done."

"Thank you. From the bottom of my heart, thank you, Señor Pellegrini." With that, he poured their wine and left them to enjoy the remainder of their evening.

Father Martine picked up his glass. "Gentlemen, I would like to propose a toast to the person responsible for our presence here in Milan this evening—to Consuella, the brightest star in the world of Italian opera."

"To Consuella," they echoed.

Francesco then raised his glass. "I would like to propose a second toast if I may, to good company."

"To good company," they all repeated, raising their glasses once more.

Father Martine just sat there for a moment or two. Then he turned to Pietro and smiled in that mischievous way of his, exclaiming, "Well! Pietro! You wily old fox, all this time you've been making these grand ambitious plans, and not a word, not even a hint. I'm going to have to keep a closer eye on you in the future."

This last remark was very much tongue-in-cheek, and Pietro, recognising it as such, replied in his usual modest manner, "Well, over the past few months, the distribution of our wines here in the Lombardy region have been very well received. The project has been ongoing for some time now. With the positive outcome and knowing we were going to be gathered here tonight, I arranged for the distributor to deliver a case. I just thought it would be a nice surprise and an ideal way for me to share my good news with you. That's all."

Francesco answered him. "Not only is it a nice surprise, it is also wonderful news. And I, for one, would like to congratulate you and wish you further success in all your future endeavours. Gentlemen, if you will,

I think this calls for one final toast. Please raise your glasses to the finest wine producer in all of Italy."

Father Martine and Antonio, raising their glasses, repeated, "To Señor Pietro Pellegrini."

As the meal progressed, the conversation inevitability turned to Consuella. Father Martine turned to Francesco, saying, "You've been involved in this project from the very start. Although I've had many discussions with Antonio here, you and I, we've never really taken the opportunity to talk, so I would be most interested in your opinion as to the best way forward. What I mean is, what would be in her best interest? What should we do to really cement her future?"

Francesco replied at length. "Well, before I talk about the future," he began, "I feel I must talk about the past; it's there we will find the key in how best to proceed. In all my time as a voice coach, I really don't think I've ever come across a talent quite like Consuella's. She really has a most beautiful voice, and when you add to that her ability to actually become the character she is portraying—it matters not whether it's *Carmen*, or *The Marriage of Figaro*, she just seems to make this transformation so effortlessly—she's magnificent.

"I've seen other great singers, but for me, Consuella outclasses them all. Another very important factor has been the management of her career to date. I am not just referring to Antonio's excellent stewardship; I'm also talking about her patrons—Sister Maria, Pietro, and your good self. Your willing participation in this endeavour has been—how should I put it?—yes, the guiding hand behind the whole enterprise. Although it was Antonio, who initiated the process, it was you, the patrons, who gave it your full support from the start. And I have to say, you did so in a very measured fashion. You set the parameters, laid down the guidelines, and clearly defined the roles each of us was to play in shaping her career.

"These included Sister Lucia as wardrobe assistant, companion, and chaperone; myself as voice coach and occasional acoustics expert; and Antonio as manager and guardian. You wisely secured her place of residence. As a matter of fact, all of the above you brought together, and they became the solid foundations on which her career has grown and flourished.

"It was a perfect template for one so young. But now, looking to the future, I'm afraid there are some parts of this particular template that, regretfully, will no longer suffice."

As Father Martine was taking all this in, Antonio and Pietro made no comment. They just listened and observed.

Father Martine broke the brief silence. "Francesco, please tell me, what changes do you see as necessary in the present circumstances for moving forward?"

"Well to start with, you are going to have to get used to Consuella not living at the convent any more. That arrangement was fine when she arrived in Milan as a young innocent eighteen-year-old. She is a fully-grown woman, just a few days short of her twenty-first birthday. To think she could go on living there and continue with Sister Lucia acting as chaperone, well the very idea, to say the least, is quite absurd."

Francesco then turned to Pietro. "Please forgive me, Pietro. I am very much aware Consuella is your daughter. My comments just now are my own thoughts on changes that need to be implemented as part of the next important stage in her future. So please, I earnestly pray you understand I mean no offence."

"None taken," Pietro assured him. "As a matter of fact, I would be very interested in any other thoughts you believe may have some relevance."

Francesco continued, "Well as I see it, two and a half years ago, it would have been very difficult for any of us to predict the likely outcome of our efforts in the project we undertook, probably more in faith than in conviction. I am excluding Antonio from that last comment. I'm sure you will agree that, from the very start, Antonio's belief, dedication and commitment were total."

Father Martine and Pietro nodded in agreement.

Francesco continued, "Looking back, I think it would be fair to assume that the results to date, have been quite successful. they have surpassed any expectations we could possibly have had when we started out on this most interesting of journeys."

He gave them a few brief moments to digest and reflect on his comments and then continued. "So going forward, if you deem it desirable for Antonio to continue on as Consuella's manager, I for my part would be prepared to involve myself more actively in assisting them both. I believe the next three years of this project may well be more financially rewarding. But I can promise you one thing. They will be very challenging. So these, then, are my reasons for offering more of my time. Consuella and Antonio are going to need it."

Father Martine queried, "Can you explain to us what you mean by very challenging?"

Francesco replied, "I believe now is as good a time as any for Antonio to give you some details on what lies ahead and to outline his thoughts as to how we should proceed. Antonio, would you be good enough to explain for our two guests what you have in mind?"

"Thank you, Francesco. The challenges, as I see them, would require Consuella to dramatically increase her workload. She will be performing at larger venues. And it would also involve a great deal of travelling, not only throughout Italy, but also to other cities across Europe."

"Okay, Antonio, that does sound challenging, but certainly not too terrifying. That is, of course, a sensible plan is in place. So can you briefly outline for Pietro and myself some details? We would give them serious consideration. We too are as anxious as I'm sure you are to reach an agreeable solution. I take it you fully accept our obligation to consult Sister Maria. Then if the three of us are of one mind, I believe we can agree on a new contract no later than tomorrow."

Turning directly to Pietro, Father Martine said, "Have I forgotten anything?"

"Nothing that I can think of. Now let's hear what Antonio has to say."

Antonio, taking a deep breath and a sip of wine from his glass, replied, "Over some months now, Francesco and I have given the matter some considerable thought. I am proposing that Francesco be appointed joint manager. He will, of course, continue his excellent role as voice coach. And in addition, he will take over the day-to-day management of Consuella's schedule here in Italy.

"I, on the other hand, will be spending more time in other European cities, negotiating concert dates and venues, thereby enabling her to embark on a long overdue European tour. The logistics of such an undertaking are quite daunting. However, I'm absolutely convinced the two of us working as a team can assist Consuella in displaying her outstanding operatic abilities to a wider European audience."

Pietro asked, "Which cities do you have in mind? And how convinced are you that she will be well received?"

"The cities we're considering include Berlin, Vienna, Madrid, Paris, and London. For some time now, we've been receiving proposals from opera companies in these and other locations. After much deliberation, we decided to defer them temporally, at least until a decision was taken by yourselves on the future management structure you wished to adopt. We thought it more prudent at the time not to burden Consuella or yourselves with these developments. It was our opinion that, to have done so, would possibly have led to an inappropriate response or even disharmony. This was something we wanted to avoid at all costs, so we stuck to the task as originally set out. We believe these objectives have been achieved, and we now have the perfect opportunity to take this project to the next exciting stage."

Father Martine remained silent. He just looked in Pietro's direction.

After a moment, Pietro spoke. "I have to say, Antonio, we feel somewhat disappointed with your decision not to share this important information with us. Well what's done is done!"

A brief silence followed. Francesco couldn't help but notice Father Martine again looking in Pietro's direction, as if he was passing on some kind of non-verbal instruction.

Pietro resumed. "What about the United States?"

"I presume you mean the United States of America."

Pietro, now beginning to grow impatient, responded, "Yes, Antonio, I do mean the United States of America."

Antonio replied, "Well, Pietro, what is it you would like to know about the United States of America?"

Pietro, now barely able to contain himself, shot back, "I would like for you to tell me, that is, if it's not too much trouble, have you had any offers from that country?"

"Well, now that you mention it, we have."

"You have what exactly?"

"We have had offers from that quarter as well."

"And your response?"

"The same as the others. But in this instance, we decided to postpone them indefinitely."

Pietro, now becoming quite agitated and about to challenge Antonio, was immediately interrupted by the timely intervention of Father Martine. "Gentlemen, gentlemen, we are all friends here and, I would like to think, sensible adults as well. May I suggest we calm down just a little and continue our discussion in a rational manner? Maybe then we can prevent this conversation from descending into some kind of farcical drama."

Francesco replied, "I couldn't agree more Father. Remember the very reason we're here this evening and let there be no more discord among us."

Antonio, turning to Pietro, said, "Please forgive my rudeness just now. It's no excuse, but the past few weeks have been quite stressful, what with our agreement coming to an end. Also there's the termination of my guardianship with Consuella's coming of age and, I suppose, my own apprehensions as to what happens next."

Pietro responded, "Antonio, no need for apologies. My main concern as a parent is for Consuella's future well-being and happiness. That's all."

"Well now that that's settled," continued Father Martine, "I can certainly see the logical and sensible approach you have taken regarding Consuella's career in Europe. I must confess, though, I am somewhat puzzled by your response to Pietro's question regarding the United States of America. Would it be possible for you to explain to us your reasons for this postponement?"

"Antonio, if I may, I would like to respond to Father Martine's question."

"By all means, Francesco," Antonio replied, somewhat relieved his friend was willing to deal with this thorny issue.

Francesco, seeing he now had everyone's attention, began by saying, "Friends, I would like to say, first of all, the initial enquiries from America excited us greatly. And I must say we were quite flattered by the interest shown from so far afield.

"However, after much discussion and deliberation, we came to the conclusion that it would not be in Consuella's best interest to pursue this option—certainly not now or, for that matter, anytime in the immediate future."

Pietro, finding his voice again, asked, "Francesco, you've explained to us the fact—that you postponed these offers indefinitely. But could you please explain for us your reasons for such a decision?"

Francesco continued, "Pietro, Father Martine, Antonio and I have the utmost respect for you both and also of course for Sister Maria. I sincerely mean no offence when I say this. But my knowledge of the operatic world is greater than yours, and the reason is that it just happens to be the path chosen for me by my father. Pietro, I would never be so presumptuous to debate with you the process of wine making, for I know your knowledge in this particular field is far greater than mine. Likewise, Father Martine, I would hesitate greatly before I would engage you in a theological discussion, for the simple reason your expertise in such matters would completely dwarf any opinions of mine. Now, concerning Sister Maria, well I won't even go there, so please bear with me if you will.

"After many discussions and, believe me, a great deal of deliberation, it was my opinion, based on my extensive knowledge of the current state of opera and how it's performed and practised in that great country, I came to the conclusion outlined earlier. I would like to add, if I may, I have been to the Grand Metropolitan Opera in New York. And I can assure you it is a most daunting arena. It is my most firmly held belief that, if we were to subject Consuella even at this stage in her career to perform at this venue, it would be for us irresponsible in the extreme and nothing less than a betrayal of the trust placed in us by Consuella and your good selves."

Pietro, still looking perplexed, responded, "Francesco, I'm quite sure your decision was based on your sense of loyalty and duty to ourselves and my daughter. But what can be so different about the Metropolitan Opera of New York and, let's say, La Scala in Milan?"

"That's an interesting question. First of all, La Scala is a smaller more intimate venue. The performers are a lot closer to the audience. The acoustics are excellent. The orchestra and chorus don't generally compete with the performers. There is a perfect balance between all these elements. Also it is most fortunate that I happen to be acquainted with a considerable number of eminent conductors, and for most of Consuella's performances, I was afforded the opportunity to confer with them beforehand. This enabled us to establish the appropriate balance between herself and the musicians. On these many, many occasions, the end result of these small but nonetheless important details have been, for me and I would like to think for most people, something I like to refer to as a true operatic experience.

"Then finally there's the audience. We Italians, when we go to the opera, we do so with a passion and an interest that is all-consuming. However, there is a downside. As an audience, we can be quite vocal in our criticism of any artist who delivers a performance we consider to be something less than perfect." Francesco sat back in his chair, giving the others the opportunity to reflect on his description of Italian opera.

Pietro, having pondered this interpretation, turned his attention once more to the United States. "You know, Francesco, I would probably agree with most of what you've explained just now. So what is it that makes the Metropolitan so different?"

"To begin with, the size of the stage alone—it doesn't allow for that intimate connection between artist and audience. I'm not saying it doesn't happen; it's just more difficult to achieve. The orchestras are generally larger, as well as the choral sections. This, on occasions, leads to an imbalance, thereby forcing performing artists to practically shout to be heard. Conductors at venues such as the Metropolitan, I'm quite certain, would not react graciously to someone such as myself making suggestions as to how they should conduct their orchestra. Perhaps they would feel it would, in some way, be an affront to their professionalism. Who knows?

"Something else that's very different, an American audience is nothing like an Italian audience. There are many, many true opera lovers in New York and, indeed, in many other parts of the United States. They attend the opera with the same sense of anticipation we do here in Italy. But in America, you also have a not insignificant number of, let's say, opera goers who attend for a variety of reasons, and very few of these have anything to do with opera."

"Can you give us some examples?" Pietro queried.

"Well, some fashion-conscious ladies attend for the sole purpose of disporting themselves in the most exquisite gowns just purchased from the top fashion houses. For others, both male and female, they often attend for no other reason than to be seen. I think they somehow believe it makes them appear somewhat more cultured in the eyes of their peers. Within these groups, there are individuals, and these are generally males, who attend for the sole purpose of doing business. These activities are generally carried on during intermissions and at the numerous after-show suppers."

Father Martine responded, "So is it your contention that all the elements you've just described, or some of them at least, when combined, affect the performance of every opera star in a negative way."

"No, certainly not every performer. It has been my experience to observe many, let's say mature European artists—sopranos, tenors, male and female, with many, many years experience behind them—doing quite well on the American stage. It's not that their voices have gotten any better. But in a number of cases, as they age, they tend to put on a little more weight. They generally become more robust, and in nearly all instances, their lung capacity increases. These factors, I suppose you could say, make them a little more indestructible. It is at this stage most performers in this situation reach the inevitable conclusion that their best years are now behind them.

"For those who take the opportunity at this late stage in their career to perform in America, the challenge doesn't hold any great fear for them, because by now they really have nothing to lose. This option, for most of them, is a more attractive proposition than remaining on the European stage, where, little by little, their fame and glory is constantly being challenged and, in the end, totally eclipsed by the young and upcoming stars."

Pietro again. "So, what really does all of this mean? And what relevance does it have for Consuella?"

"Well, first of all, it is crucially important you don't misunderstand me. I am not saying opera in America is bad or inferior to opera here in Europe. In that country, there are wonderful performers, as well as great orchestras and conductors. Most of the opera houses I've been to are truly magnificent. So I suppose what I'm really trying to say is that opera in America is essentially very different.

"Now I would like to make one final point. And it is this. If you accept my comments and observations as creditable, then I'm sure you will agree with Antonio and me that, at this pivotal stage in Consuella's development, to even consider embarking on such a course would be hugely harmful and detrimental to her as an individual and artist. Any person contemplating such a course of action would be carrying out an act of great disservice, and such a person would be responsible for causing irreparable damage to her future career as a performer.

"Gentlemen, I thank you for your patience. I sincerely hope you understand the reasons behind the opinions just expressed. They are deeply held, and I genuinely believe they are in everybody's best interest, most particularly, Consuella's. If, on the other hand, you don't agree, well then I suppose there's nothing left to say."

With these words, Francesco leaned back in his chair, raised his wine glass to nobody in particular, took a long overdue sip, set his glass on the table, and waited to see if Father Martine or Pietro were in any way inclined towards making a comment.

Instead, the only response was a studied silence.

Antonio, responded to their silence with the following: "I would just like to say that I am in complete agreement with the views and opinions expressed just now. I would also suggest that it would be incumbent on the three of you to seek Consuella's approval. As Francesco stated earlier, she is a fully-grown woman, and her willing participation is essential for the project to proceed. Now I don't mean to be rude, but if you don't agree, we would prefer you speak your minds right now. A prompt reply would save us all a lot of grief, and we can then end our evening in a civilised manner."

Father Martine turned slowly in the direction of his companion. "Well, dear friend, what thoughts do you have on the proposals and opinions put forward by our two hosts?"

"I've no problem with their analysis, nor indeed with their recommendations. I'm just wondering to myself how best to explain all of this to Sister Maria. Other than that, I'm quite happy to proceed with the proposals as outlined."

Father Martine replied, "Well that's it then. It would seem we're both happy to proceed with your plan. Don't worry about Sister Maria. I will have a word with her tomorrow morning. In such matters, she generally trusts my judgement.

"In anticipation of our meeting tomorrow, I believe you will see the three of us presenting a united front in support of your proposals. We have a preliminary contract prepared, and it is not too dissimilar from what we've been discussing so far. We can iron out the minor details and then have the final drafts drawn up for everybody's signature.

"In relation to Consuella, I totally agree. She is no longer a child and we will have to take cognizance of that in our deliberations. Pietro, if it's okay with you, I believe the best person to handle this would be Sister Maria. Can I take it you approve?"

Pietro nodded his consent. Father Martine brought this part of their evening to a close by announcing, "Well now that we've concluded our discussions on these most important topics, may I suggest some coffee and perhaps dessert?"

All agreed. As the four men sat back in their chairs, each of them took the few moments available to briefly reflect on all that had been discussed thus far.

CHAPTER 23

Francesco's Project

Having finished their desserts and whilst waiting for their coffee, Father Martine once more turned to Francesco. "Forgive my curiosity, but how does one become a voice coach?"

"Well, in my case, quite by accident. My first love was the violin. I started playing at the age of five. At sixteen, I was performing in my father's orchestra."

"Your father is a conductor?"

"Not anymore. He's been retired for some time now."

"And his name?"

"His name is Angelo Cipriano."

"I know that name. And if I'm not mistaken, I've seen your father perform. It was many years ago in Rome. As I recall, it was a most memorable, wonderful evening. So now tell me, you were playing violin in your father's orchestra. How did you make the transition from musician to voice coach?"

"Well, during my time in the orchestra, I often witnessed some very fine performers failing to project themselves properly on stage, thus preventing them from giving the sort of performance I knew they were more than capable of delivering. Occasionally taking them aside, I would go over the entire programme and assist them with their breathing, timing, and delivery. In most instances, there was a marked improvement. Word got around the operatic community, I then found more and more artists seeking my assistance. As the numbers increased, I took the decision to resign from the orchestra and set up my own school here in Milan.

"There was another even more compelling reason for this dramatic career change. It was around this time I met Carlota. Not too long after, we took the decision to marry. Well I proposed. I can only suppose she took pity on me and accepted. Then after the birth of our twin daughters, I made voice coaching my career. This for me was a more preferable option than being a musician in an orchestra, as it allowed me spend more time with my family."

"Do you think you will ever go back to performing?"

"My ambition is to form my own orchestra and become a conductor just like my father."

"Surely you'll miss playing the violin?"

"Not at all. My plan is, I suppose you could say, slightly unorthodox."

"Please explain?"

"Well first of all, I intend to carry on playing the violin, whilst leading the chorus and conducting the orchestra all at the same time."

"But that's never been done before."

"Exactly. And that's why I'm going to do it."

"But surely it would be most difficult to achieve this, for a full operatic performance, would it not?"

"That's correct. My orchestra, however, won't be performing in the traditional manner. It is my intention to perform on the main stage and invite well-known opera stars to appear as guests. They will accompany the orchestra, performing some of the best-loved arias from the most popular composers. You never know, maybe someday even Consuella will appear as a guest."

"And how long more will you continue with voice coaching?"

Francesco replied, "Consuella and Violetta, I'm hoping, will be my last students."

Father Martine, turning to Antonio and Pietro, exclaimed, "Extraordinary, how extraordinary—a violin player conducting an orchestra. I pray that God almighty lets me live long enough to witness this event."

As the four men sipped their coffee, Antonio decided to broach the subject of Consuella and himself. "I'm sure you're all aware by now that, since my return, I have not had a suitable moment to speak with Consuella about the purpose of my recent trip to Verona."

Father Martine replied, "Before we left the convent this afternoon, Sister Maria informed us she would speak with Consuella in relation to whatever it was that took place between herself and Sister Lucia. Hopefully this unpleasantness or misunderstanding will be cleared up to everyone's satisfaction."

Francesco, leaning towards Father Martine, asked, "What then?"

"I will of course brief Antonio on the outcome. If it is positive, then I would recommend that there be no further discussions. We should all of us give her the time remaining to prepare for these final performances. Then on the night of her birthday celebration, Antonio here can make his announcement and present his gift of betrothal. We of course will all act surprised but applaud heartily nonetheless."

Francesco again. "And what would your recommendation be should the outcome be, let's say, less than positive?"

"I was hoping you wouldn't ask me that question, because for me, never having had to face such a dilemma, I believe I am the person least qualified to offer any advice in the event of such an outcome."

Father Martine turned to Antonio and continued, "Antonio, dear friend, I'm sorry if I've disappointed you. It's probably the best I can do under the circumstances."

"Come, come, Father. All of you have done more than enough for me already. I have to be strong enough to accept whatever it is Consuella decides. Whatever the outcome, I will be quite prepared to carry on managing her career, if that is your wish."

Pietro decided a word from him at this particular moment would be appropriate, "Your comments just now clearly demonstrate you are a person of good intent. Let's hope everything will be resolved in a satisfactory manner. I wish there was more I could say to encourage you."

Antonio, genuinely touched, thanked him for his comforting words.

With that, Father Martine decided to conclude the evening by saying, "Tonight has been a most interesting and enjoyable experience. On behalf of myself and Pietro, I would like to thank you both for your wonderful hospitality. Now, Antonio, if you would be so kind, you may take us back to our hotel."

"All in good time, Father. We have to settle the bill, and I'm sure Mario will be most anxious to know if you enjoyed the food and the ambiance of his restaurant."

Father Martine looked around. He spotted Mario hovering nearby. Raising his hand and clicking his fingers he called out, "Mario, be a good chap and bring us the bill. We're all done here."

Mario just glared back at him without saying a word. Francesco and Antonio waited in anticipation for the next instalment between priest and restraunter. Pietro just looked on with a bemused expression. Father Martine, meanwhile, sat back in his chair with not a care in the world.

Mario, having prepared the bill, practically waltzed across the room holding the bill in both hands. He then placed it on the table directly in front of him. "There you are. Father, your bill as requested. And I do hope everything was to your satisfaction."

Growing slightly uncomfortable and not wanting to lose face, he replied rather caustically, "Well I suppose your efforts were adequate. Now, my good fellow, what am I supposed to do with this?"

"Ah there you go again, Father, just like your pupil Señor Antonio making with the jokes. Though in all sincerity I have to say, it's most heartening for me to witness you a humble friar treating your companions so generously. The church collections must be more than adequate these days. Or maybe some grateful parishioner gave you a large donation for hearing an embarrassing confession."

Antonio and Francesco, although exhibiting serious expressions of their own, were nonetheless delighted to witness Mario holding his own in the ongoing verbal joust. Pietro also found himself enjoying the spectacle as he watched his friend struggling to compete with Mario's very witty onslaught.

Father Martine, getting a sense Mario was more than ready for any remark he was likely to throw back at him, replied rather sheepishly, "Oh Mario, I'm so sorry. You must have misunderstood. You see I was merely calling for the bill. I'm sure our hosts will be happy to settle the account with your good self."

Mario, now beginning to enjoy the battle, decided to press on for victory. Speaking in his best authoritative voice, he replied, "Dear Father, let me explain. In my restaurant, the custom is the person who calls for the bill settles the account. So whenever you're ready. And by the way, there is no service charge, so any gratuity you deem appropriate will be most gratefully and humbly accepted."

Father Martine, now wishing the ground would just swallow him whole, looked over in the direction of his dining companions to see if they might be inclined to come to his assistance. Enjoying the encounter enormously, they returned his pleading gaze with serious expressions of their own and made no effort to rescue him.

As a last desperate measure to save himself further embarrassment, he decided to employ his tried and tested poor cleric routine. It had never failed him in the past. "My dear, Mario. As you can see, I'm a man of the cloth, a humble priest if you will. I'm sure you, most likely a devout Catholic, would be fully aware of my holy vow of poverty."

Mario triumphantly replied, "Well, Father, the way you were guzzling down the wine here tonight, it would never have occurred to me you were poverty-stricken. I suppose all I can do now is prevail upon Señor Francesco and Señor Antonio to rescue the situation. Other than that, the only option left for me is to take up a collection on your behalf."

With that, he picked up the bill. Bowing in front of them he continued, "Gentlemen, I do hope everything was to your satisfaction?"

Then turning to Pietro, he enquired, "Dear Señor Pellegrini, I sincerely hope you don't find my question impertinent. Was the meal to your liking? And did you enjoy your evening in my humble establishment?"

"Why yes indeed, Mario. I enjoyed it very much. The meal was excellent, would you agree, Father?"

Still smarting from the way he had been outmanoeuvred, Father Martine responded rather dryly, "Well I wouldn't go that far. The food was certainly edible. Though, I found the sauce a bit too rich for my pallet."

Mario couldn't resist. "I suppose this most likely has something to do with that vow of poverty you mentioned earlier."

His remark was followed by a stunned silence. Father Martine seemed to be in a momentary state of shock. Francesco glanced over in Pietro and Antonio's direction. The three of them suddenly burst out laughing.

Father Martine, with a sulky expression and pretending to be deeply offended, remarked, "What's so funny?"

Pietro answered him, "Dear friend, it's not often we get to experience you being lost for words. Tonight I do believe you met your match."

Looking over in Mario's direction, he replied, "Well, I really didn't want to take advantage of poor Mario here. By his own admission, he is but a humble waiter. So I decided not to be too hard on him."

Mario, with a broad smile on his face, responded, "Father, you are such a rogue. Well that's what your companions tell me. So tonight it was me Mario making with the jokes. I hope you are not too displeased. But if you are, by way of compensation, I will deduct the cost of your coffee from the bill."

Father Martine, getting into his stride, answered him, "One coffee, Mario. My, oh my. Antonio and Francesco told me of your legendary hospitality. It's really something to witness first-hand."

Mario, now finding himself at the receiving end of the wily old friar's caustic wit, responded, "Oh let's not quibble. The four coffees, no charge."

"What about the wine?"

"What about it, Father? Was not Señor Pellegrini's choice exceptional?"

"You know, Mario. I find myself in complete agreement. Señor Pellegrini's choice was indeed truly exceptional, but I'm not talking about the wine on the table."

The others looked on, enjoying the spectacle, and wondered which of the protagonists was going to win the contest.

Mario, now with a puzzled look on his face, responded, "Dear Father, if you're not referring to the wine on the table, then I'm at a loss. Could you please possibly enlighten me?"

"Why of course, Mario. I'm referring to the case of wine in your cellar. You know the one that was delivered earlier with Señor Pellegrini's compliments."

"Oh that wine. And there I was thinking the distributor had delivered it by mistake. I was of course going to contact them at the first opportunity to rectify the matter."

Father Martine, displaying a roguish smile, replied, "Of course you were, Mario. It would be most uncharitable and, dare I say, even unchristian of us to think otherwise. Wouldn't it, gentlemen?"

The others nodded in agreement. Mario, now struggling to regain his composure, replied expansively, "Truly, gentlemen, I'm most humbled by this wonderful generous gift. So the wine on the table, no charge."

Father Martine decided to squeeze him just a little further. "Let's see now. There were four bottles on the table. By my reckoning, that leaves eight in your wine cellar. Would I be correct?"

Mario just stood there, quite lost for words.

Pietro, taking pity on him, joined in. "Mario, I want you to accept the remaining wine as gift from all of us. In return, all I ask is, whenever an opportunity presents itself, I'd like you to promote the Pellegrini range— you know, a kind of marketing campaign on my behalf."

Now greatly relieved, Mario enthusiastically replied, "Dear Señor Pellegrini, it will be such an honour to perform this task on your behalf. You are truly a wonderful gentleman."

Father Martine decided to have the last word. "Mario, may I make a suggestion?"

"Would it make any difference if my answer was no?"

"Not really."

"Well then, Father, please continue. I'm all ears."

"The wine, obviously no charge. Throw in the coffees and the desserts. What do you say? Do we have ourselves a deal?"

"Yes, Father, we do indeed have ourselves a deal. You know, the moment you walked through that door, I just knew it."

"What was it you knew?"

"I just knew, Father, you and I would get on famously."

Doing some hasty arithmetic, Mario adjusted the bill. Antonio and Francesco, having enjoyed the exchanges enormously, settled the account with no further quibbling.

Mario, in his usual dramatic fashion, enthusiastically bowed. "Gentlemen, Father, it was such an honour having you here. I look forward to seeing you here again very soon." With that, he gave a final bow and departed.

Francesco stood up and shook hands with Pietro and Father Martine, saying, "Gentlemen, it was such a pleasure meeting with you this evening. And thank you for taking the time to join Antonio and myself."

Pietro replied, "It was our pleasure. Indeed it is we who should be thanking you for your wonderful hospitality. Oh and by the way, Father Martine will be celebrating Mass tomorrow morning at eight. So if you and Carlota care to attend, you would be most welcome."

Francesco responded with a mischievous smile on his face, "You should have told me this before you plied us with this wine of yours. However, I'm sure my good wife will make every effort to rouse me on time."

Pietro smiled back. "Half the time, I don't know if you are serious or just having fun at my expense. I suppose that's the reason I enjoy your company so much."

"Pietro, dear friend, tonight I think I'll just leave you guessing."

Antonio, heading for the door, called out, "If you please, gentlemen, I need to get you to your hotel as quickly as possible if we are to have any chance of waking in time for Mass tomorrow morning."

CHAPTER 24

The Convent that Same Evening

While Antonio and Francesco were entertaining Pietro and Father Martine in Mario's restaurant, Sister Maria, in the privacy of her room, reflected on the gloomy atmosphere that had been very much in evidence when they'd arrived earlier that same afternoon.

The most sensible and appropriate course of action, she decided, would be to have Consuella and Sister Lucia join her for dinner. Then, she would try and determine the extent of the problem.

Entering the dining room and seeing Sister Lucia, she sat down and joined her.

Having already started her meal and feeling slightly embarrassed, Sister Lucia apologised. "Please forgive me, Reverend Mother. I thought you had already eaten."

"Not to worry, Sister, not to worry. I'll let Sister Agostina know I'm here."

She headed for the kitchen.

"Ah there you are, Sister. Would it be possible to have a plate of that delicious food?"

"Of course, Reverend Mother. Please take a seat, and I'll bring it in straight away."

"Don't trouble yourself, Sister. Just put some on a plate, and I will take it in myself. Oh and by the way, could you possibly check with Consuella and see if she cares to join myself and Sister Lucia?"

Sister Agostina, in a timid manner, replied as she passed her the food. "She was here earlier, Reverend Mother, and has already eaten."

"That's fine. Could you just call her then and see if she would like to join us anyway?"

Sister Agostina, now beginning to exhibit some degree of stress, continued as best she could. "As far as I know, Reverend Mother, she is not in her room."

Sister Maria, becoming slightly more frustrated, decided nonetheless not to be too hard on Sister Agostina. "Oh dear me, this doesn't sound too promising. Is there any chance you actually know where she is right now?"

"Please, Reverend Mother, I hope you won't be too annoyed. All I can tell you is she left the convent, in fact it was quite some time ago."

"Thank you, Sister. There's no earthly reason for me to be annoyed with you. Consuella is the guilty party. You have nothing to reproach yourself for. If she happens to return while I'm having dinner, please let her know I wish to speak with her. Can you do that for me?"

Sister Agostina, now somewhat relieved, answered, "Of course, Reverend Mother. As soon as she returns, I will make sure to let her know."

Rejoining Sister Lucia, Sister Maria remarked, "Something very strange seems to be going on. Apparently, Consuella has taken it upon herself to go somewhere, and yet you're still here. How come?"

"Indeed, Reverend Mother, it is rather strange but, I regret to say, not so unusual."

"Dear Sister, I know there is something not quite right. I sensed it the moment I arrived. Can you enlighten me as to what's going on? Because right now, I'm somewhat confused and slightly alarmed."

Sister Lucia, not for the first time, found herself in the unenviable position of having to balance her loyalty to Consuella and her duty to her superior. She realised she had no option but to choose the latter. "Reverend Mother, this is not the first occasion. In fact, it's the third time she's left the convent unaccompanied. The first time was Saturday last. I didn't object as she told me she needed to visit Francesco for an additional coaching lesson. I subsequently found out no such meeting took place."

"What did you do then?"

"Naturally enough, when she returned I questioned her."

"Then what happened?"

"She became quite agitated and more or less told me it was none of my business. She was extremely rude to myself and to Sister Agostina. Antonio witnessed some of these exchanges. He was appalled and told her so in no uncertain terms. I, for my part, informed her I would be giving you a full report."

"Is there anything else I need to know?"

Sister Lucia updated her on all the other incidents that had taken place.

When she finished, Sister Maria, now gravely concerned, asked, "Is that it?"

"Yes, Reverend Mother, I think I've covered everything."

"Then tell me. How is the situation right now?"

Before Sister Lucia had a chance to answer, Consuella entered. "My apologies for the interruption, Reverend Mother. Sister Agostina said you wish to see me."

"Ah there you are, dear child. I will be finished with Sister In a moment or two. Please wait for me in the library. I will join you shortly."

She nervously replied, "Of course, Reverend Mother."

With her departure, Sister Maria continued, "Now, Sister, where were we? Ah yes, you were about to update me on how things currently stand."

Sister Lucia, endeavouring to end what had been a most difficult discussion for her personally, attempted to finish with something slightly more positive by saying. "In Consuella's defence, I would like you to know, she did in fact apologise to both of us. Presently, the atmosphere is not perfect, but I'm relieved to report a certain degree of civility has been re-established."

"One final question and then we'll be finished. Antonio travelled to Verona on a special mission concerning Consuella and himself. Do you know if he spoke with her anytime since he returned?"

"As far as I'm aware, no, at least not to my knowledge."

"Do you think it possible she might have had some inkling as to the reason for his journey?"

"I'm quite certain she knew."

"And you, Sister, did you have any idea as to the purpose behind his trip?"

"Would I be correct in saying Antonio journeyed to Verona to gain her father's support, and of course yours and Father Martine's, in his quest to win her hand?"

"Indeed, Sister. How perceptive. That's exactly the reason he made the journey. What would you suggest we do now?"

"It's really not my place to say, Reverend Mother. All I can hope and pray is everything works out for both of them in the end, because from the first day we arrived here, they always seemed to bring out the best in each other. And for me, it was such a joy being in their company."

"Well, Sister, all I can say is thank you for taking the time to share your thoughts. I assure you, our conversation this evening will be handled with the utmost discretion. I'm fully aware this discussion for you must have been somewhat difficult. You had to decide between your undoubted loyalty to Consuella and your vow of obedience to me. I'm glad you made the right decision. I promise, everything you've told me I'm sure will assist in resolving this unfortunate situation. On that you have my word. Again thank you. Now off you go. Get a good night's rest. I will now go and see what Consuella has to say for herself."

"Before you go, Reverend Mother, I have a request, actually two requests."

"Go on, Sister. I'm listening."

"Please don't be too hard on her. Deep down, I know there has to be some rational explanation for her unusual behaviour."

"I will certainly give it some consideration. And please, what was your second point?"

"When I entered the convent, I did so because I believed I had a vocation."

"And what vocation was that?"

"I truly believed my vocation was to be a teacher. When you requested me to accompany Consuella to Milan, I did so willingly. Now with her coming of age, I feel my role in this aspect of her life is coming to a close. So if it pleases you, I would really like to take up a teaching position here in Milan, if it were at all possible."

Sister Maria reflected for a few moments and then responded. "Dear Sister, you've done everything that's been asked of you, and you've done it in quite a remarkable way. So there's no need for you to concern yourself with the next stage of Consuella's career. That will be for others to decide. Next term, you will be teaching our young students here, and I am confident they will be very happy to have you among them. I will inform Pietro and Father Martine of your wishes."

"Thank you, Reverend Mother. This evening you have made me so happy. I really don't know what to say."

"There's no need to say anything. As a matter of fact, it's me who should be thanking you for the selfless manner in which you performed this task."

Sister Lucia, now quite emotional, stood up, made a courteous bow, and responded, "Thank you, Reverend Mother, for those kind words. They are most appreciated. They really are. I'm going to visit the chapel. I will say a special prayer for your intentions and also Consuella's. If you wish, I will awaken you for early Mass tomorrow morning."

Sister Maria stood up. "Thank you, Sister. I really do appreciate that."

They both left the dining room together. Sister Lucia made her way to the chapel. Sister Maria gave a gentle knock on the library door.

Without waiting for a reply, she entered and sat down opposite Consuella. "I hope I haven't kept you waiting too long?"

"Not at all, Reverend Mother. I was just lost in my own thoughts right now."

"Pleasant thoughts I hope?"

"Some pleasant, some conflicting."

"Would you care to share some of these thoughts? Could it be just nervousness ahead of the concerts?"

"It's not that at all. In fact, I'm quite looking forward to them.

"Well then, what is it that's troubling you so much?"

"That's just it, I really don't know. When I look back over the recent past and what has been achieved, I really should be the happiest person in the world. Instead, here I am experiencing serious doubts and anxieties about what lies ahead. It's made me quite sad and somewhat miserable."

"Consuella, please, you must banish these negative thoughts. You've enjoyed great success and good fortune in a relatively short space of time. Look at the wonderful dedicated support group you have around you. Just think of the joy you've brought to so many people, of your generosity to your family and those closest to you. Try and focus on the many positives in your life. I know in my heart, if you can do this, you will banish this negativity and feel much better."

"Thank you, Reverend Mother, I will try."

Sister Maria decided to press on as tactfully as she could. "Now, Consuella, could you perhaps tell me how things have been between Antonio and yourself since his return from Verona?"

Consuella, wondering where this was going, decided a calm response would be appropriate. "Fine, just fine, though I have to say I get the distinct impression there's something weighing heavily on his mind. On a number of occasions, the atmosphere between us was somewhat strained."

"Can you elaborate?"

"Well he always seemed to be on the verge of saying something profoundly important and then just as quickly changed the subject or dashed off on some pretext. For me, of course, it was all quite confusing, as prior to this, we were always at ease in each other's company. I always admired his confident manner, his self-assurance. and the positive attitude he brought to every situation, literally from the first day I arrived here in Milan."

Sister Maria paused for a moment and then continued. "You know Consuella, when we arrived earlier this afternoon, I couldn't help but notice that there seemed to be a strained atmosphere between yourself, Sister Maria and Antonio. So I suggested to your Father and Father Martine that I would have a private talk with you and hopefully clear up any misunderstandings."

Consuella, beginning to feel slightly uncomfortable, decided she really had no choice other than allow Sister Maria continue.

"Now, Consuella, you're not a novice under my authority. You are, I believe, a mature sensible adult. It's not my intention to lecture or reprimand you in any way. If at any time you feel unwilling or unable to respond to my questions or comments, you may terminate our discussion at any time."

Consuella, slightly more at ease, replied, "Please continue, Reverend Mother."

"During Antonio's absence, on more than one occasion, you left the convent unaccompanied. In addition to this, you misled Antonio regarding the number of coaching lessons you had with Francesco. You were extremely rude to Sisters Agostina and Lucia. And finally, the mysterious letter. When Antonio inquired out of his sense of duty, you dismissed it out of hand. As I recall, Antonio handled all correspondence on your behalf. Would you agree?"

Consuella squirmed in her chair, her eyes now rapidly blinking.

Sister Maria, noting her distress, decided to reassure her but carry on nonetheless. "Dear Consuella, I know this is difficult. All of us, at different stages in our lives, have done or said things that, in hindsight, we were not very proud of. I'm sure you know, in difficult situations such as these, confiding in someone you believe in your heart you can trust often helps. Do you have faith enough to place your trust in me?"

Consuella, deciding to go on the offensive, replied somewhat caustically, "I suppose this means you've been speaking with Sister Lucia?"

Sister Maria, despite the insolence of Consuella's last remark, calmly responded, "Yes, as a matter of fact, I have spoken with her."

"I would have thought our dear sister would have shown more loyalty to me."

Sister Maria, growing more impatient by the minute, answered rather sharply, "Consuella, you of all people should know, when Sister Lucia accompanied you to Milan, she did so under my implicit instructions. May I remind you, lest you've forgotten, she was under a vow of obedience to me as her Mother Superior? One of her many duties was to report back to me. This she did on a regular basis, I believe I can say without fear of contradiction, in all that time, she had nothing but the highest praise for you and the progress you were making. I would advise you to tread very carefully from here on."

"Please forgive me, Reverend Mother. I didn't mean to be rude just now. I've already apologised to both sisters. And yes, I wasn't completely truthful with my answers in relation to my unaccompanied journeys. On one occasion, I went to look at a property, a town house in fact, as it's most likely I will be living outside the convent in the very near future."

"And today's little excursion? What was that all about?"

"The same, Reverend Mother. It was also related to my future living arrangements."

Sister Maria, not overly surprised by this revelation, responded, "That's not such a terrible thing. We all accept you were not going to spend the rest of your life in the convent. But why all the secrecy?"

"Oh, it was just something I wanted to do on my own."

"Well, I'm certainly relieved that mystery is cleared up. Now what about the coaching lesson that never took place?"

"To my regret, I was untruthful with Sister Lucia on this occasion also. I went to meet with a very influential figure. During the course of this meeting, there was a discussion concerning my future plans."

Sister Maria, finding this piece of news slightly more alarming, inquired, "Was anything proposed or agreed to during these discussions?"

"Yes, proposals were made, but neither was any agreement reached."

"May I ask what the current situation is?"

"Just as I've outlined, proposals were made. I didn't agree to them, but neither did I reject them."

"Would I be correct in saying you are still giving these proposals some consideration?"

"Yes, Reverend Mother, I suppose you could say that."

"Tell me, Consuella. These proposals as you call them and the mysterious letter in your possession, are they by chance connected in any way?"

"If you don't mind, Reverend Mother, I'd rather not say."

Sister Maria just sat for a few moments. She couldn't help but feel, although Consuella wasn't being downright rude, her responses, however, to say the least were somewhat impertinent. "Would it be your intention maybe sometime in the immediate future to enlighten me as to the their substance or maybe even discuss the contents of the letter?"

"I will take it under consideration."

Barely able to conceal her anger, Sister Maria drew on her many years of discipline and self-control, enabling her to calmly respond, "Well, Consuella, is there anything further you wish to add?"

"No not really, Reverend Mother."

With that, Sister Maria stood up. Although trying to maintain her composure, she continued in a voice beginning to exhibit real signs of emotion. "I have to say, this evening I was hoping for a more open discussion. Regrettably, an opportunity has been lost, and that saddens me greatly. Looking at you now, I see a woman; I still can't help looking back to those early days in Verona. There you were, just a young innocent child, at all times so very graceful, so shy, and always so charming. Now look at you, all grown up before my very eyes." Trying desperately to hold back her tears, she reached her two hands out.

Consuella clasped them in her own. She too was now beginning to cry. "Oh, Reverend Mother, please tell me. Have I changed so much?"

"Consuella, change is part of growing up. It's how we change that's important. There's nothing more for me to add except to say, always remember those who love and care for you. They will always be there, even in your hour of greatest need. I know this to be true. And I believe it deep down in my heart. Now if you'll excuse me, I have an early start tomorrow."

"As you wish, Reverend Mother."

"Oh by the way, tomorrow morning. Father Martine will be celebrating eight o'clock Mass. You are more than welcome to join us if you so wish."

Consuella, about to say, *I'll consider it*, instead replied, "Thank you, Reverend Mother. I will do my best to attend."

With that, Sister Maria took her leave.

Consuella remained behind momentarily. Having waited just long enough to be sure everyone had finally retired, she closed the library door behind her and made her way silently to her room.

Lying in bed, though quite exhausted, she had great difficulty in getting to sleep. Her mind was in turmoil, awash with a mass of conflicting emotions. She asked herself over and over, why was she being so rude to those who loved and cared for her? What feelings did she have for Antonio? How, she wondered, did he feel about her? What to make of Don Barcese's proposals? Would he fulfil his promises? Should she confide in someone or just wait and see how events unfolded over the coming days?

When sleep finally came, she drifted off with an image of herself walking onto a large stage— a stage that, even in her fitful slumber, she knew was one she had never performed on before.

CHAPTER 25

The Convent Kitchen
Early Morning

Awakening from a fitful night's sleep, Consuella hastily dressed and made her way downstairs to the kitchen. As she entered, she was slightly startled by Sister Agostina's presence. "I'm so sorry, Sister. I didn't mean to disturb you."

"Not at all, Consuella. Would you care for some breakfast?"

"Thank you, Sister. A black coffee would be fine if it's not too much trouble?"

"I must say, Consuella, you're up bright and early this morning."

"Indeed, it is an early hour. There's something in need of my attention before this morning's meeting. So I need to pop out for a while."

"Will you be back in time for Mass?"

"Unfortunately no, but I will certainly do my very best to be back in time for breakfast."

Handing her the coffee, Sister Agostina replied, "Don't worry, Consuella. I'll make sure to have a nice breakfast waiting for you on your return. If you could please excuse me for a moment, there's something I need to check in the dining room."

"Take your time, Sister."

Before Sister Agostina returned, Consuella slipped out and made her way across town by cab. Arriving at Don Barcese's town house, she stood there for a few hesitant moments and then rang the doorbell and waited. She wondered, had she perhaps arrived too early? Maybe everyone was still sleeping. To her relief, Henry, the butler, opened the door.

Recognising Consuella, he immediately invited her in. "Please, Señorita Pellegrini, if you would be kind enough to take a seat in the drawing room, I will inform the master of your presence."

As she waited, Consuella thought for a moment. *What in heaven's name am I doing here? Have I gone completely mad?*

Before she had a chance to answer her own question, Don Barcese made his dramatic entrance. "Consuella my dear, what an unexpected pleasure. I can tell by your expression there's something weighing heavily on your mind. If I can be of assistance, just say the word."

"As a matter of fact, it's not your assistance I need. I would just like you to clarify some points contained in your proposals."

"What is it you would like me to explain?"

"Did you mean it when you said within three to six months of signing a contract, I would be performing on the stage of the Metropolitan Opera of New York? Also that you will charge a management fee of no more than 15 per cent? Finally, you're proposal stated that, if either party for whatever reason deem this arrangement is no longer in their best interest, that party may exit the contract forthwith without fear of litigation. Is that correct?"

"Yes, my dear, that's correct."

"But surely, Don Barcese, unless I'm very much mistaken, this document appears to be more in my favour than yours. I have to ask, why so generous?"

"Well, first of all, it's not for the money. As you can see, I'm a person of some means, so it's not that at all. My dear, Consuella, let me explain. A talent such as yours comes along maybe once in a lifetime. Over the past two years or so, I've watched your progress with great interest and am fully convinced the next stage of your career should be played out in a much wider arena. In my humble opinion, I believe I am the person most suited to perform this task."

"How do you intend to win over my patrons?"

"I've been giving that matter careful consideration for some time now."

With that, he rang the bell on the table.

Straight away, Henry entered. "You rang, master."

"Yes. In my study on the desk, there is a large Manila envelope. Please bring it here."

"Of course, master."

"You said just now you were giving the matter some thought."

"Indeed I have, my dear."

Before he had a chance to continue, Henry was back and handed him the envelope. "Will there be anything else, master? Tea, coffee, perhaps?"

"Consuella, I do apologise. Please forgive me. Would you care for some refreshments?"

"No thank you, Don Barcese. I'm just fine."

"Thank you, Henry. That will be all. Please see to it that Señorita Consuella and myself are not disturbed."

"As you wish, master."

Consuella was somewhat surprised by the curt formality between master and servant. It was something she had never experienced in her entire life.

Handing her the envelope, Don Barcese invited her to study the contents and then continued where he had left off. "As I was saying, I came to the conclusion that winning over your patrons would be an almost insurmountable task. So I decided to have this contract drawn up. It requires two signatures only, yours and mine."

Opening the envelope, she removed two sets of documents. Glancing through the first one, she could see it was a contract containing the clauses discussed earlier.

Studying her studying the document, he asked, "Is there anything you wish me to explain or clarify?"

"No. It seems to cover the points you raised earlier. Would I be correct in saying these two sets of papers are the same?"

"That's correct. And as you can see, I've already signed both documents."

"I can see that. But surely you must be aware, I'm in no position to sign anything without the consent of my guardians."

"Yes Indeed. If you were to put your signature to these contracts today, they would have no validity whatsoever. Now, if you look closer, you will see I have dated them for the day after your twenty-first birthday. By then, legally you can make whatever decision you feel is in your own best interest, If you were to sign these documents on that day, there would then no longer be any need, any need at all for you to remain under the control of your guardians, or anyone else for that matter."

Consuella replied, "Under the circumstances Don Barcese, I feel it would be good manners on my part to at least inform you that, on my return to the convent, I will be engaging in very detailed discussions concerning my future. It's most likely, by close of day, I will be under contract to Señor Antonio for some time to come."

"If that's what fate has in store for you, so be it. It will be a consoling comfort for me to know at least I tried."

"Why, that's most noble of you, Don Barcese. And I do appreciate the time you've given me this morning. Now, if you'll excuse me, I have to be getting back."

With that, Don Barcese rang the bell one more time.

On cue Henry, appeared. "Yes, master."

"Can you please tell George to bring the car around to the front door?"

"Of course, master."

"My chauffeur will deliver you safely back to the convent. And please, feel free to take the documents with you. If nothing else, they will strengthen your hand in the negotiations to come."

As she was being driven back across town, Consuella reflected on her meeting with Don Barcese. There was still something about him she couldn't quite put her finger on.

Holding the envelope close, she felt more confident about the anticipated encounter with Sister Maria.

Arriving back at the convent, she strode down the hall with a purposeful stride in her step and made a dramatic entrance as Sister Maria was in mid-sentence.

CHAPTER 26

The Chapel

Father Martine approached the altar; bowed reverently; and then, turning to the small congregation, made the sign of the cross and greeted them. "Welcome, dear friends. I'm grateful for the opportunity to celebrate Holy Mass in this beautiful chapel. Today is the feast day of Saint Beatrice. In our Christian tradition, this name has a special significance. It means 'voyager through life'. We've made a voyage together, and as we gather in this place of worship, let us offer this celebration to God, that he may grant us the grace to continue our journey in peace and harmony."

As Father Martine was speaking, Sister Maria discreetly looked around. She could see everyone was present except for one significant absentee. Consuella was nowhere to be seen. This wasn't the beginning she would have wished for on such an important occasion. She had a sense this was going to be a very long day indeed.

The Mass took no longer than twenty-five minutes. With the final blessing, Father Martine invited the guests to join him in the dining room for breakfast. As everyone made his or her way there, he signalled Sister Maria and Pietro to join him in the vestry.

As soon as they were alone, he inquired, "I'm wondering, Sister, why Consuella failed to join us. Can you shed any light on the matter?"

Sister Maria replied, "After our discussion last night, I was of the opinion she would attend."

"From your conversation, did you learn anything we should be concerned about?"

"There's no doubt in my mind she is definitely under some degree of pressure. I strongly suspect it has something to with a person she met during Antonio's absence."

Pietro, exhibiting a degree of anxiety, enquired, "Who can this person be?"

Sister Maria answered, "She informed me he was a person of some influence, and there was some talk of proposals made, though it's my understanding nothing was agreed upon."

Father Martine then gave her a brief account of their discussions with Antonio and Francesco. "Pietro and I were reasonably satisfied with the main thrust of their proposals and are happy to proceed."

Sister Maria asked him, "Then what is it you wish me to say?"

Pietro answered, "Dear Sister, we regret putting you under this kind of pressure. If I were to tell you both of them have my absolute trust and I have total confidence in their judgement, would it help in any way?"

Sister Maria replied, "Consuella is your daughter. I know how much she means to you. If you're happy to proceed, then you have my agreement.

"Oh there is one more thing. I will be making an announcement on behalf of Sister Lucia. I don't have time to go into details right now. Can I take it both of you will support me?"

Father Martine answered, "Consider it done, Sister. Now I think it's time we joined the others. Hopefully, after breakfast, we can get this meeting under way."

As they sat down, Sister Maria, still seeing no sign of Consuella, assumed she was probably in her room and had most likely overslept. Seeing Sister Agostina, she asked her to call Consuella and let her know breakfast was being served.

"Oh, I'm sorry, Mother Superior. I thought you were already aware. She was here earlier this morning, in fact before anyone else had even risen, and she had a quick breakfast and then left."

"Do you know where it was she was going at such an early hour?"

"She didn't say, Mother Superior, though from what I could tell she seemed to be in some kind of a hurry."

"Thank you, Sister. You've been most helpful."

Standing up, making sure she had everyone's attention, she exclaimed in total exasperation, "This is really is too much. While most of you probably assumed Consuella was in her room, it now appears she had an early breakfast and left the convent before any of us was even awake. Forgive me for saying this, Pietro. Your daughter's behaviour is completely irrational and, as far as I'm concerned, highly unacceptable."

"Unfortunately, I have to agree. Does anyone have any suggestions?"

Francesco responded, "It certainly looks like Consuella won't be joining us for breakfast after all. Hopefully, she'll eventually turn up. In the time available, let's go over the events of the past week. Maybe we'll find some clue that might explain her unusual behaviour.

"Sister Maria, you were the last person to speak with her. How did she seem to you?"

"She seemed to be under some considerable strain. I took this into consideration during our conversation. she acknowledged that she had been rude on a number of occasions. And in fairness. she has apologised. She made two unaccompanied journeys, one of which was yesterday evening. She informed me her reasons for doing so was to look at some properties. When I stated such an endeavour was not so unusual, she seemed somewhat relieved. We then discussed the earlier occasion of her unaccompanied journey. She seemed quite open about a meeting she said took place between herself and an influential figure."

Antonio and Francesco immediately exchanged concerned glances.

Francesco asked, "Did she say if anything of substance was discussed?"

"Well I was able to ascertain that proposals of some sort were made. When I pressed her further, though, her response was that she was considering them but had not taken any decision so far."

"Do you have any clue as to the identity of this so-called 'influential person'?"

"None whatsoever, Francesco. The strange thing is though, I have a feeling this encounter is somehow linked to the mysterious letter."

"How so?"

"Because when I questioned her about it, she became extremely evasive and slightly hostile. It was really at this stage that our discussion more or less ended."

Father Martine, beginning to feel the strain, asked, "Francesco, can you shed some light as to the possible identity of this mysterious person."

"It can only be one person. I would also agree with Sister Maria's contention; this person and the letter are inextricably linked."

"So, Francesco, can you give us a name?"

"His name is Don Marco Barcese."

Father Martine, remembering Antonio's comments from the day before, asked, "This Don Barcese, is he a person of such importance? And if he is, should we be concerned?"

Francesco replied, "He is certainly a person of great self-importance. And there is absolutely no doubt in my mind that this, indeed, is the person Consuella met. I would now urge the three of you to waste no time and deal with this potentially catastrophic situation as soon as you possibly can."

Pietro, now greatly concerned, asked, "When you use the term 'catastrophic', is it possible you're overstating the gravity of the situation my daughter may have gotten herself into?"

"If anything, Pietro, I am understating the damage this individual can inflict on your daughter."

"Please, Francesco," Sister Maria interceded. "It's not my intention to offend you. But this matter is very important to me and most definitely to Pietro and Father Martine. What is it about this person that convinces you of the potential danger he poses and the urgency for immediate action?"

"Where to start?" Francesco, having addressed the question as much to himself as to the others continued, "This Don Marco Barcese promotes himself as an impresario and expert, not only on Italian opera but on opera worldwide. The truth of the matter is somewhat quite different. He is nothing but a rogue and a charlatan to boot. He can be most charming. He wears very expensive hand-tailored suits; dines only in the best restaurants; and has a magnificent town house, a chauffeur-driven auto-mobile, and a private box in most opera houses throughout Europe.

"For many years, he has managed, or should I say mis-managed, the careers of many young and promising upcoming performers. Violetta and her father, Alberto, who are among us today, have had first-hand experience of his managerial style, and you all know what a fine singer Violetta is.

"Anyway, back to Don Barcese. In the early stage of their careers, these promising young artistes enjoyed a certain degree of success. As soon as he had total control, he exploited them in a reckless manner through one-sided contracts. Never once to my certain knowledge did he ever lift a finger or make any effort to assist even one of these performers in developing their talent. Oh no, such acts were way beyond his perception as to what constituted sound professional management.

"I could go on. But there's really no point. The only thing left for me to say is—that's of course you believe what I've just told you—that all of you must act and act immediately. Consuella's very future depends on it."

Everyone around the dining table was in total shock. Even Sister Lucia was quite stunned, and she wondered how events surrounding Consuella's actions could bring about this almost tragic state of affairs.

Father Martine, with a grim expression, slowly, very slowly looked in Antonio's direction and, in a weary voice, inquired, "Can I take it, Antonio, you would concur with Francesco's description of the individual in question?"

"Word for word," was Antonio's reply.

Father Martine just slumped back in his chair, deeply frustrated. Sister Maria, aware of the tired expression exhibited in his demeanour, decided there and then decisive action was needed and needed immediately.

"Pietro, in response to Francesco's description of this individual and all the other nonsense that's occurred, I have come to the conclusion that, as soon as Cons—"

With that, Consuella made her dramatic entrance. She was holding the large Manila envelope. Practically gliding over to a vacant chair she sat down, laid the envelope on the table, and then addressed Sister Maria. "I do apologise, Reverend Mother, for my late arrival and my untimely interruption just now as you were speaking. If I recall, you were saying something about a conclusion. Would that be correct?"

The room fell into total silence.

Father Martine sat bolt upright in his chair.

Pietro had an expression of acute embarrassment.

Sister Agostina tried to busy herself with an attempt at clearing some dishes.

Carlota was totally surprised by Consuella's uncharacteristic brazenness.

Sister Lucia remained impassive and didn't exhibit any outward sign of emotion.

Violetta and her Father just looked on dumbfounded.

Francesco and Antonio observed the various reactions. In particular, they were watching Sister Maria, who seemed to be gauging the atmosphere created just now by Consuella's dramatic entrance. They could see the brief interruption gave her a few moments to best decide the approach she would now take in bringing this overblown drama to some sort of conclusion.

"Ah there you are, my dear child. Thank you so much for joining us. No need for apologies. Why all of us here, I'm sure, have been late at least once or twice in the past. What a pity you missed Mass. It was a wonderful celebration. Also we were so terribly disappointed you were unable to join us for breakfast. Sister Agostina tells me you had breakfast earlier this morning before you left the convent, for an important meeting perhaps? Or maybe you were looking at some more properties."

Consuella, now regretting the manner and tone of her arrival, was beginning to experience some degree of discomfort with the approach Sister Maria was now adopting. Her unease and distress was clearly visible for all to see.

"Well, Consuella, I'm waiting for an answer, if it's not too much trouble?"

"It was a meeting, Reverend Mother."

"There now, that wasn't too difficult. May I enquire with whom you had this meeting?"

"I'd rather not say, Reverend Mother."

"Well maybe I can say. Could it perhaps be a certain Don Marco Barcese?" Sister Maria almost spat the name out.

Consuella burst into tears, screeching, "Why, why are you doing this to me? Do all of you hate me so much? Are you jealous of my success? What is it? What is it? Can somebody, somebody please, oh please, explain to me what is it I'm supposed to do? What is it I'm supposed to become?"

With that, she lowered her head in her hands. Gradually, her sobbing subsided. She remained still for a few brief moments. And then composing herself, she slowly resumed her upright position. Turning in Sister Maria's direction, she spoke in a barely audible and halting voice. "Yes, Reverend Mother, the person I met with this morning and on one other occasion is the individual you speak of. His name is Don Marco Barcese."

"Consuella, one more question if I may. This Don Barcese, the mysterious letter, and the envelope in your possession, are they in some way connected?"

"Yes, Reverend Mother."

"Please continue."

"The letter and this envelope were given to me by this gentleman. The contents contain proposals regarding the future management of my career."

"Thank you, Consuella. Well now that that mystery is cleared up, I suggest we take a short break and reconvene, let's say in fifteen minutes. Can I take it we're all in agreement?"

Everyone present was certainly glad and relieved this fractious episode had drawn to a conclusion of sorts. They were also hoping the discussions to follow would be somewhat less dramatic.

Consuella, in a slightly more composed state, approached Sister Maria, who was standing next to Father Martine and her father. To avoid his stern expression, she kept her head slightly bowed. Speaking very quietly, she asked, "Reverend Mother, with your permission, I would like to retire to my room if I may to freshen up."

"By all means, dear child, take your time. And we'll see you back here at ten fifteen. Oh, by the way, Consuella, Father Martine, your father and I were hoping to have a discussion with you on an unrelated topic. But time, I'm afraid, is against us. No matter. Maybe we'll have an opportunity when this morning's meeting is concluded. Now run along and make yourself pretty."

"Thank you, Reverend Mother."

As Consuella left the dining room, Sister Maria couldn't help but notice she hadn't forgotten to bring the envelope with her.

Sister Lucia decided to assist Sister Agostina, who was now busy in the kitchen. When she entered, Sister Agostina exclaimed, "Oh my goodness, I almost forgot. Thank you, Sister. Your presence has just reminded me of something very important."

With that, she dashed from the kitchen and headed for the table in the hall. There, she retrieved a large Manila envelope. Proudly marching into the dining room, she spotted Sister Maria. Making her way over she presented the envelope to her, announcing, "Mother Superior, this arrived a short while ago by special messenger. I felt it my duty to bring it to you at once."

Sister Maria, taking the envelope, could see it was addressed to all three of Consuella's guardians. Placing it on the table, she turned to her two companions. And in a weary voice, she exclaimed, "This is all we need, another set of proposals. Dear Lord in heaven, please, if it be your will, send me a sign—anything at all that might give me some indication, even a hint, that this day will eventually end just like any other. That's all I ask. Thank you, Lord."

Carlota, noticing Sister Maria's frustration, decided to give her some encouragement. "I have to congratulate you on the way you handled the situation just now. For the life of me, I really am puzzled by Consuella's behaviour. It's so unlike her. Is there anything I can do to assist?"

"There is, Carlota. I know you hadn't planned on staying for our meeting. I would appreciate it if you could. Not knowing what's in store for the next instalment of this drama, I may need your support."

"Of course I will stay."

With that, Violetta and her father approached. Alberto addressed both of them. "Dear Sister Maria, Carlota, whenever my daughter and I hear that individual's name, it still causes us some discomfort. So if we may be excused, we will take our leave."

Francesco, Antonio, Pietro, and Father Martine joined them. Francesco then spoke to both of them. "Violetta, Alberto, all of us here fully understand your reason for not wishing to remain for what is about to follow. We are all very grateful for your presence here this morning. Have a safe journey, and I hope to see both of you very soon."

Everyone present bid farewell to father and daughter.

Father Martine then decided a brisk walk was in order. "Ladies, gentlemen, I am going to take a brief stroll. Anyone care to join me?"

They all, except Antonio, declined. He responded, "Why certainly, Father. A breath of fresh air will do us both a world of good."

When they were alone, Antonio enquired, "Would it be reasonable to assume, following the drama of the last hour or so, no discussions took place between yourselves and Consuella?"

"Unfortunately no, though Sister Maria did mention to her that, after our meeting, we'd like to discuss an unrelated topic. The main task now facing you and Francesco is to make your case and convince her your proposals are sound and reasonable. The three of us will of course give you all the support we possibly can."

"Thank you, Father. I'm pretty sure we're going to need it."

As they continued walking, Antonio, in a very casual manner, remarked, "I see you were up to your old tricks again last night."

Father Martine responded with that innocent look of his. "Antonio, I'm deeply hurt and quite upset that you could say such a thing."

"Oh come now, Father. The last time you were hurt was on a football field. You know exactly what I'm talking about."

"Could it perhaps be something I may have said in the restaurant?"

"It's not so much what you said; it was more the way you were orchestrating Pietro's interrogation of Francesco and myself."

"'Orchestrating'. What an appropriate turn of phrase. You always did have a way with words. Oh all right then. Yes, I suppose you could say I was conducting that minor production."

"I know I'm going to regret asking. Is there any way you could enlighten me as to the motives behind these manoeuvres of yours?"

"It was yesterday evening before you picked us up, I decided to pose some of these questions with Pietro. I suggested he put them to the two of you in the restaurant."

"Your reasons?"

"Quite simple really. Following my discussions with you yesterday afternoon, I decided it would be better if he was asking some of the questions. Knowing most of the answers you were likely to give, I just thought he would feel more involved and be totally on my side in our discussions with Sister Maria. My objective, I'm happy to say, has been achieved. I now have two willing allies, which makes me slightly more comfortable, especially with all the intrigue surrounding Consuella and this Don Barcese. Isn't he the character you spoke of yesterday?"

"The very one, Father."

"Goodness me, who would have thought back then this creature may now have the capacity to cause such mischief, though I'm reasonably confident when she hears your exciting proposals, there shouldn't be any further need for us to concern ourselves with this Don Barcese."

"Thank you, Father. As usual, you have an answer for everything. And before you say anything, that remark was meant as a compliment."

"Antonio, I know you meant it no other way. So I will gladly accept it as such. Now I think it's time for us to return. Would you agree?"

"Of course, Father."

With that, the two of them went back inside and joined the others.

CHAPTER 27

The Dining Room

As Antonio and Father Martine rejoined the others, they were somewhat relieved to see everyone, including Consuella, was present.

Father Martine addressed the gathering. "Friends, we have come to the main purpose of our presence here this morning. During our discussions, should anyone wish to ask a question or make a point, please feel free to do so. You may remain seated for the duration, as I would like to keep the proceedings as friendly and informal as possible. Now, before Antonio and Francesco give us their proposals, Sister Maria wants to say a few words."

"Thank you, Father. First of all, whatever the outcome, Sister Lucia will have no future role. She made it known to me her wish was to resume teaching our young students here in Milan. Having given the matter some thought, I decided to grant this request. As you all know, the past two and a half years, Sister Lucia has acted as Consuella's chaperone. Not only that; she was friend, wardrobe assistant, nurse, doctor, and trusted confidant as well. Dear Sister Lucia, on behalf of us all, I would like to thank you most sincerely for everything you've done. It was quite extraordinary. I know the children will be greatly excited to see you among them once more. So, from all of us here, best wishes for your future and thank you thank you so very much."

Sister Lucia, showing her appreciation, just smiled in that modest way of hers.

"Now secondly, we were hoping to have a brief meeting with yourself Consuella to give you our thoughts on aspects of the proposals Antonio and Francesco are about to share with us. Unfortunately, that opportunity has passed. There is, however, one thing I would like to add. And I can't stress this strongly enough. Antonio stated unequivocally, for the project to move ahead successfully, it would require your willing participation and consent."

With that, Consuella, for the first time since she arrived, looked over in his direction, "Why thank you, Antonio. That was most considerate of you."

Smiling back, he replied, "You're welcome, Consuella."

Father Martine, thanking Sister Maria, invited Antonio and Francesco to outline their plans. "Now, gentlemen, please in your own time, give us your thoughts."

Antonio took everyone through the proposals. Most of the time, he directed his comments specifically towards Consuella.

When he got to the part dealing with the offers from other European cities, she interrupted him. "You mean to tell me you've had these offers for some months past and decided not to inform me."

"That's correct."

"Antonio, if this is your way of getting my willing participation, I feel somewhat disappointed."

Sister Maria could sense a storm brewing, and they hadn't even come to the part dealing with America.

Antonio, ignoring Consuella's reaction, decided to press on.

As he outlined the reasons behind their postponement of the offers from the United States, Consuella almost exploded. "You mean to tell me you took a decision of this magnitude without consulting anyone."

"No, on the contrary, I spoke at length with Francesco. He put up a most persuasive argument. This led me to the decision I took, which I'm sure you'll agree is in your best interest."

She was now practically shouting, "Francesco is a voice coach, for goodness sakes. What would he know about American opera?"

Everyone around the table was absolutely appalled. Any hopes they may have had for an agreeable outcome seemed to be truly dashed.

Sister Maria, now absolutely outraged, demanded, "You will apologise at once to Francesco for that insulting remark."

"Reverend Mother, it's my career we're discussing. I don't feel inclined to apologise to anyone."

Her father intervened. "Consuella, you are my daughter. I demand you show respect for those of us gathered around this table. You are shaming nobody but yourself by these remarks."

"When other people show respect for me, I will respond appropriately."

Father Martine, trying to rescue what was now becoming an impossible situation, intervened. "Consuella, you of all people should know everyone around this table has your best interest at heart, in particular Antonio and Francesco. Surely you can't have forgotten the dedication and the hard work they've put in over these past number of years to bring you to where you are today."

"Yes that's true. And I believe they were sufficiently rewarded for their efforts. I now have to ask myself, do Antonio and Francesco have the necessary breadth of vision to take my career to the next level? What I've heard so far doesn't exactly fill me with confidence. However, I am more than willing to consider any other proposals they may wish to present."

For several moments, no one spoke or reacted in any way. Father Martine glanced around the room. He noted the shocked expressions on the faces of everyone except Francesco. He didn't seem to be to bothered in the least by her emotional outburst.

Antonio then stood up, signalling to all present he was going to say something of some importance. "My contract, or agreement if you like, draws to a close in two days' time. Consuella has four more concerts to perform. All necessary preparations are in place. This is not a proposal. I've decided as of now to resign with immediate effect my managerial position, including my guardianship role. There are two sets of proposals on the table. When I take my leave, I suggest you take the time available to study and debate their contents among yourselves."

Addressing Sister Maria, Pietro, and Father Martine, he said, "Dear friends, I would like to take this opportunity to sincerely thank you for the faith and trust you placed in me. Not once did you question my decision-making. At all times it was comforting to know I had your unconditional support. For me that was something very special."

Father Martine, his voice thick with emotion, replied, "Antonio, my dear boy, I know I speak for the three of us. Never, not for even one solitary moment, did we doubt your integrity and commitment. It truly was commendable."

Antonio next spoke to Sister Lucia. "Well, Sister, regardless of the outcome here today, it appears your role in this exciting adventure is drawing to a close. I'm having great difficulty finding the appropriate words to describe what it was you meant to Francesco and myself. You did everything we asked of you and more. I wish you every success in your next important assignment. If you take care of your pupils even half as much as you did Consuella, they will indeed be most fortunate. From the bottom of my heart, thank you.

"Carlota, what can I say? You were always kind and ever so gracious. This is something I will never forget.

"Now to my companion and brother in arms, the title 'voice coach' does you a great disservice. You were much more than that. What was achieved could not have come about without your tireless efforts. Checking acoustics, pestering conductors—these tasks you performed with determination and total commitment. I would like to echo Father Martine's comments from last night. I pray the good Lord grants me the favour of seeing you conduct your own orchestra, hopefully some time in the not-too-distant future."

Consuella was sitting quite still, wondering if he was going to ignore her and leave.

Looking in her direction, he spoke what he believed would be his last words to her. "Well, Consuella, it seems our journey has reached its end. I feel rather sad that it's ending in, let's say unexpected circumstances. I want you to know everything I did, I did with your best interests at heart. All that's left for me to say is, I wish you every success in the years to come. Whatever happens, no matter where you find yourself, just remember this talent, this gift you posses is very special and unique. Embrace it. Keep it close. Protect it as you would a precious jewel. And please, I beg you, be on your guard and don't let others exploit it for their own selfish ends."

Moving around to her side of the table and leaning down, he took her hand in his and gave it a very gentle kiss.

Consuella, now in turmoil, was unable to speak the words she was feeling in her heart. *'Oh, Antonio, why oh why did you not speak like this when you returned from Verona? Why did you not tell me then you loved me?'*

He looked into her eyes once more, gave her a loving smile, and bowed graciously. He then walked to the door.

Father Martine practically leapt from his chair. "Antonio, please wait. I'll show you out."

As he reached Antonio, he turned to the others. "Please, don't anybody do or say anything until I return."

In the hallway, Father Martine guided Antonio towards the library. Closing the door behind them, he paced up and down, not saying a word. Finally he spoke in a voice filled with frustration. "How on God's good earth could such an outcome be possible? By now, I expected our plans to be fully agreed and implemented. Instead we have an unmitigated disaster on our hands. Has Consuella completely lost her mind?"

"I wouldn't say she's lost her mind, but I've absolutely no doubt she is being influenced in a malign way."

"Can you enlighten me?"

"Well it's obvious Don Barcese has a bigger starring role in this drama than we first suspected. Consuella more or less admitted as much. Even if only half of what Francesco told you is true, then yes, you do have a disaster on your hands."

"Antonio, what should we do now to bring some sense to this madness?"

"Oh, I'm sure you'll think of something. As for me, I've no further role to play in any decisions yourselves or Consuella make. I think I made that very clear just a few moments ago."

"I'm fully aware of what you said. I just thought it was a ploy on your part to make Consuella come to her senses."

"I'm afraid not. You know me well enough by now, Father. When I take a decision, I generally stick with it. As soon as I walk out this door, I will be closing a most interesting and memorable chapter on a part of my life that's had its ups and downs. But there were many happy occasions, and I'm truly grateful for that."

"What are you going to do? Surely you'll need to make some sort of plan."

"You could say I have half a plan."

"You have half a plan?"

"Yes. I'm going to take myself down to the central ticket office and book the next available train for Vienna."

"What's the other half of your plan?"

"I didn't tell you this, but sometime ago, I received an offer from the State Opera Company of Vienna. They invited me to become director of opera. At the time, I didn't mention it because I felt there was no point in bothering you with irrelevant details on an offer I had no intention of accepting. I sent a courteous reply declining the position. Back then I fully intended to renew my existing contract with Consuella. I received another letter. It was brief and to the point. It simply stated the position was being held open until Monday the third of October. To answer your question, the other half of my plan is to accept the offer. That's of course if it's still available."

"My goodness me, Antonio. You do realise the significance of this day.

"I do indeed. That day is Consuella's twenty-first birthday."

"Finally, what about your feelings for Consuella? Where does that part of your relationship now stand?"

"I still have strong feelings. In fact, as I finished speaking with her, we exchanged glances. And for a very brief moment, I sensed something between us. I suppose the most sensible option for me right now is to put aside all thoughts of what might have been. I once learned, when one strives for something that is unattainable; such endeavours, in most instances, end in disappointment."

"How profound. Who taught you that?"

"As a matter of fact, it was you."

"Antonio, I'm terribly sorry and greatly saddened about the way things have turned out. Promise me you'll take good care of yourself. Keep in touch and visit me often. I've no more to say except thank you, thank you, my son." With that, he reached out and gave his former pupil an emotional hug.

As they shook hands, Antonio replied, "Don't worry, Father. I'll be fine. And I promise I will keep in touch."

With that, he walked out the door and left the convent for what he believed would be the last time.

Father Martine returned to the dining room. He could see no one had moved. Taking his seat, he looked around. All he could see were gloomy faces. "Would anyone care to make a comment or say something meaningful?"

Sister Lucia was first to speak. "Please, Reverend Mother, as I've no further role in any discussions, may I be excused?"

"Of course, Sister. And once more, thank so much for all you've done."

Sister Lucia stood up. Her final words were for Consuella. "Consuella, I wish you well next week. And I hope and pray you have continuing success into the future."

Consuella emotionally replied, "Thank you, Sister. I am truly grateful and deeply indebted to you for everything you've done. All your many acts of kindness I will remember with great affection. Thank you so very much."

With that, Consuella stood up. She reached out and tearfully hugged Sister Lucia. Everyone could see this was a sad parting for both of them.

As Sister Lucia took her leave, Consuella sat down.

Sister Maria, even more annoyed, made the following remark: "It's a great pity you were unable to express similar sentiments as Antonio was about to depart. Who knows? Maybe we wouldn't be in this unfortunate position right now."

Everyone sat quietly. Nobody seemed inclined to say or do anything. The mood was now tense and sombre.

Father Martine decided someone needed to speak. "Well, dear friend, as Consuella's father, I think it only fair you be given the opportunity to speak your mind."

"I am almost too ashamed to speak. Earlier this morning, I thought we would be celebrating the next stage of my daughter's career. Instead, I am sitting here not knowing what is going to happen next. This indeed is most embarrassing."

"And you, Sister, is there anything you wish to add?"

"I've said all I need to say. When I leave this room, I will make immediate preparations for my journey back to Verona. I will not be attending any performance, nor for that matter the birthday celebration, because you see, Consuella, from here on, what you do is no longer my concern."

Consuella just sat silently with her head bowed.

"Yourself, Carlota, would you like to say something?"

"Thank you, Father. I'd rather not. I've never really played a role in any past negotiations and feel it would be rather inappropriate for me to comment."

Finally, Father Martine invited Francesco to express any thoughts he might have and to share whether he was willing to carry on in his current role even without Antonio's presence.

"Well, I don't think it's my place to offer an opinion as to what should happen next," Francesco began. "I believe Consuella made it very clear with her earlier remarks that she doesn't value my opinion very highly. To answer your second question, it was Antonio who engaged my services. My loyalties will always be first and foremost to him. Without his involvement, I have no desire to be part of any future arrangement. Consuella, it matters not to me if you find what I have to say offensive. I'm going to say it anyway."

She stiffened slightly in anticipation.

He continued, "Today, in this very room, you have done a great disservice to Antonio. More tragically, you have done a far greater disservice to yourself. Foolishly or naively, you rejected the one person who would have assisted you in achieving even greater success. You have thrown all this away. Why? You don't have to answer. Maybe it's something you might wish to discuss with Sister Maria and company after Carlota and I take our leave."

With that, he stood up. Carlota joined him.

"Consuella, despite everything that's been said, Carlota and I genuinely wish you every success in the future. We will follow your progress with interest."

"Sister Maria, Pietro, Father Martine, it was a great pleasure working on your behalf these past few years. I've enjoyed our friendship enormously, and I promise to stay in touch."

Carlota endorsed his remarks with her own comments. "I too have enjoyed our friendship. I'm happy to say I will be seeing Sister Lucia often. The next time we meet, I sincerely hope it will be under somewhat happier circumstances."

He and Carlota said their goodbyes and shook hands with everyone, including Consuella. Francesco was somewhat relieved he wouldn't be involved in what was to follow.

With their departure, Consuella and her three guardians sat silently for a few moments.

Father Martine, for the second time, found himself having to take the initiative. "Well, I suppose we should study these documents and see if we can salvage something from this calamity."

Sister Maria, in a serious tone, answered, "As I stated earlier, I will play no further part in these proceedings. I'm sorry to say this, Pietro, but your daughter has exhausted my patience."

"Regrettably, I find myself agreeing with you. I too have no desire to participate in any further discussions. I'm sorry, Father, but that's my position. So if you'll excuse me, I will take my leave with Sister Maria. Before I go, there are two final points I need to make.

"Consuella, it's my earnest wish that, one day in the future, you might realise the great disservice you have done to Sister Maria; Father Martine; and myself, your only parent. I hope and pray you'll regret the shameful manner you adopted in dismissing the proposals of Antonio and Francesco."

With that, he stood up. Sister Maria joined him. They both left the dining room, leaving a frustrated Father Martine and a very dejected Consuella behind. He focused his gaze on the two envelopes. She just sat there in a silent passive state.

Looking at her, he began by saying, "Consuella, I want you to pay close attention because, as things stand, I might be the only friend you have left."

"Dear Father, before you continue, there is something I would like you to clarify, if you can?"

"I will do my very best. Please, say what you have to say."

"The day before Antonio travelled to Verona, he told me it was of some importance. And on his return, he was hoping to have wonderful surprising news for me. Is it possible you may be able to shed some light on what it was he was referring to?"

"That's an interesting question, Consuella. Why do you ask?"

"Well it was during his absence I may have allowed myself to be influenced by the gentleman spoken of earlier."

"You mean this Don Barcese character?"

"Unfortunately yes, that's the person I'm referring to. If Antonio had not made that journey, under no circumstances would a meeting have taken place, well certainly not without Antonio's presence. If I hadn't met with this person, then it's most likely today's events might have turned out a lot differently. Sadly, I now find myself in a situation, as you so aptly put it, without friends."

"Consuella, you still don't know the reason for Antonio's trip to Verona?"

"I certainly thought it had something to do with our growing fondness for each other. I was probably a little shy and reluctant to ask. I suppose I wanted to avoid any possible disappointment in case I was mistaken."

"Oh dear me, if only you had asked, how very different today might have turned out. The reason Antonio came to Verona was to ask Sister Maria, myself, and particularly your father for permission to seek your willing consent to become his fiancée."

Her reaction was immediate. He noticed her eyes were tearful. Yet she just about managed not to cry. Also, the colour in her cheeks changed to a slight crimson.

"Are you okay, Consuella?"

"Yes, yes, Father. I'm fine. I'm fine."

Feeling somewhat awkward himself, he continued on as best he could. "Consuella, I would much rather it was Sister Maria or your father having this conversation with you right now. In affairs of the heart, I'm sorry to say I'm not much of an expert."

"Father, believe me, you're doing fine. Please carry on, please?"

"What I relayed just now, does it surprise you in any way?"

"Yes and no. You see, when he set out for Verona, I thought his mission was something close to what you've just explained. But on his return, he never raised the subject. I said as much in my conversation with Mother Superior. If only she had enlightened me or even given a hint, who knows where we might be right now?"

"We shouldn't blame Sister Maria too much. I think we're all at fault in one way or another. When he departed Verona, he did so with great enthusiasm. In fact, before he left, he purchased a most appropriate gift for you."

"Oh my goodness, how kind and thoughtful."

"Yes indeed, how kind and thoughtful. On his return to Milan, noticing the change in your demeanour, he decided to wait for an appropriate moment to make his feelings known. On our arrival, we were truly surprised to discover no discussions had taken place. How very sad it is, particularly for you and Antonio.

"He shared some of his thoughts with me. He felt you had become somewhat distant and aloof. I discussed the situation with Sister Maria, your father, and even Francesco. We came to the conclusion it was probably just nervousness on your part, what with the final concerts and your coming of age. We advised him the most appropriate course was to finalise the negotiations and get the agreement in place. We intended to then speak with you and establish exactly what your feelings were. We assumed your reaction would be positive. That being the case, we then intended to convey these happy tidings to him.

"The final part of our plan was to be executed on the night of your twenty-first birthday. Antonio was to present his gift and make his proposal in front of us all as witnesses. We would have, of course, reacted with surprise but applaud enthusiastically nonetheless. Sadly, with what has transpired, it's most regrettable nothing is now going to work out as we genuinely expected."

For a few moments, neither of them said anything. He gave her as much time as he deemed suitable to allow her take in these almost tragic revelations. In a caring tone, he then asked, "Your thoughts, Consuella?

"Oh it may be nothing, but when he came over to me and took my hand in his, we looked into each other's eyes. For that brief moment, if he had asked me there and then to run away with him, I'm absolutely certain I would have willingly done so without any hesitation whatsoever."

Father Martine just listened. Although by his own admission, he was no expert in affairs of the heart, there was no doubt in his mind she was being sincere, he was fully convinced she truly loved Antonio. "You know, Consuella, Antonio and you are probably for me the closest thing to having my own children. I feel very privileged to have played some part in your lives. I've watched the two of you growing up. It saddens me to witness and be a participant in this unfortunate state of affairs. I promise, I will do all I can to bring about a reconciliation."

Consuella, now feeling somewhat emotional, responded, "Father, do you have any insight into Antonio's feelings towards me?"

"This is the best way I can answer your question. When we left this room, he described for me what he experienced the moment he came over to you."

"Would it be possible to share it with me? If you're not comfortable with something you feel you should not divulge, I quite understand."

"On the contrary, the feelings and emotions he expressed were exactly the same as you've described just now."

"And what were those?"

"Goodness gracious me, Consuella, you poor innocent child. Do I have to draw you a diagram? Can you not see it? The two of you experienced the same emotions simultaneously. In countless plays and novels this is described as falling in love. Is it possible you've grasped the essence of what I've told you just now?"

"Indeed, I have, Father. And thank you for your perceptive insight. These revelations and your promise of assistance fills me with some hope for the future."

"Okay then, now that you're aware of how things currently stand, may I suggest we study these proposals and see where we go from here?"

"As you wish, Father." She picked up the first envelope and handed it to him. "Please, Father, I'd like you to open it."

Opening the envelope, he laid the contents on the table. He could see the proposals were quite detailed and comprehensive. "This document is most interesting and, I believe, well constructed. It's from a person by the name of Salvatore Giordano. Does this name mean anything to you?"

"Yes. This gentleman is a competent manager and, as far as I know, has a reputation for being honest and diligent."

"Any negatives?"

"I wouldn't call them negatives as such. The fact is, he doesn't represent any of the major performers and confines his activities mainly to Lombardy."

"Well then, maybe he'd be a good choice. After all, Antonio had no prior experience before he took on the role of managing your career."

"That's very true, but he did have tremendous support from yourself and Francesco."

"Okay. Let's not dismiss this proposal just yet and see what the other envelope contains."

"Very good, Father," she replied as she handed the second envelope over.

Slightly taken by surprise, he opened it and could see it contained two identical documents. Placing the first one on the table, he perused the other. From his reading, he concluded the substance seemed to be very much in her favour. With a puzzled look, he enquired, "I take it you are familiar with what's contained in these proposals?"

"Yes, Father. I've studied them in detail and am interested in any thoughts you might have?"

"My thoughts are irrelevant. However, my question is, why is this Don Barcese being so generous? From what I've heard, he has a reputation for drawing up one-sided contracts with clauses and conditions that are always more advantageous to himself."

"I questioned him on this very issue, and his reply was that I had a very special gift and he was the best person to assist me in showcasing this talent to a wider international audience."

As she was speaking, Father Martine happened to glance at the proposal and discovered, to his horror, two signatures—hers and Don Barcese's. Quickly picking up the other document, he could see identical signatures on this one also. Handing it to her, he asked, "I recognise these as your signatures. Can you tell me when you signed them and why?"

"Earlier this morning in my room following the adjournment. I thought it would somehow strengthen my hand for what was to follow."

"So, when the meeting reconvened, would I be correct in assuming you had no intention of allowing the contract with Antonio and Francesco to proceed?"

"No, Father, honestly that was not my intention. It was when he got to the part concerning America; I suppose I just lost my self-control. I'm sorry, Father, but that's the best answer I can give."

"Well, no matter. What's done is done. I'm sure even Don Barcese must know his proposals have no validity whatsoever. As you are not yet twenty-one, they would need your father's signature, as well as mine or Sister Maria's, for them to be recognised as legally binding."

"Not quite so, Father."

"Consuella, am I missing something? And if I am, can you please explain?"

"The day after tomorrow, the third of October, as you know, I celebrate my twenty-first birthday. That's the day I reach my majority, or coming of age if you like."

"Yes, yes. I know all that. Can you just get to the point of what it is you have to say?"

"Although this is the day I celebrate my birthday, the circumstances surrounding my actual birth-date are somewhat different."

Father Martine, now with a concerned look on his face, replied, "Please continue, Consuella."

"On the day I was born, the delivery left my mother extremely ill and very weak. I, too, was quite sickly. The doctor and the nursing staff were greatly concerned. Without her seeing or even holding me, I was immediately taken to intensive care. Before they did so, as a precaution they registered my birth and had me baptised. In the meantime, my mother was nursed around the clock. Gradually her condition improved, as did mine. After five days had passed, the doctor decided it was now safe for me to be reunited with my mother.

"My father, my aunt, and Sister Maria were present when the nurse brought me into the room. She placed me in my mother's arms, this being the first occasion for her to see and hold me. She wept with joy and tearfully announced to those present, 'Today is the first time for me to see and hold my precious Consuella. For me, this is the day of her birth, and for all the years to come, this is the day we will celebrate her birthday.'"

"Pray tell, Consuella, what date is that?"

"That date is the third of October. So you see, I was actually born on the twenty-ninth of September. This is the date I was baptised and registered."

After taking a few moments to absorb these revelations, Father Martine responded, "Consuella, you do realise this changes everything?"

"In what way, Father?"

"Well, to begin with, you don't need my approval, or for that matter Sister Maria's and even your father's, for any decisions you make concerning your career. Regarding these proposals, I can only ask what your intentions are. What really puzzles me is, why did not your father and Sister Maria take cognisance of this during our protracted and difficult discussions?"

"Who knows, Father? I can only suppose, with the passage of time, the third of October just merged with my birth-date."

"Consuella, as I stated earlier, this changes everything. I'm not going to express an opinion as to what you should do next. Whatever decision you make, I earnestly hope and pray it's the correct one. A final point if I may, would it be correct for me to assume you are likely to take a decision in favour of Don Barcese?"

"Yes, Father, I would prefer it was otherwise. If at some time in the future you were successful in prevailing upon Antonio to reconsider, I would then immediately remove myself from this contract."

Slightly more encouraged, Father Martine stood up. "Time is moving on. I'm sure you still have a lot to do. In the meantime, I will speak with Sister Maria and your father and see if I can convince them to stay."

"Thank you, Father. I appreciate that and also your thoughtfulness, not just now but in the past as well."

"Oh one last thing, if I am successful in persuading Sister Maria to delay her departure, do all you can to avoid her presence. I wouldn't like the current state of affairs to deteriorate any further."

"I promise, I'll do my best to avoid her."

Leaving the dining room, Father Martine went in search of Sister Maria. In the hallway, he met Sister Agostina and asked if she knew where Sister Maria and Pietro might be.

"Señor Pietro has already departed. And as far as I know, Mother Superior is in her room."

"Thank you, Sister. Would you be good enough and ask her to join me in the library?"

"Of course, Father. And please, I do hope you won't think me impertinent. But is everything all right?"

"Why do you ask, Sister?"

"As Señor Pietro was leaving, she informed him she was going to her room to pack her bag. He replied he was doing the same and would return later to collect her."

"Oh I'm sure that's not the case. If you just let her know I need to have a word, I'm sure everything will be fine."

Joining him in the library, Sister Maria immediately challenged him, "Father, I hope you didn't request my presence here to try and persuade me to reconsider the statement I made earlier?"

"Sister Maria, I of all people know such an exercise would be less than useless. So no. That's not it at all."

"If it's not that, then please explain. What is it you wish to say?"

"Thank you, Sister, I'll be very brief." He relayed the details of his discussion with Consuella concerning the contracts and her revelations surrounding the circumstances of her birth. He concluded by saying,

"Right now, I find myself wondering why Pietro and your good self didn't enlighten me in relation to these important facts?"

"Your question deserves a straight answer. I'll do my best. Several times during our discussions, the thought did cross my mind to broach the subject of her actual age. But out of consideration for her father's feelings and hers as well, I did not. I decided to do so would most likely cause further trauma to both father and daughter.

"I'm sure you're aware I was a witness to the circumstances surrounding this difficult period in their lives. Although Sophia was overjoyed to be reunited with her daughter, who was now making steady progress, sadly however her own health didn't improve. In fact, she never fully recovered, and it is probable the difficult birth of Consuella might have been a contributing factor eventually leading to her untimely death.

"I realise now I should have relayed this information to you at an earlier stage. Please accept my apologies for the oversight."

"I understand," Father Martine replied. "No apology necessary. In light of these circumstances, would it be possible the two of you might reconsider your position and stay for her birthday celebration and one performance?"

"Before I answer, may I ask you something?"

"Of course."

"Has she taken a decision regarding her future?"

"She has. And I'm sorry to say, with the limited options available, she is definitely going to choose Don Barcese."

"Oh my goodness, what have we done? If Francesco is correct in his assessment, then we have a duty to protect Consuella in any way we can. Father, I will change my decision if you can convince her to allow you to speak with this individual as soon as possible.

"Under the circumstances, I think it best Pietro and myself have no further involvement. You still have her trust, and I believe she'd be willing to have you guiding her, at least until we find some way of achieving a more satisfactory outcome."

"Thank you, Sister. I will do as you suggest. If you'll excuse me, I'll go over and let Pietro know what we've decided. And just in case you're worried, I won't be discussing any of the circumstances surrounding her birth.

"Finally, I advised her to avoid you at all costs. Should the two of you happen to bump into each other, please don't be too hard on her."

With these parting words, Father Martine left. Fortunately, Emilio was still on hand and was available to drive him to the hotel. On the journey over, he wondered, was it possible he might well be the architect of this potential catastrophe?

Maybe that fateful day when Antonio came to visit, perhaps he should have spent more time reminiscing about past times. And have allowed his young protégé to depart without involving him in his grand ambition.

He banished the thought and decided he would now have to do everything he could to somehow bring about a satisfactory conclusion, regardless of how long it was going to take.

At the hotel, he briefed Pietro on Sister Maria's change of heart and was successful in persuading him to do likewise. He then decided to call on Francesco, to see if he might have some further news.

CHAPTER 28

Antonio Calls on Francesco

Having sent a cablegram to Vienna informing the Vienna State Opera Company of his pending arrival, Antonio then went to the ticket office and made a reservation for the overnight train to Vienna. With these tasks completed, he decided to visit Francesco and brief his friend on his immediate plans.

"Welcome, Antonio. Come on in, and let's see if we can make some sense of these extraordinary events. Take a seat. I'll let Carlota know you're here."

As Carlota joined them, Francesco continued, "With your sudden departure, things certainly didn't improve. If anything, they deteriorated even further. I decided to play no further part and told them so. Carlota and I left soon after, and what happened then, I have no idea."

"You know, maybe I shouldn't be so terribly surprised at the way things have turned out."

"How so?"

"Well, from the first day I returned, Consuella's behaviour was a little strange. Even so, I certainly wasn't expecting this. There's no doubt in my mind Don Barcese has influenced her in some way.

"Still yet, I believe the fault really lies with me. Why didn't I just wait a few more days and speak with the others when they arrived? If I had done that, things might have turned out a lot differently."

Carlota joined in the conversation. "Antonio, you're not to blame. Consuella is an adult. She should have known better. Goodness knows, yourself and Francesco warned her about this individual on numerous occasions."

Francesco added, "As I see it, she only has herself to blame. Under the circumstances, when you decided to leave, I believe you made the right choice. So now tell me, have you made any plans?"

"I've decided to take my chances with the offer from Austria, assuming of course it's still available. I'm taking the overnight train tonight. I've already sent them a cable requesting a representative be there to meet me on my arrival. If everything works out as planned and we can agree on terms, I will take up the position without any hesitation.

"With no future role for me in Consuella's life or career, I think it's best I leave Milan as soon as possible. That way, I can put all of this behind me. Hopefully, my memories of Consuella and what might have been will fade if I follow a separate path in another country."

"Antonio, I fully understand the sense of hurt and disappointment you must be feeling right now. I know Father Martine will miss you greatly, as will Carlota and I. We would just like to wish you every success in whatever the future brings."

"Thank you both. I too will miss the many happy occasions we've shared. Now, Francesco, may I ask what future plans do you have? Are you going to carry on coaching aspiring artistes?"

"For the moment, yes. With two daughters to support, this activity will be my main source of income for the immediate future. But I'm determined to pursue my ambition of forming my own orchestra. When that day comes, I hope you'll do me the honour of attending my opening night."

"I promise, no matter where or when, it would be a great privilege for me to attend."

As they stood up and warmly embraced, Antonio asked one last favour of Francesco.

"Of course, Antonio, anything; just name it."

Taking the necklace from his coat pocket, he handed it to Francesco. "As you know, this was my gift of betrothal to Consuella. Would you possibly take care of it for me?"

"Of course Antonio. Don't worry. I will keep it very safe."

Thanking him, Antonio then finished by saying to both of them. "Our parting saddens me greatly. I will always cherish our friendship, and I promise to stay in touch and keep you updated on my progress."

With those concluding words, he departed. As he did so, he wondered when and under what circumstances he would meet his friends again.

CHAPTER 29

Father Martine Calls on Francesco

Father Martine rang the bell; the door was opened by Carlota.

"Welcome Father, I must say I wasn't expecting to see you so soon after the events earlier. Do please come in. I will let Francesco know you are here."

"Thank you, Carlota. I certainly wasn't expecting to be here either, but there's something I need to discuss with Francesco. By the way, how are the twins? Good I hope."

"They're getting big and bold, and their father spoils them no end."

"But, Carlota, isn't that what fathers do? Anyway, as long as they inherit their mother's good looks and charm, they'll be just fine."

She just smiled. "Father, please take yourself into the sitting room. I will bring some refreshments and let Francesco know you're here.

A few moments later, Francesco entered. "My goodness, I seem to be very popular all of a sudden. You're my second visitor today. Antonio was here and left not less than half an hour ago."

"How was he? Did he discuss his plans?"

"He did indeed. He's already been to the ticket office and will leave tonight on the overnight train to Vienna."

Father Martine, now visibly upset, replied, "How sad, how very sad. Who would have thought earlier this morning this day was going to end in such drama? You know if we put music to it, we'd have ourselves a tragic opera."

"Indeed, Father, indeed. Under the circumstances, though, I believe he made the correct decision."

229

Just then, Carlota entered. Laying the tray down, she noticed the two men's grim expressions. "Darling, is everything all right? You both look quite tense."

"Please join us, dear. I would like you to hear what Father has to say."

Father Martine gave them a brief update on what had taken place following their departure. "The most alarming part is she intends appointing Don Barcese manager. This is my reason for being here right now. I value your judgement, Francesco, so I would like your opinion on what course of action I should now take."

Francesco responded, "First of all, I need you to outline, in as much detail as you can, the exact circumstances you believe are guiding her in this calamitous direction?"

Father Martine briefed him thoroughly on the proposals and discussions between himself and Consuella. "What I've told you just now is as much as I can recall," he concluded. "So any thoughts on how best to proceed?"

"As I see it, there is probably not a lot we can do if she decides to appoint him. And from what you've told me, I would say she has already made that choice. I believe Sister Maria's suggestion is an excellent one. You should arrange a meeting as soon as possible. Consuella's presence will be absolutely essential. Your role will be that of concerned family friend, rather than guardian. Keep the two documents in your possession at all times during the discussions. This will be intimidating and should cause him some discomfort. Go through everything line by line. Challenge him at every opportunity. Insist the fee for his involvement be fixed at 10 per cent. Have it written into the contract you will be administering her financial affairs and under the terms he will be obliged to furnish a monthly progress report, including details regarding concert dates, venues, and performance fees.

Finally, for the meeting, time and place is of crucial importance. Your order has a monastery near here. This location would be ideal. It should give you a slight advantage. Arrange the discussions for as early as possible. This fellow is not an early riser. A morning conference won't be to his liking, and this should wrong-foot him somewhat.

"I have every confidence in your ability to carry out this task. Sister Maria's decision not to involve herself and Pietro any further is a wise one.

You acting alone on Consuella's behalf will ensure emotion plays no part in the proceedings. If you are successful in your efforts, at the very least, it should limit his influence to a certain degree."

Francesco concluded with a two-part question. "Do you agree with the suggestions? And how comfortable are you with taking on this difficult challenge?"

"What you've said just now is most sensible and well thought out. I will brief Consuella and ask her to make the necessary arrangements. Your faith in my ability I pray carries me through on the day. I will do everything possible to protect her interests. Now, before I leave, do either of you have any thoughts on their fractured relationship. Is their anything we can do?"

"For the moment, I think it's best Antonio proceeds with his plan. As the saying goes, absence makes the heart grow fonder. We're all aware of the affection they have for each other. Unfortunately, today's events have put considerable strain on the two of them. A brief period of separation may not be such a bad thing. It may give them an opportunity to realise their destiny is to share their future together. During this hopefully brief time frame, your task will be to guide and protect Consuella. For my part, I will keep in close contact with Antonio. An opportunity may present itself. If it does, we can then assist in bringing about a happy and lasting reconciliation. Under the circumstances, this is probably the best we can do."

Father Martine stood up. "Carlota, Francesco, please accept my heartfelt thanks for your time and patience. Your advice is gratefully accepted. Let's see if we can bring about a satisfactory conclusion as speedily as possible. Finally, before I take my leave, may I enquire, particularly in light of today's events, what are your future plans?"

"Oh I'll carry on coaching in the short term, although I suspect you are probably wondering if it is still my ambition to form my own orchestra. The answer is an emphatic yes, and I promise my very first performance will be dedicated to you. It would be a great honour if you were to attend my opening night."

"Francesco, I promise when that day comes, I'll make a special effort be there. Now, dear friends, if I may be excused, I'll call on Consuella and inform her of our plan. As soon as I have an outcome, I will contact you.

"You know, earlier this morning, Sister Maria implored the Almighty to give her some indication as to when this day was going to end. I'm beginning to realise I should have made the same prayer."

Carlota, trying to encourage him, replied, "Oh come now, Father. It's not that bad. Deep down, I suspect, you thrive on all this drama and intrigue. Now off you go and complete your mission."

Leaving Francesco's home, Father Martine travelled with Emilio back to the convent. It was now four o'clock in the afternoon. He was hoping this meeting with Consuella would be the final act in what had been a very dramatic day.

On his arrival, Sister Agostina was surprised to see him. "Please come in, Father. I will let Reverend Mother know you're here."

"Actually, it's Consuella I'm here to see. Would you be so kind and let her know I'm here? I promise I wont keep her too long."

He waited in the hallway.

When she arrived, he greeted her. "Consuella, I'm sorry for bothering you this late in the evening. But I need to discuss one or two issues concerning these proposals."

"Father, it's no bother at all. Let's go into the library. We'll have some privacy there."

He gave her the good news concerning her father and Sister Maria. He then briefed her on his conversation with Francesco and Carlota. "Consuella, if you're satisfied with these proposals and wish me to present them on your behalf, I will gladly do so. If, on the other hand, you don't, well then I'm afraid there's nothing more I can do."

Her response was not long in coming. "Father, I really do appreciate your efforts in persuading my father and Reverend Mother to change their mind. Regarding the other issue, I place myself completely in your capable hands."

"Excellent. Now, can you make contact with this fellow and arrange a meeting for eight o'clock tomorrow morning?"

"Father, I would prefer if this request were made by you personally. I feel it would carry more weight. Besides a journey by me to his residence this late in the evening would be somewhat inappropriate."

"Oh very well then. I've come this far. I suppose one more errant isn't going to kill me. I think it's best I hold on to these documents. Don't worry. I won't let them out of my sight. Now, if you give me his address, I'll be on my way. I will collect you at seven forty-five in the morning."

"Thank you, thank you, Father. One final question if I may?"

"Okay, but please be quick. I'm now getting very tired, and when I'm tired, I tend to get somewhat cranky."

"Oh, come now, Father. Why there isn't an angry bone in your body."

"Consuella, please could you just ask your question."

"Of course. I was just wondering, do you have any more news concerning Antonio?"

"Yes I do, and it saddens me to be the one telling you. Later tonight, he will leave Milan and travel to Vienna. For how long, I have no idea. Francesco Carlota and myself are of one mind. If some time in the future, a reconciliation were to become in any way probable, we would assist in every possible way to bring it about. There's really nothing more for me to say.

"Now, if you'll excuse me, I'll see if I can persuade this Don Barcese fellow to attend our meeting tomorrow."

Consuella, with tears in her eyes, replied, "Goodnight, Father. And yes, Antonio's sudden departure does indeed sadden me. I will miss him so much. I'm really quite upset and just can't find the words to say how sorry I am for the damage done today. Can you find it in your heart to forgive me?"

"There, there, Consuella. This is no time for tears. What's done is done. Now, take yourself off to your room and try not let anyone see you in this state. Get a good night's rest. I will call for you tomorrow as planned."

"I will do as you suggest, Father. And thank you thank you so much for everything you've done."

Leaving the library, he replied in a weary voice, "Don't thank me just yet, young lady. There's still a lot more to be done."

Getting into the auto-mobile, Father Martine thanked Emilio for his patience and gave him the directions. Thankful for the brief respite, he sat back and wondered what sort of reception he was likely to get from the great Don Barcese.

CHAPTER 30

Train Journey to Vienna

Arriving at the Milan Central railway station, Antonio observed the hustle and bustle of people meeting and greeting, while others were bidding farewell to family members and loved ones. Feeling a little sad and quite alone, he boarded the train for the fourteen-hour journey to Vienna. Just after he'd settled himself into his compartment, the train finally pulled out from the station. As it gathered speed, he sat by the window and watched the lights of the city fade into the distance.

His mind drifted back to the events that had taken place earlier in the day, especially the moment he had taken her hand in his. He wondered what emotions she might have experienced during the brief encounter. He decided, difficult though it might be, he would now have to erase this image from his mind permanently. Instead, he focused on the complimentary comments of Father Martine and Francesco. Their kind words at least gave him a sense he was now leaving Milan with a clear conscience and an untarnished reputation.

Two hours into the journey and with the realisation he had hardly eaten, his appetite returned. Feeling somewhat peckish he made his way to the dining car. There he joined another group of passengers. He had a pleasant meal and was rather surprised the wine list included a choice from Pietro's own vineyard. He encouraged his dining companions to accept his recommendations and was rather pleased when they took his advice.

As the train rumbled on, he found himself on first-name terms with his fellow dining companions. After the meal, they remained in the dining car enjoying a few glasses of wine. The conversation was wide ranging. The three hot topics were politics; religion; and, of course, the opera. Antonio enjoyed the diversion; it helped lift his spirits somewhat. After two pleasant hours of genial camaraderie, he bid his travelling companions goodnight, headed back to his compartment, settled down, and drifted off into a relatively peaceful night's sleep.

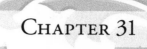

CHAPTER 31

Don Barcese's Town House, Late Evening

Having rang the bell and waiting for someone to answer, Father Martine couldn't help but notice the sheer grandeur of the place. He wondered, was the world of opera management so lucrative it allowed one to live in such opulence?

The door was opened by Henry. Never having met Father Martine before, he just stood there silently, waiting for him to speak.

"My name is Father Martine, and I need to speak with Don Barcese—that is if it's not too inconvenient?"

"I will see if the master is available. May I enquire, Father, what it is you wish to discuss?"

"Of course. I'd be most grateful if you could inform Don Barcese my business concerns Señorita Consuella Pellegrini."

"Very good, Father. Please follow me. I will show you into the drawing room and let the master know you are here."

Standing there gazing around the room, he could see it was even more impressive. A few minutes passed, and then the door suddenly opened, and Don Barcese breezed in.

"Father Martine, what a pleasure it is to finally meet you. Please take a seat. May I offer you some refreshments?"

"No thank you. I realise the hour is late, so I'll be as brief as possible. The purpose of my visit is to do with the documents you gave to Señorita Consuella earlier this morning. I would like to discuss the matter with you in more detail if you don't mind?"

"Why of course, Father. Please continue."

"Now would not be suitable. Rather, I'd like if you could meet with the of us; let's say eight o'clock tomorrow morning at our monastery, you know the one, it's just outside the city."

"May I be so bold in asking the reason for your involvement and your decision to convene this meeting at the other monastery?"

"Well, let's just say Don Barcese, I'll be there not so much as a guardian—more as a concerned family friend, if you like. The location ensures a degree of privacy for our discussions."

"Very good, Father Martine. I will of course make it my business to be there at the appointed hour. Is there anything else you wish to discuss?"

"No. That's all I need to say for now. So if I may be excused Don Barcese, I'll bid you a goodnight and be on my way."

As Don Barcese closed the door behind Father Martine, he was intrigued. Why the late evening visit? And why a meeting so early in the morning?

He wondered, was it possible the negotiations between Consuella and Señor Antonio had run into some difficulty? With this unexpected development, he decided the only option open to him was to wait for his forthcoming encounter with the friar.

He cast his mind back to the fortune teller and her comments concerning the seven of diamonds. Was it possible her predications were actually coming to pass? Was this Father Martine the difficult and formidable opponent she had spoken of?

Finally back at his hotel, Father Martine, on entering the restaurant, was surprised to see Pietro. He sat down opposite him and ordered some food.

Pietro looked at him and enquired, "You don't look too good. Are you all right?"

"Well, nothing that an Irish whisky won't fix."

Pietro called the waiter and ordered two large Jameson's. "If you don't mind, I think I'll join you."

As they sipped their drinks, Pietro continued. "This, for me, has been a very long day indeed."

"Oh my goodness me, has it really? Well, while you've been enjoying a splendid meal and the ambience of these pleasant surroundings, what do you suppose I've been doing these past few hours?"

"I really couldn't say. Would you care to enlighten me?"

"Where do I start? Yes I know. After you and Sister Maria left the dining room, I spoke at length with Consuella to try and bring some sense and clarity to the events of earlier this morning. After that, I spent the next few hours literally running around Milan between yourself, Francesco, and the famous Don Barcese. I'm sure you'll agree my day was slightly more hectic than yours."

"You actually met with this creature. What reason could you possibly have to engage with this reprehensible character?"

"This creature will most likely be managing your daughter's career in the not-too-distant future."

Pietro, in a state of shock, exclaimed, "But how? How could such a disastrous outcome be the final result of all our efforts?"

Father Martine briefed the distraught Father as best he could on everything that had transpired over the previous few hours. He finished by saying, "As you can see, the current situation is less than ideal. The only thing left is for Consuella and myself to meet this Don Barcese character first thing tomorrow morning. I promise I'll do all I can to protect her future. So now, if you'll please excuse me, I'm going to my room and see if I can get a decent night's sleep."

As they both stood up, Pietro, in a tired voice, replied, "Dear friend, I don't believe anyone could have done as much as you have today. Whatever the outcome tomorrow, I know you'll do your very best to secure the most favourable terms possible for my daughter."

With that, they both left the restaurant and bid each other goodnight.

CHAPTER 32

Antonio Arrives in Vienna

On Sunday morning, while Consuella and Father Martine were meeting with Don Barcese, Antonio's train, the Allegro Tosca, pulled into Meidling train station, Vienna. Disembarking from the train, Antonio walked along the platform towards the exit. There he saw a gentleman who was holding a large card with his name printed in bold capitals.

Approaching him he introduced himself. "Good morning, sir. My name is Antonio Fabrizio. I thank you for the courtesy you've shown in meeting me so early in the morning and at such short notice."

The person meeting him placed the card in an attaché case and introduced himself formally, "Señor Fabrizio, may I introduce myself? My name is Herr Dressler. I will now take you to the Grand Hotel. It is quite close to the Vienna State Opera House. If you wish to attend Mass, you can do so at Saint Stephen's Cathedral, which is close by. Tomorrow morning. Herr Hartmann, the managing director, and myself will join you for further discussions. So please, if you would kindly follow me, I will take you there straight away."

Antonio followed him from the station to a waiting auto-mobile. He couldn't help but notice, although Herr Dressler was polite, he was most certainly formal. During the course of the short journey to the hotel, Herr Dressler asked him inconsequential questions about his journey but never once mentioned any details about the position Antonio assumed was still on offer.

Arriving at the hotel, Herr Dressler accompanied him to the reception desk. He addressed the receptionist in a curt formal manner, informing her that Señor Fabrizio was a guest of the Vienna State Opera Company and would be staying for an indefinite period. The receptionist, bowing formally, handed him the room key. Taking the key, he in turn bowed formally as he presented it to Antonio.

"Please, Señor Fabrizio, this is your room key. I trust you will have a pleasant stay at this accommodation. Enjoy the rest of your day. Herr Hartmann and I will be here at precisely seven thirty tomorrow morning to begin our meeting."

With those parting words, he turned and promptly left the reception desk, leaving a bemused Antonio standing there in the middle of the foyer.

Just as he was about to pick up his valise, a porter came over, picked it up, and marched off. Then in mid-stride, he turned to Antonio and said, "Please, Herr Fabrizio, if you would be good enough and follow me, I will escort you to your room."

Antonio was somewhat amused at being called Herr. He nonetheless followed the porter's request.

In the privacy of his room, he unpacked his bag. Calling down to reception using the telephone on his bedside table, he enquired what time the next Mass was being celebrated. The receptionist informed him there was a Mass at ten o'clock. Checking his watch, he decided he had plenty of time to freshen up before attending.

As Antonio made his way along Corinthian Strasse, the architecture impressed him. He soon came to Saint Stephen's Cathedral, which was even grander than he imagined. During the celebration of the mass, there was a full choir and an orchestra. He concluded the Austrians could certainly match the Italians when it came to expressing themselves spiritually.

At the end of the service, he spent the remainder of the day walking through the elegant streets of the city. Back at the Grand Hotel, he had a pleasant meal and then decided to have an early night in preparation for his encounter with Herrs Dressler and Hartmann the following morning.

Having finished breakfast at seven twenty, he left the restaurant and waited in the foyer for the much-anticipated arrival of the two gentlemen from the Vienna State Opera Company. At precisely seven twenty-seven, Herr Dressler entered the hotel accompanied by another individual whom he assumed to be Herr Hartmann. As they approached, Antonio stood up to welcome them.

Herr Dressler was the first to speak. "Good morning, Señor Fabrizio. I trust you had a pleasant night's rest. If I may, I would like to introduce you to Herr Hartmann, managing director of the Vienna State Opera Company."

Antonio, about to proffer his hand by way of greeting, but seeing there was no likely reciprocal gesture from Herr Hartmann, decided a polite bow would be more appropriate.

With these stiff formalities concluded, Herr Dressler continued, "May I ask, Señor Fabrizio, have you eaten breakfast?"

Antonio replied, trying to inject some life into the formal exchanges, "Indeed I have, Herr Dressler, and it was most splendid. How about yourself and Herr Hartmann, have you eaten yet?"

Herr Dressler answered him matter-of-factly. "Indeed we have. This means we can get down to business straight away. Why don't we all sit down, relax, have some coffee, and begin our discussions."

A somewhat relieved Antonio waited for Herr Hartmann to take a seat. Herr Dressler insisted on Antonio sitting next to Herr Hartmann before taking his own seat. A waiter came by to take their order.

"You must forgive us, Señor Fabrizio. We Austrians, on most occasions, can be somewhat formal. But I can promise you once you get to know us, I am more than confident you will be quite comfortable in our company. Now, before we present our proposals to you, are there any questions you have for us?"

Antonio, slightly more at ease, replied, "Well gentlemen, I was greatly flattered on being offered this prestigious position not only once but twice. Can you explain your reasons?"

Herr Hartmann answered him. "Señor Fabrizio, we have watched your progress at La Scala with great interest. In our opinion, you have achieved enormous success in the important role you played in that great institution. It is our belief the experience you've gained there will assist us in developing the Vienna State Opera Company, thereby making it into one of the most prestigious opera houses in Europe."

Antonio, without hesitation, replied, "Gentlemen, I would like to thank you most sincerely for the confidence you have shown in my ability to carry out this task. I humbly accept this challenge. And I promise, I will do my utmost to assist you in achieving your ambition for the Vienna State Opera Company."

A delighted Herr Hartmann stood up, this time exchanging a warm handshake with Antonio. He enthusiastically responded, "Excellent, excellent, Señor Antonio. I will leave yourself and Herr Grossman to iron out the contractual arrangements. So if I may be excused, there is another appointment I need to keep. Once again, Señor Antonio, thank you, thank you so very much."

With a formal bow, Herr Hartman took his leave. Herr Grossman took Antonio through the contract line by line. With their business concluded, Herr Grossman stood to attention and bowed in that formal manner of his. Then with a broad smile, he took Antonio's hand. Shaking it enthusiastically he said, "Señor Antonio, I am overjoyed and delighted you have joined us. I am confident you will achieve great things in our State Opera Company. I will take my leave and allow you to enjoy the rest of your day in our beautiful city, Vienna. I will see you tomorrow morning at eight o'clock. Then we can start implementing your plans and suggestions."

With Herr Grossman's departure, Antonio sat at his table for some moments reflecting on all that had taken place over the past forty-eight hours. He came to the conclusion he would no longer have any influence over future events in Milan or Verona. His main objective now was to put all his energy and experience into the challenge he had just accepted.

CHAPTER 33

Consuella and Father Martine Meet with Don Barcese

The next morning at seven thirty, Father Martine arrived at the convent and collected Consuella.

The ever-reliable Emilio drove them the short distance to the monastery. Father Martine, noticing her nervous disposition, decided to put her mind at ease. "Good morning, Consuella. How are you feeling today?"

"Good morning, Father. You know, I can't recall ever feeling this apprehensive. I am quite nervous."

"Okay then, just try and relax. I'll do the talking. All you have to do is observe. If by chance I say or do anything that gives you cause for concern or if you have a question or a point you need to make, all you have to do is catch my attention. We can then excuse ourselves and go into the adjoining room. Actually, a minor interruption could well be to our advantage and may just unnerve him a little."

Arriving at the monastery Father Martine informed Father Edmundo they were expecting a visitor, and as soon as he arrived, he was to be shown into the visitors' room. Meanwhile, he escorted Consuella into the adjoining room and then explained to her, "When he arrives, we'll leave him sitting there for a few minutes before we make our entrance. When we do, I'll greet him. You just politely nod and take a seat at the far end of the table. I will take a seat that doesn't allow him address you directly. Are you comfortable with that?"

"I just want these discussions to conclude as speedily as possible. I have every faith in your abilities, Father. That's the reason I am placing my fate and future in your capable hands."

Moments later, Father Edmundo entered and announced the arrival of Don Barcese.

"Very good, Father. Please inform our guest Señorita Consuella and myself will join him shortly."

Father Edmundo did as requested.

Father Martine had one final word with Consuella. "Now, Consuella, before we go in, I just want to ask. Next week you have your final performances under what were past management structures. Have you any thoughts?"

"I know for sure I'll be very sad in the certain knowledge Antonio won't be present."

"That's indeed very sad, but you'll have to come to terms with that reality, at least for the immediate future. All I can hope and pray is that it won't be for too long. Now I think we've kept our guest waiting long enough. Let's go in and get this over with."

Father Martine made sure he had the documents, and they made their entrance. As he greeted Don Barcese, Consuella just nodded politely and sat down.

"Welcome, Don Barcese. Thank you for being so punctual. I do hope we haven't kept you waiting too long. Please, please, take a seat."

As he was speaking, Father Martine deliberately led Don Barcese to a seat he believed would keep him at a slight disadvantage and an appropriate distance from Consuella. Taking one of the documents from the envelope, he placed it on the table in front of him and then began. "I take it these proposals are yours. And may I enquire why it is you wish to take over the management of Señorita Consuella's career?"

"Why yes indeed, Father, the proposals are mine. And I believe you will find them fair and reasonable. To answer your second question, my reasons for wishing to manage Señorita Consuella's career are quite simple. Over the past few years, I've followed her progress with great interest. In my humble opinion, she is by far the most accomplished soprano to have come along in at least a decade.

"To date, Señor Antonio has managed her career in an exemplary fashion. Now, though, I find myself asking, does he have the breadth of vision to take this exciting project to the next exciting level?"

Father Martine, hearing echoes of Consuella's remarks from the previous day, very calmly asked him to explain in greater detail what exactly he meant 'by breadth of vision' and 'next level'."

"Dear Father Martine, Señor Antonio is a capable manager, and I am acutely aware the high regard you have for him as an individual and former pupil. His managerial achievements to date, although impressive, have been limited to some cities and other provincial centres here in Italy. The next logical step is to make the transition from national stage to a much wider international arena and audience. This is what I mean when I use the term 'next level'. The challenges ahead would be quite daunting. Señor Antonio's inexperience at this level suggests to me he just doesn't have the breadth of vision to take this project forward. I trust this explanation clarifies the points raised by your good self?"

"Indeed it does, Don Barcese. Now tell me if you will, do you believe you have the necessary qualifications to meet these challenges? And please can you explain what exactly you mean when you use the term 'international arena'?"

"I will indeed, Father. In the past I've had the great pleasure of managing the careers of many prominent operatic artistes here in Italy. Many of them under my guidance have performed in the major capitols of Europe and even in a number of theatres in the United States of America— one of these being the Metropolitan Opera in New York. That's what I mean when I use the term 'international arena'. The experience I've gained guiding and managing many fine performers at these prestigious venues, I believe answers any question concerning not only my ability, but also my suitability."

Father Martine, looking directly into Don Barcese's eyes, responded, "Why yes indeed. I suppose it does really. But you know, Don Barcese, I've often asked myself the question, where are all these performers now?"

Don Barcese now had the distinct impression the wily old friar was trying to provoke him with that last remark. He decided nevertheless to remain passive and just politely answer the questions as they were put to him.

Before moving on, Father Martine very unobtrusively made eye contact with Consuella. Nodding her head ever so slightly, she indicated her willingness to proceed.

"Okay then. Let's move on, shall we?"

Don Barcese, without saying a word, just smiled. He opened his hands palms up, indicating he was ready to proceed.

Father Martine took up where he had left off. "Now back to these proposals of yours. I've read over the two documents. Would I be correct in my assertion they are both originals and identical word for word?"

"Yes indeed, Father. They are as you say."

"There's a clause here that states, if either party wishes to terminate the arrangement, etcetera, etcetera. Please clarify exactly what this means?"

"Of course, what I was endeavouring to achieve in this instance was to make the contract as attractive as possible, thereby demonstrating my motives as being totally unselfish."

"Don Barcese, I would like to remind you, in case it's slipped your mind, the documents I have here before me are a set of proposals, nothing more. I would be obliged if you could refrain from referring to them as a contract."

"My apologies, Father Martine. I assure you it will not happen again."

Father Martine, as he continued, could see Don Barcese was beginning to feel the pressure. He was squirming somewhat uncomfortably in his chair as he was making his apology. "Now this section dealing with payment states there will be a management fee of not more than fifteen per cent, am I correct?"

"Yes indeed, Father Martine, you are quite correct."

"Why so generous?"

"Well as I explained to Señorita Consuella—"

Father Martine yet again cut him short. "Please, Don Barcese, what you said to Consuella is irrelevant. Just explain it to me."

"My apologies. The reason for the modest management fee is quite simple. At this stage in my life, I just happen to be a person of substantial means."

"What, did you inherit a gold mine?"

"No, no, dear Father. I have some business interests outside the world of opera, and over the past number of years, let's just say I've been most fortunate. Or as a person of the cloth such as your good self might say, I've been very blessed. So you see, it's not about the money; it's not that at all. What it's really about is giving Señorita Consuella the best professional management possible, as well as a set of terms and conditions I believe won't be matched by any other potential candidate."

Believing he had put forward a compelling argument in furthering his cause, Don Barcese sat back in his chair feeling rather good about himself in a smug kind of way. For the first time since he sat down at this table in this monastery, he was beginning to feel he was at least clawing back some of the ground conceded earlier.

Father Martine picked up the document and the envelope. "If you could excuse us for a few brief moments, I would like to discuss one or two matters with Consuella if that is acceptable."

"Of course, Father. Please, take all the time you need."

Father Martine rose from his chair. He guided Consuella into the adjoining room and asked her for her thoughts on how she felt the discussions were progressing.

"Father, this morning I really didn't know what to expect. The excellent manner in which you've handled these proceedings so far, I have to say, impressed me greatly. I never realised you were such a skilful negotiator."

"Well, Consuella, the priesthood isn't too much different from most other professions. Running a monastery, I've had to fight with bishops, deal with overzealous committees, flatter potential donors, and much more besides. To survive, I've had to deal with many sets of different circumstances. That's all I'm doing here, nothing more nothing less. Now, let's take ourselves back in there and see if we can achieve something that actually benefits you.

"Thank you for your patience, Don Barcese," he announced as the two of them returned.

Again laying one of the documents down before him and keeping the other close by, he continued more or less where he had left off. "I couldn't help but notice both sets of documents bear your signature." He purposely omitted the fact they also had Consuella's. "Also, they are dated for the day after tomorrow, the fourth of October in fact. Why so?"

Don Barcese completely caught off guard by the forthright challenge concerning these two significant points found himself floundering somewhat. Struggling to come up with a plausible answer, he decided his only option was to brazen it out. "As a businessman, I find myself nowadays signing so many documents, I'm sorry to say I must have signed these in error without reading the contents."

"What about the date? How do you explain that?"

"I must have gotten my calendar mixed up and mistakenly put down an incorrect one. I suppose you could say that was rather careless of me."

"Why yes indeed, I suppose I could say that, couldn't I? Or maybe, Don Barcese, I could say you were being very clever. Now I am going to tell you what I believe your true intention was. So please, listen carefully, as I am only going to say this once.

"It is my contention you drew up these proposals knowing Consuella was still below the legal age to enter into a legally binding agreement. You signed both sets and dated them for the day after her twenty-first birthday. You then gave them to her in the hope she would sign them on the day after her coming of age.

"Well I'm sorry to inform you, Don Barcese, these documents have no validity whatsoever. Why I may as well just throw them in the dustbin. Would you care to comment, as I would like an answer if it's not too much trouble?"

"Father Martine, you have me at a disadvantage. your analysis and interpretation, I have to say, are not incorrect."

Father Martine noted the double negative in his reply. Many years of tough negotiations told him Don Barcese was now experiencing some degree of pressure, and it showed.

"Dear Father, my only defence is my motives were honourable, though my methods were less so. I would like to apologise to yourself and, of course, to Senorita Consuella for the subterfuge."

Father Martine took the document. Placing it in the envelope, he then rang the bell. Almost immediately, Father Edmundo entered.

"Ah there you are, Father. Could you please take this envelope and lock it away in my office?"

"Of course, Father. Will there be anything else?"

"Don Barcese, please forgive my bad manners. I should of course have asked earlier. Would you care for some refreshments, tea, coffee perhaps?"

"A black coffee would be most welcome."

"Anything else? Some food perhaps or maybe a snack?"

"No thank you. The black coffee will be just fine, no milk no sugar."

"Father Edmundo, if you'd be so good, please bring a cold lemonade for Consuella; a mint tea for myself; and a black coffee, no milk no sugar for our guest."

With Father Edmundo's departure, Don Barcese was wondering, what next? He was very much aware Father Martine most definitely had the upper hand. His plan to entice Consuella to sign on the appointed day was well and truly dashed. The contracts may as well be in the dustbin for all the good they were going to do him now.

He was still somewhat puzzled as to why he was still here and why Father Martine hadn't dismissed him by now. A thought began to germinate in that crafty brain of his. Maybe, just maybe the negotiations with Señor Antonio might have stalled or run into some sort of difficulty. All he could do now was wait and see what tricks this troublesome friar might have up that long sleeve of his.

Consuella, having sat quietly during the exchanges, was beginning to see a different Don Barcese. In her eyes, he no longer seemed to be the brash confident man about town impresario. After witnessing the forensic way Father Martine had stripped him down layer by layer, she came to the conclusion he was just an ordinary human being, not much different from any other.

There should be no earthly reason for her to be intimidated by him in any future encounter. She also drew the conclusion her future well-being was firmly in the hands of this wonderful saintly warrior sitting beside her.

Father Edmundo returned and set the tray down. "Will there be anything else, Father?"

"No thank you, Father. This is just fine. You may leave now, and again you'll see to it we're not disturbed."

As Father Edmundo left, Father Martine resumed. "Don Barcese, before I bring our meeting to a close, it would be bad manners on my part if I didn't offer you an opportunity to respond to the points raised in our discussions just now. Please, in your own time, you may ask me any questions you may deem relevant."

"Thank you, Father. I have one question, and it is this, are you any closer to a final decision concerning the management of Señorita Consuella's career?"

"Let's just say all possibilities are being considered. Now, before you take your leave, may I make a suggestion?"

"Of course, Father, please. When you're ready, I'm most anxious to hear your suggestion."

"I would like you to prepare another set of proposals with the following inclusions—a management fee of 10 per cent, a list of all the venues and dates you intend to negotiate for all performances covering a twelve-month time period, and a clause stating you will furnish a written monthly progress report including financial statements. Insert a paragraph stating all fees minus documented expenses will be lodged into a bank account of my choosing. The final clause must be quite specific. It is to clearly state Consuella will perform here in Italy on no fewer than twenty occasions in any calendar year. These concerts are to be evenly split between La Scala, the Arena Verona, and other possible venues Consuella and I deem appropriate. Most importantly it is imperative you include space for three signatures. And finally, please prepare three sets of documents. I think that covers everything. Do you have any questions?"

Don Barcese waited a few brief moments before responding. He was convinced, at this delicate stage in the negotiations, a misplaced word could ruin any slim chance he might still have of achieving his ultimate operatic goal. "These inclusions, as outlined, certainly to me don't appear to be unreasonable. I will take cognizance of them when drawing up the documents in question."

Again Father Martine noted the double negative. He then asked how soon the new documents would be ready.

"Oh it shouldn't take more than a few days," Don Barcese answered.

"I'm afraid that won't be good enough, Don Barcese."

"I'm sorry, have I said something that's caused offence?"

"No not at all. I just want you to be aware a final decision will be made one way or the other no later than twelve midnight tomorrow. So it's really up to you what course of action you take between now and then. I think it's fair to say our meeting is now concluded. On behalf of Consuella and myself, I would like to thank you for your presence here this morning and the courtesy extended not only to me, but also to Consuella.

"Now if we may be excused I have to get this young lady back to the convent. Can I take it you'll be attending the performances next week?"

"Most certainly. I wouldn't miss them for the world."

Standing up, Don Barcese came around to Father Martine's side of the table. "And now, Father, it's my turn to thank you for your time and the pleasant manner adopted during our discussions."

He extended his hand. Father Martine reciprocated with a brief but not unfriendly handshake. Consuella took her place beside Father Martine. Don Barcese, facing her for the first time since the start of their meeting, repeated the gesture. Hesitating for a moment, she then extended her hand for a brief handshake.

Father Martine rang the bell. On cue, Father Edmundo entered.

"There you are, Father. Would you be good enough and show our guest to the door. Once again, Don Barcese, thank you for your and time and presence here this morning."

Trying his best to sound sincere, Don Barcese responded, "Thank you, Father. It was my pleasure."

His last words were for Consuella. "I'm very much looking forward to your concerts next week. I'm absolutely certain you will give of your best."

She answered him in a confident manner. "Why thank you, Don Barcese. That's most gracious of you."

With those being the last words spoken, Father Edmundo escorted Don Barcese from the room.

Father Martine just flopped down into his chair quite exhausted. Turning to Consuella, in a weary voice, he exclaimed, "My dear child, sometimes I wonder, would my life be any easier if I hadn't plotted and schemed in persuading Sister Maria and your dear father to allow you come to Milan?"

"Oh come now, Father, let's have some breakfast. Then you can accompany me back to the convent. I'll have a short rest. Reverend Mother, I'm sure, will contact Francesco and my father. You will then be able to update them on all that's happened this morning."

"You know Consuella, sometimes, only sometimes, you can be wise beyond your years. I'm happy to say today is one of those days. Come on, wise young lady, let's have some breakfast."

While being driven back to his town house, Don Barcese was seething with rage; this monk had humiliated him in front of Consuella of all people. His overriding objective right now was to prepare a new set of documents and deliver them within the time frame specified. He made a silent pledge to himself. One day he would have his revenge on this interfering troubling priest.

CHAPTER 34

The Convent Late Morning

Arriving back at the convent before midday, Father Martine took Consuella to one side. "Now, Consuella, It's not like you have to avoid anyone in particular. We've all endured a great deal of stress over the past twenty-four hours or so. I'm suggesting, no, I'm insisting, you go to your room and get some rest. Meanwhile, I'll try to get the others together and bring them up to date."

As she departed, Sister Agostina emerged from the dining room.

Father Martine greeted her in a friendly fashion. "Ah, Sister, there you are. I was wondering, would you happen to know where Reverend Mother might be?"

"She's in the library, Father. Would you like me to let her know you're here?"

"Thank you, Sister. That won't be necessary. I'll just go in and join her there."

As he entered, he was somewhat surprised to see not just Sister Maria. Pietro and Francesco were also present. "This is a happy coincidence," he said. "On my way over, I was just thinking it would be a good idea for the four of us to come together. I wanted to bring you up to date on my meeting with Don Barcese."

Sister Maria replied, "It was me, Father. I took the liberty of contacting them. I thought it might save time."

"Well done, Sister. I know you're all pretty tired, myself included. I'll be as brief as possible."

He relayed the events as they had unfolded earlier in the morning and the situation as it presently stood. He finished by saying, "So tomorrow by twelve midnight, Don Barcese has to deliver three sets of documents

252

to me personally—that's if he has serious intentions regarding the future management of Consuella's career."

Francesco was the first to respond. "Excellent, Father. I don't think anyone could have done any better under these extraordinary circumstances."

Sister Maria and Pietro nodded in agreement.

Francesco, preparing to leave, made a final point. "I suppose all we can do now is wait and see how Don Barcese plays his hand."

Sister Maria added, "Yes indeed. I believe that's all we can do. Thank you, Francesco, for making yourself available at such short notice. Now before you go, a question if I may?"

"Of course, Sister. Ask your question."

"Despite all the turmoil, in particular Consuella's ungenerous remarks, will you be attending her birthday celebration and, more importantly, her final concerts."

"Absolutely, Carlota and I will attend. And for the last few performance, I'll be there well before the curtain rises to assist her. I will be doing this as much for Antonio's sake as for hers. Although he was treated badly by Consula, I believe he would still like her to finish the season in a splendid fashion."

He noticed Pietro seemed to be somewhat upset. Placing an arm around his shoulder he continued, "Come now, Pietro. No need to be sad. Despite all that's happened, your daughter is still a remarkable young lady."

Pietro answered him. "Francesco, what you said just now didn't upset me. I was thinking of Antonio and what might have been between himself and my daughter. More than anyone, he should be here for all of this. Instead, all we know is he's somewhere in Austria. It really is such a shame."

Father Martine took him gently by the arm. "Come on, dear friend. I think it's time for us to head back to our hotel. Who knows? Maybe, just maybe, this tale may yet have a happy ending."

As they were leaving, he invited Francesco to join them. "Francesco, Emilio, God bless him, is still available. So if you care to ride with us, you're more than welcome."

"Thank you Father, I don't mind if I do."

With that, the three said their goodbyes to Sister Maria and took their leave.

When they arrived at the hotel, Father Martine invited Francesco to join them for some tea. Pietro, feeling quite exhausted, excused himself and bid them farewell.

As the two men took their seats in the lounge, Francesco enquired, "Well, now that you've finally met the famous Don Barcese, I'm most curious to know your opinion."

"He is certainly a skilled negotiator, and most of the time, he was polite and courteous. He made a great effort to portray himself as an affable agreeable character whose only concern was Consuella's welfare. I have to say, your advice was most helpful, for most of the time I managed to keep him on the back foot. I think he was none too pleased."

"That's good very good. Anything else worthy of note?"

"His residence was most impressive. I never realised the world of opera management paid so handsomely."

"Oh it pays pretty well, but not that well. The area he lives in is the most exclusive neighbourhood in the city. His next-door neighbour is Grand Duke Sergei Mikhailovic. He is a first cousin of Tsar Nicholas II. When he's in town, he's normally accompanied by his mistress, the famous ballerina Mathilda Kschessinskaya. His neighbours on the other side are Lord and Lady Trimbleston. Farther down the avenue, the Sultan of Brunei has a residence.

"When Don Barcese purchased his palazzo, he decided to make some structural changes. He brought his architect over to London. He was a lover of all things British, particularly the aristocracy and their town houses. He instructed him to make countless sketches of the most impressive facades around Kensington and Mayfair. Before he returned, his final acquisitions were the hiring of a butler named Henry, a chauffeur named George, and even a parlour maid who goes by the name of Mildred.

"Back in Italy, extensive renovations were carried out, and his mansion was eventually finished in the regency style so typical of the finest London town houses. All he was missing now was a title. Unfortunately for him, a title was something his money was unable to procure. To maintain a home in that part of Milan, one has to be very rich indeed."

"So how come he happens to enjoy such a lavish lifestyle? Is he really that wealthy?"

"He is probably one of the richest individuals in Milan. The source of his wealth has been a talking point for some time now. It still remains a mystery and, on his part, a very well-kept secret."

"How extraordinary. Well, we'll just have to wait and see if he shows up with the relevant documents."

"Don't worry. He'll show up for sure. To have Consuella under his management will be a real feather in his cap.

"Well, I think I'd better be going. I look forward to seeing you at this birthday celebration—that's if you can use the term 'celebration'. I think 'wake' would be a more appropriate description for what lies in store. Would you agree?"

"I'd have to agree. It will certainly be a very subdued affair, and unfortunately we can't change what's happened. To think, just two nights ago, the four of us, including Antonio, were enjoying a friendly meal while discussing what we believed would be a very bright future for both of them."

"Indeed, it just goes to show you can only be sure of today. What tomorrow brings is not ours to command."

"How right you are, Francesco, how very right you are."

CHAPTER 35

Monday Morning

The following day, Monday, Father Martine celebrated Mass in the convent chapel. He was relieved to see Consuella in attendance. After Mass, he and Pietro joined the others for breakfast.

As they ate, he noticed a degree of good manners and civility had been restored. There was, however, a slight tension still hanging in the air. His immediate concern was an inappropriate word, even if sincerely spoken, might just land them back where they had been the previous Friday.

He made an attempt at some inconsequential small talk to brighten things up. "Now, Consuella, can I ask, how did your dress rehearsal go? Good I hope?"

"It was more than good; it was excellent. The costumes for next week's production are the best I've seen. And I'm most grateful Sister Lucia accompanied me there and back."

He decided to keep the conversation going. "Well it's certainly pleases me to see your association with our good sister ending on a high note."

Sister Maria joined in. "What an interesting expression, Father."

"What expression, Sister?"

"Your expression just now. 'High note'—kind of operatic, don't you think?"

"Why yes, Sister, I suppose you could say that. But you know what I mean."

Pietro responded, "Of course we do, Father." He then addressed Sister Lucia. "Tell me, Sister, are you looking forward to resuming your teaching career?"

"Indeed I am, Señor Pietro, though for me it's more a vocation than a career."

Father Martine added, "Very well spoken, Sister, very well spoken indeed. And now that this journey you've made is nearing its end, do you have any special memories or perhaps something you wish to share?"

"Dear friends, when I started out on this journey, more out of a sense of duty and my vow of obedience than anything else, I really had no idea what to expect. Over the past two and a half years, I've been to most opera houses throughout the land. If I had a voice, I could sing you every aria and chorus. I know them all by heart. I can even name the composers and titles of most operas. For me, it was an education in geography and music. Most importantly though, it was wonderful being a companion to Consuella."

Everyone around the table was quite taken by her eloquent words. Pietro responded, "You know, Sister, I don't think I ever fully realised how important a role you played in my daughter's career. Today, in front of my dear friends and Consuella, from the bottom of my heart, thank you."

Consuella looked over in her direction. They both exchanged smiles of genuine affection. Sister Maria and Father Martine were somewhat relieved the gloom had finally been lifted.

As they finished breakfast, Sister Agostina entered to clear the dishes.

To everyone's surprise Consuella set about assisting with the task. "Thank you, Sister, for a delicious breakfast. Please, allow me help you with these."

The others, slightly amused, just looked on.

Father Martine, standing up, addressed Pietro. "Well, dear friend, I think it's time for us to head back."

Once they'd said their goodbyes, Sister Maria accompanied them to the door. "Forgive me, Father. I didn't want to mention that individual's name during breakfast. Do you think he's likely to show up sometime today?"

"Francesco seems to think he will, and he knows this character better than I. So to answer your question, I believe he will."

"Everything depends on you, Father. You will do your best? Promise me you will."

Before Father Martine had a chance to answer, Pietro responded, "There now, Sister, getting yourself upset isn't going to help. You know Father Martine is the best person to handle this difficult business."

"Of course, Pietro. You're absolutely right. My apologies, Father. I've probably gone and upset you now."

"Not at all, not at all. You know me better than that. Let's just see how the rest of the day goes. I promise, if there are any developments, I will certainly let you know."

With those parting words, the two of them headed out to the automobile. Sister Maria made her way back to the dining room. She still had one or two questions for Consuella.

Returning to her chair, she was pleasantly surprised to see Consuella and Sister Lucia chatting away as they helped Sister Agostina. With the chores completed, they both sat down.

Sister Maria began by saying, "That was a pleasant morning, and I would like to thank both of you for making it so. And to think that after next week the two of you will be following different paths. Sister you will take up your teaching post and you Consuella will be leaving us to venture into the big world out there. I will certainly miss the many happy occasions we've shared in the past. I've always known this day was eventually going to come. The thing is, I'm feeling rather sad because I never really thought it was going to be this difficult."

Consuella, trying to control her own feelings, responded, "Please, Reverend Mother, don't be too upset. Our relationship is not ending. It's just entering a different phase; that's all. And now that Sister Lucia is taking up her new role, you will most likely see her more often than before. No matter where my career takes me, I will always return to perform in Milan and Verona, so there will be many opportunities for us to see each other. Of that I am quite certain."

"Thank you, Consuella. I do hope you won't mind, but there's something I need to ask that's been weighing heavily on my mind."

"Please, Reverend Mother, ask any question you wish."

"Have you decided on a date for leaving the convent? Have you made alternative living arrangements? My reason for asking is out of concern for your well-being and safety."

Before Consuella answered, Sister Lucia thought it might be appropriate if she were to excuse herself. "My apologies for the interruption, Reverend Mother, I will leave the two of you alone so you can continue your conversation in private."

Consuella answered, "Please, Sister, I would like you to stay. I think it's important you also have full knowledge of my intentions going forward. Who knows? Maybe someday in the future I may need your assistance as well.

"Saturday next, I will be moving to a town house. The location is a short distance from La Scala. It provides a degree of privacy, and this particular aspect was a factor in my decision."

Sister Maria asked, "Have you purchased the property?"

"For the moment, I'm renting. Six months from now, I will make a more permanent decision."

They chatted on for another short while. The rest of the day passed off in a reasonably relaxed fashion.

CHAPTER 36

The Birthday

Tuesday morning, the third of October, Dominique, Paolo, and Adamo arrived from Verona. Later that same evening, everyone gathered to celebrate Consuella's twenty-first birthday. Antonio's absence was obvious for all to see. The occasion, although an important milestone in Consuella's life, certainly didn't quite have the expected celebratory mood about it.

Sister Maria prevailed upon Father Martine to say a few words marking the occasion. Looking at her with an expression that asked why me, he nevertheless began making an unscripted speech. "Ladies and gentlemen, I would just like to say, it's such a joy to see all of you here this evening, a loving family, close friends, and even colleagues from the operatic community gathered here for this very special occasion. As you know, we are here to celebrate Consuella's twenty-first birthday. She has officially reached her coming of age and is now officially an adult. Consuella, all of us present sincerely wish you a very happy birthday and continued success in your future."

Everyone stood up and sang "Happy Birthday". Just as the birthday song ended, an usher entered and placed a magnificent bouquet of flowers in front of Consuella.

Francesco, for a moment fearing this might be Don Barcese's usual flattering gesture, very casually lifted the card. Silently reading it, he was relieved and pleasantly surprised. Glancing over in Sister Maria and Father Martine's direction, his positive expression dispelled their fears.

Standing up, he then addressed Consuella. "Consuella, accompanying this beautiful bouquet, there is a card with some brief words dedicated to you. If you wish, I will read them for you."

"Of course, Francesco. I'm so excited. Please, please read them."

"To Consuella on this very special day, a birthday greeting to you from me. These flowers were chosen because of their beauty, but no matter how beautiful, they will never match the beauty of your smile and the warmth in your heart. Best wishes for a successful, splendid filled future. Kindest regards, Antonio."

Francesco handed her the card. "I think you may wish to keep this. Unfortunately, these blooms will fade, but the sentiments expressed never will."

Now completely overcome, in a pitiful state and with tears in her eyes, she accepted the card and held it close to her heart. Looking at her, Francesco could clearly see the effect Antonio's gesture had on her.

There was an awkward silence. Sister Maria thought now was as good a time as any to explain Antonio's absence. She asked Francesco if he was willing to do so. He agreed.

"Dear friends," he began. "I'm sure most of you are asking yourselves why Antonio is not with us on this special occasion. He is at this very moment in Austria. His reason for being there I will now explain. The Vienna State Opera Company some while back invited him to accept the post of director of opera."

There was an audible gasp throughout the room.

Francesco gave everyone just enough time to absorb this startling revelation and then continued, "Sadly for us, his intention is to accept this offer. My reason for sharing this unwelcome news with you here this evening is to simply avoid idle gossip and useless speculation. This would be most unhelpful and is certainly something Consuella could do without right now.

"As of yet, no decision has been made regarding the future management of Consuella's career, though I can say a number of options are being considered. Father Martine, with his wealth of knowledge, is advising Consuella on suitable practical alternatives. This is all I have to say on the matter. I'm now asking you to respect Consuella's privacy. Thank you for your time and patience."

As he took his seat, he signalled the musicians to resume playing. He was hoping this might encourage couples to take to the floor. Maybe some music and dancing might just dispel the gloom and bring back some semblance of gaiety to what was left of the evening.

Adamo requested Violetta to take his hand for a waltz. Dominique and Paolo joined them. Consuella sat there feeling quite alone.

At that moment, Stefano Pavello approached. He was the young tenor who had shared the honours with her on the day of the auditions. "Consuella, would you do me the honour of accompanying me on the dance floor?"

"Of course, Stefano. And if your dancing is as good as your singing, we can then demonstrate for all to see our other hidden talents."

Father Martine looked over in Carlota's direction and then asked her husband, "Francesco, shouldn't you be dancing with your charming wife?"

"Father, at best, I'm a competent voice coach and an average musician. The waltz is an acrobatic feat I've never quite mastered. The last occasion Carlota and I danced was on our wedding night, and she still has the marks to prove it."

With a smile on her face she added, "Believe me, Father. My husband is telling the truth. I'll just watch the dancing and enjoy the music."

Sister Maria, somewhat relieved Francesco's explanation regarding Antonio's absence was now behind them, still had concerns in relation to the contract. She discreetly asked Father Martine if there had been any developments.

"Not just yet. There's two hours left before the deadline. Let's be patient just another short while and see what happens."

At eleven fifteen, the restaurant manager approached. "My apologies for disturbing you, Father Martine. Don Barcese is in the foyer. He asked me to let you know of his presence."

"Did he say anything else?"

"No. And I didn't feel it was my place to ask."

"Very good. Please inform him I'll be with him shortly."

"Of course, Father. I'll let him know right away."

Francesco looked at him. "Well, Father, it would seem the moment of truth has arrived. Any thoughts?"

"Not really. I'll just go out and see if he has the documents as requested."

Sister Maria and Pietro didn't make any comment. Consuella, having returned to her seat, decided all she could now do was wait.

Entering the foyer, Father Martine approached Don Barcese and greeted him in a reasonably friendly manner. "Ah there you are, Don Barcese. What brings you here at this late hour?"

"Please accept my apologies, Father Martine. I hope I'm not disturbing you on this important occasion. By the way, how is Señorita Consuella? Is she enjoying her birthday celebration?"

"Indeed she is. Now I don't mean to be rude, but if you can just get to the point, I would appreciate it."

"Of course, Father. I'll be as brief as possible. These are the documents we discussed. I've had them drawn up as per your instructions. I just wanted to make sure and deliver them personally within the time frame specified."

"Thank you, Don Barcese. I'll study these over the coming days and let you know my thoughts."

Taken aback and somewhat annoyed by Father Martine's curt response, Don Barcese decided to proceed cautiously nonetheless. "Please, Father, it was my understanding you would be making a decision no later than twelve midnight tonight."

"You are indeed correct. A decision will be made within that time frame. However, I don't recall telling you when you would have an answer."

"As usual, Father, I stand corrected. You of course made no such promise. Please forgive me for being so presumptuous."

"Not at all, Don Barcese. No need to apologise. We're both sensible adults. Good manners dictate I should at the very least let you know my intentions. So please listen carefully. Consuella has three more performances under the existing arrangement, her last being this coming Friday. I will be in attendance for the duration, and Señor Francesco will be assisting. Saturday next at ten thirty, if you care to join Consuella and myself at this hotel, I will then let you know my decision. That's all I have to say for now. So if I can be excused, I need to return to my guests. Once again, Don Barcese, thank you for your efforts. Goodnight and have a safe journey."

With the documents in his possession, Father Martine headed back into the banqueting room, leaving a very subdued Don Barcese behind. Don Barcese knew full well there was nothing, absolutely nothing he could do but wait until the following Saturday to find out what fate had in store for him.

Father Martine returned to his guests. Taking a seat beside Pietro, he smiled over in Sister Maria and Francesco's direction.

"Don't worry, Pietro. Before I meet with this individual Saturday next, I will go through these documents with Francesco. The two of us will see to it we have the best possible terms for Consuella."

The evening drew to a close. Everyone seemed reasonably happy that the birthday celebration was a reasonably happy occasion.

The following morning, Sister Maria, Pietro, Dominique, Paolo, and Adamo bid a fond and sad farewell to Consuella. Father Martine remained. His task was to ensure himself and Francesco would be there to guide and support Consuella over the coming days.

The following Saturday, as agreed, Don Barcese made his way to the hotel for his meeting with Consuella and Father Martine. As he entered, he spotted the two of them sitting in the lobby. "Good morning, Senorita Consuella. Good morning, Father Martine. I do sincerely hope I have not kept you waiting?"

"Not at all, Don Barcese. Please, if you will, take a seat."

As he sat down, Don Barcese could see Father Martine had the documents in front of him on the table. He decided the best option was to say nothing and wait for him to open the discussion.

"Well, Don Barcese, everything seems to be in order. So I'm happy to inform you, we have ourselves a contract. As you can see, the three documents have been signed by Consuella and myself. May I ask when you intend to commence Consuella's next schedule of performances?"

"With your permission, Father Martine, I would like to start straight away—that is, of course, if Señorita Consuella has no objections."

Consuella answered him. "Don Barcese, please, if you will, Father Martine and I would like to know which cities outside of Italy I am scheduled to perform in and how soon."

"Dear Señorita Consuella, this coming Tuesday, with your permission and Father Martine's approval, we will depart Milan and travel by train to Berlin and then onto Madrid, Paris, and finally London. This extensive tour will take us up to mid-December. I promise to have you back in Italy by then to enable you to honour your commitment to Sister Maria and Father Martine for the carol services in Verona."

"Why thank you, Don Barcese. That is most thoughtful of you. Father, do you have any questions?"

"Just one. Can you tell us what plans, if any, do you have regarding the United States of America?"

"I am glad you asked me that, Father. Early next January, with yours and Señorita Consuella's approval of course, I have booked a passage for our journey to New York. Señorita Consuella will perform on six occasions in the Grand Metropolitan Opera. Before her appearance at this most prestigious venue, I have booked a series of concerts in Boston and Philadelphia. My reason for arranging the tour in this way, is to give her an opportunity to get used to an American audience. There is no doubt in my mind that, when this extensive tour is completed, Señorita Consuella will be the most adored and popular soprano in the world."

"Very good, Don Barcese. That does sound impressive. Now I just want to remind you, regarding the terms of our contract, I will be expecting you to stick rigidly to the terms as agreed. Finally, what plans do you have for Consuella on your return to Italy?"

"We will return in early March. It is my intention to allow Señorita Consuella to rest and enjoy some time with her family. I am certain there will be lots for all of you to discuss following what I sincerely believe will be a hugely successful tour. In late March, I have booked Señorita Consuella to make her triumphant return to La Scala, where she will play the heroine's role In Verdi's *La Traviata*."

"Very good, Don Barcese. So now, if you will excuse us, we have to take our leave. There is much preparation required for Consuella's journey next Tuesday. What time is the train departing?"

"Early morning, eight o'clock."

"Well that's it then until Tuesday next. Don't worry. I will see to it Consuella gets to the train station on time."

They both stood up and took their leave without any further comment.

A very relieved Don Barcese sat back in his chair. He reflected on what had just transpired between himself and Father Martine. He was also quite pleased with himself. He had now finally achieved his goal of bringing Consuella within his orbit. Again, he cast his mind back to the card reading episode involving the gypsy lady. Events certainly seemed to be going his way, and this pleased him enormously.

CHAPTER 37

The European Tour

Tuesday morning whilst taking Consuella to the train station, Father Martine could clearly see the concerned look in her demeanour, despite the fact she was trying valiantly to project an outward air of confidence.

"Well, Consuella, any last minute thoughts before you embark on this new and hopefully exciting chapter in your career?"

"You know, Father, this morning just before you collected me, I was thinking how wonderful my life has been—that is, until I went and ruined it all through my arrogance and stupidity."

"Come now, Consuella. Don't be too hard on yourself. Just try and focus on the challenges ahead and give of your best. I believe that's all you can do until an opportunity presents itself for us to find a better solution, hopefully sometime in the near future."

"Thank you, Father. As always, your comforting words give me hope and encouragement. I promise, I will do my very best."

As they arrived at the train station, they found an anxious Don Barcese waiting on the platform, tickets in hand. He greeted them enthusiastically, "Welcome, Señorita Consuella. Welcome, Father Martine, you have been most diligent in getting here on time. This forthcoming tour, I believe, will be an exciting and rewarding experience for our young star."

Father Martine, looking Don Barcese directly in the eye, replied, "As long as it is a safe and successful tour, Don Barcese, there is really nothing more for me to say except. I expect you to take excellent care of this young lady, and I think it would be a good idea to dispense with the formalities from here on in. It won't be necessary for you to adopt the title 'Señorita' when addressing Consuella. I will be awaiting your weekly reports on her progress. I think we're done for now."

With that, he turned to Consuella. "My dear child, take good care of yourself. Make all of us proud, as I know you will. And don't forget to keep in touch, especially with your dear papa and Sister Maria. With God's blessing, we will see you back here in Verona for our Christmas carol service."

"I promise you, Father, I will. Thank you, thank you so very much for all the care and consideration you've given me for so many years past. Goodbye, Father, goodbye."

Father Martine waited until they boarded the train. He then took his leave from the station with mixed feelings of sadness and slight apprehension. He came to the conclusion there was very little he could now do to protect Consuella, except to hope and pray Don Barcese kept his promise to act professionally during this her first tour outside the borders of Italy.

During the remaining weeks of October through November and into the early weeks of December, Consuella's journey and progress through Europe was quite spectacular. In Berlin, she performed in the famous Konigliches Opera House. From there, it was on to Cologne, where she performed in the Luiv Opera.

The audiences in both cities took her to their hearts. They were reminded of another great Italian operatic soprano by the name of Lina Cavalieri, who, at age thirty-six, was many years older than Consuella. She now mainly performed on the New York stage with the great Enrico Caruso.

From Cologne, it was then on to Paris. There, she performed the lead role in Puccini's opera *Manon Lescaut* at the world famous Palais Garnier. For Consuella, Paris was an enchanting city. She was quite overwhelmed by its beauty and style.

Don Barcese, ever mindful of his responsibility and Father Martine's final words on their departure from Verona, performed his duties in an exemplary fashion. He wanted to be certain no negative reports reached her father and the Reverend Mother back in Verona. He himself kept Father Martine up to date on Consuella's progress through Europe.

The next stage of their journey took them to Barcelona. There she performed in the Gran Teatre del Liceu, where she sang and played the part of the housekeeper Berta in Rossini's *The Barber of Seville*. This opera was a particular favourite with Spanish audiences.

For her final performances in Spain, the venue was the Royal Theatre in Madrid, where George Bizet's four-act opera *Carmen* was being staged. Consuella took the part of Micaela and delighted the audience singing the aria "Habanera".

The next and final stage of this grand European tour took them to London.

On the boat journey from Cherbourg to Southampton, Consuella took time to reflect on her journey thus far. Although she would have been much happier if it was Antonio escorting her, she had to admit Don Barcese, despite his somewhat overbearing manner, was doing everything possible to ensure the tour was a successful one.

At this stage, she decided to express her appreciation for his efforts. "Don Barcese, it would be remiss of me if I failed to compliment you on your efforts and professionalism thus far. I have written to my Father and Reverend Mother informing them of this fact. I've also let them know our journey to date has been most rewarding."

"Why thank you, Consuella. I very much appreciate your kind words just now. I'm sure you'll be pleased to know I have kept Father Martine up to date on what I can only say has been your tremendous progress so far. It was truly something to behold. However, the final and most daunting part of your tour still awaits you on the stage of the Royal Opera House, Covent Garden, and London."

London was indeed her greatest challenge to date. Not only would she be appearing in front of royalty. On top of that, she was to perform in two operas and sing in the English language. *The Pirates of Penzance* and *The Mikado* by Gilbert and Sullivan were the two most popular comic operas among British audiences.

Don Barcese booked the services of an English language coach to assist Consuella for her roles in both operas. It was a major challenge. Nevertheless, the perseverance and resolute determination she adopted in her preparations enabled her to deliver remarkable performances. The Covent Garden audience was most impressed, as was a much-relieved Don Barcese.

It was now early December. Consuella's European tour had now concluded, and she and Don Barcese journeyed back to Italy. Don Barcese, ever mindful of Father Martine's parting words, made it an absolute priority to have Consuella back in Verona as promised.

At the train station, Father Martine was waiting to greet them as they disembarked. "Welcome home, Consuella. Did you have a comfortable journey? And tell me, how do you feel now that you've completed your first tour of Europe?"

"I'm just fine, Father. The tour was wonderful and so exciting, though it's still so good to be back home."

Turning to Don Barcese, he said, "Well, Don Barcese, I would like to take this opportunity to thank you for keeping your word. I do appreciate it. And may I ask, will you be present for our Christmas carol service?"

"Unfortunately no, Father. I need to get back to Milan. So I will now place Consuella into your capable hands, as I'm sure her family and your good self must be looking forward to having her back home. With your permission, Father, I will now take my leave."

"Of course, Don Barcese. Once again, thank you for your efforts to date. I take it we will meet again early January?"

"Indeed, Father, I will send you details of Consuella's forthcoming schedule for the journey to America. So now, Consuella, enjoy the Christmas season with your family, and I will see you in January."

"Why thank you, Don Barcese. Before my forthcoming trip to America, there is one more European city I would like to perform in."

Don Barcese, quite taken aback by this unexpected development, responded calmly, "Which city do you have in mind, Consuella?"

"I would very much like to perform in Vienna."

"There are many fine opera houses in Vienna. Do you have any particular one in mind?"

"Why yes. I would like to perform in the Vienna Court Opera House."

A surprised Father Martine decided a timely intervention was required. "Don Barcese, if you have no objections, I believe I can prevail upon Señor Antonio to facilitate Consuella's request. After all, he is director of opera at that most prestigious venue. Also, if you agree, I would prefer it if Señor Francesco were to accompany her. What do you say?"

"Of course, Father. I will leave this task in your capable hands. In the meantime I will make the necessary travel arrangements for the forthcoming American tour. All that's left for me to do now is wish both of you a happy and peaceful Christmas. I look forward to seeing you both January next."

Don Barcese took his leave and boarded the train for Milan. During the course of his journey, he was surprised and somewhat annoyed with this last-minute decision of Consuella's. He was also none too pleased with Father Martine's decision to involve Señor Antonio and his troublesome companion. He decided there was nothing more he could do except make the arrangements for the forthcoming trip to America. He was determined to secure top billing for her at the Grand Metropolitan in New York. This, he believed, would put paid to any further interference from the mischievous friar, Señor Antonio, and that interfering voice coach.

As Consuella and Father Martine journeyed to her father's home, he raised the matter with her. "You know, Consuella, I was slightly surprised by your sudden decision just now., I would have been in a much better position to deal with this issue if I'd have had some prior notice of your intentions. Can you explain?"

"Again, Father, I'm in your debt. It was only when Don Barcese was about to depart. It was only then the thought struck me. I just suddenly felt that I would very much like to meet Antonio once more, particularly before my journey to America. Your timely intervention, I'm happy to say, makes this wish of mine probably more likely. What do you say, dear Father, can you do this for me?"

"Okay, Consuella. I will speak with Francesco. I'm pretty sure he will be able to prevail upon Antonio to make the necessary arrangements on your behalf. I also thought it would be preferable if Francesco were to accompany you instead of Don Barcese. I don't think Antonio would be overly excited at the prospect of having to meet with him. So let's leave it at that for the time being. I will speak with you again when there are further developments. For the moment, I think it best not to trouble your dear father and Sister Maria. I don't want to make the situation any more complicated than it needs be."

"Of course, Father. I will do as you suggest. Now tell me all about your plans for this year's carol service."

Arriving at her father's house, Consuella was over-joyed to see all of her family waiting to well-come her home. She hugged her father and greeted everyone enthusiastically. They were all eager to hear everything about her very successful European tour.

The carol service and the Christmas celebration was a splendid happy occasion for Consuella and all of the family. She was particularly delighted to meet with Carlota, Francesco, and their twin girls. Another pleasant surprise was the presence of Violetta and her father. A delighted Adamo made a point of sitting between father and daughter during the Christmas lunch. Pietro was so happy to have his youngest daughter home again. He cherished the time they now had together. He decided not to dwell too much on the fact that, in a very short while, his daughter would be very far away.

As they finished dinner, Father Martine stood up from the table. He requested that Consuella and Francesco join him. "Pietro, may I have the use of your sitting room for a few moments? There is something I need to discuss with Consuella and Francesco."

"By all means, Father. Please take all the time you need. And I won't even ask what scheme you and Francesco are planning right now."

The three of them smiled by way of response and left the dining room. As they closed the door behind them, Pietro couldn't help but tease Sister Maria. "Well, Sister, it mustn't be all that important, because, if it was, they would surely have had to involve you, would you agree?"

Sister Maria replied, quite tongue-in-cheek, "Well, Pietro, now that your daughter is an international star of some renown, what further need would she possibly have for my inadequate services and advice, a provincial nun who's never travelled beyond the borders of Italy?"

In the sitting room, Father Martine discussed the possibility with Francesco, of him making the trip to Vienna with Consuella.

Francesco responded, "First of all, I will need to contact Antonio. If he is agreeable, Carlota and I will accompany her. It's my belief that this would be more acceptable to him, rather than having Don Barcese turning up with Consuella in Vienna."

"My sentiments exactly. I will leave everything in your capable hands. Consuella, you can see Francesco and I are of one mind regarding this issue. Is there anything you wish to add?"

"No, Father. I agree with both of you. It would be best if Carlota and Francesco were to accompany me. I would feel so much more comfortable and would be ever so grateful to have them as travelling companions.

Thank you, Francesco, I really do appreciate the effort you are willing to make on my behalf."

"No need to thank me Consuella. After I have spoken with Antonio, I will get back to Father and discuss our travel arrangements."

With that, the three returned to the dining room and joined the others.

CHAPTER 38

Vienna, January 1912

As previously arranged, Carlota and Francesco travelled with Consuella from Verona to Vienna on the third of January. This was going to be the first opportunity for Francesco to meet with Antonio since the time of his sudden departure from Milan. Consuella, on the other hand, seemed to be somewhat nervous.

Carlota, ever vigilant, decided to engage her in some harmless chit-chat, which might dispel the slight anxiety she seemed to be experiencing. "Well, Consuella, here we are, the three of us travelling together to Vienna. I'm sure you must be quite excited at the prospect of performing at the Vienna Court Opera and, of course, the opportunity you will have to meet with Antonio."

Consuella answered in a hesitant manner. "You know, Carlota, even though this is something I truly wanted to do, I am now somewhat apprehensive—not about the forthcoming performances but, rather, at the thought of meeting Antonio. I still have feelings of guilt regarding the unfair manner in which I treated him in the past."

"There now, Consuella. Don't be too disheartened. When Francesco spoke to Antonio, he responded positively regarding your request, didn't he, darling?"

Francesco, who had been sitting quietly reading his book, decided to assist his wife in her efforts. "Consuella, when I spoke by telephone with Antonio regarding this matter, his response was most enthusiastic. And he stated that he had every confidence in your ability to perform to the highest standard in what is regarded as the most prestigious opera venue, second only to La Scala. He also promised me that he will be at the train station to welcome us on our arrival. Does that seem to you like he is holding some kind of grudge for actions that are now a thing of the past? So now I would like you two ladies to enjoy the remainder of the journey, and if you have no objections, I would like to continue reading my book."

They both smiled in response.

Carlota took Consuella's hand in hers. "My dear Consuella, I want you to just try and relax. Let's enjoy the remainder of our journey together. You know Francesco would not have spoken those words just now if they were untrue. So now, do you faith in your former voice coach?"

"Thank you, Carlota. You and Francesco have set my mind at ease. Please don't worry too much about me. I promise I'll be fine."

As previously arranged, Antonio was waiting for them as their train pulled into Meidling Train Station. As they disembarked, Antonio greeted them. He exchanged warm handshakes with Carlota and Francesco. Consuella, again slightly nervous, remained standing behind Carlota, wondering to herself if Antonio was going to say something.

She didn't have very long to wait. He took one look at her and exclaimed, "Francesco, this must be the young soprano you spoke of."

Then turning to Consuella with a friendly smile, he continued, "Welcome to Vienna, Señorita Consuella. I do hope you enjoyed your journey. Are you looking forward to performing at the Vienna Court Opera?"

Consuella at first didn't quite know how to react. Looking over in Carlota and Francesco's direction, she could see them smiling. She now realised this was Antonio's way of avoiding any potential embarrassment for either of them. She responded in kind, "Why thank you, Señor Antonio. The journey was indeed delightful, and yes, I am looking forward to performing in that great theatre."

Francesco, satisfied that this meeting between Consuella and Antonio had gotten off to a positive start, made the following suggestion: "Antonio, why don't you take us to the hotel. Carlota and Consuella can have a rest. Then you and I can catch up on all that's been happening since we last met."

At the hotel, Francesco joined Antonio in the dining room. "We're all checked in, Antonio. The two ladies have gone to their rooms. So now, how have you been since we last met?"

"I have to say, Francesco, I'm very pleased with how things have gone for me here. I'm doing my best to build a new life for myself, so I really should be grateful."

"What are your thoughts now that you have met Consuella?"

"For me, there is one thing that will never change. My feelings for Consuella are the same today as they always were. I'm just curious why she wanted to come to Vienna of all places."

"Carlota and I haven't spoken with her in any great detail on the subject. My own view is that she very much wanted to see you before her pending trip to America. She will be there for the best part of three months. I can't say for certain, but I get a sense she still has an emotional and affectionate attachment to you. I suppose now you'll need to decide what to do between now and our departure."

"Thank you, Francesco. I will indeed give the matter very careful consideration over the coming days. Now the big question, how is the great Don Barcese behaving himself?"

"Surprisingly well from what I've heard. I believe we have your teacher to thank for this individual's stewardship of Consuella's career these past few months. Before they departed for Germany and the other destinations, Father Martine made it abundantly clear he would be paying very close attention to Consuella's progress. It would seem Don Barcese, for once in his life, met someone who was more than able to deal with his arrogant behaviour. The tour, it seems, was a great success. Now, how are things going for you in your new exalted position as director of opera here in Vienna?"

"Well, I have to say quite splendidly. At times it has been challenging, though on these occasions, I have drawn on the many lessons you've taught me over the years."

"Excellent, excellent. Now I think we should get ourselves ready for Consuella's performance later tonight. What do you say?"

"As you say, Francesco. I will be waiting at the theatre for you at eight o'clock tonight."

With that, Antonio bid his friend farewell and took his leave.

The three-night run of Mozart's *Marriage of Figaro* was a great success. When the final curtain closed, Antonio met Carlota and Francesco in the foyer.

Carlota was overjoyed and complimented him. "Antonio, thank you so much for the wonderful production you put on here this evening. La Scala would be most envious of what you have achieved here these past three nights. It was truly marvellous. Don't you agree, darling?"

Francesco answered in his usual understated manner, "Why yes, I would have to agree with you, my dear. The acoustics were wonderful; the orchestra was superb; the soprano, well what can I say, I suppose she was adequate."

Antonio smilingly responded, "Carlota, Francesco, if the two of you wish to make your way to the hotel, there are one or two items I have to deal with here. When Consuella has changed out of her costume, I will accompany her back. Then the four of us can have an enjoyable meal together. You have an early train journey back tomorrow morning; this evening will be our last opportunity to be together, though hopefully we can all meet again when Consuella returns from America."

Carlota and Francesco took their leave. Antonio headed for Consuella's dressing room. Knocking on the door softly, he called out her name, "Consuella, it's me, Antonio. When you are ready, if you wish, I will escort you to your hotel. Carlota and Francesco have gone ahead."

As she heard his voice, her heart skipped a beat. "Antonio, please come in. I am almost ready."

He entered the dressing room and closed the door behind him. Taking one look at her as she was fixing her hair, he realised there and then, his feelings and the love he deeply held for her, had not changed in any way, since the day of his departure from Verona. "Consuella, congratulations on the wonderful performances. You now have many fans here in Vienna. Well done."

Turning towards him, she smilingly replied, "And what about you, Antonio? Are you still a fan?"

"Always, always," he replied as he reached out and embraced her.

She put her arms around him and tearfully responded, "Antonio, dearest Antonio, please, please forgive me for being so terribly cruel to you. I've missed you so much and I've never stopped loving you, not for even one single moment."

The two of them remained in each other's arm for several moments, just silently and lovingly embracing each other.

Meanwhile, Carlota and Francesco, as agreed, waited in the hotel dining room. Carlota, sitting there patiently, posed the following question: "Darling, do you have any thoughts on what might be possible between Consuella and Antonio now that they have met each other again?"

"You know, dear, in life, anything is possible. I think the best thing for us to do is just observe and see what happens. On the train journey home, an opportunity may present itself for you to gauge more accurately how things now stand between them. I do know for certain she will travel to America. When she returns, I think we will have a much better sense of where their relationship is going."

Before Carlota had a chance to respond, Consuella and Antonio entered the dining room. As they took their seats, Carlota couldn't help but notice the radiant expression on Consuella's face. Antonio also seemed to be in a very happy frame of mind.

The four of them had a most enjoyable evening. The table talk was mainly about Consuella's performances and the audience's positive reaction. There was no talk of her forthcoming tour of America and certainly no mention of any future plans the two of them may have discussed.

As the evening drew to a close, Antonio bid them goodnight. "Carlota, Francesco, it was truly wonderful seeing you again."

He then turned to Consuella. "Consuella, I would like to wish you every success on your journey to America. If your performances there are even half as good they were here in Vienna, you will make your family very proud and the three of us also. Have a safe and pleasant journey."

Carlota paid close attention to the manner of Consuella's response. "Thank you, dearest Antonio. From the bottom of my heart, thank you. This short trip has meant so much to me. I will carry this fond memory with me until, hopefully, we can meet again very soon."

As she was speaking, he held out his two hands and took hers in his. Carlota and Francesco could clearly see that this parting, for both of them, was sad and yet bliss-full. There seemed to be a hope in their eyes that their parting would not be for too long. With that, Antonio took his leave. Consuella just stood there watching him as he left. She had a warm smile on her face. To Carlota this was, without doubt, a loving gaze.

Early the following morning, the trio made the journey back to Verona. Carlota decided to try and ascertain how things now stood between Consuella and Antonio. "I have to say, Consuella, Antonio looks very well. What do you think?"

"Yes indeed, Carlota. He does look really well. And I have to say, he is still as handsome as ever."

"You know, Consuella, this reminds me of a previous train journey we made together in the past. We were on our way back from Dominique's wedding, do you remember?"

"Of course I remember. On that particular occasion, you were deliberately teasing Antonio."

"Well the reason I teased Antonio back then was to see your reaction. I'm happy to say I was not disappointed."

"I'm curious, Carlota, why are you raising this matter now?"

Carlota decided now was an opportunity for her to find out the current status of Consuella and Antonio's relationship. "Last night in the hotel, as Antonio was preparing to take his leave, I had the exact same thought as I had on that train journey. I just thought you and Antonio make a lovely couple; that's all."

"You know, Carlota, I have to agree with you. I also think we make a lovely couple. As for the future, well, I think I'll just keep you and Francesco guessing. Who knows? Maybe when I return from America, Antonio and I might just have surprising news for you. I will also be giving careful consideration to a totally unrelated matter."

"May I enquire as to what this unrelated matter might be?"

"Of course, Carlota, though I feel Francesco may well be more interested than yourself. On my return, I will be making a decision as to whether Don Barcese will have any future involvement in my career."

Carlota was happy with her response. She was now convinced that the love and affection Consuella and Antonio had had for each other in the past had not in any way diminished over the short time span they had been apart. She also felt there was no need for her to involve herself in the issue concerning the future management of Consuella's career. She believed her husband would pursue this later statement of Consuella's in his own way.

Francesco, who had been quietly listening to their conversation, responded to her remarks concerning the future management of her career. "You mentioned Don Barcese just now. May I enquire what plans, if any, you might have in this regard?"

"You may well indeed, Francesco. I have to say, in all honesty, he has done a reasonable job up to now. On my return from America, he has me scheduled to appear in Milan. It is my intention to terminate the contract on completion of these three performances."

"Have you given any thought as to who might be a suitable candidate to replace him?"

Consuella answered him with a mischievous smile, "Oh a certain Señor Fabrizio from Vienna might be a worthy candidate for the position. Let's just wait and see what happens. What do you say?"

Carlota and Francesco didn't respond. They just smiled.

The remainder of the journey passed off pleasantly enough. There was no further discussion concerning herself and Antonio.

CHAPTER 39

The American Tour

Back in Verona, Consuella spent two precious days with her father, Dominique, Paolo, and Adamo. She spoke only briefly about her trip to Vienna and hardly mentioned Antonio at all. Everyone was dying with curiosity.

Before Carlota and Francesco departed for Milan, Carlota dropped one or two hints to the family, as to what might happen between Consuella and Antonio on her return from America. This seemed to satisfy everyone, well at least momentarily.

On the evening of Thursday, 11 January, Don Barcese arrived in Verona. Father Martine met with him at his hotel. "Welcome, Don Barcese. I trust you had a pleasant journey from Milan. And what a pity, if you had been here earlier, you would have met Señor Cipriano and his charming wife, Carlota."

"Oh what a shame. No matter. I trust everything went according to plan in Vienna. And how is Señor Antonio? Keeping well I hope?"

"He's fine, just fine. And yes, everything did go splendidly for Consuella. So now, let's get down to business. My time is precious, as I'm sure yours is also."

"Of course, Father. We will travel from Verona tomorrow. I have booked return passage on the SS *George Washington* from Genoa to New York this coming Saturday. We will return early March in time for four scheduled performances at La Scala. I will see to it Consuella has reasonable time to recover from her journey prior to this. It is quite a long voyage, four and a half thousand nautical miles to be exact. But have no fear. I will take good care of Consuella. You have my word on that."

"Of that I've no doubt, Don Barcese. Once you keep me updated on progress, I don't think we will have any problems. So I look forward to meeting you tomorrow at the train station. I will make sure to have Consuella there on time."

With that, Father Martine bid him farewell and left.

The following morning, Don Barcese waited at the train station as agreed. In the distance, he could see the pair making their way along the platform. On second glance, he was totally surprised and slightly shocked to see a larger group of people accompanying Consuella and Father Martine.

"Ah there you are, Don Barcese. I would like to introduce you to Señor Pellegrini; his daughter Dominique; her husband, Paolo; and Adamo, Consuella's older brother."

Don Barcese bowed gratuitously. He shook hands with Pietro and replied as convincingly as he could, "It is a great honour to finally meet you, Señor Pellegrini. You must be very proud of Consuella and all she has achieved in her career to date."

"Yes indeed, Don Barcese, and I will always be indebted to Señor Antonio. He was the one who discovered her potential and assisted her in achieving the success she so rightly deserves. I trust you will take excellent care of my daughter over the coming weeks?"

Ignoring the comments concerning Antonio, Don Barcese replied, "Of course, Señor Pellegrini, I will do my utmost to protect your daughter and bring her back safely."

After some emotional farewells, Don Barcese and Consuella boarded the train for Genoa. There, they would board the ship for the long voyage to America.

Don Barcese had booked a series of performances in three major cities. The first two venues were the Boston Opera House in Massachusetts and the Philadelphia Opera House in Pennsylvania. And then, finally, to complete her American tour, she was scheduled to perform in the world-famous Metropolitan Opera of New York.

The tour had been a wonderful experience for her. Don Barcese had done his job diligently enough, though Consuella had a sense he certainly wasn't making the same efforts on her behalf as he had previously done during her European tour. He booked excellent accommodation for her in the best hotels and made sure to accompany her on time to and from all venues.

On most occasions, particularly in New York, he always seemed to be meeting with individuals who certainly didn't strike her as opera enthusiasts. Little did she know, these individuals were associates of his from his home-town in Sicily.

Don Barcese, on the other hand, had a sense that his stewardship of her career was possibly coming to an end. He hadn't forgotten her father's words about Señor Antonio. He wondered what, if anything, might have taken place between Consuella and her former manager during her trip to Vienna.

He decided there was nothing he could do to change what he believed was going to be the inevitable outcome of his very short tenure as her manager. He consoled himself in the knowledge that he had, at the very least, outmanoeuvred Antonio and the interfering voice coach in achieving this goal, even if it was going to be short-lived as now seemed likely.

CHAPTER 40

Consuella Returns to Milan

By late March, Consuella and Don Barcese travelled from New York to Genoa. The American tour had exhausted her, and the voyage left her feeling quite ill. She spent two precious days with her family. Although they were over-joyed to have her once more among them. They were somewhat concerned regarding the delicate state she seemed to be in. Still feeling unwell, she nevertheless made the journey to Milan. At La Scala, she was scheduled to perform a three-night run of Verdi's *La Traviata*, commencing Sunday, 31 March.

Violetta Mollinaro had been chosen to play the part of the servant girl, Annina. Consuella was to play the leading role of the courtesan, the aptly named Violetta. She was genuinely looking forward to performing with her friend in this much-loved opera.

Francesco was in the audience. His main purpose for attending was to observe Consuella. He would then be in a better position to up-date Father Martine on her progress. As he sat down, he spotted Don Barcese in his private box; his arrogant demeanour and sense of his own self-importance were still very much in evidence.

Don Barcese, looking rather pleased with himself, was fully confident the audience would give Consuella a rapturous welcome. After all, this was her first performance in Milan since her return from a very successful American tour. Tonight, there was no doubt in his mind, he would finally be recognised as the most distinguished and influential impresario in the world of Italian opera.

Just before the opening curtain, Don Barcese's associate Carlo happened to be hanging around the foyer. Ever vigilant, he spotted a police inspector in conversation with two officers. He drifted over in their direction, curious to find out what they might be discussing. What he overheard alarmed him greatly.

Wasting no time, Carlo entered Don Barcese's box. Leaning down, he whispered quietly into his ear, making sure his guests could not overhear. "Don Barcese, whatever you do, just stay calm and look straight ahead. Act as if everything is normal. There are two police officers in the theatre. I overheard their superior instructing them to keep you under surveillance until the end of the third act. Their orders are to arrest you as soon as you leave the theatre."

Completely panic-stricken, Don Barcese nevertheless managed to whisper back, "Thank you, Carlo. You go out and keep a close eye. Tell George to bring the auto-mobile around and wait. There's nothing I can do right now, though I'll try and think of something before the end of the evening."

Carlo did as he was instructed. Don Barcese, in the meantime, sat there desperately trying to think of some way he might avoid this looming catastrophe. As the orchestra burst into life and the curtain opened on the first act, he made a desperate effort to mask his concern. With a beaming smile on his face, he looked all around him, trying to create the impression he was enjoying himself enormously with not a care in the world.

The orchestra was delightful and the performers, likewise. Francesco could see from the audience's reaction everyone certainly seemed to be enjoying the performance. He paid close attention to Consuella. Although her voice was as beautiful as ever, he did however detect she was having some difficulty with her delivery, particularly on the high notes.

As act one was drawing to a close, Consuella took her place on stage to sing "Sempre Libera". This aria literally meant "Always Free". Two minutes into her solo, she hesitated for a moment, missing a note. She looked anxiously to the conductor. Being a thorough professional, he quickly rebalanced the musicians in an effort to cover her mistake. The audience didn't seem to notice. Francesco certainly did.

Trying desperately to carry on and finish the piece, Consuella suddenly lost her voice. For a frozen moment, she just stared into the auditorium and then collapsed precariously close to the edge of the stage. The orchestra immediately stopped playing. The stage manager, Gianni Donati, ordered that the curtains be closed and the house lights switched on. The other members of the cast, greatly concerned, rushed over to render assistance. They decided the best thing to do was take Consuella as gently as possible from the stage to her dressing room.

There were loud gasps from the audience, as well as total confusion. The crowd waited anxiously and somewhat impatiently for something to happen. Francesco glanced up in the direction of the private boxes. There was no sign of Don Barcese; also, his curtains were partially closed. Francesco quickly made his way backstage

In the midst of the chaos and confusion, Don Barcese seized his opportunity. He drew the curtains slightly and slipped out of the theatre. George drove him to a secret location. He then gave George specific instructions. "Whatever you do, don't go back to my residence tonight. Take this key, and when you get an opportunity, give it to Alfred. There's a possibility I may have to leave Italy. If that's the case, Alfred will take care of you and Mildred. So go and make sure you don't tell anyone of my whereabouts."

George did as instructed. Don Barcese then took a cab to another location. It wasn't that he didn't trust George. He just wanted to be doubly sure and avoid arrest at any cost, which would enable him to plan his escape.

Meanwhile, back at the theatre, a fretful Gianni Donati didn't know what to do next.

Francesco took him to one side. "Gianni, I want you to go out on stage. Apologise for the brief interruption. Explain to the audience that Señorita Consuella is okay but, regrettably, will be unable to carry on. Ask them to remain seated and reassure them the second act will commence in fifteen minutes."

"But, Señor Francesco, we have nobody to replace Señorita Consuella."

"Yes we do. Violetta Mollinaro will take her place."

"Señor Francesco, are you sure she can do it?"

"I was never more certain. Now, Gianni go out there and make the announcement. I'll make sure Violetta is ready."

He headed straight away to Consuella's dressing room, knowing Violetta would be there. On entering, he could see the stress and confusion for himself. Surprisingly, there was no sign of Don Barcese. He beckoned Violetta to come over.

"How is she?" he asked rather anxiously.

"We gave her smelling salts and some water. She's in a slightly better state, though there's no chance she'll be able to continue."

"Okay, I'll take care of Consuella and see to it she gets home safely. Now what I want you to do is go straight away to your dressing room. I'll have the wardrobe assistant bring you a costume. Change into it immediately and be ready to go on stage. I want you to take Consuella's place."

"Francesco, I couldn't possibly do this to Consuella. Tonight's performance will have to be cancelled. There's really nothing more to be done."

"Listen to me, Violetta. If this performance is cancelled, that audience out there won't easily forget. If act two and three go ahead, which they have to, then despite this minor disruption, those opera lovers will put this minor inconvenience behind them."

"Okay, Francesco. I'm quite nervous, but I will do it. Please wish me luck."

"Don't worry, Violetta. You'll be fine. And remember, you're doing this for Consuella."

To the relief of Gianni Donati, Violetta and the cast took their places on stage for act two and three. Francesco couldn't help but draw the conclusion, that it was somewhat ironic. Here was Consuella going through the exact same trauma endured by Violetta some four years earlier, and here was Violetta stepping in to rescue the situation on her behalf. It didn't surprise him in the least that the architect of Consuella's breakdown and humiliation was nowhere to be seen.

The audience, despite the disruption, settled down and enjoyed the remainder of the evening. Francesco, reasonably satisfied normality had been restored, headed back to Consuella. He was relieved to see the house nurse in attendance.

"How is she, nurse? Is there anything I can do?"

"She's very weak and most likely suffering from shock. I've given her a sedative. She needs to be taken home right away. As a precaution, I would advise she see her doctor as soon as possible."

"Thank you, Nurse. I'll see to it. If you can get her ready, I'll organise a cab and get her home as quickly as I can."

He asked one of the attendants to call a cab and have it wait at the side entrance. The nurse helped him escort her very gently from the theatre. Once they were inside and just as Francesco was about to give the driver instructions,

Consuella, in a barely audible voice pleaded, "Francesco, I don't want to be taken home. Please, take me to Sister Lucia. She will know what to do."

On the way to the convent and very aware of her fragile state, Francesco nevertheless delicately inquired if she could give some clue that might explain why her manager, Don Barcese, had failed to come to her assistance.

Despite her weakened state, she managed to answer and then made a request. "It doesn't surprise me in the least. During the tour of America, he seemed to become more disinterested in my progress as each day passed. He just did about enough to avoid any possible repercussions from Father Martine."

"Okay, Consuella. Try and relax a little. We haven't too far to go. Now what is it you wish me to do?"

"You know the opt-out clause in my contract. When we arrive at the convent, could you possibly go over to his residence and terminate our agreement? This is something I had intended to do anyway."

"Okay. Let's first get you there safely and then see what happens."

On reaching the convent, Sister Agostina opened the door. She was quite startled to see Francesco standing there supporting a very weak Consuella. Guiding her to the nearest chair, she then hurried to fetch Sister Lucia and Sister Colombina. Both of them were quite shocked to see Consuella in this distressed state. They immediately took her to the infirmary.

Francesco waited in the hallway. Some fifteen minutes passed before Sister Lucia returned. "Francesco, thank you. You did the right thing bringing her here. She's asleep now. Someone will be in attendance throughout the night. The doctor will be here first thing in the morning. There is probably not much more we can do in the meantime."

"That's fine, Sister Lucia. At least now she's in safe hands. If you can excuse me, there's something I need to attend to right away on Consuella's behalf. Carlota and I will call as soon as we can tomorrow. I will then explain everything to you and Sister Colombina.

"In the meantime, can you telephone Sister Maria and let her know what's happened? Make sure she notifies Pietro and Father Martine. When I get an opportunity I will make contact with Antonio."

With that, he bid her goodnight, got back into the cab, and gave the driver directions to Don Barcese's town house.

CHAPTER 41

Inspector Albasini

Arriving at Don Barcese's residence, Francesco was surprised and somewhat puzzled. There were a number of police officers present.

As he approached, one of them asked, "Excuse me, señor. I need to ask, what business do you have here?"

"Certainly, officer. I have some urgent business to discuss with Don Barcese. I would appreciate it if you allow me proceed."

"I'm sorry, señor. My instructions are clear; nobody can enter without permission and proper identification."

"I understand. May I enquire who is in charge?"

"Inspector Albasini, señor."

"My name is Francesco Cipriano. Could you possibly let him know I'm here?"

"One moment, señor. I'll see if he's available."

After a few brief moments, the officer returned. "Just go straight in, Señor Cipriano. Inspector Albasini will see you right away."

As he entered, Francesco was greeted by Sergio Albasini, inspector of the Department of Public Security. "Francesco, you're the last person I would expect to see calling on Don Barcese. What brings you here at this late hour?"

"It's a personal matter, Sergio."

"Well I'm sorry to disappointment you, Francesco. As you can see, I'm also waiting for him. If and when he turns up, he will be immediately arrested."

"What's this horrendous crime he's committed? Did he steal the funds from the church poor box?"

"That wouldn't surprise me in the least. I'm afraid his criminality is some-what more serious than that. He's deeply involved in the illegal arms trade."

Francesco was literally stunned by Sergio's revelation. "He what?! You mean to tell me Don Barcese is an arms dealer."

"It's true. He's been involved in this activity for some five years now. We've been watching him closely for the past three years or so. We were never really able to gather sufficient evidence against him until four days ago. The captain of the ship used for transporting and delivering the arms made a fatal error. He landed several consignments of arms on the North African coast. All of the purchasers turned up. Bar one. He decided to reload this consignment and bring it back to Italy. This was something Don Barcese never allowed under any circumstances.

"Up to then, we never intercepted the vessel. In all instances, we knew full well no arms would be found. On this occasion, however, our agents in North Africa set a trap. They posed as revolutionaries. Made a prepaid purchase and, on the day of collection, deliberately failed to show up.

"On entering our territorial waters, the ship was boarded by the Customs and Border Protection Police, under our instructions. They seized the arms and the money, then detained the captain and the crew. Within twelve hours, the skipper gave us the vital information we needed to arrest Don Barcese and charge him with serious arm trafficking offences.

"We had him under surveillance earlier this evening. In the confusion following that unfortunate incident involving Señorita Consuella, he managed to slip away. When we apprehend him, it will certainly be the end of his prestigious involvement in the operatic world.

"Anyway, your reason for being here. Can I ask what it's about?"

"Well, it concerns Señorita Consuella. With the incident earlier, I rendered some assistance. She requested I come over here and terminate her contract. From what you've just told me, I believe this contract is now most definitely and irrevocably terminated."

"Of that, you need have no doubt. Tell me, how is she doing now?"

"I took her to the convent. Sister Lucia is looking after her. The doctor will be calling first thing tomorrow morning. Hopefully, she'll be okay after a day or two."

"Francesco, if there's any further news, I'll certainly let you know."

On his way home, Francesco was thinking about the seriousness of what Sergio Albasini had just revealed concerning Don Barcese. On reflection, he really wasn't all that surprised, although it certainly was a grave matter. He couldn't help but smile, thinking back to one of his exchanges with Mario, who, probably unknowingly, branded Don Barcese a Sicilian gangster.

The following morning, Francesco and Carlota arrived at the convent to check on Consuella. Sister Lucia joined them in the drawing room. Carlota anxiously asked, "How is she this morning? Has the doctor been over?"

"She had a restful night," Sister Lucia told them. "The doctor was here earlier. He's put her on a course of fairly strong medication. He recommended she take an immediate break from performing—at least until she shows positive signs of recovering."

Francesco asked, "Have Sister Maria and her father been notified?"

"Sister Colombina telephoned her this morning. There is one other thing, Francesco."

"Go on, Sister. We're listening."

"For her convalescence, Consuella wants it to take place at the convent in Verona."

"What did the doctor have to say?"

"He said in two days time, she could travel, provided she is accompanied by someone who would be able to take care of her for the journey."

"What does that have to do with Carlota and me?"

"She has requested Carlota and yourself perform this task."

Carlota asked, "What about the twins?"

"While you're away. They'd be welcome to stay with me here at the convent."

Francesco looked at his wife. "Well, darling, what do you think?"

"I'll have a word with them. If they're happy with this plan, then we'll do it."

"Thank you, Carlota. And don't worry; I'll take good care of the two girls."

Carlota and Francesco took their leave to prepare for the journey to Verona. Later that same morning, Francesco telephoned Antonio and gave him the news concerning Consuella.

CHAPTER 42

Carlota and Francesco Accompany Consuella to Verona

On Thursday, 4 April, Carlota, Francesco, and the twins arrived at the convent. Sister Lucia welcomed them and showed them into the drawing room.

Sister Colombina joined them and greeted them warmly. "Welcome, Carlota. Welcome, Francesco. Good morning, children. Now please, take a seat. Sister Lucia and I will go and see if Consuella is ready."

While they were gone, Sister Agostina brought in some refreshments. Some moments later the two sisters returned with Consuella. Carlota was quite shocked by her appearance. She could clearly see how ill she actually was. The first thought that came to mind was the occasion on which she had met a very fragile Violetta Mollinaro. Taking her by the arm, she helped her to a chair.

Francesco asked Sister Lucia if there were any special instructions. "Has the doctor issued any particular advice for the journey?"

"She's already had her medication. This is a letter for the doctor in Verona. It's the doctor's diagnosis of her condition. He said to keep her warm for the duration of the trip and that she will probably sleep for most of it. That's about as much as I can tell you, Francesco. I know you and Carlota will take very good care of her. Carlota, don't worry about Adriana and Carla. Instead of me taking care of them, I think they will be taking care of me."

Carlota smiled in response. "Thank you, Sister. I think we should take our leave now. The most important thing is to get this young lady to Verona, so she can make a full recovery. I for one want to hear her sing again very, very soon."

With that, Carlota and Francesco gently escorted Consuella to the auto-mobile. Before leaving, Consuella, although in a fragile state, tearfully thanked Sister Lucia. "Dear Sister, thank you for all you've done for me, not just on this occasion, but also in the past. Please keep me in your prayers."

During the journey, as the doctor had predicted, Consuella slept for most of the trip. On their arrival in Verona, Father Martine was waiting for them at the station. When they got to the convent, Carlota and Sister Maria assisted her to her room. Francesco, Pietro, and Father Martine waited in the dining room.

Pietro was in a distressed state, so Father Martine opened the conversation. "Francesco, we're deeply grateful to you and Carlota. If you hadn't been on hand to offer assistance, I fear poor Consuella would be in a much worse state now. What about this Don Barcese character, any news of him?"

"When Sister Maria and Carlota return, I'll give you a full update."

Sister Maria and Carlota joined them. Francesco handed her the letter. "This is a letter from the doctor. You might wish to give it to the doctor here. How is she now?"

Sister Maria answered, "We have her settled in. Dr Vanzetti will be here first thing tomorrow morning."

Father Martine continued where he had left off. "Now, Francesco, can you take us through the events that led to this sorry state of affairs?"

Francesco brought them through everything that had taken place following Consuella's collapse, including Sergio Albasini's revelations concerning Don Barcese. The three of them were quite shocked.

Father Martine asked, "So where is this criminal now? Are the police confident they will apprehend him?"

"All I can say is they have a number of officers watching the train stations and ports to prevent him slipping out of the country. Let's hope their efforts are successful. If nothing else, we can at least be thankful this scoundrel will have no further impact on Consuella's life or career."

"What about Antonio? Have you made contact with him yet?"

"Yes, I have already spoken with him. He'll be here tomorrow morning. Pietro has kindly invited Carlota and myself to stay with him tonight.

When Antonio arrives, I will bring him up to date on all that has taken place, and see were things might just go from there."

"That's good. Maybe now a reconciliation between them might just be possible."

Carlota and Sister Maria gave him a surprised look. Carlota responded, "You know, Father, I've always admired your optimism. But do you not think that talk of a reconciliation just now might be somewhat premature? Consuella is in a very delicate state. I believe our overriding objective should be to do all we can to make sure she makes a full recovery. Would you agree, Father?"

He replied quite sheepishly, "Of course, Carlota. As usual, I stand corrected. Please, forgive my impetuous remarks just now."

"I forgive you, Father. Now if you gentlemen will excuse us, Sister Maria and I are going to check on our patient."

While they were having these discussions, little did any of them realise Don Barcese had already left Italy and was now in Berlin.

CHAPTER 43

Don Barcese Leaves Italy

Having cleverly disguised himself, Don Barcese managed to avoid the border checks. He crossed over into Austria and, from there, travelled by train to Germany. On his arrival in Berlin, he made an appointment for the following day with Herr Berthold Schuster, the manager and vice president of the Berlin National Bank.

Entering the bank, he was immediately escorted to the boardroom. He was surprised to see Herr Schuster standing to attention. The manager was a tall, handsome, smartly dressed individual with blond hair; if Don Barcese was to make a guess, he would have put his age at no more than forty-five. Beside Herr Schuster was an exceptionally pretty female. She too seemed to be standing to attention, notebook, pencil, and file in hand, ready for action.

Herr Schuster greeted him in Italian. "Welcome, welcome, Don Barcese. May I say what an honour and such an unexpected pleasure to see you here in Berlin."

Don Barcese was thinking to himself during this effusive greeting that Herr Schuster was not going to be pleased for very much longer. He decided, nonetheless, to allow him to continue with the pleasantries.

"And now if I may," said Herr Schuster, "I would like to introduce you to my able assistant, Frau Kirstin Engel. Frau Engel will be taking notes of our meeting. Without her, it would be most difficult for me to function. She is meticulously efficient."

Without saying a word, Frau Engel bowed in a very precise manner. Don Barcese returned her gesture with an approving smile and a mangled German thankyou. She nevertheless maintained her military style posture and made no response.

With the formalities now completed, Herr Schuster continued. "Please, if you will, Don Barcese, please take a seat, and we can begin."

"Do you mean I can sit at any seat of my choosing?"

"Why of course, Don Barcese, please sit wherever makes you most comfortable. I know we Germans have a reputation for being stiff and formal, but there are occasions when we can be spontaneous and sometimes even quite frivolous. So please choose a seat you feel suits you best."

Don Barcese made his way to the other side of the table. He selected the middle chair and sat down. Herr Schuster sat down in the chair directly opposite. Frau Engel set the file down in front of her boss. Ever mindful of her subordinate status she did not opt to sit at the boardroom table. Instead, she placed a chair slightly behind his left shoulder and sat bolt upright, pencil and notebook at the ready.

Before the meeting commenced, Don Barcese took the briefest moment to observe. He had a strong sense that, if he were to make a sudden movement or gesture, Frau Engel would most likely leap across that broad table and, in one fell swoop, stab him in the neck with that pencil of hers. He was in no doubt he would be dead before his body hit the floor.

Just as this thought was running through his mind, he looked over in her direction. She returned his gaze. This time, she had a slight imperious expression. He couldn't help but feel she was reading his thoughts, and it made him somewhat uncomfortable. Raising his hand to his mouth, he coughed in a slightly self-conscious manner and then turned his face to one side to avoid her penetrating stare.

"Don Barcese," Herr Schuster began. "Now that we are all seated, we can begin our meeting. So, in your own time, please proceed."

"Thank you, Herr Schuster. Could you please bring me up to date on the exact sums in both accounts?"

"Of course," he replied. Opening the file, he scanned the first page and ran his index finger down a column of figures. He repeated this process with the second page, and then, turning to Frau Engel, he spoke in German. As he did so she was busy making notes.

Don Barcese found himself at a disadvantage. He didn't understand the German language except for one or two phrases. And his position at the opposite side of the table didn't afford him an opportunity to observe what Frau Engel was recording in that notebook of hers.

"Ah there we are. Thank you for your patience, Don Barcese. I will now give you a detailed summary on the current status of the accounts." Herr Schuster held out his left hand, and Frau Engel handed him the notebook.

Placing it on the table, he began, "In your current account, there is the sum of one million nine hundred and sixty thousand German marks. On deposit, the amount is eleven million seven hundred and forty-three thousand German marks. And according to Frau Kirstin's calculations the value of the funds in both accounts comes to a total of thirteen million seven hundred and three thousand German marks."

Don Barcese sat for a few moments without making any comment or gesture. Herr Schuster also sat motionless. He was wondering to himself what thoughts might be going through Don Barcese's mind. Was he perhaps going to make a withdrawal? Or maybe he was about to make a lodgement?

Don Barcese leaned forward. "Thank you, Herr Schuster. Thank you, Frau Kirstin. You have both been most diligent."

They acknowledged his gesture with a formal bow.

Don Barcese then asked, "Now, would it be possible for you to calculate that sum in American dollars?"

Without batting an eyelid, Herr Schuster handed the notebook back to Frau Kirstin. Taking it, she turned over a new page and began jotting down figures. Having completed her sums, she handed it back.

"Thank you, Frau Kirstin. I just do not know how I would manage if I didn't have your pretty brain working so effortlessly on my behalf."

She allowed herself a brief smile but remained silent nonetheless.

"Now let me see what my able assistant has produced. Ah yes. Here we are. The total sum comes to three hundred and twenty six thousand two hundred and sixty two American dollars precisely."

Don Barcese didn't respond. Instead, he was thinking how best to inform Herr Schuster his presence at the bank was for one purpose only, and that purpose was to withdraw all of his money in American dollars.

Herr Schuster, on the other hand, was trying to figure out why Don Barcese wanted to know the dollar value of his funds. Could it be possible he was thinking of making some investments in America? He decided to probe a little further and see if he could ascertain what Don Barcese had in mind. "Please, Don Barcese, I don't mean to be impertinent, but your request just now. Is it possible you may be thinking of using some of your funds for investment purposes in the United States?"

"How perceptive you are, Herr Schuster. That is exactly my intention."

"Excellent, excellent. We have a section that specialises in advising important clients such as yourself. At the best of times, these sorts of transactions can be most complicated. So should you wish to invest in real estate or other commodities such as oil and gas, we have a team of experts who can produce a portfolio of options for your approval. With your permission, I will make the necessary arrangements. I can promise you, you won't be disappointed."

"Why thank you, Herr Schuster, but that will not be necessary. You see, I have many business associates in America, so I have decided to withdraw all of my money and close both accounts. I am planning on travelling to the United States very soon, and it is most likely I will not be returning to Europe for some considerable time. So if you would be kind enough and make the necessary arrangements, I would be most grateful."

"Again, you must forgive me, Don Barcese. You have taken me quite by surprise. I certainly was not expecting such an outcome. This large amount of cash, particularly in American dollars, would not be available at such short notice."

"I quite understand, Herr Schuster. So would it be possible to give me a time frame in order for us to conclude our business?"

"Would the day after tomorrow be acceptable?"

"Then the day after tomorrow it is. I will be here at midday, I am very much looking forward to concluding our business in an amicable fashion, Now, if I may, I would like to take this opportunity to thank you, Herr Schuster, and of course Frau Kirstin for the time you have given me and also the courteous manner adopted by both of you in our discussions."

As he stood up, they both stood up in unison. Bowing formally they each shook his hand with, of course, Frau Kirstin not offering hers until her boss had done so first. Don Barcese then walked from the bank. He climbed into the Mercedes auto-mobile he had hired for the duration of his stay. As the driver drove him to his hotel, he just kept running that figure over in his mind. 326,000 American dollars plus. Sitting back and enjoying the luxury of the splendid motor vehicle, he felt rather pleased with himself. Despite the recent setbacks in Italy and the fact it was most likely he would never have the opportunity to return, he was happy in the knowledge all of his past contingency planning would now afford him the opportunity to seek out new and exciting projects in America.

He fully realised, of course, that he would sorely miss all the great performances at La Scala. He concluded, however, the Metropolitan of New York was an acceptable alternative, particularly now that the great Arturo Toscanini was a much-celebrated conductor in that great cathedral of opera.

Arriving at the bank midday Friday expecting to be shown into Herr Schuster's office, he was, instead, escorted to a secure room that had all the appearances of a very large vault. Herr Schuster and the indomitable Frau Kirstin were already waiting. He also saw a tall beefy-looking individual standing directly behind them holding what appeared to be some sort of attaché case. To one side, there was a table with neatly stacked blocks of cash.

Dispensing with formalities, Herr Schuster immediately got down to business. "Good afternoon, Don Barcese." Then, placing both hands on the table, he continued, "Here are your funds in American denominated bills as per your instructions. Would you like some time to check for yourself?"

"Oh I don't think that will be necessary. As you have said yourself, Herr Schuster, you Germans have a reputation for being stiff and formal. But it is also widely accepted, your compatriots have a name for being very efficient and remarkably ethical in their business dealings."

"Why thank you, Don Barcese. You are most kind. Frau Kirstin has already checked the total amount due, and I can assure you it is correct to the very last dollar."

Don Barcese, in a rather sardonic tone, replied, "Why I wouldn't, under any circumstances, doubt Frau Kirstin's integrity, not for a single moment. So please, what's next?"

Frau Kirstin produced some documents, handed them to her boss, and then took one backward step. He could tell by her demeanour she was none too pleased with his last remark.

"What's next, Don Barcese, is most simple," continued Herr Schuster. "I have some documents for you to sign, and then Karl will place the bills into the lockable attaché case, which the bank has provided. Frau Kirstin will of course see to it everything is done in accordance with procedure. Karl will then escort you from the bank to your auto-mobile. After all, we would not like it if anything nasty happened to you when you stepped outside."

Don Barcese shot a quick glance in his direction. He wondered if the remark was a feeble attempt at humour, or maybe it was nothing more than sarcasm. Dismissing the thought, he stepped forward to sign the documents.

Herr Schuster placed the documents on the table then continued, "There are three documents in duplicate. And of course, as you can see, I have already signed them so as not to waste your precious time. If you are satisfied with the content, then all you need do is sign your name on the line second from the bottom. Frau Kirstin will witness your signature, and then our business here today will be complete."

Taking the papers, Don Barcese scanned them thoroughly. The first was his authorisation for the bank to close his accounts, the second covered administrative and currency conversion fees, totalling 548,120 marks. The final document briefly stated the total amount of American dollars being handed over was full and final payment of all outstanding monies due.

"Can you give me a breakdown of the fees?"

"Of course. There is an administrative fee of two and a half per cent and a one and a half per cent commission charge on the currency conversion. On the document it is shown in German marks. In American currency, it totals thirteen thousand and fifty-one dollars. The remaining sum on the table minus the fee and the conversion charge is a grand total of three hundred and thirteen thousand two hundred and eleven dollars precisely."

Making no comment, Don Barcese signed the documents. Frau Kirstin moved to the table, witnessed his signature on all three copies, and then placed them in an envelope and resumed her position.

Herr Schuster issued an instruction in German.

The burly-looking individual stepped forward, set the attaché case down on the table, and began placing the bundles inside. Frau Kirstin again stepped forward and supervised the process until it was completed. She produced a set of keys, locked the case, and formally handed the keys to Don Barcese.

He graciously accepted and, in this instance, decided to make one more effort to thank her. Again in fractured German, he uttered the following. "Thank you, thank you, Fra!! sorry I mean Frau Kirstin."

Standing there looking at him, she remained silent for a moment or two. He was now beginning to regret his pathetic attempt at trying to appear sophisticated in her presence.

Finally she replied in flawless Italian, "Why thank you, Don Barcese. You are most gracious. And I do appreciate your valiant attempt at our native language just now. It is most commendable."

Her linguistic skills both surprised and impressed him, though he wasn't quite sure if she was thanking him or insulting him. He decided remaining silent was probably the best option.

Herr Schuster brought proceedings to a close. "Well then, I believe our business here today is finally done. Karl will now accompany you to your vehicle. I would just like to say on behalf of the bank; Frau Kirstin; and, of course, my humble self, it was a great pleasure doing business with you these years past. We wish you a bon voyage and every success in the United States of America."

"Why thank you, Herr Schuster, Frau Kirstin. I will carry those kind thoughts with me on my long voyage to America."

With that, Don Barcese walked from the bank. As he approached the auto-mobile, the chauffeur was on hand to open the door. Karl placed the attaché case on the rear seat. Don Barcese thanked him and slipped him a 100-mark note. Karl responded with a broad grin, showing his appreciation.

Back at his hotel, he watched as the concierge deposited the case in the safe. He then sent a cable to his bank in Paris. He notified them he would be there on Monday, 8 April. He gave specific instructions for all his cash to be ready for withdrawal in American denominated bills. He was determined to avoid the excruciating procedures he'd experienced with Herr Schuster and Frau Kirstin.

That same evening, he dined alone in the hotel restaurant. Returning to his suite, he decided an early night was a sensible option, given that he had an early start the following morning for the next stage of his journey.

At Anhalter station, he purchased his ticket and boarded the eight o'clock train for the eleven-hour journey to Paris. In the comfort of his private compartment, he began formulating the strategy he would adopt in America.

His plan was to renew his acquaintance with a fellow Sicilian by the name of Nicholas Terranova. He was one of the individuals Consuella had observed during their time in New York. Terranova, like Don Barcese, had left Sicily in the late nineteenth century, though in his case, he'd emigrated to America and joined his step-brother who was already in New York.

By this time, a criminal organisation had already emerged on the scene. It went by the name Koza Nostra and operated mainly out of Brooklyn and East Harlem. These two districts housed the largest proportion of Italian immigrants in the city. Nicholas had joined "the family", as the group was now generally referred to by its associates.

He'd made a name for himself as an enforcer. Very quickly, he had risen through the ranks and become an under-boss. By 1910, he was the major boss of one of the five New York families. Don Barcese had no intention of joining their ranks; his place of residence would be Park Avenue. Nevertheless, he believed his association with this important crime figure would be very useful indeed, particularly in the lucrative trade of arms dealing. With this thought in mind, he sat back, relaxed, and enjoyed the view of the rolling countryside as the train steamed on at full speed.

On his arrival in Paris, he checked into the Ritz Hotel. Again following the same procedure, he made certain his attaché case was securely locked away in the hotel safe. The following day being Sunday, he enjoyed a late breakfast and took a leisurely stroll along the wide boulevards close to his hotel. That evening, he attended a performance of Verdi's *Simon Boccanegra* at the Opera Garnier.

Félia Litvinne, a Russian-born soprano of some renown sang the part of Amelia. As he listened, his thoughts drifted back to Consuella. There was still no doubt in his mind she was the greatest soprano of them all. He wondered if he had been in any way responsible for her recent humiliating on-stage breakdown. He fully realised slipping out of the theatre that evening in order to avoid his own arrest most certainly meant their contract was now irrevocably terminated.

He decided, however, there was nothing, absolutely nothing he could do now. He took some comfort in the certain knowledge the so-called voice coach and that meddlesome friar would be on hand to assist her in the trauma she was now most likely experiencing.

With the final curtain, he left the theatre and made the short journey back to his hotel.

The following morning Monday, 8 April, his first stop was the shipping line's booking office. There, he booked a first-class cabin aboard a magnificent ocean-going liner for the six-day transatlantic voyage leaving Wednesday evening from the port of Cherbourg in Brittany. Its destination was pier fifty-nine in New York City.

With his travel arrangements now finalised, he made the short journey to the Bank Societe Generale. There he was formally greeted in Italian by Monsieur Dominique Joubert, a tall elegantly dressed individual aged mid to late forties, with black slicked down hair, sallow oily skin, and dark penetrating eyes.

"Please, if you will, Don Barcese, just follow me. Everything is prepared as per your instructions."

Monsieur Joubert guided him to a private office. There on a table was an attaché case with the American dollars already neatly stacked inside. Doing some quick mental arithmetic, Don Barcese calculated the number of bundles was about three-quarters of what was in the other attaché case.

Satisfied with his inspection, he turned to his companion. "Thank you, Monsieur Joubert. You have been most efficient. Do you have a total for me?"

Remaining somewhat aloof, Monsieur Joubert set about his task in a charmless manner. "On the table, there is a sum of one hundred and eighty six thousand American dollars. This sum represents the total amount from your account, minus bank charges of course."

"Of course," echoed Don Barcese, adopting a caustic manner of his own. He was now of the opinion this Frenchman had as much personality as a dead fish. Nevertheless, he was reasonably happy the business at hand was moving along at a satisfactory pace. "Now, do you have any papers for me to sign?"

Monsieur Joubert, without making a reply, pointed to a one-page document on the table, took a pen from his waistcoat pocket, and handed it to him. After a quick perusal, Don Barcese, satisfied everything was in order including the fees, signed the paper. He handed it to Monsieur

Joubert, who just folded it and placed it somewhat carelessly in his jacket pocket. He then extended his hand one last time. For a split second Don Barcese thought he was being offered some form of goodwill handshake. He very quickly realised, however, Monsieur Joubert was merely waiting for his pen to be returned. With the attaché case securely locked and the keys handed over, Don Barcese bid farewell to Monsieur Joubert and took his leave from the Bank Societe Generale.

He stayed one more night in Paris. The following morning Tuesday, he settled his account and collected his suitcase and the other two most important items from the safe. From there, he was driven to Paris North train station. He boarded the train and settled into his compartment for the four-hour journey to Cherbourg.

CHAPTER 44

The Port of Cherbourg

On his arrival in Cherbourg, Don Barcese had to make do with a room in a rather weather-beaten hotel near the seafront. As there was no safe, his only option was to stay in his room and protect his money. There was a small balcony with a view of the harbour and the Atlantic Ocean beyond. He ordered a meal and a bottle of wine. To his surprise, the food and the wine where quite exceptional.

Reflecting on his earlier encounter with Monsieur Joubert, he came to the conclusion the French may well be ill-mannered and somewhat arrogant, but at least they made up for these character defects with good food and fine wine. Having finished his meal, he sat on the balcony and gazed out on the ocean. He found himself wondering what this voyage had in store for him, what sort of life he would have in New York, and whether he would at some time in the future have an opportunity to return to his native land. With these lingering thoughts, he bolted all the doors and slept with the two attaché cases close by.

The next morning, he awoke to the sound of trawlers leaving the small port. They were heading for the fishing grounds out in the Atlantic. Opening the doors onto his balcony, he saw the scene below was one of frenetic activity. In the harbour, crafts of varying shapes and sizes jostled for position at the dock. A virtual army of labourers were busy loading and unloading goods of every possible description on and off the vessels.

He made the decision to stay in his room at least until he saw his ship approaching the harbour. He ordered breakfast and spent the remainder of the day observing the activities taking place on the bustling streets below his window. That same evening, just before five o'clock out on the horizon, a large ship came into view. He paid close attention as it drew closer. Despite the many occasions he had crossed the ocean, this vessel was by far the most impressive he had ever seen. At precisely six o'clock, the liner dropped anchor some distance from the harbour. The small port just didn't have the capacity to accommodate it. The quay was thronged with large crowds marvelling at the majestic sight sitting serenely out in the bay.

Promptly settling his account, he engaged the services of a porter to assist him with his luggage. The two attaché cases he carried himself. On his arrival at the boarding area, there was great excitement as families and friends were bidding emotional farewells to loved ones. Having no time for this sentimental nonsense, he just breezed past to the top of the queue.

The White Star Line had laid on two vessels, named *Traffic* and *Nomadic*, for the sole purpose of ferrying passengers out to the ship. The first-class ticket holders, of which he was one, were given priority treatment and transferred ahead of the remaining second- and third-class travellers, who had to wait their turn. Once on board, he was greeted by a steward, who showed him to his suite. He was delighted to discover his first-class status entitled him to the services of a maid and valet, who, between them, had a few phrases of Italian. Happy in the knowledge his luggage and, more importantly, the cases containing his money were securely stowed, he locked the door and took a stroll on the promenade deck. He paid little or no attention to the lower classes still scrambling to come aboard. Instead, he mingled and exchanged pleasantries with his fellow travellers.

One such individual he encountered was a person by the name of Victor Giglio, a most charming handsome twenty-four-year-old American citizen of Italian descent. Don Barcese was delighted to make his acquaintance, particularly due to the fact Victor was fluent in both English and Italian. He questioned him ever so politely, merely to gauge if he was a person of some significance. "Victor, I can clearly see for myself you are certainly a fine well-dressed young gentleman. May I be so bold and inquire as to the nature of your business and the reason you are making this voyage to New York?"

Victor replied quite modestly, "You are too kind, Don Barcese. But you see, I'm just a humble valet, nothing more. I've been travelling through Europe with my employer. He very much wanted to make the return journey on this particular vessel, so that's it really."

Slightly taken aback by the young man's revelation and more out of curiosity than anything else, he decided to probe a little further, "Please, Victor, I don't mean to be impolite, your employer, would he perhaps be a person of some importance?"

"Well, most people who know him would certainly be of that opinion. On the other hand, my employer most definitely does not see himself in that light. As a matter of fact, he firmly believes he is no different from any other individual, just maybe more fortunate than some, that's it really."

"Your employer must truly be a remarkable human being. I would be most interested in meeting him sometime during our voyage."

"Oh I am sure an opportunity will present itself. When it does, it would be an honour for me to introduce you to Mister Guggenheim."

"Victor, did you just say Mister Guggenheim?"

"Yes, that is correct. Benjamin Guggenheim is my employer. Do you perhaps know him?"

"Well, I certainly know of him. He is probably one of the most important businessmen in America. In fact, I did see him on one occasion last year. He was among the audience at the Metropolitan Opera House in New York."

Victor replied enthusiastically, "Yes, I remember that event very well. I had the privilege of being with him on that particular occasion. If I recall correctly, it was a performance of Verdi's *Il Travatore.*"

"Well, Victor, there is certainly nothing wrong with your memory, and it would seem you are quite knowledgeable when it comes to the opera."

Victor, smiling in appreciation, replied, "Thank you, Don Barcese, for those kind words. I must take my leave now. It was an honour for me to make your acquaintance. I will certainly mention you to my employer. I am certain an opportunity will present itself for you to meet him during the course of the voyage."

As they parted company and despite his own cynical selfish nature, Don Barcese found himself taking quite a liking to young Victor. For a moment or two, he thought back on his earlier life of squalor and deprivation. This was the environment that had shaped him as an individual; of this he was certain. He wondered how different his life would have been if he had grown up not necessarily in a wealthy household, but just maybe in a loving and caring one. Would he have perhaps turned out something like this splendid young man he had been talking to these past few moments?

At precisely ten minutes past eight that same evening, the ship weighed anchor and headed out to sea. Its next port of call was Queens-town on the south-east coast of Ireland. He joined the other passengers in the first-class dining room for a sumptuous meal. Everybody seemed to be in high spirits. The evening passed with passengers sipping cocktails whilst being entertained by a group of very fine musicians. They were also busy exchanging greetings and forging new friendships. At about twelve midnight, feeling rather tired after a rather long day, he excused himself and bid his fellow dining companions goodnight. Returning to his suite, he settled himself in bed and fell asleep almost immediately.

CHAPTER 45

The Journey from Queens-Town

At Queens-town harbour the following morning, the procedure was much the same, though on this occasion the number of passengers embarking was much less than in Cherbourg. They numbered 123. Within this group, only two among them held first-class tickets. The rest were mainly farm labourers, together with a smaller number of domestic servants.

These poor wretched individuals fleeing poverty, persecution, and discrimination in their own homeland were desperately seeking a new life and a brighter future. Witnessing the scenes below him, Don Barcese paid closer attention. The pain and suffering in their faces was clearly evident. Their eyes though told a different story; in those eyes, he could see a hope and a determination to carve out a better life for themselves in a far-off land. His mind drifted back to Victor's earlier comments in relation to his employer's philosophy regarding the human condition. These poor disadvantaged creatures were no different from Benjamin Guggenheim or himself for that matter. They just happened to be less fortunate; it was that simple.

In the early afternoon, with 2,228 passengers and crew on board, the majestic liner sailed from the port of Queens-town and headed into the Atlantic Ocean for its six-day voyage to New York. Taking a leisurely stroll on deck, Don Barcese was feeling ever so relaxed and somewhat relieved. It was now nearly three weeks since that fateful night in Milan. He believed himself to have been remarkably lucky in making his escape from what would have been his certain arrest and incarceration. It was thanks to the ever-resourceful Carlo, who had tipped him off on the evening in question. That had made it possible for him to slip away during the confusion following Consuella's collapse on stage.

These two unrelated incidents, the first somewhat fortuitous, the second almost tragic convinced him that fate was most definitely working in his favour. Now here he stood on the threshold of a new and exciting chapter in his life, travelling first class in the company of aristocrats and business tycoons. Not only that, in his suite, he had almost half a million American dollars. Pausing for a moment, he once more gazed on the mass of humanity below him in third class. He consoled himself in that self-important arrogant way of his. *Yes indeed, some people are more fortunate, definitely more fortunate than others; and for better or worse, that is the world we inhabit.*

The days passed by pleasantly enough. A familiar routine was now well established. Breakfast in the morning was followed by leisurely strolls on deck exchanging pleasantries and engaging in harmless chit-chat with fellow passengers. Lunch in the afternoon, in his case, preceded a short nap before dressing formally for dinner in the evening. Saturday, 13 April, on entering the restaurant, he spotted young Victor sitting at a table in the company of two female passengers and another gentleman. He surmised this person had to be none other than Victor's employer, Benjamin Guggenheim.

Victor, seeing him enter, gave him a friendly wave. He acknowledged the greeting as he headed in the direction of his own table. Victor whispered something into his boss's ear. Benjamin Guggenheim glanced over in Don Barcese's direction and then gave his valet what appeared to be a nod of approval. Rising from his chair, Victor made his way over to where Don Barcese was now seated.

"My apologies, Don Barcese, for disturbing you just now. My employer has requested me to see if you would care to join us for dinner."

"Why thank you, Victor. I am deeply honoured. So please, lead the way. I will be right behind you."

On reaching the table, Victor made the introductions in Italian and English. "Don Barcese, it is my great pleasure to introduce my employer, Mr Benjamin Guggenheim; his travelling companion, Madame Aubart; and her maid, Mademoiselle Sagesser."

As they were exchanging greetings, Don Barcese surmised Victor's description "travelling companion" was his polite way of informing him Madame Aubert was, in fact, Benjamin Guggenheim's mistress.

The evening passed off pleasantly enough. The table talk was somewhat laboured due to the fact Benjamin Guggenheim did not speak Italian, and Don Barcese had a very limited grasp of the English language. Victor, however, just about managed to keep the conversation flowing as best he could in a bilingual fashion.

Sometime around eleven o'clock, Don Barcese thanked his host for the wonderful hospitality. He bowed courteously to Madame Aubert and her maid before taking his leave.

The next day being Sunday, religious services were held for those who wished to attend. Ironically, the safety drill was cancelled to facilitate this event. Apart from this, the well-established routine continued.

The seas were calm, though there was a noticeable drop in air temperature. Most passengers now wore heavier garments and topcoats while taking their afternoon strolls. Later that evening, Don Barcese, as usual, had a pleasant meal. Taking his leave from the dining room and just before returning to his suite, he took a moment to look up at the night sky. There wasn't a cloud in sight. As he gazed at the stars in the heavens, he had a sense they were guiding him to his destiny.

In the comfort of his suite, his valet had already laid out his pyjamas and dressing gown. His clothes for the following morning were freshly pressed and hanging in the wardrobe. Then just as he was about to change, he heard a sudden thud and then a crunching sound. It lasted no more than maybe three or four minutes. Looking at his watch, he noted the time. It was precisely eleven forty. At eleven fifty, as a precautionary measure, the captain gave the order for passengers and crew alike to don life jackets. His valet returned. He was wearing his own life jacket. He handed one to Don Barcese and requested that he put it on. Now slightly alarmed, Don Barcese nevertheless followed the valet's advice and then headed out onto a very crowded deck.

His fellow passengers, most of whom were already wearing their life vests, were milling around in some degree of confusion. He could clearly see the concerned expressions on their faces, though as far as he could tell there was no real sense of panic, certainly not at this stage. Making his way laboriously through the throng, he spotted Victor a short distance away. He pushed and shoved his way through the mass of bodies to reach him.

On doing so, he asked in a breathless voice, "Victor, thank goodness I have found you. I can't understand a word anyone is saying. Can you perhaps tell me what is happening? Is the ship in some kind of danger? And why do we have to wear these ridiculous life preservers?"

"Don Barcese, I can assure you there is no need for you to be concerned. The life vests are merely a precaution. On any vessel, whenever an incident such as the one we have just experienced occurs, the captain in charge always issues the order for every person on board to follow this procedure. As I said before, it is a standard safety measure, nothing more."

"Well thank goodness for that. Do you have any inkling as to what happened back there?"

"I have just spoken with one of the ship's officers. He told me there was a minor collision, that's all. Apparently the ship's starboard side brushed up against an iceberg as it was taking evasive action to avert a head-on collision. Probably a few bumps and bruises—I can assure you it is nothing more serious than that."

"Thank you, Victor, for those comforting words. I suppose we can take off these ridiculous life vests now."

"Not just yet. We have to wait for the all-clear. Please be patient. It should not take too much longer. Then everything, I am sure, will return to normal."

Victor departed and made his way along the crowded deck in an attempt to reach his boss's suite.

Don Barcese decided to wait around. He spent the following ten minutes or so observing the activities of the crew and waited anxiously for the anticipated all-clear announcement.

Meanwhile, Thomas Andrews, a naval architect and engineer, was carrying out his own inspection. As head of the design team, his presence on board was to monitor the ship's performance on this, her maiden voyage.

Just before midnight, he joined the captain, who was now on the bridge.

"Well, Mr Andrews, have you completed your inspection?"

"Yes, Sir, I have."

"And your assessment of the damage?"

"Not good. In fact, the damage sustained is quite severe. On striking the iceberg, four watertight compartments in the hull section were breeched.

The water is now causing extensive flooding in compartments five and six. Within the hour, all six compartments will be completely flooded. If it were three or even four, we could stay afloat and limp on, but with six, this ship will most definitely sink. Of that, I am absolutely certain."

With a grim expression, Captain Smith questioned him further. "How much time do we have, Mr Andrews?"

"By my estimate, this ship will sink in approximately two hours."

Captain Smith, now somewhat alarmed, remained silent for a moment or two and then continued. "What do you advise, Mr Andrews?"

Without hesitation, he replied, "Immediate evacuation, Sir."

Turning to First Officer William Murdoch, Captain Smith gave the command, "Mr Murdoch, uncover the lifeboats and prepare for immediate evacuation, women and children first."

As first officer, Murdoch mustered his crew and set about his task. Captain Smith gave the following instructions to Chief Officer Henry Wilde and Second Officer Charles Lightholler: "Gentlemen, see to it distress flares are set off immediately and have the wireless room send out distress signals continuously to all shipping in the surrounding area."

Then, turning once more to Thomas Andrews, he inquired, "How many life boats do we have on board, Mr Andrews?"

"Sixteen lifeboats in total, Sir, and four collapsible craft."

"How many persons will we be capable of evacuating?"

"If all twenty were successfully launched and if each one had the requisite number on board, my estimate is the number of survivors could be eleven hundred."

"But, Mr Andrews, there are in excess of two thousand two hundred souls on board. You were the person in charge of the design team. So please explain, why are there not sufficient lifeboats?"

"With all due respect, Captain, that is a question you may wish to ask the directors of the White Star Line. At the design stage, I set the requirement at thirty-two. The directors were of the opinion this number was not ascetically pleasing, so they ordered the reduction. I strenuously protested but was overruled."

"Thank you, Mr Andrews, I will now do my duty. So help me God, I will."

At twelve twenty-five, some forty-five minutes from the time of the collision, in confusion lifeboat number seven was the first to be launched. Over the next forty minutes, another four were lowered into the water. By one o'clock, everyone on board, including Don Barcese, was fully aware of the looming disaster. At ten minutes past one, he witnessed a most cowardly act of self-preservation. As lifeboat number one was being made ready, Sir Edmund Duff Gordon sought permission to board, falsely claiming his wife, Lady Lucy Christiana, was gravely ill. The order was given and the lifeboat was eventually lowered with the reprehensible Duff Gordon and his wife on board.

The managing director of the shipping line, J. Bruce Ismay, one of the persons responsible for the executive decision to reduce the number of lifeboats, without a shred of remorse committed an act even more heinous and cowardly than Duff Gordon's shameful behaviour. Disguising himself as a woman, he boarded one of the collapsible lifeboats and got away, thereby saving his own life, while many hundreds of passengers, as a direct consequence of his and his associates' criminal negligence, remained stranded on the stricken vessel.

In stark contrast to these two despicable incidents, Don Barcese witnessed some acts of selfless heroism and bravery. Two in particular had a profound effect on him. Isidore Strauss, the second wealthiest person on board and joint owner with his brother Nathan of Macy's Department Store in New York, accompanied his beloved wife Ida and assisted her onto lifeboat number eight. He himself was offered a place by her side. The offer may have been due to his pre-eminence as one of the most important passengers on board. Or maybe it was simply the fact that, at sixty-seven years of age, he was deemed by the crew in charge as a deserving candidate for evacuation.

Isidore flatly refused. "Gentlemen, if I were to board this craft in order to save my own life while women and children more deserving of me remain, what sort of life would I have? What sort of human being would I become? Thank you, gentlemen. Now carry on. Do your duty, and I will do mine."

Just as the crew was preparing to launch, Ida stood up and called out to her husband, "Isidore, you are my husband. We have been married for forty-one years. In all that time, you have never left my side. I will not be separated from you now."

Removing herself from the lifeboat as quickly as she could, she embraced Isidore, and with tears in her eyes she whispered lovingly into his ear, "My darling, whatever fate has in store for us, let us face it together."

Don Barcese watched as Isidore and Ida departed from the boat deck. They seated themselves near the grand staircase and held hands while the musicians played on. In one final act of kindness, Ida Strauss gave her place on board the departing craft to her maid Ellen Bird.

At one forty-five, John Jacob Astor, the wealthiest passenger on board, accompanied his young wife, Madeline, who was five months pregnant to lifeboat number four. He could have put forward his wife's pregnancy as a legitimate reason for him to accompany her. This he did not do. Instead, he saw to it his distraught wife; her nurse, Caroline Louise Endres; and her maid, Rosalie Bidois, got safely on board. He made certain she was as comfortable as possible under what were, for his young expectant bride, truly horrendous circumstances. John Jacob Astor kissed Madeline one last time.

He was truly broken-hearted to see her being taken away from him in this manner. As the lifeboat moved slowly away, he watched until it vanished from sight. He knew, deep down in his heart, he would never see his young wife again. He was also greatly saddened by the realisation he would not be there by her side for the birth of their first child. He stood alone for a few moments silently praying, not for his own deliverance; his prayers instead were offered for his wife and unborn child. He slowly regained his composure. His ability to do so was due to the fact he had previously served in the military as a lieutenant colonel and had seen action in the Spanish-American War.

As Colonel John Jacob Astor IV prepared to leave the launching area, William Murdoch, having witnessed his brave act and also aware of his military service, stood to attention, saluted him, and spoke the following words: "It is an honour and a privilege to salute you, Colonel Astor. You are a brave officer and a true gentleman."

He paused for a moment and then asked, "And you, sir, what is your name?"

"My name is William Murdoch, sir. I am first officer aboard this vessel."

"Well, First Officer Murdoch, I salute you and your gallant crew. Your brave efforts under these appalling conditions are truly heroic. This tragedy is not of your doing. I will leave you now and let you get on with your important work."

He left the boat deck in the certain knowledge he would not be counted among the survivors.

Between one forty-five and one fifty-five, Don Barcese watched as the last two remaining lifeboats were lowered. For the briefest of moments he was tempted to board one of them and maybe save his own life. Instead, with a resigned expression, he silently looked on as they departed.

With the bow section sinking lower, it caused the stern to rise up, leaving the ship at a precarious angle. With some difficulty, he moved along until he reached the grand staircase. He watched as the orchestra continued playing cheerful gay tunes. Although he was no sentimentalist, he was impressed by the bravery of these eight musicians. Their music seemed to have a calming effect on the nerves of those still trapped on board.

Time was fast running out. For Don Barcese, the experience was somewhat different. The events taking place before his eyes—the cowardly, the heroic, and the tragic—were just like small dramas being played in slow motion. He wondered if this was God's way of showing him the good and bad in people. Could it be possible he was being given one final opportunity to redeem himself as a human being?

Moving along the sloping deck, at precisely two o'clock, he met Victor one last time. The valet was in the company of his boss. The two of them were both in evening dress minus their life vests. They seemed to be enjoying themselves enormously, sitting there sipping brandy with not a care in the world.

Victor greeted him in his usual friendly manner. "There you are, Don Barcese. I was wondering where you got to. Would you care to join us?"

To him, the scene seemed somewhat surreal. In an attempt at normalcy, he answered, "Please, Victor, I don't wish to intrude. I am sure Madame Aubert and Mademoiselle Sagesser will be joining you very soon. By the way, where are the two ladies? Are they safe?"

"As to their whereabouts and safety, all I can tell you, Don Barcese, is less than half an hour ago, Mr Guggenheim and myself assisted them in getting aboard lifeboat number nine. Hopefully, they are some distance from the ship right now. After that, we assisted in the evacuation of other women and children."

"What about you and your employer, do you have any plans to get off this ship and save yourselves?"

Victor put the question to his boss, who immediately replied.

"My employer has asked me to convey the following," Victor then told Don Barcese. "He would be happy to leave this vessel, but not until every woman and child on board have been safely evacuated. These values he learned at a very young age, so for him, there is really no dilemma. To be worthy of the title 'gentleman', he feels duty-bound to conduct himself in an honourable fashion. This he will do, even if it means sacrificing his own life in the process."

While Victor was relaying these facts, Benjamin Guggenheim watched closely to gauge the manner of Don Barcese's reaction.

"What about yourself, Victor? Are you obligated to follow this praiseworthy, though I have to add foolhardy, example? Do you feel you have a duty to your employer similar to the one he believes binds him to his privileged upbringing and upper-class status, even if it means losing your own precious life in the process?"

Victor, with a generous smile, replied, "Forgive me, Don Barcese, I do believe you may have misjudged my employer. That is not the situation at all. He has placed no obligation on me whatsoever. I have freely chosen to stay by his side. Where he goes, I go. Where he leads, I follow. It is that simple."

Benjamin Guggenheim then added a comment and Victor translated. "My employer wishes you to know, there is a vessel making its way here to render assistance. If it makes it on time, we may yet be saved. If, on the other hand, it does not, we have already made our decision."

"Pray tell, Victor, is it possible you can enlighten me as to your decision in the event the less favourable outcome is visited upon us?"

"In that case we will go down with the ship as two gentlemen who performed their duty under difficult circumstances; nothing more, nothing less."

Pausing for a moment, Don Barcese couldn't help but admire the honesty and courage of these two brave men who were prepared to sacrifice their own lives rather than live as cowards. He was now beginning to understand, a person's worth was measured by what was in his or her heart; by how the person lived his or her life; and, most importantly, by how one treated his or her fellow human beings. Wealth and privilege, poverty and powerlessness had nothing to do with it. With this revelation dawning on him, he smiled and remained momentarily silent.

Victor, now somewhat confused asked, "I'm sorry, Don Barcese, but have I said something that has amused you?"

"No, no, Victor. On the contrary, my reason for smiling is quite simple. When I boarded this vessel, I had, let's say certain views on a person's place in society, the human condition if you will. I believed money made a person important and respectable; poverty, on the other hand, rendered a person useless and most certainly less worthy of respect. Over these past few days and tonight in particular, I have learned that every human being is entitled to dignity and respect whatever their status. I have you and Señor Guggenheim to thank for revealing these truths to me. I am deeply grateful. The tragedy is, it is most unlikely I will have an opportunity to practise these new-found virtues."

Victor quickly explained to his boss.

Benjamin Guggenheim spoke for the last time.

Victor interpreted. "Don Barcese, at this particular moment, it matters not how you have lived your life. There is nothing you can do to change the past. There is, however, something you can do to determine what sort of person you can be. You do not have to perform heroic deeds; all you need do is not die a coward."

Probably for the first time in his entire life, Don Barcese found himself speaking truly from his heart. "Victor, Señor Guggenheim, my humble thanks for your kind words of wisdom and your noble deeds. They have given me the courage to accept whatever fate awaits me. I bid you farewell and pray that God continues watching over you."

With these parting words, he made his way very slowly back to his suite. Once inside, he somehow managed to sit on the bed. He opened the two attaché cases. The steep angle caused the contents to spill out over the bed and onto the floor. As he watched, he just smiled and came to the conclusion that God most certainly did have a sense of humour. The money now scattered over the bed and floor was the sum total of his wretched existence. It represented all the betrayals, the scheming, the cheating, and the downright dishonesty; these were the methods employed over a lifetime in his pursuit of wealth and privilege.

The irony was God was allowing him take the money with him. There was certainly no danger of anyone breaking into his cabin and stealing it away. With the ship now entering its final death throes, he just sat there staring at what was now worthless paper. His mind drifted back to the encounter with the gypsy woman. He fully realised her prophetic words were now coming to pass.

Your wealth, Don Barcese, will not diminish during your lifetime. It may comfort you to know, that, when you come to the end of your life's journey, your money will be close by.

Her final words concerning a sea voyage were now indelibly etched in his mind.

All I can tell you, Don Barcese, is your voyage will be a short one.

There was a sudden grinding tearing sound of metal being ripped apart. He knew these were his final moments. This was his fate, and there was no possible way he could avoid it. The bow section was completely submerged, causing the stern to rise up out of the water. The strain was so great the ship quite literally broke apart in midships. The front half of the stricken vessel vanished almost immediately beneath the waves. The stern, for a brief moment, stood almost upright in the water, as if defying the very heavens. Then suddenly, it plunged four hundred meters to the ocean floor.

There were 705 survivors. On that dreadful night more than 1,500 unfortunate souls tragically perished, Don Barcese being one among them. In life, he was not particularly honourable or even trustworthy. Without a doubt, he was most certainly a scoundrel, but even for a rogue such as him, in his final hours, there was a redemption of sorts. Over the course of this appalling tragedy, Don Barcese may not have performed heroically. But neither did he die in a cowardly fashion.

CHAPTER 46

Meanwhile in Verona

Consuella's weak condition was now a matter of some concern. Having attended to her, Dr Vanzetti called the family together to give them an update on her condition. Antonio was also present, in the company of Carlota, Sister Maria, Francesco, and Father Martine.

When they were all gathered, the doctor continued, "It's not my intention to alarm you unnecessarily. Presently, all I can tell you is Consuella's current weakened state will need a very long period of convalescence. She has requested that it takes place here at the convent. She believes Sister Maria and the other nuns will take excellent care of her.

For the time being, it would be preferable she have as few visitors as possible. If you wish, Pietro, you may go in and see your daughter, but please don't stay too long. That's all I can tell you for the moment. Sister Maria, I will take my leave now. I will call again the day after tomorrow. In the meantime, if I'm needed, don't hesitate to contact me."

As Dr Vanzetti departed, Sister Maria brought Pietro in to see Consuella. He was quite taken aback at how fragile she looked. He nevertheless tried to mask his concern with a loving smile as he greeted his youngest daughter. "My dearest Consuella, I want you to rest here until you feel well enough to come home. I have every faith in Sister Maria to take excellent care of you. So don't worry. I will come and see you often." He leaned down and gently kissed her affectionately on her forehead.

"Dearest Papa, I'm so sorry for causing you all this worry. And thank you for letting me stay here. I promise, I will try my best to get well very soon. And please thank Dominique, Paolo, and Adamo for being here with you. I really do appreciate it.

"Reverend Mother told me that Antonio travelled all the way from Vienna. Please, Papa, please thank him on my behalf. Also, will you please thank Carlota and Francesco for taking care of me? Hopefully, I will be able to talk with all of them soon."

"Okay, my Consuella, rest now. I will say a special prayer every day until you are fully recovered."

Masking his tears, he gently let go of her hand and silently left the room. When he joined the others, they could clearly see how upset he was. Nobody spoke; instead they just waited silently, until he regained his composure.

Dominique placed her father's hand in hers. "Dearest Papa, I think we should leave now and let our dear Consuella rest. You know Sister Maria will take excellent care of her. So please don't worry. With God's blessing she will be singing for us again very soon."

Pietro stood up, still holding his eldest daughter's hand. He replied, "Yes, Dominique, it's best we leave now and allow Sister Maria get on with the task of looking after our dear Consuella. Sister Maria, as always, I am in your debt. I know you will take very good care of my daughter. Thank you. From the bottom of my heart, thank you.

"Carlota, Francesco, Consuella asked me to convey her deepest appreciation for your selfless efforts on her behalf. Antonio, thank you for making the journey here. She is deeply touched by your presence, and her wish is to speak with you sometime soon."

With Pietro's departure, Sister Maria and Carlota went into Consuella's room and sat at her bedside for a short period.

Antonio took this opportunity to raise the issue regarding the current status of her management arrangements.

Francesco responded, "If it's okay with you, Father, I will bring Antonio up to date on how things presently stand."

Father Martine nodded his approval.

"As things now stand, Antonio, Consuella's contractual arrangements are well and truly terminated."

He then briefly explained all that had taken place since their journey back from America, including his discussion with Inspector Albassini. "That's as much as I can tell you for the moment, Antonio. If I receive further news, I will of course let you and Father Martine know immediately."

The following day, Carlota and Francesco returned to Milan.

Antonio called to the convent to check on Consuella's condition. On his arrival, he met with Sister Maria and spoke with her. "Dear Sister, would it be at all possible for me to see Consuella—even for the briefest of moments? I will be travelling back to Vienna this evening, and I would dearly like to wish her well before my departure."

She asked him to wait while she went into to see if Consuella would be able to receive him.

"Consuella, Antonio is outside. He is leaving today and asked me if it were possible for him to see you just briefly before he departs."

Although still very weak, she nodded her approval.

Sister Maria returned to an anxious Antonio. "Antonio, she is still quite weak, though I could tell by her expression that she would also like to see you. So please, be mindful of her delicate state. You may go in now."

As he entered, Antonio could clearly see how fragile she actually was. He sat on the chair beside her bed and reached out his hand. He delicately placed it on hers and smiled ever so gently.

Slowly she turned her head in his direction. Her eyes momentarily brightened, and in a voice now almost a whisper, she said, "What took you so long, Antonio? Is it possible you no longer love me?"

Holding back his tears, he lovingly replied, "My dearest Consuella, I have never stopped loving you, not even for one single moment. So please get well very soon. It wouldn't be acceptable for my future bride to be looking unwell on our wedding day."

"Antonio, are you proposing marriage? Well if you are, I might just take pity on you and accept. Who knows? I might even allow you take charge of my career."

Although she was still smiling, he could see their brief time together had tired her considerably. Still holding her hand, he leaned over and gently kissed her on the cheek. Even in her delicate state, her eyes sparkled in response to his loving gesture.

Closing the bedroom door very gently behind him, he thanked Sister Maria for the precious few moments he was able to spend with his beloved Consuella.

Very mindful of the emotions he was now experiencing, Sister Maria offered some words of consolation. "Antonio, have a safe journey and please don't worry yourself too much. You know Consuella is in safe hands. We will do our utmost to assist her in making a full recovery. I will make sure Father Martine keeps you updated on her progress."

With that, Antonio thanked her once more and then departed to make the long, lonely train journey back to Vienna. He was now determined more than ever that, as soon as she was fully recovered, he would stand with her at the wedding altar.

Some weeks later, Inspector Albasini contacted Francesco and asked him to drop by his office. On his arrival, Francesco found Sergio Albasini seated at his desk. The inspector invited him to take a seat.

"Well, Sergio, I hope you have good news for me. Have you caught that scoundrel yet?"

"No, Francesco, we haven't apprehended him. And I'm sorry to say, Don Barcese will not be facing charges anytime in the future. In fact, he won't be brought before the courts here in Italy or anywhere else for that matter."

"So where is he now? Don't tell me you have no clue as to his whereabouts."

"Oh we know where he is all right; well, we're pretty certain we know."

"Sergio, you have my full attention. I promise, no more interruptions."

"Thank you, Francesco. I'll be as brief as possible. Some weeks ago, mid-April in fact, there was a major maritime disaster off the coast of Newfoundland. You may have read about it in the newspapers. Anyway, our embassy in Washington received the passenger manifest and the names of the survivors, due to the fact there were a number of Italian nationals on board."

"Does this tragedy have some bearing on our conversation just now?"

"Don Barcese was listed as a passenger; he was not, however, counted among those who survived."

"So tell me, Sergio, where does this leave your investigation now?"

"We are as certain as we possibly can be that Don Barcese perished during the sinking of this vessel. So basically, our file on him is now closed."

"Thank you, Sergio. I appreciate you giving me the news so promptly. You know, I suppose all I can really say on the life he lived is this: Although he was most definitely an unsavoury character, in my wildest dreams, I would never have wished for him to meet his end in such a tragic fashion.

"By the way, what was the name of the vessel again? It seems to have slipped my mind."

"It was a British vessel from the White Star Line. Apparently, it was the most luxurious passenger liner ever built. It was named *Titanic*, and this disaster struck only days into its maiden voyage."

"My goodness, all those poor souls. How tragic, how very tragic. Anyway, Sergio, many thanks for the update. When I travel to Verona, I will let the others know of these developments."

"By the way, Francesco. How is Señorita Consuella doing?"

"She is being taken care of by the sisters at the convent in Verona. Hopefully, it won't be too long until she returns to the stage. Once again, Sergio, thank you. I can see you're busy, so I'll see myself out."

Having bid farewell to Inspector Albasini, Francesco's next task was to travel to Verona and check on Consuella's progress. He also intended to inform everyone of the tragic events involving Don Barcese.

Early in July, he travelled to Verona. He was somewhat surprised that Consuella's condition hadn't improved all that much. Sister Maria brought everyone up to date on how things were progressing. Along with Francesco. Pietro, Father Martine, and Antonio were also present.

"Dr Vanzetti has been attending on a regular basis. It is his opinion that she still needs total rest. For the time being, he doesn't want her to receive visitors. He believes the care she is presently receiving will benefit her. And, hopefully, in a couple of weeks from now, we should see a marked improvement in her condition."

Francesco inquired whether the doctor had expressed an opinion as to when she might be able to perform again. "Did he give any indication as to when she will be ready to return to the stage?"

Sister Maria answered, "Just now, it would be some-what inappropriate discussing Consuella's possible return to the stage. For now the best thing to do is pray she makes a full recovery."

In late September, to everyone's relief, there was a marked improvement in Consuella's condition. It was now possible for her to receive visitors more frequently and take regular strolls in the convent grounds.

For her twenty-second birthday, everybody was present in an effort to try and make it a special day. Violetta and her father were also in attendance. They all sang "Happy Birthday" and presented her with a birthday cake. There were no candles.

On this occasion, Adamo renewed his acquaintance with Violetta. Carlota quietly observed and could clearly see that both of them were remarkably comfortable in each other's company.

Antonio, despite his busy schedule, travelled to Verona as frequently as possible. During these visits, he spent many precious moments with Consuella. On one such occasion, they discussed when would be the most suitable time to announce their marriage plans. They agreed to wait until she was well enough to perform again and then announce their intentions in December. They decided on a date in late January 1913 for the forthcoming wedding.

Antonio made a special trip to Milan and requested that Francesco temporarily take care of Consuella's return to the stage, at least until he could decide what he needed to do concerning his position with the Vienna Court Opera. Francesco, without hesitation agreed to his request.

Antonio thanked his friend for his support. "Francesco, as usual, you are always there for me when I need you. Thank you so much. I really do appreciate it."

"Not at all, Antonio. I will schedule a number of performances for Consuella, nothing too challenging and certainly not too much travelling. The important thing for now is to ensure her return is gradual. Over the coming months, we will be in a much better position to decide what's best for her going forward. Now, what about you? Are you going to continue your work in Vienna?"

"My contractual obligations take me up to October 1915; it would be very difficult for me to terminate this arrangement in the interim. So I might have to prevail upon you to manage Consuella's schedule until then."

"Don't worry, Antonio. I'll handle everything until you make a final decision. Now, what about you and Consuella? Do you have any plans? Or am I being just too inquisitive?"

"Not at all, Francesco. Let's just say there might be an announcement sooner than you think. I might even prevail upon you to return that item you've been taking care of for me."

"Okay, Antonio, I won't press you anymore on the subject. And don't worry about your gift of betrothal. I've been holding onto it in anticipation a moment such as this might arise. So don't disappoint me. I'll say no more except that my dear wife, and everyone else for that matter, is most curious as to what happens next with Consuella and your good self. No matter; another few weeks of suspense won't do them any harm. Anyway, I think we're done for now. Don't worry too much, I will make certain to keep you up to date on your beloved Consuella's progress. Everything will be just fine. Now have a safe trip, and hopefully, we'll meet again very soon."

Antonio bid his friend farewell and travelled back to Vienna happy in the knowledge that things were going to work out after all.

Over the coming months Francesco scheduled a number of performances for Consuella. Her progress was slow but steady; opera enthusiasts were delighted to see her performing again. As December approached, Francesco made sure to have her back in Verona for the Christmas carol service. This was something he knew would mean so much to her family, as well as to Sister Maria and Father Martine. Antonio made a special effort to be there, as this was the occasion on which he and Consuella intended to announce their future plans.

On the afternoon prior to the carol service, they all gathered at Pietro's home for lunch. Everyone was surprised and delighted to see Dominique and Paola proudly holding a beautiful baby girl. After many words of congratulations from all present, Pietro announced how proud he was to be a grandfather. "Dear friends, today is such a happy day for me, not only do I have my daughter Consuella back home in Verona; I am also delighted to announce the arrival of an additional member to the Pellegrini household."

Looking over in Dominique and Paolo's direction, he continued. "It gives me a great sense of joy to introduce you to my first granddaughter, Sophia Pellegrini Gasparini. The name Sophia, as I'm sure all of you are aware, is also that of my dear departed wife, so this is a double honour for me and the Pellegrini household."

With that, Dominique went over to her Father and placed baby Sophia in his arms.

As she did so, Carlota whispered quietly to Sister Maria, "This is wonderful; I didn't know that Dominique was even pregnant."

Sister Maria discreetly replied, "Actually, Carlota, young Sophia is adopted. Isn't it wonderful, though, to see how proud Pietro is to be holding his adopted granddaughter? It's as if she was his own flesh and blood, don't you agree?"

"Indeed I do, Sister. It is truly a wonderful sight to behold—grandfather and granddaughter together in a household that has had to deal with so much trauma in the past. Hopefully for all the family, a brighter future beckons."

Consuella, who was sitting next to Antonio, just smiled lovingly at her father as she watched him cuddling baby Sophia. She then spoke very quietly to Antonio. "Dearest Antonio, isn't it wonderful to see how happy a day this is for my family? Let's not make our announcement just yet. Today is Dominique and Paolo's day. We can share our news with everyone before you journey back to Vienna. What do you say, darling?"

Antonio, with a slight frown, just glanced in her direction. Then with a broad smile, he replied, "Well if it makes you happy, darling, I suppose I have no other choice except to agree. But don't keep me waiting too long. The suspense and anticipation is beginning to take its toll on my fragile emotional state."

As he was speaking, they both held hands and lovingly gazed into each other's eyes. Nobody paid much attention to the two smitten lovers; everyone instead was still marvelling at the sight of Pietro holding his precious granddaughter.

Later that evening, Consuella sang all the beautiful carols in the chapel. Although somewhat tired, she gave a magnificent performance nonetheless. After the service, she returned to her father's home. Feeling somewhat exhausted, she went to her room and fell asleep almost immediately. No one was too concerned; they put it down to the excitement of the day and the fact she was still recovering from her long illness.

The following morning Carlota, Francesco and Antonio called to Pietro's home. They came to wish everyone a happy Christmas before their departure. The thoughts running through Antonio's mind centred on how everyone might react when he and Consuella made their announcement.

On their arrival, Pietro greeted them. The family was gathered together, and there was a festive atmosphere in the air. Sister Maria and Father Martine were also present.

Carlota looked around. Seeing no sign of Consuella, she asked, "Where is Consuella?"

Pietro replied, "The excitement yesterday, and most likely the carol service, left her very tired. She went straight to bed last night when we arrived home. Dominique, will you see if she is awake? I'm sure she'll want to see our guests before they depart."

As Dominique went to see if Consuella was awake, Carlota congratulated Pietro. "Well, Pietro, I can certainly see how proud you are of your beautiful granddaughter and how happy you must be that she is named after your dearest Sophia."

"Thank you, Carlota, for those thoughtful, kind words; they do mean so much to me."

With that, Dominique emerged from Consuella's room. She was in total shock and could barely speak. Looking in her father's direction, she tearfully blurted out, "Papa, Papa, there is something wrong with Consuella. Please, Papa, please. We have to do something. She's not moving; she's not moving."

Everyone reacted in a startled fashion, Pietro immediately jumped up. Sister Maria joined him. Before they entered Consuella's room, she hurriedly spoke to Father Martine. "Father, please contact Dr Vanzetti immediately. Tell him it's an emergency. Carlota, can you come in with us? We need to see what can be done before the doctor gets here."

The family was in a dreadful state of shock. Paolo did his best to comfort his distraught wife. Luckily, baby Sophia was in her crib sleeping. Adamo too was very upset. He just sat there feeling quite helpless, not knowing what to do.

Having made contact with the doctor, Father Martine joined a concerned looking Francesco. He could also see Antonio was now in a very distressed state. He instinctively knew something needed to be said—anything, anything at all to lessen the gravity of the situation Consuella might now be facing. "Antonio, I can see how very concerned you are right now. Please be patient for a few moments more. The doctor will be here very soon. Carlota and Sister Maria are with her now, so she's in good hands. It's probably nothing more than a bout of fatigue following the excitement of yesterday and her performance last night."

Although grateful for the consoling words, Antonio nevertheless found himself unable to respond. He just sat there and remained silent. The only thoughts going through his mind were of his beloved Consuella.

When Dr Vanzetti arrived, Adamo led him to Consuella's room. Carlota, Sister Maria, and Pietro came out. Everyone could see the concerned expressions on their faces. Nobody spoke. They just sat and waited to see what the doctor might have to say.

Some moments later, the doctor emerged and asked Pietro to join him in another room.

Pietro in a some-what distressed state responded, "Doctor, I would like if Sister Maria was present to hear what it is you have to tell me."

"Of course, Pietro. I fully understand."

On entering the adjoining room, Dr Vanzetti asked Pietro and Sister Maria to be seated and then began by saying, "Pietro, I have examined Consuella. Regrettably, I have to inform you her condition is not good. In fact, your daughter is very ill and needs to be hospitalised right away."

"Doctor, does this have anything to do with her previous illness?"

"No. I'm afraid it is something more serious than her previous condition. That's why I feel she should be taken to the hospital as quickly as possible. I will go and arrange for an ambulance to call as a matter of urgency. In the meantime, someone needs to be in attendance until the ambulance gets here."

Sister Maria responded, "Thank you, Doctor. Carlota and I will stay with her until then."

When Dr Vanzetti left, Sister Maria and Carlota went into Consuella's bedroom to watch over her. Carlota was quite taken aback at how fragile she looked.

Outside, Dominique and Paolo stayed close to Pietro in an effort to give him some small comfort. Adamo went outside to await the arrival of the ambulance. Father Martine and Francesco just sat silently by Antonio's side. They instinctively knew this was not a time for words, comforting or otherwise.

After the arrival of the ambulance, Consuella was transferred to Saint Mary's Hospital. Sister Maria and Carlota accompanied her on the short journey. She was immediately placed into intensive care. The others followed on separately.

Again Dr Vanzetti spoke with the family. "Consuella is sleeping now. We have given her some medication, and her condition is slightly more stable. Tomorrow morning, we will carry out a series of tests to try and determine what has led to this deterioration in her condition. That's really all I can tell you for the moment. I think it best if you were to leave now and allow her get some rest. In the meantime, she will be under constant observation."

Pietro was too distraught to speak. He looked over in Sister Maria's direction. She responded on his behalf, "Thank you, Doctor. We will depart now so you and your staff can do what's needed for her."

With that, they all left the hospital and made their way back to Pietro's home. Dominique took her father to his room. He was quite exhausted. She thought it best for him to try and at least get some rest.

Father Martine decided some words were now needed. "I think you will all agree, this is not the sort of Christmas we were expecting. I suppose under the circumstances, Consuella being in the hospital under the care of the nursing staff is definitely the best option. There's nothing more we can do now, except to hope and pray that she makes a speedy recovery.

"Carlota, Francesco, you've missed your morning train. There is an afternoon departure; if you wish, I will take you. Antonio, I think it's probably best for you to return to Vienna this evening. There is nothing more any of us can do for now, and I believe the family would appreciate some private time together."

Carlota and Francesco gathered their bags, said their goodbyes, and walked to the door. Antonio reluctantly joined them.

At the train station, they bid each other a sad farewell. Carlota and Francesco boarded their train. Father Martine then accompanied Antonio to his train.

As they walked along the platform, Father Martine decided to offer some comforting words. "Antonio, don't be too discouraged. Hopefully, in a few days from now, Consuella will be feeling much better. I suppose we should at least be grateful for the excellent care she is receiving right now. I will of course keep in touch and let you know how she is progressing. God willing everything will be fine, so try not to worry too much and have a safe journey."

"Thank you, Father. I will do my best, even though I feel bad leaving in this way. When you get to see Consuella, will you please explain how reluctant I was taking my leave like this?"

"Of course I will, Antonio. I will most definitely let her know it was my suggestion. And have no fear; she will understand."

"There is one more thing I need to tell you before I depart."

"Yes, Antonio, you have my attention please continue."

"Today Consuella and I were going to make an announcement."

"Go on, Antonio. I'm listening."

"Today we were going to announce the date of our wedding. Does this revelation surprise you?"

Father Martine looked at him. For a moment or two, he didn't say anything. Then he replied, "My dear Antonio, that doesn't surprise me in the least. As a matter of fact, we were all wondering when this day would come. All I can say is, Consuella now has a very good reason for making a full recovery. Have I your permission to share this wonderful news with her father and Sister Maria?"

"Of course. So now I'll be going. Goodbye, Father. You promise to keep me up to date on her progress?"

"I promise, Antonio. We'll talk very soon. You have my word on that. Now off you go. Have a safe and restful journey."

As Father Martine left the station, he wondered if there was some cruel fate yet again pulling Consuella and Antonio apart. He dismissed the thought and decided to hope and pray that a brighter future might yet dawn for the two of them.

CHAPTER 47

Saint Mary's Hospital, January 1913

During Consuella's confinement, there was no real improvement in her condition; to everyone's concern, she remained very weak. Towards the end of January, while Sister Maria and Pietro were by her bedside, she pleaded with her father, "Dear Papa, I would like to spend the next few days at the convent. Please, please let Reverend Mother take me there."

"Okay, Consuella, but first we will have to see what the doctor has to say. If he agrees, then it might be possible. So rest now and we'll see what happens."

Sister Maria and Pietro discussed the situation with Dr Vanzetti. They told him of her request and sought his opinion.

He responded, "As things currently stand, her condition has not improved. We have done all we possibly can. I am at a loss as to what more can be done. So if this is her wish, I will make the necessary arrangements."

The following day, Consuella was brought back to the convent. Sister Maria made certain her room was as comfortable and welcoming as possible.

Later that same afternoon, Father Martine came by. Seeing Sister Maria and Pietro, he knew straight away the situation was not good. He sat down beside Pietro and asked, "Dear friend, is there anything you need me to do right now?"

With tears in his eyes, Pietro answered him, "Father I would be most grateful if you could possibly contact Carlota, Francesco, and Antonio, and also if you would the young Señorita Violetta. I think it is a matter of some urgency that they get here as quickly as possible."

"Of course, Pietro. I will attend to it straight away."

The following day, Father Martine collected Carlota, Violetta, Francesco, and Alberto from the train station.

Sister Maria greeted them on their arrival. "Thank you for getting here so quickly. Pietro and the family are inside."

Carlota asked, "How is she, Sister. Is there anything we can do?"

"I'm afraid the only thing we can do now is pray. It breaks my heart to tell you this, but I'm afraid our dear Consuella is growing weaker by the hour."

Francesco asked her about Antonio. "Has Antonio been notified?"

"Father Martine spoke with him; he will be here first thing tomorrow morning."

Sister Maria brought everyone into the room; Pietro and the family were present. They were holding a silent vigil. Consuella was resting and seemed quite calm.

She opened her eyes in a welcoming gesture. As Carlota and Violetta moved closer, she smiled and whispered, "Dearest Carlota, thank you for coming, and please make sure to take good care of your dear husband, Francesco. He is truly a wonderful generous thoughtful person. Violetta, it would indeed make me very happy if you were to take pity on my poor brother Adamo. Marry him as soon as possible. For I know he loves you very much."

Carlota and Violetta, knowing these were probably her last words to both of them, with tears in their eyes, the two of them just lovingly smiled by way of response.

As the evening drew to a close, there was now no doubt in anyone's mind that Consuella only had a very short time left. At Pietro's request, Father Martine recited the prayers for the dying.

The following morning, as soon as he arrived, Antonio was taken straight away to Consuella's room. The scene that greeted him was truly heartbreaking.

On seeing him, Sister Maria quietly suggested to the others that Consuella might like to have a few private moments with Antonio. As quietly as they possibly could, they followed her from the room and waited outside.

Sitting by the bedside, Antonio reached out and gently caressed her cheek.

Despite her delicate state, she managed to smile. "You are late, Antonio. You promised to marry me. Poor me; here I am still single and all alone. I am beginning to wonder if you ever really loved me."

Trying to hold back his tears and then taking her hand, he gently held it in his. "My dearest Consuella," he replied, "please forgive my late arrival. I got here as quickly as I could, because there is something I need to tell you; it is also something my heart needs to tell you. You are my true love. You are my first love, and for as long as we both shall live, you will be my only love."

"Thank you, my dearest darling, you too are my true love. There is now something I need you to do for me."

"Of course, my precious darling. Just tell me whatever it is you wish me to do."

"Come closer, Antonio. It is a secret. I will whisper it."

He leaned closer and listened intently as she whispered in his ear. As she finished, she made one final request. "My dearest darling, you promise you will do this for me?"

His heart now breaking and unable to hold back his tears, he lovingly replied, "My dearest Consuella, I will honour your wish until the day I die. It will be our secret."

With a smile on her face, she gazed into his eyes. "My dearest Antonio. I never stopped loving you, not for one single moment. And I will always love you."

Slowly laying her head back down on the pillow, she gave him one last smile and closed her eyes.

He sat quietly by her bedside for several minutes. He just wanted to spend these last precious moments with his beloved Consuella.

Composing himself, he picked up the bell from the table and gently rang it. Sister Maria and Pietro entered. They could now see and fully understand. The only reason she had hung on so bravely was so she could see and say a final farewell to her beloved Antonio one last time.

Pietro was truly heartbroken; his precious daughter was now gone from him forever. Sister Maria guided him to the chair on the opposite side of the bed from where a broken-hearted Antonio was just sitting there, silently holding his own vigil for his now departed Consuella.

Sister Maria quietly leaving the bedroom gathered everyone together. With tearful eyes and in a voice full of emotion, she spoke the following words, "Our dearest Consuella has now left us. She waited just long enough, so that she could see and say a final farewell to her beloved Antonio one last time. Father, I think we should give Pietro and Antonio these few moments with her before we go in. Will you then say the final prayers?"

"Of course, Sister, just let me know when you deem it appropriate."

Sister Maria entered the bedroom. Everyone silently filed in behind her.

Father Martine began the prayers. "Dear Lord, today we say farewell to our precious Consuella, a dutiful daughter to her dear father, Pietro, a loving sister to Dominique and Adamo. She brought so much joy during her short time among us. We will never forget her generosity, her grace, and her charm. But most of all, we will never forget her beautiful angelic voice. So today, dear Lord, with great sadness and profound sorrow, we place our dearest Consuella into your loving care. Amen."

On Thursday, 13 January, Consuella was finally laid to rest. Her wish was to be buried beside her Mother in the cemetery close to the convent. With everyone gathered at the graveside, Father Martine recited the prayers.

As the casket was being lowered Carlota spoke briefly with Sister Maria. "Sister, I have written a short poem in commemoration of Consuella. With your consent, if I may, I would like to read it."

"Carlotta, this is a most thoughtful gesture. Please read your poem. You have my permission, and I know her grieving father will approve."

Taking her place close to Pietro and the family, Carlota unfolded a single piece of paper and began:

"By my graveside do not grieve.
I am not there I had to leave,
I'm with my Saviour in Heaven above,
I've told the Angels of our love,
I am the breeze on the windswept plain,
In the morning spring, I am the rain,
Do not kneel there do not cry,
I am not there I did not die."

As Carlota finished reciting the poem, Pietro took her hand in his. "Carlota, your words, your poem encapsulates everything my Consuella was during her short life. This gift of words you have given to my family on this saddest of days, I promise, will forever be remembered and treasured in our household. Thank you."

Carlota bowed graciously to Pietro and the remainder of the family. Taking a step back, she could see Francesco with his arm around Antonio, who was inconsolable. Stepping closer and taking his hand, she comforted him by saying, "Dearest Antonio, the inspiration for this short poem was Consuella and you. The deep love you both had for each other will be remembered through these simple words."

Trying very hard to somehow compose himself, he tearfully answered, "Carlota, what do I do now? What do I do without my dearest beloved Consuella?"

Carlota, holding him in a loving caring embrace, replied, "In one of those verses, Antonio, there was a message especially meant for you: 'I am with my Saviour in Heaven above. I have told the Angels of our love.'

"Carlota, I will try to remember those very beautiful consoling words in the difficult weeks and months ahead. Thank you, from the bottom of my broken heart, I thank you."

With the funeral service now over, the family, together with many members of the community, slowly made their way from the cemetery. Antonio, wanting to be alone in his devastating grief, decided to leave Verona as soon as was possible and do so without causing offence.

Before his departure, he spoke briefly to Francesco. "Francesco, if you could, I would like you to say goodbye to everyone, especially Father Martine, on my behalf. I don't think I can stay another moment in Verona. Without Consuella, it's just something that I would be unable to bear. I am only now learning what it is to be truly broken-hearted. Goodbye, my dear friend. Thank you for all the past years of truly wonderful companionship."

"Don't worry, Antonio. I will do as you wish. I completely understand your reasons. When you feel able to talk, let me know. I will make myself available. God bless you, Antonio. Have a safe journey. Until we meet again, try and take good care of yourself."

With Antonio's departure, Francesco spoke with Father Martine and explained the reason behind Antonio's sudden departure. Although he was quite upset, he fully understood. He then wondered to himself, when and under what circumstances would he would see his pupil again.

Chapter 48

The Letter

For the remainder of 1913, Antonio remained in Austria and immersed himself in his work at the Vienna Court Opera. As the third of October approached, without letting anybody know, he made the journey back to Verona. In the early hours of the morning, he knelt down by the graveside, laid a single white rose in front of the headstone, and prayed silently for his beloved Consuella. Before anyone else arrived to visit the graveside, he had already departed.

Meanwhile in Milan, Francesco finally realised his ambition of forming his own orchestra. Violetta kept her promise and married Adamo in early November. Mindful of the fact the family were still in mourning, she and Adamo opted for a quiet ceremony. Father Martine performed the wedding service. The only guests other than family were Carlota; Francesco; and their twin daughters.

As time passed, Sister Maria and Father Martine spent as much time as possible with Pietro. Although still deeply traumatised, he did his best to come to terms with the loss of his precious Consuella. His granddaughter, Sophia, was a source of great comfort to him during these difficult days.

Towards the end of November, Dominique gave her father the happy news that she was three months pregnant. Six months later, on 25 May 1914, she gave birth to a beautiful healthy boy. At the christening, Father Martine asked Dominique and Paolo if they had decided on a name. In unison, they both answered. The chosen name for their newly born son would be Pietro.

On 28 June 1914, a catastrophic event occurred, which changed the map and landscape of Europe forever. On that day, the archduke of the Austrian Hungarian Empire, Franz Ferdinand, and his wife the duchess were assassinated in Sarajevo. One month later, a terrible devastating war broke out between Austria and Serbia.

Germany came to the support of Austria-Hungary and went to war with Russia. Great Britain and France soon joined the conflict in support of Russia. Italy found itself in a difficult position for the remaining part of that year. However, in May 1915, Italy finally declared war on Austria.

With Italy's entry into the conflict, Antonio, being an Italian national, found his position with the Vienna Court Opera no longer tenable. Although still grieving the loss of his beloved Consuella, he reluctantly returned to Italy and volunteered for service in the army. He was given the rank of captain and put in charge of an infantry detachment.

Before his departure for the battlefield, he paid one last visit to Francesco.

On his arrival, Carlota was greatly surprised to see him standing on the doorstep in military uniform. "Antonio, my goodness me, what an unexpected surprise. I had no idea you were back here in Italy. Please come in. I will let Francesco know straight away. He will be so excited."

Leading him into the sitting room, she immediately dashed off to fetch her husband.

On entering the room, Francesco could see the anxious worried expression on his friend's face. He greeted him warmly nonetheless. "Antonio, I fully realise it was probably most difficult for you coming here today. So if there is anything you wish to tell me, I promise I will listen very carefully without interruption."

"Thank you, Francesco. I appreciate your gesture. As you can see, I am no longer involved with the Vienna Court Opera. I tendered my resignation some weeks back. I have volunteered for military service. In two days from now, I will be heading to the battle-front. So I really wanted to see you one last time and say farewell before my departure."

"Thank you, Antonio. I do appreciate your thoughtful gesture, and I do know your words are truly sincere."

"Francesco, in all our years of friendship, you have never let me down. So before I leave, there are two favours I need to ask of you, because you are the one person I know I can depend on in any circumstance."

"Of course, Antonio. Make your requests. I promise I will listen most carefully."

"My younger sister, who now resides in America, is my only living relative. This is her mailing address. I have given my commanding officer your details as my next of kin. Should I be injured or, for that matter, fail to return, the military command would notify you in writing. If you receive a communication pertaining to either of these two possibilities, you would be performing a great personal service on my behalf if you were to then notify my sister."

"Antonio, I am honoured you have chosen me as your next of kin. It is my fervent wish, however, that it will not be necessary for me to carry out such a task. Carlota and I will pray daily for your safe return. Now to your second request. In your own time, Antonio, please continue."

Taking a sealed envelope from his coat pocket and handing it to his friend, Antonio continued, "My second request is the most important one. This letter, as you can see, is addressed to Father Martine. I would be eternally grateful if you were to pass it on to him, but only in the event of my death on the battlefield."

Francesco took the letter, locked it in a secure drawer, and then replied, "Antonio, I give you my solemn word. If either of these events come to pass, and I fervently pray they do not, your wishes as outlined just now will be honoured by me. This I promise."

As he was preparing to leave, he made one final request. "Francesco, there is one last important task you might be able to perform on my behalf."

"Just name it, Antonio. I will do my very best to do what it is you ask."

"Last October, I visited Consuella's graveside."

"Did you happen to meet with your teacher on that particular occasion?"

"No. I did not meet with anyone. I just wanted to spend some private moments alone in the cemetery. I placed a white rose on the grave and said a silent prayer. If for some reason I do not return, would you be able to perform this task on my behalf each year on the day of her birthday? It would mean so much to me."

"Antonio, dear friend, if for any reason you are unable to be in Verona on this important day, I will do my utmost to honour your wish. Now before your departure, there is something I need you to do, not especially for me but more particularly for yourself."

"Of course, Francesco. Just name it?"

"I would like you to sit down at this desk and write a brief letter to Father Martine, informing him that you have joined the armed forces of our beloved country. I believe this would be nothing more than good manners on your part. At the very least, this is something I strongly feel you should do. If you agree, I will see to it he receives your communication."

"Francesco, forgive my thoughtlessness just now. You are of course quite correct. This is the least I can do. May I borrow a pen and paper?"

Antonio composed a carefully worded letter thanking his teacher for all his acts of kindness and thoughtfulness over the past number of years. He asked his forgiveness and understanding for not being in touch. He mentioned that he was now in the army and finished by asking his teacher to remember him in his prayers. Francesco handed him an envelope. He wrote down the address, placing the letter in the envelope, and handed it back. "Thank you, Francesco, for reminding me what good manners are."

As Francesco smiled in response, Carlota joined them. Antonio bid them a heartfelt goodbye. They were both quite sad and somewhat emotional as they bid him farewell.

During a bloody campaign that lasted from June 1915 to November 1916, five major battles were fought between the Italians and the Austrians in the Isonzo and Vipava valley regions. There were in excess of ninety thousand casualties.

In August, during a particularly brutal encounter, Antonio and his detachment became isolated from the remainder of their battalion. Although heavily outnumbered, they put up fierce resistance and bravely defended their position until they were finally overwhelmed by the sheer weight of the opposing enemy forces.

In mid-1916, Francesco received the letter he was dreading most; the envelope bore a military seal. Before he opened it, he made sure Carlota was by his side. What he read was brief and to the point:

> We regret to inform you, Captain Antonio Fabrizio was fatally wounded while fighting on behalf of the Italian nation. Please accept our condolences on this sad occasion. In recognition of his heroism, he has been posthumously awarded the medal for military valour. His remains are buried in the military cemetery in the province of Trento.

As Francesco placed the communiqué on the table in front of him, Carlota could see he was deeply upset. Just then, their two daughters, Adriana and Carla, entered. They knew straight away that something terrible had just occurred.

Adriana asked her mother, "Mama, is something wrong with Papa? He doesn't look too good."

"Dear children, just this very moment, your father has received some heartbreaking news. His dearest friend Antonio, whom both of you know so well, has tragically died in this dreadful cruel war."

His two daughters, with tears in their eyes, went over to their father and lovingly hugged him.

Carla spoke for both of them. "Dearest Papa, we both know how terribly upset you must be. Poor sweet Antonio. He meant so much to you. We always thought of him as your younger brother. You loved him so much, and he adored you. For you Papa, we too are also deeply saddened."

Francesco just held his two precious daughters closely. He was grateful for having them so near during these heartbreaking moments. Carlota observed this touching scene. She was so proud of her two daughters. The love they both had for their father was clearly evident, and she was grateful for this blessing.

Adriana took her mother's hand in hers, saying, "Mama, we will leave you and Papa alone now. The two of you most likely need to discuss what needs to be done." The two girls left the room to allow their parents some quiet moments together.

Carlota placed her two arms around her husband's shoulders and silently held him in a loving embrace.

After a few brief moments, Francesco regained his composure. Opening the drawer, he placed the envelope on the table. "My dear, when Antonio was last with us, he entrusted this letter into my care. It's a letter he wrote to Father Martine. He asked me to deliver it to him should he fail to return from battle. He also asked me to write to his younger sister."

Carlotta sat down beside her husband as he composed some compassionate words of condolences for Antonio's only living relative.

The following morning, Carlota and the two girls accompanied Francesco to the train station. They knew the task facing him would not be an easy one. His two daughters and Carlota hugged him as he was about to board the train. Carlota had some encouraging words for her husband as he finally departed. "Take care my darling. Have a safe journey and pass on our good wishes to Father Martine."

Before departing Milan, Francesco had taken a conscious decision not to notify Father Martine in advance. He believed arriving unannounced was probably the most appropriate manner in dealing with what he was certain would be an emotional experience for both of them.

Arriving at the monastery in the late afternoon, Francesco was met by a very surprised Father Damiano, who nonetheless greeted him enthusiastically. "Señor Francesco, what an unexpected surprise. Father Martine didn't mention that you would be paying us a visit. Please come on in, and I will let him know you are here."

"Thank you, Father. By the way, is it possible you can break the news to him gently? You see, I didn't give him any prior notice regarding my journey here."

"Very good, Señor Francesco. Take a seat in the library. You know where it is. I will go and very gently let him know you're here."

Francesco sat down, he chose a seat close to the large bay window, knowing this was Father Martine's favourite spot; he thought it might just make what was to follow a little more bearable. Pressing his hand to his breast pocket rather self-consciously, he just wanted to make sure the letter was still there.

A few minutes passed. Father Martine entered in an excited state. "Francesco, what a most unusual, though I'm delighted to say pleasant surprise. How are Carlota and the twins? Any word from Antonio? Have you heard from him these past few months?"

Francesco responded as calmly as possible. "Carlota and my two girls are just fine, and they asked me to pass on their best wishes to your good self. Regarding your dearest pupil Antonio. Sometime back, he requested me that under a particular set of circumstances I was to pass this letter on to you. These circumstances have now come to pass. So I think it best you read this letter first."

Francesco handed him the letter. All he could now do was sit silently as Father Martine began reading:

'Dear Father,

If you are reading this, my last and final letter to you, it means I have already departed this life. When I volunteered for military service, I asked my dear friend Francesco to keep it safe and only pass it on to you in the event of my death. When I died and how I died, I cannot tell you. If Francesco is with you as you are reading this, he might be able to shed some light on the manner of my passing. I pray that I served my country in an honourable fashion and that I have not brought shame on myself or behaved in a cowardly fashion.

Please forgive me, Father, for not coming to visit you. It was just too difficult for me to return to Verona knowing my beloved Consuella was no longer there.

I want you to know that I have always been deeply grateful for the kindness you showed to me as your pupil and also for the abiding love you instilled in me for the opera. I could not have achieved the success I enjoyed without your guiding hand, your tireless efforts, and your tremendous support. For these many acts of generosity, I will be eternally grateful. As you know, dear Father, in my short life, for me there was only one true love. Please say a daily prayer for Consuella and also for me your obedient pupil, that we will be united for all eternity in heaven. Her final last words to me and the request she made has been our secret. What she revealed on the tragic day of our final parting is also the main reason for me not returning to Verona.'

Putting the unfinished letter to one side, Father Martine was now having some difficulty trying to maintain some degree of composure. He indicated his distress and revealed he was too upset to carry on reading. Francesco, very much aware how difficult it was for him, just sat quietly to give him these few moments to silently grieve.

"Thank you, Francesco, for giving me these precious moments to absorb this heartbreaking news. My apologies for not finishing this, Antonio's last letter to me. The remainder is just some personal words. I am sure you will understand. You more than anyone knew what Antonio meant to me. He was like a precious son—always obedient, always so charming. How tragic that Consuella and Antonio have been taken away from us while they were still so young. I will offer my heartfelt prayers every day that they are reunited in heaven. I suppose that is as much as I can do for them now."

"Indeed, Father, that is as much as any of us can now do to keep their memory alive. Although they are no longer with us, we will still have the memories for all the days to come."

The two of them just sat silently for some moments, reflecting on Antonio and his first and only love, Consuella.

After a few brief moments, Father Martine asked, "Have you any plans to visit Antonio's graveside?"

."Yes, before I make my journey back to Milan, it is my intention to visit his grave, say a prayer and bid a final fare-well."

"May I make a suggestion Francesco?"

"Of course Father, what is it you wish to suggest?."

"Why don't you stay here tonight. Tomorrow the two of us can make the journey together and pay our final respects.

"That's an excellent suggestion Father. I believe the two of us visiting the grave-side together will render our sad mission just that little bit more bearable."

"Very good Francesco, Father Damiano will show you to your room. In the meantime I will contact Sister Maria and Pietro and give them the sad news of Antonio's passing."

The following morning, Father Martine and Francesco travelled by train to the military cemetry in the Trento region. There they said some prayers and paid their final respects to Antonio. A loyal friend and a beloved pupil. At the train station, they parted company and bid each other a sad fare-well. Father Martine made the lonely journey back to Verona, Francesco travelled back to his family in Milan.

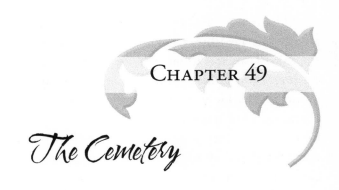

CHAPTER 49

The Cemetery

On 3 October 1918, Francesco entered the cemetery. There was a steady rainfall. As he knelt down beside the graveside, he sheltered beneath an umbrella. Placing a single white rose beside the headstone and about to say a prayer, he was interrupted by a female voice.

"Excuse me, señor. Is it possible you may be at the wrong graveside? I don't think I've seen you here before."

Without looking up and still partially covered by the umbrella, Francesco replied, "Well let me see now, señora. The name on this headstone is that of Señorita Consuella Pellegrini, would you agree?"

"Yes indeed, señor, that is correct. Can you tell me, did you by chance know her?"

"I did indeed. In fact, I knew her very well."

"May I ask how you knew her?"

"Señorita Consuella was my pupil."

"But surely that can't be, señor. My sister was taught by the nuns here at the convent."

"I do apologise if I've misled you when I said she was my pupil. I should have been more specific; in fact, I was her voice coach."

"Oh please forgive me, Señor Francesco. It's me, Dominique. I do apologise. I did not recognise you just now."

As she was speaking, the rain stopped. Francesco stood up and folded his umbrella. Standing there in front of him was Dominique and beside her a young girl, perhaps six or seven years of age.

"That's okay, Dominique. I should have identified myself when you spoke just now, but you see I was lost in my own thoughts for those few moments. This being Consuella's birthday, I wanted to pay my respects

344

and say a prayer. Now, how have you been? And who is this pretty señorita standing next to you?"

"I'm fine, Señor Francesco. We all still miss Consuella terribly, but life goes on, and we have to do the best we can. This pretty señorita beside me is my daughter, Sophia."

"Ah yes, I remember now. It was around Christmas time some years back. The joy on your father's face as he held her in his arms, was such a wonderful sight to behold. By the way, how is he? Keeping well I hope?"

"Consuella's sad passing left him broken-hearted; he will never get over it. The only consolation for him now is his three grandchildren—Sophia standing here before you; my son, Pietro Junior; and young Alberto, the son of Violetta and Adamo. The three of them have brought much comfort into my dear Papa's life. But what about you, Francesco? What have you been doing all these years? How are Carlota and the twins? They must be all grown up by now."

"Carlota is doing voluntary work at the military hospital in Milan. Adriana will complete her medical studies next year, and Carla is a high school teacher. Hopefully this war will end soon so our country can get back to some sort of normality. Some time back, I started my orchestra. We entertain the troops whenever we can, and presently, we perform mainly in Milan. When this terrible war is over, I intend to take my orchestra on tour throughout Europe and hopefully America. Anyway, please pass on my good wishes to your father."

"Well, Francesco, you might wish to do that yourself. For as we speak, they are coming down the pathway from the convent. I'm sure the four of you will have lots to talk about."

As they entered the cemetery and walked towards the graveside, Pietro spotted Dominique in conversation with Francesco. In the distance, he didn't recognise him. He pointed them out to Sister Maria. "Sister, there's a gentleman talking with Dominique at the graveside. At this distance, I don't recognise him. I wonder who it could be.

Sister Maria, looking in their direction, immediately recognised Francesco. "If my eyes are not deceiving me, I do believe that's Francesco."

Father Martine, still as alert as ever, exclaimed, "Sister, did you say Francesco? My goodness, we haven't seen him for quite some time, I wonder what brings him all the way to Verona."

When they reached the graveside, Francesco greeted Sister Maria and Pietro.

Father Martine shook his hand enthusiastically. "Francesco, it's so good to see you. How is Carlota? My goodness me, how long has it been since we last met?"

"Too long, Father. Carlota is just fine. She was a little tired this morning after our train journey yesterday evening. She's having a rest back at the hotel, so I decided to visit the graveside and pay my respects. I have to say, it's nice to see all of you again, even on this sad occasion."

"Ah yes indeed, Francesco. Today is a sad day for all of us, particularly Pietro. We visit the graveside often, but on her birthday, it is always so much more difficult."

Sister Maria joined in by suggesting, "Father, why don't you start the prayers. Then we can all go back to the convent, have some breakfast, and catch up on all of Francesco's news since he was last here in Verona."

They stood around the graveside holding hands. Sophia stood between her mother and grandfather.

Father Martine began the prayers: "Almighty Father, we are gathered here today to remember Consuella, a dutiful daughter, a loving sister, an outstanding student gifted with an angelic voice. Our prayer today, dear Lord, is that our dearest Consuella has found lasting peace and is present with you in your heavenly kingdom in the company of all your angels and saints on this her birthday anniversary. Amen."

With the prayers completed, they headed back to the convent. During breakfast, Francesco brought them up to date on all the news from Milan.

When they were done, Pietro stood up and announced, "Thank you, Sister, for a wonderful breakfast. I need to get back, so if I may be excused, I will take my leave with Dominique and Sophia. May I offer you a lift, Francesco?"

"Not at all, Pietro. I'll stay a while. I'd like to catch up with Sister Maria and Father Martine on all that's been happening here in Verona since we last met."

Father Martine joined in. "Don't worry, Pietro. I'll see to it Francesco gets back to his hotel when we're done here."

"Very good. I'll leave the three of you to it then. By the way, Francesco, later this afternoon, Violetta, Adamo, young Alberto, and Alberto Senior will be paying us a visit. Would you and Carlota care to join us?"

"Why thank you, Pietro. I'm looking forward to it already."

"Excellent. Sister Maria, Father Martine, I take it the two of you will also come over."

"Of course we'll be there," Sister Maria answered.

With Pietro, Dominique, and young Sophia's departure, Sister Maria continued, "You know, Francesco, I sometimes think back on the many occasions we spent in the company of Consuella and Antonio. Isn't it so terribly sad and somewhat tragic that the two of them—so young, so warm, and so very charming, with their whole lives ahead of them—are no longer with us."

"Yes indeed, Sister, it is indeed very sad, very sad indeed. While we're on the subject of Consuella, when Pietro and Dominique were here, I couldn't help but notice, that young child Sophia, bears a remarkable likeness to Consuella."

Sister Maria, with a concerned expression, looked in Father Martine's direction. He decided he needed to respond matter-of-factly to Francesco's observation.

"Why yes indeed, Francesco, how perceptive of you. In that young child, there's no mistaking the Pellegrini genes."

Francesco didn't immediately reply. He just sat there reflecting on Father Martine's comments. He could also see the two of them had anxious expressions of their own. After a few brief moments, he responded, "You know, Father, unless my memory is playing tricks on me, I seem to recall sometime back, in fact some years ago, Carlota telling me that that child was adopted by Dominique and Paolo. Would I be correct?"

Sister Maria remained silent.

Father Martine, now quite flustered, responded somewhat unconvincingly, "Why yes, Francesco, you are of course absolutely correct. That child, Sophia, as you quite rightly remember, was indeed adopted by Dominique and Paolo. Isn't it quite remarkable the likeness she bears to Consuella? What a coincidence, don't you think?"

Francesco made no reply; he just waited to see which one of them was now going to say something.

Sister Maria finally spoke. Her words were to Father Martine. "Father, would you care to explain to Francesco? Or perhaps should I?"

"I think it best, Sister, if you were to explain."

Sister Maria remained silent for a moment or two. She then hesitantly addressed Francesco. "The two points you made, Francesco, are quite correct. Firstly, young Sophia does bear a remarkable likeness to our dear departed Consuella. And secondly, she was indeed adopted by Dominique and Paolo. But these two facts are only two small parts of a much bigger and more tragic tale. I will now do my best to explain in greater detail. That young child, Sophia is, in fact, Consuella's daughter."

Francesco was quite stunned by this revelation. He decided however not to interrupt and allow Sister Maria continue with her narrative.

"That child's father is Antonio. So you see, Consuella and Antonio are in fact Sophia's actual parents. I will now take you to the very beginning— to the very time these heartbreaking events occurred.

"That night Consuella collapsed on stage in Milan, you were present and assisted her; you then brought her to Sister Lucia. Her collapse that evening wasn't due to any neglect on Don Barcese's part. Instead, it was because she was already three months pregnant with Antonio's child. The doctor who attended her that particular evening gave you a handwritten note in a sealed envelope and asked you to give it to the doctor here in Verona. You and Carlota brought her here for what you probably thought would be a short period of convalescence.

"After being attended to by Dr Vanzetti and following a few days rest, she shared her secret with me and begged me not to say anything to her father. She was fearful of the shame he would have to endure seeing his youngest daughter giving birth to a baby while she was as yet still unmarried.

"Francesco, you yourself are aware that here in Catholic Italy, young girls who find themselves in this unfortunate predicament generally suffer the humiliation of being ostracised in their own community. And in nearly all cases, they suffer great personal trauma. I'm sorry to say, we here in the Catholic Church have often been known to take a very hard line on young girls who find themselves in this unfortunate situation.

"I decided to assist Consuella in keeping her pregnancy secret from the family and even Antonio. Dr Vanzetti, for his part, reluctantly agreed to abide by the code of doctor–patient confidentiality. Consuella did not object when I suggested I needed to confide in Father Martine. She fully accepted we would need his assistance if we were to have any chance of following through with her intentions. Over the following months, it wasn't so terribly difficult. It's amazing what can be concealed with large pillows and blankets.

"Following the birth in early September of that year, Father Martine baptised the baby girl. Consuella chose the name Sophia. At the christening, there were only the three of us present. It was heartbreaking for Consuella. The fact she could not share the occasion with her dear Father, her family, and especially her beloved Antonio was indeed, for her, deeply upsetting.

"After six weeks, with Consuella's agreement, I placed baby Sophia into the care of our sisters who run an orphanage not too far from Verona. Consuella had a plan, and it was this. She was hoping that some time in the near future, I might be able to persuade Dominique to adopt Sophia. Her reasoning was that her daughter would then have an opportunity to grow up in the Pellegrini household.

"Consuella had a sense she was not going to recover from what was a difficult birth. Her fervent wish was that Sophia would enjoy the loving care of her family. She especially wanted her dear Papa to have the experience of having a granddaughter—even if he was to never know that this child was his own biological granddaughter.

"Father Martine and I played our part in what we believed was an honourable deception. I pray the good Lord will not judge us too harshly for our role in this tragedy. All I can tell you is, for Consuella, the events I've described to you just now were truly heartbreaking.

"Over the following three months, Consuella's health fluctuated. She did have some good days. In fact, thanks to your efforts, she was able to return to the stage very briefly and perform. More often than not, though, she had bad days. On the good days, she was able to take short strolls in the grounds. Visits from her family, Antonio, Carlota, and your good-self were happy occasions for her. Unfortunately, they usually left her feeling quite exhausted. But she cherished those moments nonetheless.

"From September until early December, whenever an opportunity arose, I took her to visit Sophia. These occasions spent embracing and holding her daughter, Antonio's daughter, were always so special.

Throughout this sad bitter-sweet period, she never lost sight of her goal—that one day her precious daughter would be accepted into the Pellegrini household.

"Fortuitously, it was around the early part of December when Dominique and Paolo came to see me to discuss the possibility of adopting; Dominique was experiencing some difficulties in conceiving. I saw this as the perfect opportunity for Consuella to achieve her objective. I took Dominique and Paolo to the orphanage. When they saw Sophia their decision was immediate. They took to her immediately. On learning she was named Sophia, they were overjoyed. They brought her home just before Christmas to introduce her to the family. Both you and Carlota were there. You most likely remember Pietro holding his adopted granddaughter in his arms, without realising that they were in fact biologically connected.

"Consuella was now getting weaker by the day. But with this positive development, she remained calm and serene to the very end. The family, although preparing as best they could for her imminent passing, were broken-hearted and devastated nonetheless. At her graveside that day, I will always remember Carlota reading that beautiful sad poem. It really was most touching.

"As time passed, Dominique gave birth to a beautiful boy. The name they chose was Pietro; this was their way of honouring her father. Sometime later, as you know, Violetta and Adamo married. Violetta, to everyone's delight, gave birth to a son. At his christening he was given the name Alberto. These events gave Pietro some degree of comfort. Although he would never get over the loss of his beloved daughter, his three grandchildren brought much-needed comfort into his life and gave him a reason to live.

"We fully accept we should have confided in you long before now. Please accept our deepest apologies. We always intended to reveal this sad tale to you. I suppose we were waiting for the appropriate opportunity to do so. I do hope you understand and forgive us for any negligence on our part."

"No apologies necessary, Sister. I'm just wondering, the fact that Antonio knew Sophia was his daughter, did he ever discuss this with either of you?"

Sister Maria, without answering, looked over in Father Martine's direction.

In response to Francesco's last question, he took up where she had left off. "On that last tragic day, the day of her death, you may remember we were all gathered by her bedside. When Antonio arrived, we left the room to give himself and Consuella some private moments together. In those final heartbroken moments, she confided in Antonio. She revealed that Sophia was their daughter; she begged his forgiveness for not having revealed this truth to him when she knew she was carrying his child. Now fully realising that this would be the last time for her to see her beloved Antonio, she explained her reasons for doing what she had done regarding their daughter's future.

"Her dying wish was that he would allow Sophia to be raised by Dominique and Paolo in the Pellegrini household. I fully realise, Francesco, that these facts I am revealing just now might be, for you, somewhat surprising. So if you have any questions, please feel free to ask. I will do my best to answer you as honestly as I possibly can.

Francesco sat quietly for some moments reflecting on what Father Martine had just relayed. He then asked, "Did Antonio ever discuss these revelations with either of you?"

Father Martine replied, "He never discussed any of this with either of us."

"Then how did you come to know all of these details concerning their last and final farewell? As I recall, Antonio left Verona that very day. The only person he spoke to after the funeral service was me. He has only been back to Verona once, and that was in October 1913. I know for certain he did not meet with you on that particular occasion. I'm somewhat baffled. Can you possibly explain?"

Father Martine took a deep breath and then continued. "You remember back when you handed me the letter written by Antonio; he had given it to you around the time he had volunteered for military service. His request to you was that, in the event of his death during this terrible war, you would be responsible for delivering this, his very last letter to me. On that very day, I read it in your presence. On realising this letter was his farewell to me, I was truly broken-hearted.

"I am sure you may recall Francesco, I did not finish reading it. I gave you some lame excuse that the remainder was just some personal words from Antonio to me. In fact, it was much more than that. He wrote in great detail concerning his final heart-breaking farewell to Consuella and her dying wish that their precious daughter be raised in the Pellegrini household.

"Although very distressed and broken-hearted, he nevertheless promised he would honour this, her last wish. This he did. He never spoke to anyone about the promise he made, and instead he committed his thoughts and feelings in the letter he gave to you.

"When I read his heartbreaking account of what transpired between the two of them, I knew in my heart that they loved each other very deeply. This pact, if you like, he took to the grave with him. Through this letter, though, he was letting me know the love and devotion he had for his beloved Consuella, and the love Consuella had for him.

"That's really all I can tell you, Francesco. I'm sorry you had to find this out under what I can only say are unusual circumstances. I'm truly sorry. And I do hope you understand it was never our intention to deceive you."

"Father, I think I might have reacted in the same way facing the same dilemma as you did. Please, don't be too hard on yourself. What's done is done. All we can do now is keep the memory of Consuella and Antonio in our thoughts and prayers. The two of them had such a dramatic impact on all of us during the many happy years they shared their lives with us."

"Sometimes I find myself wondering how things might have turned out if Consuella hadn't died so tragically young. I suppose all we can really do now is remember them fondly for the joy they gave us during their short lifetime. Well, Sister, dear Father, I think it's time for me to be heading back to the hotel and see how my beloved wife is doing."

Sister Maria asked, "Francesco, forgive me for asking, but will you be sharing this tragic tale with Carlota?"

"Sister, you know me well enough by now. I have never kept a secret from my wife. You both know her very well, she will not think any less of you and will treat these sad tidings with the utmost discretion. You have my solemn word on that; you know you can place your trust in both of us. That's really all I can say. So sad, so very sad."

With that, Father Martine called Emilio to take Francesco to his hotel. Francesco bid farewell to Sister Maria, and Father Martine accompanied him on the short journey. Arriving at the hotel, they said their goodbyes and agreed that four o'clock would be a suitable time for their journey to Pietro's home later that same afternoon.

CHAPTER 50

Pietro's Household
Late Afternoon

Just before four o'clock that same afternoon, Emilio drove Sister Maria and Father Martine over to the hotel. They picked up Carlota and Francesco and then made the journey to Pietro's home. On the way, Sister Maria raised the subject of their earlier conversation with Francesco.

"Forgive me for asking, Carlota, did Francesco speak with you concerning Consuella and Sophia?"

"He did. And you know, Sister, I wasn't so terribly surprised by these revelations. I do believe the very difficult decision taken by Consuella back then must have been truly heart-breaking in the extreme. Francesco has told me that Sophia seems to be a happy child and that her grandfather absolutely adores her. So in the end, it would appear a positive outcome has been achieved."

Sister Maria and Father Martine were greatly relieved by Carlota's comments, though her following remarks left them feeling somewhat uncomfortable. "However," she added, "there is one final task Francesco needs to perform to bring final closure to this final tragic chapter in Consuella's and Antonio's very sad short life."

Father Martine, with a pained expression, asked, "Carlota can you give us some clue as to the substance of what it is Francesco intends? And does it perhaps involve young Sophia?"

Carlota looked to her husband to see if he was inclined to make a comment.

Francesco replied, "Yes indeed, Father. This task I need to perform involves Sophia and her birth parents, Consuella and Antonio. When my task is completed I will have an interesting surprise for Pietro and his

353

family. For the moment, I don't wish to comment further. I do hope you understand. What I have to say and the task I need to perform will be done with everyone present, so I would prefer if we could just leave it at that until we are all gathered together. That's really all I wish to say for the moment."

Sister Maria and Father Martine knew to probe further would be a useless exercise. The remainder of the journey was made without any further discussion.

On their arrival, Pietro greeted them enthusiastically. Dominique and Paolo, with their two children, made a special effort in welcoming them as well. Carlota and Francesco were delighted to see Violetta and her father, Alberto. Adamo was proudly holding his son, Alberto Junior. Carlota greeted Violetta and Adamo warmly while Francesco spoke with her Father. Sister Maria and Father Martine, despite their worried expressions, nevertheless greeted the family enthusiastically.

Pietro then made the following announcement: "Well, now that we are all finally gathered together, let us sit down and have some lunch. Then after we have eaten, we can catch up on all that has been happening since we last met. Father, would you care to say grace?"

"Yes indeed, Pietro. Dear friends, we are gathered here in the company of our Heavenly Father, so let us give thanks for the wonderful food we are about to enjoy. Amen."

During the course of the meal, they all chatted amicably among themselves. Despite it being a sad occasion for the Pellegrini household, everyone did their very best to remain positive. Carlota observed Sophia, who was sitting close to her grandfather. She could clearly see the resemblance between this child and Consuella. She then looked over in her husband's direction. She instinctively knew he was ready to speak.

Getting everyone's attention, she began by announcing, "Dear friends, my dear husband, Francesco, wishes to say some words and carry out a task, which he believes may be of some importance to this household. Pietro, Francesco will only do so if he has your approval."

Pietro answered her as a very anxious Sister Maria and an even more anxious Father Martine looked on apprehensively. "Carlota, your husband is a person who, from the first day we met, has always had my trust. So my dear friend Francesco, whenever you are ready, I am sure everyone gathered here is most interested in what it is you wish to say and probably a little curious concerning this task you need to perform. So please, whenever you are ready, please proceed."

Francesco remained seated. Taking the case containing the necklace from the inside pocket of his jacket, he placed it on the table in front of him and opened it. He began by saying, "Some of you seated at this table have seen this necklace before. For those of you who have not, I will now explain. This was Antonio's gift of betrothal to Consuella. It was a deeply held expression of the love he felt for her. Sadly and more tragically, he never did get to present it to her.

"On the evening he left Milan, he placed it in my care and requested that I keep it safe until he made a decision as to it's future use. This beautiful necklace has been in my possession since that fateful day. On many occasions, I have often wondered what should I do with it. Should I sell it and donate the proceeds to charity?

"Somehow I found myself unable to carry this through. I felt there had to be a better way. So I held onto it in the hope that maybe someday an opportunity would present itself for me to pass it on to someone who would cherish the memory of Consuella and Antonio."

As he was speaking, everyone around the table was paying rapt attention, particularly Sister Maria and Father Martine. Pietro's granddaughter was now sitting on her grandfather's knee. He held her very close as Francesco continued.

"Today, in this household, I believe I have found the answer. Pietro, if I may, I would like to entrust this necklace into your care, and when you deem it appropriate, I would like for you to present it to your granddaughter, Sophia. As she is the youngest female in the Pellegrini household, I believe she is the most suitable recipient. When you present it to her, I would be truly grateful if you were to tell her the story of Consuella and Antonio, and also the deep love they had for each other.

"Some day in the future she too will most likely marry. And in time, if she is blessed with a daughter of her own, she will then pass on this necklace and tell her own precious child the sad love story of Consuella and Antonio, thereby ensuring this tragic tale of love lost and love gained will be passed on to the generations yet to come."

Francesco placed the necklace back in it's box. He passed it across the table to Pietro, who very gently picked it up and emotionally replied,

"Francesco dear friend, your gesture today on this Consuella's birthday is not only thoughtful; it is also most appropriate and deeply moving. I will keep this precious gift and present it to my dearest granddaughter, Sophia, on the day of her confirmation. Thank you, Francesco. From the bottom of my heart, thank you so very much."

A much-relieved Father Martine stood up and spoke the following words: "Your words and your heartfelt gesture are truly commendable, Francesco. I know in my heart they are deeply appreciated by my dearest companion, Pietro, and all of us gathered here on this sad yet special day. Consuella and Antonio, during their tragically short lifetimes, brought us sorrow and joy in equal measure. Of that there is no doubt. But still, we are truly grateful for those joyful fleeting moments and the profound affect their presence had on our daily lives. Thank you, dear friend. Thank you so much."

Francesco responded, "Thank you, Father. You may remember earlier this afternoon I mentioned I would have a surprise. I think now would be the right moment to share it. And if I may add, I believe it is something all of us gathered here will lovingly remember and cherish, especially Pietro, Sister Maria, and your good self."

Francesco then turned to Carlota. She took an envelope from her bag and handed it to him. As he opened the envelope, he gave the following explanation: "The object I have here in my hand, as most of you will recognise, is a phonograph record. Here in Italy, this developing technology has been growing in popularity for some time now. In November 1912, during the time Consuella was performing in Milan, I brought her to a recording studio. With my piano accompaniment, her voice was recorded singing a beautiful aria. A disc was made and presented to us. Consuella left it with me for safekeeping.

"Over the passage of time, I somehow forgot about it. Thankfully, a few months back, my dear wife, Carlota, reminded me of its existence. I brought the disc to a recording studio and asked the engineers if it would be possible to remaster the recording with additional orchestration. The results of their efforts, I am happy to say, turned out rather well. With your permission, Pietro, I would now like to play this disc for you; for your precious granddaughter, Sophia; and for all here present."

Pietro, still holding his granddaughter closely, nodded his approval.

Francesco, standing by the phonograph machine, turned it on. Then very gently, placed the disc on the revolving turntable. Everyone listened in total rapture to the beautiful sound of Consuella's voice filling the room singing the magnificent aria "Vissi D'arte" from Puccini's famous opera, *Tosca*.

Father Martine, feeling quite emotional, stood close to Pietro, who now had tears in his eyes while still holding his precious granddaughter, Sophia. As they and everyone else in that room on that fateful day listened to Consuella's heavenly voice, they immediately knew, during these bittersweet moments of pure operatic joy, that they would have the great privilege of listening to their beloved Consuella sing this beautiful aria—not just on this poignant day but for all the days yet to come.

THE END

Lightning Source UK Ltd.
Milton Keynes UK
UKHW03f0734270418
321588UK00015B/51/P